PRAISE FOR ELLEN MEISTER

Divorce Towers

"Ellen Meister's *Divorce Towers* is utterly charming. From the first paragraph to the very last line, it is filled with wit and sex and truth and the unexpected . . . This book will make you laugh, spit up your coffee, and yes, cry . . . sometimes in the very same chapter. Do yourself a favor, buy this book, curl up with it, and let it transport you for a few hours and a few days. It's that good. A must read."

—Amy Ferris, author of *Mighty Gorgeous,*
A Little Book About Messy Love

"Word of warning: once you start this delightful book, you're not going to stop reading till it's finished."

—Jeff Arch, author of *Attachments*, screenwriter of *Sleepless in Seattle*

"[Long Island's] literary light shines her beam on Beverly Hills this time around, with the story of Addison Torres, who abandons the wreckage of her life in New York to take a job as a concierge in an upscale LA high-rise. Oy, the entitled residents! The schemes and the scandals! The eligible bachelors! If only Addison hadn't taken a vow of celibacy and sworn off romance."

—*Newsday*

"Original, clever, entertaining, expertly crafted, and of special appeal to readers with an interest in contemporary romance fiction . . ."

—*Midwest Book Review*

T0356229

Take My Husband

"A darkly comedic farce . . . Understanding that marriages can't always weather decades' worth of ebbs and flows, Meister's protagonist makes a strong case for communicating one's wants and needs early and loudly."

—*Booklist* (Starred Review)

"A laugh riot . . . Meister's comedic gifts keep the pages turning."

—*Newsday*

"An entertaining saga of love lost and found, *Take My Husband* merges the edginess of a thriller with the soul of a romantic comedy, a winning combination sure to appeal to readers across the literary spectrum."

—Shelf Awareness

The Rooftop Party

"A wickedly entertaining rom-com / murder mystery from start to finish. It promises to be a contender for beach read of the year."

—BookReporter

"Meister creates an engaging mystery in the unique setting of the home-shopping world. It's as fun to watch Dana piece together the clues as it is to see the behind-the-scenes details of her life as a TV host. Dana juggles a relationship, family drama, and a high-profile job, making her likable and easy to root for. Meister imbues her (and many other characters) with a quick wit and plenty of laugh-worthy lines. Perfect for readers who like their mysteries light on the murder but heavy on the humor."

—*Kirkus Reviews*

"A fast and fun read with an engaging heroine and supporting cast."

—*Library Journal*

Love Sold Separately

"Witty, clever, and full of original characters, it kept me up reading way past my bedtime! A great romp of a read."

—Candace Bushnell, bestselling author of *Sex and the City* and *Is There Still Sex in the City?*

Dorothy Parker Drank Here

"Meister's Dorothy Parker is just as sharp, witty, and pleasantly mean as fans would expect. Her humanity shines through, though, along with her humor . . . a surprisingly emotional novel. Not even death can keep Dorothy Parker down in this sad and funny story."

—*Kirkus Reviews*

"If you're not a fan of Parker's or Meister's already, you soon will be."

—BookReporter

Farewell, Dorothy Parker

"Meister skillfully translates the rapier-like wit of the Algonquin Round Table to modern-day New York . . . [with] pathos, nuanced characters, plenty of rapid-fire one-liners, and a heartrending denouement."

—*Publishers Weekly*

"Delicious entertainment."

—Cleveland *Plain Dealer*

The Other Life

Joyride

ALSO BY ELLEN MEISTER

Joyride

A novel

ELLEN MEISTER

Montlake

Published by Montlake, Seattle

www.apub.com

Amazon, the Amazon logo, and Montlake are trademarks of Amazon.com, Inc., or its affiliates.

EU product safety contact:
Amazon Media EU S. à r.l.
38, avenue John F. Kennedy, L-1855 Luxembourg
amazonpublishing-gpsr@amazon.com

ISBN-13: 9781662529108 (paperback)
ISBN-13: 9781662529092 (digital)

Cover design by Caroline Teagle Johnson
Cover image: © nicolecioe, © syntika, © Val_Iva, © Vladimir Malahov / Getty

Printed in the United States of America

In loving memory of my father, Gerry Meister,
a raconteur extraordinaire who inspired me every day
with his wit, intelligence, and boundless compassion.

Hope is the thing with feathers
That perches in the soul,
And sings the tune without the words,
And never stops at all
—Emily Dickinson

Prologue

Sid Marcus knew he was in trouble the moment he entered the restaurant and Platt told him he looked good. In fact, Sid looked like hell. The humiliation of getting booted from the entertainment industry and losing everything had taken a toll on his face, turning him into an old man almost overnight. That morning, when he decided not to shave, he'd reasoned the scruffy growth hid the worst of it, and figured he could pull off the look of an aging hipster. Or maybe a beguilingly scraggy Paul Newman. But one accidental glance at his reflection in a storefront window on his way to lunch let him know he'd been wrong on all counts. Instead of looking borderline eccentric, he looked borderline homeless, which was uncomfortably close to the truth.

Of course, Platt wasn't supposed to know that. He was supposed to think Sid was a sure bet—a godlike comedy writer who could deliver the next baby Jesus, only funnier. But Gerald Platt acted like he was talking to the incontinent grandpa you had to be kind to because you wanted to soften him up for the hard truth that he was never going home again. *Why, I don't smell anything at all, Grandpa. And look how nicely you hold your spoon.*

Fuck that. Sid needed to go home again. Or at least to the kind of success he'd once had. This was his shot at redemption.

Unfortunately, no one ever optioned a pitch based on pity. Just the opposite. The alpha dog had to believe the writer was a hound in heat—with a long line of salivating producers giving chase—and he was just the lucky son of a bitch who would get to make an offer.

Nervous, Sid gave himself a little pep talk. *You can do this. You're an Emmy winner, for chrissake. And your idea really is hot shit. Platt would be an idiot not to buy it.*

Banal as it was, it worked. Sid launched into the pitch with all jets fired, turning on the charm and charisma. And he knocked it over the fence and straight to the moon. He got Platt to smile, to laugh, to ask the right questions. And Sid was ready with all the right answers.

When it was done, Sid Marcus took a steadying breath and waited while Platt leaned back and laced his fingers over his belly like an old robber baron.

This is it, Sid thought. But then Gerald Platt uttered the worst word a writer can hear.

"Interesting."

Interesting? It was such a knee in the gut Sid wanted to double over and slink away like a kicked dog. Or maybe start his career over again as a novelist. But there was too much at stake for him to give up. *You can salvage this,* he told himself. *Keep going. Make him see your vision.*

So he granted Platt a knowing grin, as if they were already in cahoots on the blockbuster potential of this project, and got ready to explain who he envisioned in the starring roles. And that's when his eyes landed on the woman at the next table. At first, he thought he had to be wrong. It was a hallucination, born of desperation. But no, it was her. He swallowed against a knot of regret and wiped his sweaty palms on his pants.

"You were saying?" Platt asked.

And just like that, Sid was the fusty old grandpa—toothless and feeble. He said nothing—just sat there dumbly, unable to focus on anything but her. *Do something,* he told himself, but it was no use. He was inert, watching slack jawed as she paid her check, headed for the door, and walked out of his life.

Again.

Chapter 1

If you'd met Joybird Martin even once, you'd have no trouble guessing which of the vehicles idling in front of the Merrill Lynch building was hers. It was the pale-blue Honda Accord—earnest and dependable—standing out like a cheerful plastic bead in a string of colossal black pearls. The car in front of her pulled out, and Joybird edged forward, unintimidated by the gleaming Navigators, Range Rovers, Escalades, and other behemoths jockeying for position on the Lower Manhattan roadway.

She didn't think of herself as aggressive, just determined to be in a convenient spot for her Uber customer, because she knew these Wall Street types were easily agitated. And Joybird Martin did not want to be the source of anyone's angst. She wanted—from the soft center of her tender heart—to be the one who delivered bliss.

She put in her earbuds and opened the Duolingo app on her phone to practice some Spanish while waiting for her rider. The cacophony of New York City's horns, motors, and underground rumbles was immediately replaced by the app's gentle intonations. "*Mi padre es elegante,*" said the disembodied female. Joybird did her sincere best to repeat it with the same accent. Still, she laughed, because no, he most certainly wasn't.

She continued listening to the soothing voice. "*Mi padre es inteligente,*" it said. *Fair enough,* Joybird thought, and clicked through to the next part of the *familia* section.

There was a knock on the passenger-side window. She rolled it down and gave the man a smile, trying not to startle at his appearance. He wasn't just handsome—he was heartthrob handsome. Like a cross between a young Denzel Washington and that actor with a French name she suddenly couldn't remember. Only this guy sported stylishly futuristic glasses, as if he had something to prove. Joybird tried to settle herself. So what if he was tall, dark, and smoldering? It meant nothing to her.

"I'm Devon Cato," he said in a voice as assertive as a newscaster's. He was wearing an impeccable Italian suit and the stoic expression of someone repressing pain. "Can you unlock the door?" His face remained tight.

"Of course!" Joybird chirped, anxious to turn his mood around. She reached for the unlock button so fast she accidentally double pressed, unlocking and relocking before he had a chance to open the door. It took her a few extra tries to let him in as he yanked on the handle.

"I'm so sorry!" she said, flustered and embarrassed as he finally slid into the back seat. Joybird's rattled reaction unnerved her, as she wasn't the type of person who became unglued by a pretty face. *It just took you by surprise,* she told herself, and managed a deep breath.

They had a brief exchange to verify her rider's destination in Park Slope, Brooklyn. She knew the building—a pricey modern condo with its own gym, incongruous amid the historic brownstones. She glanced at his reflection in the rearview mirror and noticed how sullen and closed off he looked.

"What interesting eyeglasses!" she gushed, hoping the compliment would soften his mood.

He adjusted them on his face, looking dubious about the flattery. "Thank you."

"Are you a stockbroker or something?" She smiled, hoping he would understand she was really quite friendly and hadn't meant to lock him out of the car.

"Why do you need to know?" he asked, and she realized he thought she wanted something from him.

"I just like to make conversation," she said, and pointed toward her phone. "That's why I'm studying Spanish."

"You're studying Spanish to converse with strangers?" He squinted as if trying to figure her out.

"*Sí,*" she said, giving a polite beep to the driver of a Lincoln Navigator that had just boxed her in. "You know, there's so much negativity around—I thought it would be a positive gesture."

Disarmed, he let out a small laugh, releasing some of his tension. "That's very . . . sweet."

The Lincoln SUV pulled up, and she edged out behind it, merging into traffic.

The man tapped at his phone as if searching for something. "Uber says your name is . . . Joybird?"

She nodded, feeling more grounded as she glanced at his face again before directing her focus back to the road. "That's me," she said.

"For real? Your parents named you Joybird?"

"My mom was a poet," she explained. It was the answer she'd been giving nearly her whole life.

He nodded, processing the information. "And maybe a little prescient."

"You mean because I'm so upbeat?"

"Yes," he said, a catch of surprise in his voice. Probably because he didn't expect her to know what *prescient* meant. She got that a lot—people underestimating her based on her cheerfulness. But it was her philosophy that you didn't have to be stupid to be happy.

"Tell me about your day," she said. It was her favorite way of engaging her riders. And since he had seemed so despondent, she thought he might want to talk about it.

He scoffed. "Trust me, you don't want to know about my day."

"But I do!" she insisted.

He went silent for a long moment as he looked out the window. Then he released an extended breath. "One of our accounts blew up because my idiot boss wouldn't take my recommendation."

"That sounds bad."

"Catastrophic."

Joybird turned right onto West Street. "So what now?" she asked, hoping to draw him out. "How do you fix it?"

"Can't. We lost their business."

She chewed on that for a minute and could tell he was retreating into the silence, going to a dark place. She needed to jolt him toward the light.

"Are you good at what you do?" she asked, her voice clear and loud against the Manhattan traffic.

"I'd better be."

"I mean, you get results, right? It's quantifiable?" She took another glance at him in the rearview, and he was staring right back, looking surprised. Something had distracted him.

"Do you know your eyes are the same color as your car?" he asked.

It didn't sound like flirting—just an observation, sharing a fact he thought she should know. Still, the compliment sent a rise of heat up her neck.

"I guess," Joybird said, not exactly agreeing, because her eyes weren't really the same color as her car. Still, she knew that people were sometimes struck by the crisp blueness of her irises, especially since her complexion, which she got from her mother, leaned toward olive. She continued driving, hoping he would go back to her question. After a minute, she glanced at him again, expectantly, and he responded.

"My department does pretty well," he said. "So, yes, it's quantifiable."

"Okay, then! You'll be able to get more clients."

"Maybe. If we work our asses off."

"There you go—it'll be okay."

He chuckled.

"But I'm right," she pressed, almost insisting on his agreement.

He laughed again. "I guess you are."

She went quiet for a moment, focusing on the merge toward the Brooklyn Bridge.

He leaned forward. "So is this what you do—drive people around and try to cheer them up?"

"Not bad, huh?"

"Maybe you should do it for a living."

"Yes!" she said, almost shaking the steering wheel with enthusiasm. "Exactly. I just finished a course on life coaching, and now I'm practicing my skills."

Devon Cato sat back as if he were in a boardroom. "I heard there's a lot of money in life coaching." He rested his arms across the span of the back seat.

Joybird shrugged. "I'm more interested in helping people."

"That's very noble," he said, "but it doesn't pay the rent."

She let out a prolonged sigh, thinking about the pile of unpaid bills tucked into the corner of her kitchen cabinet, wedged against a stack of yellowing Tupperware. "It doesn't," she agreed.

"So what's the plan?"

Joybird had to center herself before answering. In fact, her plan had stalled, and she was trying not to let it derail her. "I've been saving money to rent a space and hang out my shingle. It's just . . . taking a little longer than I expected."

"And why's that?"

She sensed the car to her left trying to nose into her lane and slowed down to create a space for him.

"My dad moved in with me," she said, "and I had to get rid of my roommate. Things are a little tight right now."

"He's not kicking in?"

Joybird bit her lip, trying to find a way to respond without making her father sound like a freeloader, because he wasn't. In fact, he'd had a remarkable career. "He's down on his luck. We'll work it out."

"Unemployed?"

Joybird held tight to the steering wheel as the lanes narrowed, her shoulders stiffening. A truck barreled past, barely an inch from her side-view mirror. She exhaled. "It's hard to find work in his field."

"Which is?"

Now she had a good idea why this guy was so successful—he was focused and intense. Joybird took a sharp inhale to answer his question. This was the part people always had a big reaction to. "He's been a TV writer for over thirty years."

Her rider looked intrigued. "Would I know any of his shows?"

She rattled off the top sitcoms listed on his IMDb page—a practiced speech.

"Whoa, shit," Devon said, impressed. "He must be loaded."

Joybird shook her head. "Three divorces, a crooked manager, and a lot of bad decisions landed him on my stoop, broke."

"But with that résumé—"

"The TV industry has changed," she said, hoping he wouldn't press the issue. The truth was, Joybird didn't exactly know why her father had become so toxic in Hollywood, and didn't want to know. There were hints it had to do with some #MeToo misbehavior, and that was enough.

"I have an idea for you," Devon said.

She glanced at him again in the rearview mirror. "I'm listening."

"Why don't you do the life coaching from your car? I mean, like what you did for me, only you would charge for it."

"Against the rules."

"I don't mean as an Uber driver—I mean as an entrepreneur, the sole proprietor of your own private company. You could call it . . . Joybird's Coaching Coach."

"Or just JoyRide," she said with a laugh. It wasn't something she could take seriously.

"Even better! I can already see it on a website. I mean, the domain's probably not available, but you can work something out with that. I have a guy who does websites really cheap—he can automate the whole thing for you."

She could tell he was convinced it was a winning idea, and didn't want to hurt his feelings. But she also didn't want him to get carried away with his business plans. "Your enthusiasm means a lot to me," she said, "but I don't think it would work. I do appreciate the thought, though!" She kept her voice light, upbeat.

"Don't be so quick to shoot it down," he said. "It could work."

Joybird suppressed a sigh. Devon Cato didn't know the first thing about life coaching. When people spent money on that kind of help, they wanted a lovely office. Something substantial and confidence inspiring, with potted plants and a white-noise machine. Or maybe a Zoom call from the comfort of their own home—not the back seat of a ten-year-old Honda.

"Okay," she fibbed, "I'll think about it." Because what else could she say?

When they reached his building, he got out of the back seat, shut the door, and rapped on the passenger-side window again. But this time, it looked like he was actually seeing her, not just trying to get her attention.

"Yes?" she asked, gliding the glass downward.

He took a moment to study her face, and she shifted in her seat, self-conscious. This man wasn't just looking at her; he was seeing her. A tiny smile brightened his face, and Joybird tucked her dark hair behind her ear—a useless gesture, since she was wearing a ponytail. Suddenly, she remembered the name of the actor he resembled—Regé-Jean Page. She touched her neck.

"Your eyes are really dramatic," he said. "You know that?"

There was that heat again. She offered a nervous laugh, hoping it would end the conversation. "Thank you," she said, and readjusted her blouse, which she realized was too tight across her chest.

"So what do you like to do when you're not driving around, cheering people up?"

"What do you mean?" she asked nervously. She did, in fact, know what he meant, but couldn't think of what to say. This was so uncomfortable. Did this fancy Wall Street guy with the movie-star face actually think she was his type?

"I mean, what do you do for your own fun? Surely there's more to you than just coaching people out of their crappy moods."

"Not much more," she said, hoping he would find her boring and uncool. Not the kind of party girl he was used to.

"Maybe we can fix that," he said. "How would you like to have dinner sometime?" He took a business card from his pocket and held it toward her.

She stared past the card, imagining exactly how that would play out—a ridiculously expensive restaurant with ridiculously expensive designer food and a room full of ridiculously wealthy patrons. She'd feel self-conscious and out of place, and he'd realize immediately he had made a mistake. Joybird looked through the windshield, avoiding his face. She was happy to help him lead a better life, but she couldn't possibly date such a man.

He flapped the card, indicating she should take it.

"No," Joybird blurted, glancing toward him. "I'm sorry, no."

"You have a boyfriend?"

"It's not that . . . it's . . . you and me would never . . . I can't." She was, she knew, her mother's daughter—drawn to artists, poets, idealists. Ambition unsettled her. She made brief eye contact with Devon to see if he understood, but a dark cloud passed over his face.

"You think I'm too shallow for you." He sounded more disappointed than angry, but there was a decided edge to his voice as he flicked his card through her open window. She watched it land on the passenger seat before looking back at him. He let out a defeated sigh, then turned and walked toward his building.

This was a nightmare. She had just hurt someone . . . someone who assumed she'd thought she was better than him. Joybird couldn't imagine anything worse and felt a literal pain in the center of her chest.

"Devon!" she called, but he didn't turn around. Oh, god, he was even more upset than he had been when he got into her car, and it was her fault. Joybird's breathing got so fast she couldn't fill her lungs. Any minute now, she would start to get that faraway feeling where she floated out of her body.

But there wasn't any way to fix this. And so she had no choice but to leave. Joybird took a juddering breath, put the car in gear, and stepped on the gas. She would just keep going until she calmed down.

But no, she thought. This would not do. She had to make this right.

Joybird hit the brakes, put the car in reverse, and backed up, coming to a quick stop in front of his building.

"It's not because you're shallow!" she called out the open window, and a woman pushing a toddler in a stroller slowed to stare at her.

Devon Cato stopped walking but didn't turn around.

"It's because you're a . . . a . . . a *stockbroker!*" she called. "I'm sorry. You're a nice man, and that's a perfectly respectable job, but we're just not compatible."

He paused at the entrance to his building, and she thought she saw his shoulders shaking. Was he crying? As he opened the door, he turned halfway around and called, "I'm not a stockbroker." Then he slipped inside, letting the door shut behind him.

Chapter 2

Joybird picked up his card and saw that Devon Cato's title was *Equity Analyst*. She wasn't exactly sure what that was, but she knew it had something to do with investments. As far as she was concerned, the differences between that and a stockbroker were negligible. He was a slick Wall Street guy. He valued money—making it and spending it. And she just couldn't imagine getting close to someone who felt compelled to buy a pair of thousand-dollar eyeglasses every time the style wind shifted. Not when there were so many people in need.

On the other hand, men like Noah Pearlman, the thickly bearded barista who got her involved with the Brooklyn chapter of Mightier than the Sword—an organization that helped people who wanted to express their marginalization through writing—nearly made her swoon. She'd spent her whole life dreaming of a man like Noah—someone bighearted, with a passion for helping the less fortunate. For months, she had been trying to work up the nerve to ask him out, hoping he would beat her to it.

She ripped Devon Cato's card in half and dropped it into the trash bag hanging from her console. Then she tapped into her Uber app, finding a nearby rider. After that, she drove two more customers to local destinations before finally going back home, where she parked in an outdoor lot around the corner from her brownstone apartment and dropped her tiny trash bag into a fetid garbage drum by the fence.

Joybird exited the lot into a velvety September night, bright with streetlights and a friendly full moon. There were people about—including a heavyset man leaning against a building as he fed a slice of pizza into his mouth, a raucous family spilling out of a corner café, and an elderly couple holding hands. Hungry and tired, Joybird tried to force herself to be present and appreciate the warm hum of humanity in her Brooklyn Heights neighborhood, but something tugged at her insides. When she stopped to pick up a piece of litter someone had dropped—nearly bumping into a man with trendy glasses too big for his small face—she realized what it was. Devon Cato. She feared her explanation had made him feel worse, not better, as she had judged him for his values—the literal content of his character.

Joybird paused on the sidewalk, wondering if she should go back to the parking lot to retrieve his torn business card so she could call to apologize. But no. That wouldn't help, because her feelings hadn't changed. All she could say was that she was sorry she'd hurt him. The classic nonapology apology.

While she walked home, Joybird tried to coach herself back to happiness. After all, she had done her best. And next time, she would do better. That was all there was to it.

As soon as she unlocked the outer door to her building, Joybird heard the beat of loud music, and the volume increased as she ascended the stairs to her second-floor apartment. Her chest tightened. What the heck was her father up to? She put her key in the lock and opened the door to the aural assault of Alice Cooper blaring "School's Out." She could feel the bass in her belly, rumbling like indigestion.

"What on earth, Dad?" she called over the music.

He sat in the recliner in the middle of the living room, his eyes closed, and didn't hear her. She flicked the light switch on and off, and he looked up, giving her a small wave of acknowledgment.

"Dad!" she shouted.

"You want me to turn it down?"

"For god's sake." She walked over to the expensive sound system he had brought with him from LA and clicked it off.

"I was listening to that," he complained.

"I have neighbors."

He snorted. "Tell me about it. Beatnik Betty has been blasting Joni Mitchell all day."

By "Beatnik Betty," he meant Betty Simon, their upstairs neighbor. Joybird liked to think there was at least a little affection in it—his way of acknowledging that the retired journalist still clung to her flower child ideals.

Joybird dropped her car keys into the tray by the door. She had been squeezing them so hard there was a dent in her palm. "Is that what this is about?" she asked, rubbing her hand.

"Three Joni Mitchell albums in a row," he complained.

As far as Joybird could tell, her father resented the disrespect more than the music. Or what he perceived as disrespect, anyway. Since his fall from grace, Sid Marcus had been quick to feel victimized, insisting that life had dealt him a crappy hand, skimming the best cards for someone else. At one point, Joybird had gently suggested that as a white guy from Connecticut who was more privileged than the vast majority of humanity, he'd been dealt at least a couple of aces. Still, he clung to his victimhood like a favorite charm.

Joybird shook her head, summoning patience. "You *like* Joni Mitchell."

"That's not the point. Who listens to three Joni Mitchell albums in a row?"

"Anybody who wants to," she said.

"Well *I* didn't want to."

Joybird went to the kitchen sink and washed her hands, flexing her fingers under the cool water. "You could have just asked her to lower it," she said. It was an open floor plan, so they were only separated by a small countertop peninsula.

"I did. In my own way."

Joybird ignored him, as she hadn't eaten dinner and her empty stomach rumbled with need. She opened the refrigerator and peered inside.

"I ordered Thai," he called over.

She was grateful, but at the same time she hoped he hadn't ordered anything too expensive. Joybird had given her father the password to her laptop so that he could use her accounts to order in, and the money came directly out of her thinning bank balance.

"I got those noodles you like," he said.

She looked at him and saw a plea in his clear blue eyes. He was trying to please her, to be more compassionate, and Joybird appreciated it. She understood it was a struggle for him to get outside his own head.

"Thank you, Dad," she said gently, and he relaxed into satisfaction.

She found the right plastic container, opened it, and sniffed. Spicy drunken noodles—her favorite. She grabbed a fork and dug in, too hungry to bother heating it up.

"So good," she said, her mouth full.

"Also, crispy duck," he said, excited.

Joybird sighed. It was the most expensive thing on the menu, and there were perfectly reasonable alternatives. But her father had been rich for so long he'd forgotten how to be mindful of a budget. Besides, he was trying to make her happy, so how could she be cross with him?

Joybird stuffed another bite of noodles in her mouth as she walked into the living room.

"Stick it in the microwave," he said, clearly trying to be helpful.

"It's fine." She lowered herself into the seat next to him and shoveled several more forkfuls into her mouth. "You do anything today?" she asked, noticing that he was wearing a different pair of drawstring pants than he had when she'd left that morning. She took it as a sign he might have gotten dressed and gone out at some point, though he still hadn't shaved.

"Went into Manhattan," he said.

Joybird looked at him quizzically. A few weeks ago, she had tried to show him how to use the subway payment app she'd put on his phone, but he'd struggled with it, complaining that he didn't know what the fuck was wrong with tokens. Now she tried to picture him navigating his way through the turnstile and onto the R train to midtown.

"Really?" she pressed.

"You remember Gerald Platt?" he asked. "We had lunch."

The name meant nothing to her, but she assumed he was someone in the TV industry. "That's great, Dad."

"Son of a bitch said my pitch was *interesting*."

She swallowed another large bite of the spicy noodles, and her forehead prickled with sweat. She would need something to drink. "The nerve," she said, trying to make him laugh. His face stayed tight.

"'Interesting' is Hollywood for 'fuck off,'" he explained.

She nodded and understood that it probably was. Clearly, he was getting agitated. "You want to talk about it?"

He squeezed his eyes shut as if in pain, and Joybird gave him a minute to see if he wanted to open up. When it was clear he'd retreated, she took out her phone and started tapping out a text to her upstairs neighbor.

"What are you doing?" he asked.

"Apologizing to Betty."

"For what?"

"Dad, you were practically tormenting her."

"But in a funny way," he said, as if that was what truly mattered.

"You think harassing someone is funny?" she asked, and immediately regretted it. Surely there was a gentler way to make her point.

"Kind of," he said. "But what do I know? My idea of comedy is apparently worth shit."

"Don't do that," she begged, worried he was slipping into a dark place. She would have to remember to be more careful with her words.

"Please," he said dismissively. "I'm about as good at comedy as I am keeping a marriage together."

"Dad, come on."

He rubbed his forehead. "I've made a mess of everything. And now I've pissed you off by bothering your neighbor."

"I'm not pissed off, I swear."

He held up his hand. "I understand. Really. I'm not an easy person to live with. I promise I'll be out of your hair just as soon as—"

"Stop it! I don't want you to leave," she said, and meant it. The thought of losing him again—especially when it was her own fault—made her fingers go cold. Joybird struggled to keep her breath even. Why hadn't she found a better way to make her point? Her father had suffered so much rejection, and she was the one person he counted on to be there, no matter what. Now she couldn't think of a thing to say that would convince him he was loved and wanted.

Joybird began to hyperventilate as she felt herself starting to float away. It had been a lifelong problem for her, this tendency to disassociate when she couldn't cope. Or not lifelong exactly. It had started when she lost her mother. But that was over twenty years ago, and she still hadn't found a way to control it. *Breathe,* she told herself. *Just breathe. Stay grounded.*

Suddenly, she felt two strong hands on her shoulders. Her father was standing behind her, trying to help. It felt like forgiveness, and just like that, she came back into her body.

"You okay, Birdie?" he asked softly, using his nickname for her.

Joybird didn't know how he'd been so attuned to her distress, but she felt grateful. She reached over and touched his hand. "I like having you here, Daddy." It was so heartfelt that she didn't care if it made her sound like a child. Still, she braced herself for some gentle ribbing.

"You want a beer?" he asked, letting it go.

She nodded, and he went into the kitchen to retrieve two bottles of Sam Adams from the refrigerator. He handed her one, and she took a desperate sip. He lowered himself into the recliner, and for several minutes, they sat silently as they drank.

"You were right about the loud music," he said. "I was being a dick."

Joybird glanced over, and he still looked painfully glum. "It's okay," she reassured him. "You were upset from your meeting with that Platt guy."

He shook his head. "It's not Platt," he admitted, taking a long pull of his beer.

"What, then?"

"Doesn't matter."

"Of course it matters."

He stared absently at the label, then tipped his head back, took another swig, and pulled the bottle from his mouth with a soft pop. She waited, sensing he was getting ready to open up about something.

"You can talk to me," she assured him.

He nodded and took a slow breath. "Did I ever tell you about Donna DeLuca?"

"I don't think so."

He went quiet, as if trying to figure out where to begin. Joybird waited.

"Prettiest girl at Paxton Prep," he finally said, referring to the private high school in Connecticut he had attended. "Face like a goddess. Picture Cindy Crawford with a little Sophia Loren thrown in. And smarter than every fucking guy in my class put together."

"Did you go out with her or something?" Joybird asked, trying to understand why this ancient history had upset him.

"I kissed her once, at a party. Possibly the single greatest moment of my life. But we were both stoned, and afterwards . . . I don't know. I choked. I never asked her out, though I rehearsed it every day for two years."

Joybird's phone vibrated, and she picked it up to read the response from Betty. She glanced up at her father, feeling torn. On the one hand, she was tired, as that momentary panic attack had depleted her. All she really wanted to do now was hear her father out and go to sleep without upsetting him again. But on the other, she wanted to tell her friend that yes, it would be fine if she came down. After all, she adored Betty and didn't think it would be right to reject her request after she'd endured her father's musical hostility. So she typed back a smiley face followed by Yes!

"Betty?" her father asked, nodding toward the phone.

"She's stopping by."

"Fuck me."

"Don't be like that," Joybird said. "Tell me more about Donna DeLuca."

He took another sip of his beer and put it down hard on the side table. "I missed my chance . . . again." Avoiding Joybird's eyes, he glanced out the window into a night so aggressively dark it seemed to suck the streetlights into the ether.

"What are you talking about?" she asked.

He couldn't respond, and she saw that he was choking back tears.

"Sid," she pressed, calling him by his first name. Or rather, his assumed name. Unlike Joybird, he did not go by the name on his birth certificate, which was John Martin. He'd changed it when he started writing for television, certain no one would think a guy with a name like John Martin could be funny. And so he became Sid Marcus, letting people assume he was a tough Jewish kid from Brooklyn instead of a privileged Connecticut preppie.

"Dad," she said quietly. "Talk to me."

"I saw her in the city today. Having a business lunch at another table."

"Are you sure it was her?"

He nodded. "Stared at her long enough to be certain. She looks . . . the same. I mean older, of course. But that presence. That face. It still kills me."

"Did you talk to her?"

He swallowed, struggling to respond. "I didn't do a fucking thing. Then just like that, she was gone. Donna DeLuca."

"You sound so heartbroken," she said, thinking about her reticence with her own crush, Noah Pearlman. She would have to fix that.

"If you had asked me any time in the last forty years what I would do if I ever saw Donna again . . ." He trailed off, sounding hopeless.

At that, Joybird's inner child poked at her scarred heart, reminding her of what it felt like when he'd walked out all those years ago. She'd been too young to understand why her parents had split up, and struggled to cope. Even then, she had a predilection for silver linings, and settled on the romantic notion that the marital problems were temporary—perhaps even a symptom of loving each other *too* much. Then, when her mother died—forever severing the possibility of a reconciliation with her father—young Joybird told herself their love story was an exquisite tragedy.

Of course, she grew to understand it had been a childish fantasy. Her father's ambition had driven him away—the lure of tinsel too strong to keep him in New York, existing on the ragged fringes of Bohemia. Learning about Donna brought it all back, and Joybird had to remind herself that she was a grown-up and could deal with her father's feelings for another woman.

"Finish that thought," she prompted him.

"Why?" he asked. "What's the point?"

"Because finding her shouldn't be that hard, and maybe you could reach out on Facebook or something."

"Birdie," he said, "you think I haven't been looking for Donna on Facebook since the day I first typed *password* as my password?"

"Please tell me your password isn't *password*," she said.

"Not anymore."

She relaxed. "Thank god."

"Now it's my birthday."

"Dad!" she said, alarmed.

"I'm kidding. Jesus, I'm not an idiot." He let out a long, sad sigh. "Except when it comes to Donna DeLuca."

Chapter 3

Donna DeLuca.

Sid Marcus rubbed his temples as if he could massage away his own stupidity. How could he have done it? How could he have let the opportunity slip by again? It would have been so easy to go after her, to hell with Gerald Platt. But he'd just sat there—inert, mute, powerless.

"There has to be some way to find her," his daughter said.

"I don't even know her married name."

Her eyes went wide in concern, but she instantly collected herself. Sid understood. His daughter was alarmed at the idea he might pursue a married woman, but she wanted to tread carefully so as not to hurt his feelings. And that was the big difference between them. He almost never stopped to rein himself in. But damn it, he was trying.

"Well, if Donna's married," she said gently, "maybe you shouldn't—"

"Divorced," he explained. "At least that's what I heard through the grapevine."

Joybird considered this. "I had no idea you carried a torch all these years," she admitted.

"Of course you didn't," he said, the acid of guilt churning in his gut as he thought about their many years of separation. He'd left this kid twice. Once, when he walked out on her mother and fled to LA, and then a second time, after her mother had died and he couldn't seem to manage being a responsible parent, convincing himself she was better off with her grandparents.

Now, he hoped to make up for it. There was so much he wanted to give her.

"I wonder if you never really stopped looking for her," Joybird said in that blunt way she had of probing a person's heart.

She was, he knew, talking about his three marriages, but this wasn't a conversation he wanted to have with his kid. So he said, "Don't be an idiot," even though he knew it was unkind. It was a knee-jerk reaction—a way to control the conversation—and exactly the sort of thing he wanted to get a handle on. "What I mean is," he added, trying to soften his tone, "if I was looking for Donna, I would have stayed on the East Coast."

"I meant on a subconscious level," she clarified.

He waved it away, not eager to be psychoanalyzed. "Point is," he said, "I've reached a dead end. Without her last name—"

"I'm sure one of your old classmates would know it."

"I've lost touch with everyone."

"What about Mike Hillier?" she asked, somehow remembering the friend he'd followed out to LA all those years ago.

"Dead."

"Mike Hillier is dead?" she echoed, surprised. "I'm sorry."

He shrugged. "Guy was a dick."

"Wasn't there another friend?" She squinted, trying to remember the name. "For some reason I think his name is Ruby, but that can't be right."

"Reuben," he said. "You're thinking of Reuben Ross."

"That sounds familiar," she said.

"I can't believe you remember that fucking guy."

"He was over at the house."

"Well, forget him," he practically spit. "Forget Reuben Ross."

She studied his face. "You had a falling out?"

"I don't want to talk about it." He folded his arms for punctuation, but he could tell Joybird wasn't done. Fortunately, the buzzer rang in two quick bursts, indicating the arrival of Betty Simon, the Joni Mitchell fan from upstairs. Joybird opened the door.

Betty was in her early seventies, a retired journalist with wiry white hair and dangly earrings. She wore a Grateful Dead T-shirt and black jeans, and had a plate balanced on her hand. Though she was a few years older than Sid, he knew her type—an old hippie who'd clung proudly to her flower child ideals through all these decades. She probably still had a fringed jacket in her closet with a George McGovern button pinned to the front.

"I'm so sorry about the music," Joybird said, glancing over her shoulder at him.

"I was enjoying it," Betty said. "I'm just sorry I upset the old boy."

He grunted a laugh at being called *old boy*, even though he knew she was trying to get a rise out of him.

"I brought a peace offering," Betty said to Sid, holding out the plate she carried.

When he made no move to rise from his chair, Joybird took it from her. "Brownies," she observed, looking down. "How sweet of you."

"They'd better be laced," Sid muttered.

"The only recipe I know," Betty admitted.

At that, Sid stood, rubbing his hands together at the thought of getting stoned. "I'll put on some Grateful Dead."

Chapter 4

Joybird needed to get some sleep, so she left the two boomers munching their brownies, combing through her father's collection of vinyl records, and went into her bedroom. A short time later, as she drifted to sleep listening to the gentle guitar intro to "Sugar Magnolia," Joybird decided the universe had given her a gift. She might not be able to repair the damage she had done to Devon Cato, but she now had a path to fix the one person she'd been trying to make happy her entire life. All she had to do was find Donna DeLuca.

The next morning, Joybird surveyed the mess—record albums strewn across the living room floor, brownie crumbs congregating beneath the stereo, empty beer bottles on almost every surface. In the kitchen, cabinet doors had been left wide open as if there had been a raid. A pizza box sat precariously balanced on the small café table in the corner, next to an empty take-out tin. It wasn't hard for Joybird to figure out exactly what had happened: her father and Betty had scrounged for snacks, found nothing they liked, and ordered in from Grimaldi's.

She closed the cabinets, swept the floor, gathered the beer bottles, threw out the empty pasta tin, and left the record albums for her father to clean up. Then she made a pot of coffee and took the last slice of pizza from the box so it wouldn't go to waste. After warming it in the toaster oven, Joybird sat down to have it for breakfast. She took a few bites, wiped the orangey oil off her fingertips, and opened her laptop. There was work to do.

She quickly discovered that her father had been right about locating Donna DeLuca on Facebook. It was impossible. There were literally dozens of people with that name and no guarantee any of them was actually her. Finding Reuben Ross—who might have kept track of Donna—wasn't much easier, especially since Joybird wasn't sure how he spelled his first name. After going down one rabbit hole after another for nearly two hours, she had to get dressed and start driving. This wasn't defeat—merely a pause, putting her mission on hold because her rent was almost due and there were several bills on autopay that were about to drain her checking account. It was time to make some money.

Driving an Uber was never supposed to be a long-term gig. After the state senator she'd worked for lost his seat, Joybird decided she was done with politics. Not that she stopped believing in the important work of local Democrats, but she wanted to be more hands-on when it came to helping people. At first, the legislative-aide job was perfect. Joybird loved answering phones in the senator's Brooklyn office and figuring out how to help constituents with their problems. It was hectic and invigorating. When she was promoted to office manager, she was thrilled at the recognition. And though she tried telling herself the administrative work was just as important as anything else, it offered little fulfillment. So when the senator lost the primary to a younger and more progressive candidate, Joybird decided to pursue her dream of being a life coach. She was thirty-one and couldn't see any reason to put off starting the next chapter of her life. All she needed was to finish the online course she had begun and a little time to sock away some cash.

She had been on track too . . . until her father's career collapsed and he told her he needed a place to stay while he got back on his feet. There had been nothing to do but help her roommate, Zabeen, find other accommodations, and let the once-great Sid Marcus work out of her apartment rent-free.

As Joybird closed her laptop, her father shuffled into the kitchen in his incongruous Dolce & Gabbana bathrobe, which probably cost more than her entire wardrobe. A holdover from his successful days in

Hollywood, the black-and-gold jacquard wraparound made his lazy grooming look defiantly eccentric.

"Working on something?" he asked, pointing to the computer.

"Not really," she lied. Her goal was to find Donna DeLuca in secret and then surprise him. She could imagine the look on his face, and the very thought made her heart as buoyant as a life preserver.

"Like father, like daughter," he said, then opened the empty pizza box. "Where's that slice?"

She looked down at her plate, where all that was left was a crust. His eyes followed hers.

"And I thought you loved me," he said.

Joybird felt a squeeze of remorse. "Sorry. Were you saving it?"

"There's nothing to eat in this joint."

"You should have gone shopping," she said gently.

"Why?"

"So you'd have something for breakfast."

"I *had* pizza."

She sighed, wishing he didn't always feel so victimized by life. "What about Cheerios?"

"I'd rather go back to bed."

Joybird poured a cup of coffee and handed it to him. "Why don't you work on your script?" she said. "I have to get ready to go."

"Wait a minute," he begged, looking guilty. "I forgot I was supposed to ask how your day was yesterday."

Joybird put a hand on his shoulder to let him know she appreciated the inquiry. "Pretty good," she said, wrestling with guilt of her own. It was hard to focus on all the folks she had helped—people who reached their destinations feeling considerably better—and not on the one she had hurt.

"No annoying assholes?"

She hesitated, searching his face for sympathy. It wasn't his strength, for sure, but he was making an effort.

"Well?" he pressed.

Nodding thoughtfully, Joybird decided it would help to talk about it. "The only asshole was me," she admitted.

"*You?*" he asked. "What'd you do, take some poor schmuck's last slice of pizza?"

Joybird let out a breath and poured herself another cup of coffee. "Some stockbroker guy asked me out, and I rejected him."

"Must have been a real prick," he offered, and Joybird knew he was trying to be sympathetic.

She sat down. "He wasn't. Not at all."

"A fatty?"

She pictured Devon's symmetrical face, his sharp cheekbones, the big dark eyes behind those glasses. "He was actually very handsome."

"So why won't you go out with him?"

"There's more to attraction than looks," she said.

"To who?" he asked. "Stevie Wonder?"

"To lots of people."

"Not male people."

"Plenty of men would disagree with that," Joybird insisted.

Sid shook his head. "Only when they're trying to score with an ugly chick," he explained.

"Ah," she said, certain she'd snared him in his own faulty logic. "If looks are the only criteria, why would they want to sleep with an 'ugly chick'?"

He picked up the leftover crust from her plate and bit into it. "Desperation. If they had a choice, they'd go after the hot one. Every time."

"Well, I'm not going after Devon Cato."

"What's wrong with him?"

Joybird sipped her coffee and thought about his beautiful face and intoxicating cologne, faltering for just a moment before remembering his slick suit, his designer glasses, and his pricey condo. "He's a Wall Street guy," she said quickly. "You want some toast?"

Sid rubbed his eyes, his expression turning morose, as if he were retreating someplace painful.

"Dad?" she prodded.

"Huh?" he said, as if he'd been too far away to hear.

"Toast?"

"Whatever."

Joybird went to the freezer and retrieved a loaf of whole wheat bread. She unstuck the top two slices and put them in the toaster oven.

"You thinking about Donna?" she asked.

He shook her off, as if struggling to find his way back to their conversation. "Tell me about the Wall Street guy," he said. "Why didn't you like him?"

Joybird's confusion over her parents' failed marriage came flooding back to her, culminating in one of the few visual memories from her childhood that remained vivid—her mother weeping at the kitchen table after her father had left.

She turned back to him, refocusing. "Can you picture me with a stockbroker type?" she asked.

"Why not?"

"Different values, Dad," Joybird said, turning the toaster dial to medium-light.

Frustrated, he gestured toward the heavens. "I raised a fucking commie."

"I'm not a commie," she said. *And you didn't raise me,* she nearly added.

After Joybird's parents divorced, her father moved to Los Angeles and she stayed in Brooklyn with her mother. Then when she was eight and her mom died, he came and got her, bringing her back to California to live with him, his new wife, and his baby son in their fancy Malibu home. For a few years, things were pretty good. But then the show he worked on got canceled, and his wife left, taking Joybird's half brother with her. Sid and Joybird came back to the East Coast and moved in with his parents in Connecticut while he did freelance jobs punching up other people's scripts. Less than a year later, he got a new writing gig and went back to LA. This time, he didn't take Joybird with him.

She was moved into her other grandparents' house in Queens, and that became her home until she went away to college. In the meantime, her father remarried and often went weeks without remembering to call.

"Then what do you have against money?" he asked. "Trust me, there's a lot to be said for having a few bucks in the bank." He tightened the sash on his bathrobe.

"I don't have anything against money," she said, thinking about her dwindling savings. "I just want someone who shares my values."

"I get it," he said. "But I want to know you're taken care of. If I hadn't lost everything—"

"I can take care of myself, Dad," she told him. "Don't worry about me."

Sid nodded, but she could tell he didn't accept her assurance. To her father, a happy life in a modest Brooklyn apartment was far from aspirational. He wanted her to be at least as wealthy as his ex-wives. She understood that, on some level, he felt like he owed that to her. Joybird hoped she could show him it wasn't true.

"How'd you let the poor guy down?" he asked.

"I told him I couldn't go out with him. Unfortunately, he took it personally."

"So he *is* fat," her father said, trying to hold back a laugh. "I knew it!"

"Stop," she demanded.

"No offense, Birdie, but I love when you PC types can't even—"

"Dad!" she insisted. "*No.* He's not overweight. And even if he was, it wouldn't make a difference to me."

"That sounds awfully defensive," he taunted. "Did I hit a nerve?"

Joybird rolled her eyes. She would never get used to the teasing he enjoyed so much.

The toaster dinged, and he didn't make a move. With a sigh, Joybird retrieved the slices and put them on a plate. She pushed it onto the table in front of him.

"You forgot the butter," he said.

Joybird sat down and folded her arms, wrapping herself in righteous indignation.

"Now you're pissed?" he said. "Come on. Give me a break. I was playing around."

No, she thought, *I'm not going to give you a break.* Because if he'd made even the slightest effort to get to know her, he'd understand how ridiculous his accusation was. She valued people based on their character, not on their looks, not on their possessions, and certainly not on their money. Still, she felt a wriggle of unease, because hadn't she judged Devon Cato based on his job? No, she decided. That didn't count, because she wasn't looking down on him—just acknowledging they were incompatible.

"I thought you PC types liked to own your own shit," he added.

"There's nothing to own here," she insisted.

He got up, opened the refrigerator, and retrieved the butter. "Yeah?" he said. "Ever date a fat guy?"

In fact, she had dated several guys her father would have considered unattractive and unworthy. But she simply told him it was none of his business, deciding she didn't have to justify herself to him.

Sid sat down at the table and ran a smear of butter across his toast. "I rest my case," he said, and bit into it.

Joybird sighed. She knew she had the facts that would convince any judge or jury, but she simply said, "Just once in a while, you should try not thinking the worst of people."

He finished chewing and took a sip of his coffee. "Where's the fun in that?" he asked.

Chapter 5

Sid finished his toast, finished his coffee, and even finished his morning shuffle to the deli to pick up the *New York Times*. Now there was nothing to do but thumb through the paper, taking as long as he could so he wouldn't have to face his script, which he knew was not nearly as funny or edgy as it needed to be.

Donna. She had done this to him. Or, no, that wasn't really fair. It was him. He had done this to himself, going practically fetal at the sight of her.

Still, what was the point of dwelling on it? He had to focus. He had to do the work.

In the past, there had been people he could have called. People to bounce ideas off, people willing to read the script, give him notes, and rip into him if he needed it. Hell, in the past, he'd be writing under contract, collaborating with a room full of talented jackasses—one funnier than the next—and not pounding out a spec script like some damned neophyte who just discovered Final Draft.

The irony was that during all those insufferable hours in the writers' room, he'd believed that if he could just be unleashed—with the freedom to create on his own—he'd produce a masterpiece. And maybe he could have. Maybe if he hadn't seen her again, he'd have already finished a rewrite and been on his way, instead of reliving that moment again and again and again.

He tried telling himself it was the pressure. That was why he froze—he was just so focused on making things right with his daughter that he couldn't get out of his own way. Sid desperately wanted to strike gold with this script so he could take care of her. And then maybe he could relax at last and write the novel he'd always dreamed of. He'd been thinking about it for decades, more focused on the respect it would earn him than the story itself. He imagined something literary but with enough humor to keep the reader engaged. He envisioned glowing endorsements from writers like Richard Russo and John Irving. Deep down, Sid knew the book would have to be about Donna in some way. Maybe not specifically, but the focus would be on second chances. And the main character wouldn't be a Hollywood comedy writer—he'd be some poor schmuck who never left Connecticut, never went after what he wanted. The title would be *Rocky Hill*, after a little town outside Hartford. Sid had no particular connection to the place, but he liked the name and its inferences.

Eventually, he'd find the time to do it, but for now Sid had to focus on selling his TV pilot. Platt had been his best shot. Then the bastard called his pitch "interesting," and it took all the air from his tires. So by the time he laid eyes on Donna, he had driven straight into a ditch.

He had to get his focus back. It was all for Joybird, after all. When he'd first arrived in New York, Sid led her to believe he had nowhere else to go so she'd take him in. In truth, he'd had options. Okay, option. Singular. After Heather threw him out, he moved to a small apartment in LA and started seeing Lauren, a makeup artist with a hoarse laugh and a quick temper. They'd known each other for years, and when his big deal fell through and the money dried up, she invited him to live with her. He talked himself into believing it was a good move, even though it wasn't love—not for either of them. It was loneliness, and they both knew it. *Maybe,* he'd told himself, *it's better this way.* Aside from her barks and his bites, they got along pretty well, and the sex was exciting. Maybe it would even last.

But then The Thing happened. The non–heart attack. His cardiologist had been pretty blasé about the whole episode—as if getting a stent was about as serious as a root canal—but it felt serious to Sid. When it all started, with chest pain that sent him to the hospital, he had imagined Joybird getting the news her old man had died, and then learning there was nothing left for her. So even as Lauren held his hand and told him she would be there for him no matter what, he knew it was time to make up for all the shit he'd caused in Joybird's life. He decided he would go back east to forge a connection. He wouldn't tell Joybird about the issue with his heart, as the last thing he wanted was a relationship based on pity. And since the cardiologist assured him he was practically as good as new, there was no reason she needed to know. So all he had to do was mend their relationship. And meanwhile, he'd write the best damned script of his life and set her up so she could leave her crap apartment behind and not have to spend the rest of her life worrying about buying pizza one slice at a time.

Unfortunately, nothing was working out as he had planned. His determination to teach her how to toughen up for this messed-up world was falling on willfully deaf ears. That kid. Dear god. She was destined to be crushed, and it about killed him.

Money would help, but the only way to get it would be to write a pilot so strong those bastards would have to buy it.

Sid glanced over at his laptop, sitting there inert and taunting, daring him to open his script or check his email. But either one would be depressing. He was still waiting to hear from an old friend who'd landed a great showrunner gig. Sid knew better than to beg for a job, so he'd simply reached out for an agent referral. Not a big ask, but the guy probably knew Sid had been ditched by his long-term rep when the shit hit the fan. By this point—a week later—Sid had nearly given up on expecting a reply.

Forget the email, he told himself. *Find a way to fix this anemic script. Deep down, you know what it needs. Just keep digging.*

Sid Marcus understood that one of his greatest talents as a writer was the ability to give his own work a fresh read. He had a specific trick for it, going into a zone to imagine himself as someone else. The key was to find someone he understood and admired, someone with a good critical eye. Then he'd simply read the script *as* that person. It had always served him well. That is, until recently. But maybe it was a good day to try again. He leaned back in the chair and closed his eyes, combing through his mental Rolodex to find someone appropriate—someone sharp, funny, and fresh. At last, he landed on Adam Henderson, an impressive young writer he'd worked with a decade ago. The kid—now well into his forties—had incredible radar for what needed to be cut and replaced, and was currently one of the hottest producers around.

Just as Sid opened his laptop, his phone buzzed with a text. It was Betty, asking if he wanted to grab a bite. He glanced at his script, wondering what the old broad would think of it. She was a retired reporter with discerning taste and a keen eye for bullshit. Maybe one of these days he'd ask her to read it.

For now, though, the script could wait. Sid closed his computer and picked up his phone to tap out a reply: Fuck yeah.

Chapter 6

Joybird restocked the snacks and water bottles in the back of her car before settling into the driver's seat, where she opened the Uber Driver app on her phone. Equipped with geo-positioning technology, it read her location and sent her to a Brooklyn Heights address just a few blocks away. Her day was off to a busy start, as she brought an elderly woman home from her granddaughter's house and then a young woman to work in Manhattan, followed by an elderly couple returning from a doctor's appointment.

Later, she got a notification to pick up someone named Corinne from one of the fanciest Sutton Place addresses. When an angular blonde woman emerged from the building and walked toward the car, Joybird was surprised. Usually when she got a rider from such an exclusive enclave, it was an employee who worked for someone in the building. But this woman was dressed in a Chanel blazer and dark sunglasses, with a Birkin bag over the crook of her arm. Just the type who would have her own chauffeur.

"So how does this work?" the woman said when she slid into the back seat. Her voice sounded shaky, as if she'd been crying. "I've never taken an Uber before." Joybird noted a distinct air of Old Money.

"You're Corinne, right?"

"Corinne Wilbanks," the woman confirmed.

"Everything is done through the app," Joybird said. "It's pretty stress-free."

"I see. One of my people helped me with that, so I wasn't aware." Corinne looked down at a slip of paper in her hand and confirmed the address in the Murray Hill section of Manhattan, which Joybird already had in her phone.

"There are mints back there," Joybird said. "And candy. Please help yourself."

Her rider didn't say anything, but Joybird heard a sniffle. She glanced in the rearview mirror to see the woman take a tissue from her purse and surreptitiously wipe her nose.

"I'm not in the habit of crying in front of people," Corinne mumbled.

"It's fine. Everyone cries sometimes."

"Do they?" She seemed genuinely curious but a little dubious, as if this had never occurred to her before.

"Of course!" Joybird chirped. A cheerful tone was always her secret weapon.

Corinne straightened her back. "Well. My father doesn't."

Joybird tried to picture her own father crying and couldn't conjure the image. He was more of a ranter than a weeper. "I guess mine doesn't either," she said. "But I consider raging his form of crying."

"Daddy is like that too," Corinne said, staring out the window, and Joybird took it as an opening.

"You two don't get along?" she asked.

Corinne let out a steadying breath. "It's Daddy's fault I'm on this little jaunt. He's cutting me off, and I have to look for a new place."

"Sorry to hear it."

"I'm not destitute, you understand," Corinne said sharply, as if Joybird had accused her of something. "I simply need to make some . . . adjustments."

Joybird nodded, assuming this woman was heiress to an old fortune that dwindled with each generation. If her father was cutting her off, it probably just meant she would need to dig into her own inheritance.

"Is that where I'm taking you—to look at a new apartment?"

"I'm meeting a Realtor there."

"Murray Hill's a nice area," Joybird offered.

Corinne gave an exasperated sigh. "I've never lived downtown before." She paused to dab at her nose. *"Never."*

At the next red light, Joybird glanced back at the woman's stoic visage and decided there was something almost anthropological about studying someone who considered the aspirational neighborhood of Murray Hill *déclassé*. The woman took off her sunglasses, and it was clear she had spent some time crying, as her eyelids looked raw and pink.

"Have you always lived on Sutton Place?" Joybird asked.

"Not always, but mostly. My family owns a few properties in the area."

"Where else have you lived?" Joybird pressed, figuring there was something in the "not always" she might want to chat about.

"An Upper East Side high-rise for a few years with my ex. He's in Brooklyn now."

"That's where I live," Joybird said, trying to open a new topic.

Corinne barely acknowledged the remark as she wiped daintily at her nose.

"Are you at all excited about finding a new place?" Joybird tried.

"Excited?" the woman repeated, as if the word sounded only vaguely familiar.

"Maybe it would help if you thought about it as an adventure, a fresh start."

Corinne sniffled heroically, and Joybird bit her lip, trying to think of another tactic to turn the woman's mood around.

"I bet this Murray Hill place is lovely," she said. "What do you know about it?"

"Two bedrooms plus a maid's room."

That's three bedrooms, Joybird thought, *for one person.* "Sounds like a lot of space," she offered.

"But all of my friends are on the Upper East Side," Corinne argued, as if the location was a deal killer.

Joybird knew how provincial New Yorkers could be, but this sounded a little extreme. "It's not like you're moving to Wisconsin."

"To *my* friends it is."

"So you'll visit *them*," Joybird said. "And you'll make new friends."

"Does one make new friends at forty-two?"

"Why not?"

Corinne waved away the comment, took out her phone, and made a call. "It's me," she said quietly. "No, Daddy wouldn't budge . . . Are you kidding? Mother just sat there staring into her tea. I'm on my way now to look at an . . . Oh, I wish . . . Do you really want me to? Because this could take a while . . . Yes, okay . . . I miss you too . . . When is she coming back?" She lowered her voice to a throaty whisper. "The black ones . . . Of course, silly . . . Stop, I'm in an Uber . . . Kenny, I'm serious . . . Okay, I'll see you later."

Joybird kept her eyes on the road, pretending she hadn't heard what sounded like a rendezvous with a married man. At the very least, it seemed to brighten the woman's spirits.

A few minutes later, they arrived at the building on East Twenty-Ninth Street. "Well, this looks pretty," Joybird said as she pulled to the curb.

Corinne put her sunglasses back on. "Listen, I don't imagine it will take very long for me to see the apartment. Could I trouble you to wait for me?"

"Sure, not a problem. Or you could just arrange for another Uber when you're done. Whatever you like."

"I would like you to wait. In fact, could I hire you for the day? I have several apartments to see."

Joybird paused, surprised. She hadn't thought she'd made any sort of impression, but maybe she had. Maybe Corinne Wilbanks was eager for the friendly companionship. Or maybe Joybird just represented a convenience. Either way, the problem was that she would need to do it privately, off the Uber app. She knew that plenty of other drivers did this, but she wasn't sure how to suggest it. "I'd like to," she said. "But it's a little complicated."

"Can't I just hire you privately? How much do you usually make in a day?" Corinne's voice was more forceful than it had been, and Joybird understood that she had experience negotiating with workers to get what she wanted.

"About two hundred dollars, depending on how long I drive."

"I'll pay you three hundred, cash. Does that sound fair?"

"More than fair," Joybird said, genuinely delighted at her good fortune. She would not only be bringing home a windfall, but she would be engaging with someone who could truly benefit from some life coaching.

"Good," pronounced Corinne Wilbanks. Then she smoothed out her jacket and went into the building.

While she waited, Joybird used her phone to access a people-finding app and continued her search for her father's old friend Reuben Ross. She limited her inquiry to New York, and after several minutes, she located a man in Forest Hills, Queens, who was the right age. The website listed the first names of his relatives: Carol, Gregory, Natalie. Joybird recalled playing with the Rosses' son—a chubby boy named Greg. She smiled. This was the Reuben Ross she was looking for.

The rear door of Joybird's car swung open, and Corinne Wilbanks got in. "Dreadful," she muttered.

"The apartment?" Joybird asked. "What was wrong with it?"

"It doesn't even have baseboard molding."

Joybird turned to face her. "Is that important to you?"

Corinne took off her glasses and pinched the bridge of her nose. "I don't know *what's* important to me." Her cell phone rang, and she answered the call. Joybird turned back toward the windshield to give her some privacy.

"Aldo!" she oozed into the phone. "I didn't expect to . . . Yes, ghastly . . . A few more, if I have the strength . . . No, I made plans . . .

Really?" She gave a throaty laugh. "You're *bad* . . . I shouldn't . . . How could I say no to that? I'll call you later."

She got off the phone and spent several minutes texting. Joybird wondered if Corinne was canceling her tryst with Kenny to spend time with Aldo. She was vaguely relieved, since it seemed pretty clear Kenny was married. Not that it was any of her business, but it was hard not to get invested. Also, she was imagining herself as Corinne's life coach, wondering how she might steer this woman to make better choices.

"I have three more apartments to see in this area alone," Corinne said to her. "I wish there was some way to narrow it down. How do people decide if they want the one with the big bedroom, the one with the marble bath, the one with the sunken living room? I know people prioritize, but . . . I haven't done this for so long."

"Maybe I can help you figure out what you want," Joybird said. "Tell me what you like to do in your spare time."

Corinne's cell phone rang, and she held up a manicured finger. "Just a minute," she said. "I have to take this."

Joybird took out her own phone and checked her email and social media accounts, trying to create a wall of privacy. But Corinne's voice was hard to ignore.

"I'm sorry," she said. "A text was just easier—I'm looking at apartments . . . Don't be mad . . . Kenny, come on. We can do it tomorrow . . . I am not! Stop it . . . Stop it . . . Well, fuck you, too, then." Her voice rose to a restrained scream as she seethed through her teeth. "Fuck you, fuck you, fuck you!"

Joybird was shocked to hear this very controlled woman become so unhinged. But then Corinne dropped the phone back in her purse and regained her composure. "What were we saying?" she asked in a perfectly modulated tone of voice.

Joybird took a few steadying breaths, as the woman's fury had unsettled her. She turned to face the back seat. "Is . . . uh . . . everything okay?" she asked.

Corinne waved off her concern. "I get involved with men who are like children. Now, we were discussing something. My activities?"

"I was asking what you like to do in your spare time."

"Well," Corinne said, her voice becoming more formal. "That's hard to say. I mean, I'm involved with several foundations, and my social life is all wrapped up in my work."

"What about your creative outlets?"

Corinne looked surprised. "How did you know I was creative?"

"I could just tell," Joybird said. In truth, everyone thought they were creative but rarely got to talk about it. In her experience, the question made people feel special.

"You know, I used to paint. A long time ago."

"What did you paint?"

"Mostly landscapes. Lush, lush landscapes. With slashes of unexpected color. My teacher said I had a gift."

"Why did you stop?" Joybird pressed.

"I guess . . . I don't know. I just got busy with other things. And my father always said it was a colossal waste of time."

"Do you want to get back to it?"

Corinne took off her glasses and stared into space. Joybird could sense a powerful personal examination coming on, and gave her time.

"Painting," Corinne whispered reverently, and her eyes filled with tears. She closed them and held up her bony hand. "I see a canvas. A green meadow and a pale-yellow sky tinged with bright coral and just a small scrape of bloodred. It's pulsing. It's inside me."

It sounded like rapture. And okay, maybe a little bit deranged. But perhaps this very lost woman was actually on her way to finding some clarity.

"I think I have to do this!" Corinne gushed. "I think I have to paint again!"

"Well, that's wonderful," Joybird said, because if Corinne Wilbanks had some kind of mental illness, expressing herself would surely help. "And it gives you a focus for your apartment search. You'll want someplace with big windows and great light . . . and a room you can use for a studio."

"Yes!" Corinne cried. "I'll call Regina."

Corinne phoned her Realtor, and after explaining what she wanted—a sunny place, but not on the West Side—Joybird drove her to a high-rise in the east thirties, near the river, and waited in the car while Corinne went in. When she came out twenty minutes later, she told Joybird she had signed a lease and left a deposit. She seemed ecstatic.

"You have changed my life!" she gushed. "I don't even know how to thank you."

For a moment, Joybird couldn't speak. This was exactly what she had always wanted to do, and it filled her. She swallowed against a bulge in her throat. "I'm so . . . glad."

"You know, I've been seeing a therapist for ten years, and she's never helped me this much. You should consider that profession. You'd be wonderful. I imagine it pays more than driving a car service, yes?"

"Actually, I studied to be a life coach. That's my career goal."

"Oh, you should do it! You must!"

The compliment was like a soothing salve. "Thank you. It's just going to take me a little time, but I'll get there."

Corinne leaned forward and handed her cell phone to Joybird. "Put your number in my phone, and I'll send you a text so you'll have my number too. I'm going to recommend you to all my friends. You'll have a full calendar in no time!"

Joybird hesitated. She hadn't envisioned herself with a client base of people who were already so privileged. But she supposed it couldn't hurt to jump-start her business with some fancy clients . . . especially if she could truly help them. And so she tapped her number into Corinne Wilbanks's phone and handed it back to her.

"My friend Maya is going up to Connecticut next week," Corinne said. "I bet she would pay you good money to drive her if you could help her sort out her life. She's trying to figure out if she should leave her husband."

"Wow," Joybird whispered, absorbing the idea of being hired specifically as a mobile life coach, as Devon Cato had suggested. Was it really possible? Could she really turn this into a business? Joybird pondered this as she drove Corinne to Aldo's apartment, where the excited woman went inside to celebrate.

While she waited, Joybird dashed to a nearby deli to buy herself a sandwich. Back in the car, she opened the people-finding app where she'd found Reuben Ross's phone number. As she ate, Joybird thought about how she would explain who she was and what kind of information she sought about Donna DeLuca. When she was confident she could get it all out without sounding like a stalker, she called the number. Unfortunately, it rang and rang and rang. It didn't even go to voicemail. Perhaps it was an old listing. She might have to come up with another plan to find her father's lost love.

Nearly two hours later, Corinne staggered toward the car, drunk. Joybird got out to help her into the back seat. She assumed the half-baked passenger would want to go straight home and sleep it off, but she didn't. She wanted to meet some friends at a bar around the corner from where she lived on Sutton Place. Joybird tried, gently, to talk her out of it, but Corinne was adamant.

Before she left the car, Corinne pressed three hundred dollars into Joybird's hand. "I can't wait to start painting again," she slurred. "I think it's going to be so . . . so . . . good for me."

"I think so too," Joybird said.

"And also," Corinne added, "Daddy will just shit."

Chapter 7

With more time, Joybird would have coached Corinne to live for her own fulfillment, not for revenge on her father. But she hoped—no, she *knew*—that the physical distance from him, together with the creative expression of painting, would lead the troubled woman down a better path.

For Joybird, of course, physical distance from her own father had been a different story, as she had been too young, and it had gone on too long. But she was over all that now, having decided that she didn't want to dwell in the negativity of abandonment. Anyway, it was never too late to start over, and with her whole beating heart, Joybird believed that their current proximity in that cramped apartment was a chance to connect—to have the kind of relationship she'd always dreamed of. She just had to try a little harder, and they'd both get their happily-ever-afters.

But for now, she had her mind on something else—she was mulling Devon Cato's idea about turning her Honda into a therapy office. Maybe she'd been too quick to dismiss it. *Maybe it could work.* She felt such an ebullient tingle at the thought that she stopped to rein herself in. She needed a way to examine this objectively.

When she got home, Joybird was delighted to find her father and Betty in the living room, happily listening to the Beatles song "Here, There and Everywhere."

"Dad! Betty!" she exclaimed exuberantly, just as she noticed the enticing aroma of something garlicky simmering on the stove. The scene stirred a primal response in Joybird, like the fulfillment of a wish she didn't even know she had. Her eyes went damp.

"This is . . . *beautiful!*" she blurted, nearly choking with emotion at the homey domesticity she'd happened upon.

Betty greeted her warmly, but Sid looked perplexed.

"Beautiful?" he asked, and she knew he was confused by her near rapture. To him, they were simply a couple of aging boomers trying to get comfortable on cheap furniture from Ikea.

"The two of you," Joybird explained. "The blossoming of this friendship." It was the best she could do, trying to put the feeling into words. But it was like attempting to explain a work of art that shimmered with emotion.

She dropped her keys by the door, hung her sweater on the narrow coatrack, and turned back to see her father pick up a bong she hadn't noticed before. He clicked a lighter and took a long hit.

With the smoke still in his lungs, he turned to Betty and spoke. "We're smoking weed, and *she's* the one who's high."

"I just meant it's good to see you getting along," Joybird said, walking back her effusiveness. She crossed to the kitchen to see what was on the stove.

"Don't get excited," Sid called. "I'd be friends with Harvey Weinstein if he brought me free pot."

Joybird gave an exasperated sigh. "Harvey Weinstein, Dad? Really?"

"I was going to say Mussolini," he explained. "But Harvey Weinstein is funnier."

Joybird ignored his comment and looked in the pan to see what was cooking. It was a chicken-and-mushroom dish in a brownish cream sauce, and it smelled heavenly. She found her wooden spoon and gave the simmering pot a stir to make sure nothing stuck to the bottom. "Did you get any writing done today?" she asked over her shoulder.

"Not unless you count that Harvey Weinstein joke," he said.

"I'm sure tomorrow will be better," Joybird offered, trying to sound positive. She could sense he needed encouragement.

"What's the point?" he asked. "Mussolini would have an easier time selling a script than Sid Marcus."

Betty let her head roll back, a faraway look in her eyes. "Have you met him?" she said to Sid.

"Mussolini?" he asked, sounding confused and looking more stoned than he had a minute earlier.

"Harvey Weinstein."

Sid nodded, thinking. "No," he said, "but I once slept with a girl he fucked." He reached for the bong. "I guess that's not really saying much since he—"

"For god's sake, Dad!" Joybird said, covering her ears.

"My daughter has delicate sensibilities," Sid explained to Betty.

Joybird came into the room and took a seat on the sofa facing them. "Are you guys too stoned for a serious conversation?"

Sid scoffed. "What's more serious than fu—"

"Enough," Betty scolded. Then she reached out and patted Joybird's knee. "Something wrong?"

"Not wrong, no," Joybird said, and hesitated, glancing at her father. He looked fairly calm, so she continued, hoping he wouldn't feel compelled to deflate her enthusiasm. "It's actually something I'm getting excited about."

Sid turned to Betty. "Do you know she was asked out by a rich stockbroker and she turned him down because he's fat?"

Betty squinted at him, dubious, before turning to Joybird. "That's not true, is it?"

"Of course not!"

"So you *are* going out with him?" she asked.

Joybird shook her head, frustrated. "No, I'm just not *not* going out with him because he's fat. I mean, he's not fat, but that has nothing to do with it. I'm not going out with him because he's not my type."

"I actually followed all that," Betty admitted.

Joybird knew it was the kind of thing a stoned person would say, and she studied Betty's face. "Maybe we should have this conversation another time," she said, but her neighbor's expression was eager and attentive enough to put her at ease.

"It's about my career," she finally said. "You know how I've been struggling to save money to rent an office so I can open a life-coaching practice—"

"Watch out," Sid warned, putting down the bong. "She's going to ask for money."

Joybird sighed. Her father's mood seemed to be darkening. Maybe it had been a mistake to bring up his work. "I'm not asking for money," she explained, "just advice."

"Go on," Betty said gently.

"Well, I've been coaching while I drive, counseling my passengers right there in the car. And it's been working beautifully. I've helped a lot of people. Today I had this woman who was so lost, and I got her on track."

"You may have a real gift for this," Betty said.

"Thing is, I've been thinking about hanging my shingle in my Honda. I mean, opening up a private practice where I would coach people while driving them to their destinations."

Sid snorted, and Joybird took the bong to move it out of his reach.

"I got the idea from that Wall Street guy," she continued. "He was very smart and thought I should open my own business as a mobile life coach."

"Hate to point this out," her father said, "but you're already doing that."

"Yeah, but I'm hardly making any money. In effect, I'm giving away the life coaching for free. If my riders were clients, I could be doing it professionally. I know that sounds kind of mercenary, but . . ."

"It's not mercenary to get paid what you're worth," Betty told her.

"She doesn't have the street smarts for business," Sid interjected. "The kid'll get eaten alive."

Joybird studied him, feeling wounded. Did her father really think so little of her?

"Don't be so negative," Betty scolded him.

Joybird took a long breath, trying to relax the knot that had formed in her throat. "I'm thinking of calling it JoyRide—*your life coach on wheels*."

"See?" her father said, as if Joybird had just proved his point. "That sucks."

"Don't listen to him," Betty reassured her. "He's so bitter about his own failures, he hates to see others succeed."

"He has a lot of issues to work through," Joybird agreed.

"Hey!" Sid protested, looking hurt. "I'm *right here!*"

Betty pointed a finger at Sid. "Knock it off."

"What did I do?"

Betty shook her head. "First you hurt her feelings—then you played the victim. I call that being a *dick*."

Joybird was shocked Betty called her father out like that, and she felt her chest tighten as she waited for him to implode. She shifted on the couch and glanced around, wondering if she should just retreat to her room. But Sid, whose eyes were going hazy, simply shook his head.

"I'm just watching out for her," he insisted. "She needs a little tough love."

"That's the opposite of what she needs," Betty said, then turned to Joybird. "He really does mean well, but he's such a bitter old bastard, it gets in the way."

Sid gave an aggressive exhale. "I have a lot to be bitter about," he said.

"Oh, right," Betty said sarcastically, "the world's been very unfair to you. Poor Sid."

He stood, and Joybird could sense he was on the precipice, deciding between rage and resignation. She gripped her knees.

"In LA, people didn't talk to me like that!"

"Well, maybe they should have," Betty said calmly.

He opened his mouth and then closed it, looking as if his fuel had been siphoned. "Oh, fuck it," he said dismissively. "I'm hungry. You girls work this out. I'm getting something to eat."

As he walked off toward the kitchen, Betty turned to Joybird. "Kiddo," she said, "I think it's a marvelous idea. Let's figure out how to make this work."

Chapter 8

Less than three weeks later, harnessing everything she had learned from her online courses, Joybird had a website called JoyRideLifeCoach.com. When visitors entered the site, they were greeted by a cheerful banner photo of her standing in front of the sky-blue Honda, her dark wavy hair released from its ponytail, blowing upward as if pointing straight at heaven. The photographer had achieved the effect by shooting her from below, which also made her look larger than life . . . or at least taller than her five-foot-three frame. She was happy with the result, but the photographer—a friend of Betty's—wanted to retouch it, making her olive skin pinker, her blue eyes brighter, her wild hair a bit tamer. The suggestion surprised Joybird, who thought the photo was fine as is. No, better than fine. Her smile looked authentically exuberant—exactly what she was going for. The photo would stay untouched.

Most important of all, the site was easy to use, thanks to a reasonably priced online service for life coaches. One click and visitors accessed a page that let them fill out a brief intake form, request their combination coaching session / car service, and enter their payment information.

The day it went live, Joybird posted about it on social media, emailed some friends—many of whom promised to share the link far and wide—and sent a text to Corinne Wilbanks, the wealthy socialite turned artist. She'd even emailed the link to Noah Pearlman, and she knew it was only a matter of time before he sent his enthusiastic well-wishes. It seemed everyone liked the site. Everyone but her father, that is. He told Joybird it felt so woke it should come with its own rainbow flag and compost heap.

"Don't you like anything about it?" she asked.

"Yeah, it doesn't have my name on it."

"Dad," she pleaded.

"Okay, okay," he conceded. "It's very . . . upbeat. It suits you. And it'll never attract assholes like me, which is a good thing."

She kissed him on the head, grateful he was trying. She knew it hadn't been easy for him and that he'd been churning with self-loathing after missing his chance with Donna DeLuca, feeling like he'd never succeed at anything again. And it was getting worse. Trying to break the habit of taking it out on others was turning him into a walking cauldron of acid.

Still, she got him to concede that her new business had a decent shot. After all, there were already three clients scheduled for her first day of business—a young man who wanted career advice, an older woman who needed help with her jealous friends, and a teenage girl named Riley Wilbanks. Joybird assumed she was related to Corinne—perhaps a niece. In the "I'd like to discuss" section, she'd typed in: *I am surrounded by philistines.* Joybird could hardly wait.

Amid all the excitement, she continued trying to find Donna DeLuca, keeping it a secret from her father. She called the number for his old friend Reuben Ross several more times, and never reached anyone. Betty suggested she comb through her father's old high school yearbook so that she could identify other classmates and try to reach them. But that relic had gotten lost somewhere in the tumult of three divorces, so Joybird contacted Paxton Academy and arranged to purchase the 1972 edition. They promised it would arrive in a few weeks.

Joybird hoped it would be sooner than that, because she knew her father's mood was deteriorating despite his best efforts to hide it. For one thing, she rarely saw him working on his script, though he promised he was mentally writing even when he wasn't in front of his computer. She worried it was just an excuse for staring into space.

For now, though, there was something else on Joybird's mind. Before she transported her first official client, she wanted to thank the person who'd given her the idea: Devon Cato. It would also be the perfect opportunity to apologize for her unkindness, which had been weighing on her.

Since she had thrown away his business card, calling him wasn't an option. She decided that was okay because she really wanted to thank him in person. All Joybird had to do was park outside the Merrill Lynch building at close of business and wait for him to come out.

She arrived earlier than she had the day she'd been his Uber driver. Exiting her car, Joybird watched as a steady stream of office workers poured from the building, carrying handbags and briefcases and backpacks. Most walked in the direction of the subway, some got into waiting cars, and none were Devon Cato.

She kept checking the time. Five thirty. Five forty-nine. Six o'clock. Six twenty. Joybird squinted at the sky, trying to understand why she felt such crushing disappointment at the thought of missing him. With a shiver, she recalled the way he'd looked at her when he leaned in through the window, and the rise of heat made the truth impossible to ignore.

She shook it off and got into her car. It was time to leave.

Before pulling out of the space, though, she gave one last glance at the door and saw a square-shouldered form that looked like him. And just like that, her reticence evaporated. She bolted out of the car and stood in front of it.

"Devon!" she called excitedly. "Devon!"

He glanced from right to left before his eyes landed on her. Then he paused as if deciding what to do.

Smiling, she stepped aside to reveal the JoyRide decal on the passenger door, which she indicated with a dramatic flourish, like a TV hostess. Devon stared, and then a grin spread across his face. He walked toward her.

"I took your advice," she said, beaming. "I realized you were right, and figured I would come by to thank you in person. I hope you're not still mad at me."

He looked confused.

"You weren't mad?" she asked.

Devon rocked his head from side to side, considering it. "More disappointed than mad, but I let it go."

"You sure?" she asked. "Because it looked like you were crying."

He paused, then bit back a smile. "You thought I was *crying*?"

Joybird closed her eyes, recalling his shaking shoulders. "Were you laughing?"

"It *was* pretty funny," he said.

Joybird shifted her weight, considering what to say. She didn't want to challenge him, especially since she'd come to make amends, but she needed clarity. "You think I'm . . . comical?" she asked.

He held his thumb and forefinger a millimeter apart to indicate that yes, he thought she was a tiny bit comical for her bias against stockbrokers. She frowned.

"Shit," he said. "Now I hurt *your* feelings."

Ridicule was a bitter pill, so she simply decided not to swallow it. This, she believed, was exactly the kind of choice one could make in life if one wanted to be happy.

"I guess we're even," she said, her voice friendly. "Besides, it makes sense that you would find my values ridiculous."

"If it makes you feel better, I was impressed by your earnestness. It's refreshing."

She studied him, trying to decide if he was being condescending. But no, he looked genuinely delighted by her.

"Do you have a car waiting for you?" she asked, indicating the line of SUVs.

"I was heading to the subway," he said. "I'm not in the habit of taking Ubers home from work . . . unless I've had such a shitty day I can't face the R train."

She pointed to her car. "Can I give you a ride home then?"

"As a client?"

She shook her head. "As a friend I owe a favor to. Front seat. No charge."

"Best offer I've had all day."

"Great!" she bubbled, so effusively that he laughed. But not in derision. It was more like her happiness was contagious.

They got in the car and clicked in their seat belts. As Joybird turned the ignition, she asked him what happened with his department. "Did you get that client back?"

He gave a soft chuff. "That was never going to happen."

"Oh, I'm sorry, I—"

"But we got two more," he added. "And one is a real whale."

Joybird brought her hands together in delight. She loved when the universe came through like that. "You must be so relieved."

"I don't know if 'relieved' is the right word. It's not like I get to relax."

"Why not?"

"Because I will never stop having to prove myself."

Now Joybird frowned. That was a lot of stress to live under. "Are you sure this is what you want to do for a living?" she asked.

He waved off her comment. "Never mind. Tell me something about you."

She put the car in gear and looked into her side-view mirror. Clearly, he'd had enough on the topic of his job, and she understood. He wanted to take his mind off it. "What do you want to know?" she asked.

The scent of his cologne wafted toward her. It was delicate but distinctively earthy and organic, like juniper, with a hint of sweetness. She figured it must have been expensive stuff, lasting all day like that. It was so appealing, she wanted to ask him what it was called, but she thought he might misinterpret her interest.

"What keeps you up at night?" he said.

She glanced at him. It was an excellent question to get a person talking. She would try to remember it for her coaching sessions.

"Mostly my dad," she replied, relaying what he'd told her about Donna DeLuca. She explained how she had been trying to locate the woman, and how close she thought she was when she found Reuben Ross's phone number.

"You seem pretty invested in your father's happiness," he observed.

"I just hate to see him sad," she admitted. "His pain is so . . . palpable."

Joybird glanced at his face, wondering if he'd be judgmental. A lot of people found her empathy a sign of weakness—something she needed to fix. But Devon just nodded. She looked back at the road.

"I feel the same about my mom," he told her, looking down.

"Is she depressed?"

He went silent for a moment. "She was sick for a while. Watching her go through chemo was just . . ." He coughed, as if trying to cover for the tears welling. Joybird put a hand on his arm.

"Is she okay?"

He let out a long breath, recovering. "Thank god."

"Do you want to talk about it?"

"I want to talk about this guy who can help you find your father's mystery woman." Devon took out his phone and tried to look up Reuben Ross on another app. But the number he found was the same one she'd been calling.

"It looks like this is still his current address, though," he said.

"I know," she said. "I was wondering if he disconnected his landline."

"Point is, you know where the guy lives."

She stole another glance at Devon's profile. "You think I should write him a letter?"

He hesitated, as if he were waiting for her to take another guess. Joybird shifted her focus as she merged onto the Brooklyn Bridge. "What then?" she said.

55

"He lives in Forest Hills."

"And?" she asked. Joybird had noticed the address too. It was the fanciest neighborhood in Queens.

"And if you take the BQE, we could be there in thirty minutes."

She looked at him again, then back at the road. "You think I should just show up? Unannounced?"

"Worked with me, didn't it?"

"Just to clarify," Joybird said as she changed lanes to get out from behind a slow-moving car with a wood plank tied to the roof, "you want me to go there right now . . . and you'll come with me?"

He pushed his phone into the holder on her dashboard. "I programmed in the address."

Chapter 9

Aside from a slowdown on the Brooklyn–Queens Expressway—the highway with the worst traffic but, to Joybird's mind, the most glorious view of Manhattan's skyline—the trip to Reuben Ross's tree-canopied street in Forest Hills Gardens was easy. And then, there she was, parked in front of his majestic brick colonial in the JoyRide Honda.

"I guess we should just knock on the door," she said, feeling suddenly shy about this intrusion.

Devon shook his head. "Not we, *you*."

"You're not coming with me?" she asked, anxious and disappointed. She hadn't anticipated doing it alone.

"I'll be here for moral support," he said. "Trust me, you have a better shot without me."

When she blinked in confusion, he added, "I'm a Black man, Joybird. And this is an older white couple. Put two and two together."

Her hand flew to her chest. "I don't think you should assume they're racist," she said, hoping she didn't sound too terribly naive.

"Just playing the odds."

Joybird's stomach clenched at his discomfort, and her first instinct was to say something to make him feel better. But what? As much as she believed in the inherent goodness of people, she had to defer to Devon on this. He lived those odds every day. So she simply said, "You sure?"

"Don't worry about me," he reassured her, pulling his phone from the dashboard. "I owe someone on the West Coast a call. Besides, this is *your* quest."

She hesitated.

"Go," he said.

And so she did. Joybird took a deep, fortifying breath, walked up the path to the front door, and pushed the buzzer on the video doorbell. Within moments, a male voice came over the speaker.

"Who is it?"

"Mr. Ross?" she said. "I don't know if you remember me, but my name is Joybird Martin. My father is—"

"Oh!" said the voice. "One minute."

Seconds later, the heavy wooden door swung open and there stood Reuben Ross. He was slight and trim, with thinning gray hair in a neat, short cut that complemented his pleasantly shaped head. Compared to her father, he looked expensively groomed, wearing a pale-yellow sweater and dark-indigo jeans with cognac-colored loafers and no socks.

"Joybird!" he said, sounding surprised. "Look at you!"

Clearly, he needed no reminder of who she was. That was the great thing about having an unusual name. It stuck with people. His warm tone put her at ease.

"Hello, Mr. Ross," she said, realizing that he had looked a lot bigger when she was a child. Now, he was barely taller than she was. She wouldn't have recognized him, of course, though his voice sounded familiar.

"This is such a delightful surprise, although . . ." A look of alarm swept his face. "Is your father—"

"Oh, no," she interrupted, realizing he thought she might have come with grim news. "He's fine."

"Well, come here, then," he said, and pulled her in for a hug.

"Carol," he called behind him. "Look who's here! It's Joybird. John Martin's daughter."

A heavily perfumed woman with dyed black hair appeared from the back of the house. She wore a dark sweater and matching slacks, with a chunky statement necklace of turquoise and pink.

"John Martin?" she said, making a face, and Joybird felt a little sick. It seemed clear that this woman did not have warm feelings toward her father. Joybird hoped Carol Ross felt no need to open up about her bitterness.

"It's nice to see you again," Joybird said, smiling. "What a striking necklace!"

"Thank you," Carol said, touching the piece on her neck as if to remind herself what it looked like. Her expression went softer, but still wary. "It's been so long." She gave Joybird a quick, stiff hug.

"I'm so sorry to bother you," Joybird said.

"No, no!" Reuben said. "Come in, come in."

As he led her past a curved staircase, through black-painted French doors into a cozy wood-paneled den, Joybird explained that she had tried to call the phone number she'd found online, but couldn't get through.

"The landline," Reuben said. "Greg convinced us to disconnect it last year. He kept saying 'Dad, what do you need it for?' So we got rid of it." He indicated the brown velvet sofa, and Joybird let herself sink into it. It was a feather affair, too soft and too low, and she felt swallowed. The scent of cooking wafted into the room, and Joybird realized she had probably interrupted their dinner.

"I don't want to take too much of your time," she said as the couple sat in wingback chairs opposite her. "It's just that I'm on a quest to help my father locate an old high school friend, and I thought you might be able to help. He's been a little depressed and . . ." She paused, trying to find the right words.

"Oh, I get it," Reuben jumped in. "I know his career took a hit." He gave his wife a look. "We keep up with the Paxton grapevine. Or I do, anyway."

Joybird understood that he had access to information she didn't, and assumed the couple knew more than she did about the scandal that derailed her father's career. It wasn't something she wanted to hear, so she steered the conversation away.

"You might not know this," Joybird continued, "but he's back in New York. And he recently brushed past a woman he knew from Paxton and regrets not approaching her. I thought if I could find her, it might really cheer him up."

Carol frowned and crossed her arms, but Reuben seemed genuinely interested. "Who was it?" he asked.

"Her maiden name was Donna DeLuca."

"Donna DeLuca," he repeated. "Pretty girl. I think John had a terrible crush on her."

Carol made a soft snuffing sound, but Joybird ignored it.

"Definitely," Joybird said to Reuben, smiling. "I don't suppose you know anyone who's in touch with her?"

He sucked air, thinking. "Afraid not."

"What about her married name? Do you know what she goes by now?"

"I don't recall," he said. "But I should have it somewhere." Reuben turned to his wife. "Do you remember the printout I got from the twenty-fifth reunion? It had the names of everyone who came. And I'm sure Donna was there."

She scoffed. "That was decades ago, Reuben."

"I think it's in my office," he said, standing. "I might have stuck it in a photo album. I'll see if I can find it."

He walked briskly from the room, and Carol said, "Don't get your hopes up. He's pretty organized, but twenty years is a long time."

"I'm grateful for any help," Joybird said.

Carol sat back and crossed her legs, studying Joybird. "So he's back in New York."

Joybird nodded. "Staying with me for a while. He's working on a new pilot." She left out that he was doing it on spec, not under contract. And that most of the work consisted of mumbling to himself.

"Good for him, I guess," Carol said.

Her tone seemed pointedly aloof, and Joybird decided to counterbalance it with cheerful chatter. "It's been a long time since Dad and I were under the same roof," she said, hoping Carol understood that there was a lot of history to repair. "We're sort of getting to know each other again."

"I bet there's a *lot* you don't know about your father."

Now she was borderline hostile, and it was clear that Carol Ross wanted an opening to let loose on old grievances. Joybird wasn't eager to give it to her. Anyway, she was sure whatever had happened wasn't really all that bad, and assumed her father had just rubbed Carol the wrong way.

"Mrs. Ross," Joybird said, "I don't want to keep you. If you're busy with dinner or something . . . I can wait in the car."

Carol seemed to consider it, but she glanced in the direction her husband had gone and changed her mind. "It's fine. Are you hungry?"

"Oh, no. I . . . I have a friend waiting. I really don't want to take up too much of your time."

Carol Ross nodded stiffly, clearly not willing to ask Joybird to invite her friend into the house and prolong the visit. After an awkward silence, she said, "You know, we really were so sorry when your mother passed."

Joybird put a grateful hand on her heart. "Thank you."

"It was a touching funeral," Carol said, looking as if she were recalling it. "Heartbreaking."

"I don't remember too much of it," Joybird admitted. In fact, she hadn't even known the Rosses were there. Mostly, she recalled being around lots of grown-ups talking softly. Someone gave her one of those large cellophane-covered candy-store lollipops with swirls of colors. Her father told her not to open it until later, and she'd spent the whole funeral staring at it, running her finger over the ridges of rainbow she could feel through the plastic.

"Oh, that's right," Carol said, her expression turning sympathetic. "You were just a little girl—the same age as our son, Greg. Reuben and I were so sad for you."

"It was nice that you came," Joybird offered, trying to keep the kindness flowing.

"You know, you look like her."

Joybird felt her eyes water. No one ever spoke about her mother, and she didn't press it. It was just so much easier not to. "I can't always conjure her face," she admitted.

"She was a pretty girl, like you. I always wondered what she saw in—" She stopped herself. "I'm sorry, I shouldn't have said that."

"It's okay," Joybird said. "I know he's difficult. He has a lot of demons. But I think if I can find Donna for him . . ." She trailed off, and a few minutes later, Reuben came back into the room, empty handed.

"I know I have it somewhere," he said. "I'm sure I saw it recently. I just don't want to keep you while I look for it. Is it okay if I call you when I find it?"

"Sure," Joybird said, trying not to feel too deflated. She believed that he really would look for it, but she had hoped for a quick resolution, as it looked like her father was deteriorating by the day.

Carol handed her a pad and a pen, and Joybird wrote down her phone number and email address.

"We were fans of *Down Here*," Carol said, referring to the biggest hit her father had worked on—the one that had earned him an Emmy.

Joybird nodded, understanding that Carol was trying to make amends for her earlier hostility. It was a good sign, and she wondered if she could get the couple to forgive him. In Joybird's mind, he could use some friends. After they helped her find Donna DeLuca, she would invite them over for dinner as a thank-you.

"You've both been so kind," she said, struggling to rise from the aggressively soft sofa.

Reuben put out a hand to help her. "That couch is a beast," he said.

Joybird headed toward the door, but Carol stopped her. "Hold on a second, honey. I have something for you." She went to the antique wooden chest in the corner of the room, opened the bottom drawer, and retrieved an old photo album. She pulled out a picture and handed it to Joybird.

It was the four of them—Carol and Reuben with her mother and father. They were seated at a table, dressed up, and the photographer had caught them laughing. Her mother looked so amused that Joybird felt it in her very center, a mixture of happiness and sorrow that was almost unbearable.

"Mom," Joybird whispered, staring reverently at the image.

"I think your father had just said something to make us laugh," Carol explained. She turned to Reuben. "Do you remember what it was?"

He shook his head in response, adding, "But it was probably off color."

Joybird studied the picture, recalling how she used to think about the love between her parents. She'd spent so many years convincing herself it was a figment of her imagination that this felt somehow validating. There really had been something special between them, and for a short but beautiful time, their little family had been perfect.

Chapter 10

Joybird got into the car and told Devon everything that had transpired with the Rosses. When she showed him the photo Carol had given her, he shined his phone's flashlight on it.

"That's Reuben and Carol," she said, pointing at the image, "and that's my dad and mom."

He studied it for a moment, glancing from the picture to Joybird. "You look so much like her. I bet you laugh like her too."

Joybird stared down at the photo, her throat tightening as she tried to remember her mother's laugh. Nothing came to her. Not a single sound. She couldn't even conjure her mother's voice—just a few blurry images and the feeling of being safe and loved.

"You okay?" Devon asked, a hand on her shoulder.

Joybird closed her eyes and took a jagged breath, letting go of her grief and relaxing into the warmth of his touch. When she started thinking how comforting it would feel to melt into his arms, she caught herself and sat up straight.

"I was eight when she died."

He went quiet, and a plane passed low overhead, filling the silence. "I'm sorry," he finally said, his voice soft, sympathetic.

Joybird glanced away, trying to find her happier self.

"Thank you," she said, looking back at him. She kept her tone light, as she didn't think it was fair to bring Devon down like this. He had been so kind to take this trip with her. Besides, she barely knew him, and this was intimate emotional terrain. She slipped the picture into her purse.

"What's wrong?" he asked.

She shook her head. "I don't know. It just seems . . . unfair."

He nodded. "It's hard to lose a parent so young."

"I mean unfair to *her*," Joybird clarified. "She missed so much."

"It *is* unfair," he agreed.

She looked at Devon's face, studying his soft eyes. "I want more for him. For my dad. I think he can be happy like that again."

"His happiness means a lot to you."

Devon's tone was kind and without judgment, but even the gentle statement made her question why she was so determined to brighten her father's world. Then a memory came back: she and her mother sitting on the floor together in front of the sofa, watching one of her Muppet videos.

Why did Daddy leave? she had asked.

Her mother took her hand and kissed it. *He wasn't happy, sweetheart,* she'd said.

Joybird had accepted the explanation because it was such a simple equation—people should do what made them happy. She'd only wished that she and her mother had been enough for him.

"Are you worried you won't find Donna DeLuca?" Devon asked. "Because I'd like to help."

Joybird understood that he was probably projecting some of his own yearning to bring his mother joy, and this touched her. For a money guy, he had a good heart. "I'm not worried," she said. "Mr. Ross will come through with her last name—I just know it."

"How are you so sure?"

"He seemed very eager to help."

Devon smiled, his eyes catching a glint of light. "Where did you get such an optimistic worldview?"

Joybird nodded. She'd heard that question before. "It's a choice. I make that decision every day."

She started the car and pulled away from the curb. When she was barely half a block down the street, he rubbed his belly and asked if she was hungry. She was. But going out to dinner felt dangerously like a date, especially after such an unguarded conversation, and Joybird didn't want to give him the wrong idea. And also—if she was being honest with herself—she didn't want to be in a situation that might stir even more feelings for him. She envisioned candlelight and soft music, a conversation that grew more and more intimate. He might even reach out for her hand. Or place a heavy palm on her knee. Joybird lowered her window an inch to let in some air.

"I don't know," she said. "It's getting late."

"Oh, come on," he pleaded. "I know this Italian place on Queens Boulevard. My parents used to go there. You'll love it."

No, she thought. Because even if he didn't make a move, he'd sense her attraction and would call her the next day and ask for a second date. Then she'd be in that awkward position again, trying to explain that they were incompatible. But she was hungry, and enjoying his company, so she came up with a plan.

"I'll tell you what," Joybird said. "I'll go if you let me pay, to thank you." There. It wouldn't be a date, but a courtesy.

He looked at her as if she had just suggested they sign up for seats on the space shuttle. "Not a chance," he said, twisting the gold ring on his pinkie.

"Why not?"

"Because you just started a new business. And your dad is still mooching off you. Come on, Joybird. Let me take you out for dinner."

"I . . ." She searched for words, wondering if there was any way to accept while making it clear that romance would not be on the menu. "You've been so kind, and I'd feel terrible spending your money."

"I'll put it on my Amex Black Card and write it off as a business expense."

She stole a quick glance at his profile. Was he trying to impress her? Because the last thing in the world she cared about was whether he was rich enough for a fancy credit card. She latched on to it, deciding it was a sign that she needed to resist the temptation to get any closer to him. She simply refused to be sucked into a life that involved status symbols and tax write-offs.

"I'm sorry," she said. "I'm really just too tired."

"Seriously?"

"Let's just get back." She turned the corner, navigating toward the Jackie Robinson Parkway.

Devon set his jaw. "Suit yourself," he muttered.

He sounded hurt. She felt it in the maw of her empty belly. But there was nothing to do but drive back to Brooklyn and try to keep her voice cheerful.

Aside from occasional references to the directions, there wasn't much to say. When they reached his building, he wished her luck and got out of the car. It was a cold end to a warm night, and guilt tugged at her. She hadn't meant to hurt him. Again.

"Thank you, Devon," she called out the window, hoping he understood she was genuinely grateful.

He waved without turning back, then disappeared into the shadows. Joybird put the car in gear and drove away, breathing in the enduring essence of his cologne. She had enjoyed being with him and tried to ignore his appeal as she focused on the irrefutable fact that they were incompatible. But as she drove, Joybird thought about his generosity and wondered if she had been too harsh. Slowly, the scent of his fragrance dissipated, until its earthy overtones floated into the ether, leaving nothing but a lingering undertone of regret.

Joybird glanced at her purse, picturing the photo inside, wishing she could ask her mother if she'd done the right thing. But regret was an unproductive emotion, so Joybird released it somewhere on Atlantic Avenue. By the time she turned into her parking lot, she was certain rejecting Devon's dinner invitation had been the right thing to do. This way, there would be no temptation from either of them to pursue a doomed relationship. Of course, if she got a lead on Donna DeLuca, she would call to let him know. But that was just a courtesy, because he had put his number into her phone for that express purpose. Beyond that, it would be best if they kept their distance and took no chances with the potent chemistry between them.

And anyway, her love life had just taken a positive turn in the form of a text from Noah Pearlman that had nothing to do with her volunteer literacy work. He asked if she was free for breakfast in the morning. Joybird thought the idea of a breakfast date was sweet and romantic—a way to get to know each other better in a low-pressure environment. As she walked from the parking lot to her apartment, she typed her response:

Have a late morning client appointment, but I'm free before 10

Joybird smiled, wondering what he might suggest. A quaint café? A picnic in the park? There was a quick reply:

Can you pick me up at 7:30? I could use a hand

This was confusing, and Joybird felt her buoyant mood spring a leak. She wrote back:

A hand?

His response took several minutes, and when it came in, it was detailed:

Folks at Brooklyn Heights Hunger Program letting me do a breakout writing session after their community breakfast. Could use a little help. And would love to see you!

So it wasn't a date after all. Joybird deflated, but she tried to pick herself up by focusing on his final sentence. She read it and reread it, deciding it was indeed genuine. If he had merely wanted to be polite, he would have said, "It would be nice to see you." But he'd gone a step further, using "love" and an exclamation mark. There was nothing casual about that, especially since the reply had taken so long it was obvious he'd given it careful thought. This was, she decided, a very good sign.

Chapter 11

Sid took another sip of Jack Daniels and closed his eyes. "Landslide" by Fleetwood Mac was blasting from the stereo, and he let it wash over him.

In his head, he was editing and rewriting, trying to get everything perfect. But he wasn't working on a scene from his script—he was revising his restaurant encounter with Donna DeLuca, finding a route to a happy ending. In this version, Sid would approach her table and say her name. She'd look up at him with those searing eyes he'd been thinking about for over forty years.

"John?"

"It's me," he'd reply, as cool as Humphrey Bogart.

Here, her face would brighten. "But of course it's Sid now, isn't it?"

Sid erased the image of Bogart. This wasn't an old noir film. It was a modern rom-com, colorful and bouncy. Donna would smile and give him her number, and they'd begin dating. The next part would play out in a corny montage that ended in a bedroom scene—two lovers united at last. Afterward, she'd admit she'd carried a torch for him, too, and they'd laugh about it as the music swelled and the credits rolled.

Sid took a juddering breath. If only. If only he hadn't been too beaten down and ashamed to face her.

He heard a noise and looked up, surprised to see his daughter had entered the apartment with a bag of groceries. He lowered the music, embarrassed at being caught communing with Stevie Nicks like some teenage girl.

"Oh good, you got food," he said, surreptitiously wiping his damp eyes. "I hope you bought some decent cheese."

If she knew he was posturing, she didn't let on. "I just stopped at the place on the corner," she said, putting the bag on the kitchen counter. "There isn't much of a selection."

"I'll take what you got."

"I got cream cheese and cheddar cheese."

"Fuck me."

"You just said—"

"I know what I said," he told her. He hadn't meant to be such a dick, but he'd lost control. Sid looked at his glass as if to blame it for turning him mean. He was supposed to be connecting with his daughter, and he just kept making things worse. Maybe he just wasn't good enough for this fatherhood thing.

"What are you drinking?" she asked.

The question rankled him because it was laced with judgment. She knew exactly what he was drinking.

"Sometimes a guy just needs a belt," he said, avoiding eye contact. "You don't have to get all pissy about it."

"I'm not," she protested. "I just . . . I think it's okay to let yourself feel sad once in a while."

It was exactly what his ex-wife would have said. Why did women always do that? He'd feel sad when he damn well wanted to feel sad. For now, he just needed to be a little drunk.

"Thank you, Oprah," he muttered.

"I was trying to help." She set the cheese and some crackers on the table, then turned to him, her eyes soft with concern. "You just seem so unhappy, Dad."

"What have I got to be happy about?"

"Sit with me," she said, pulling out a chair at the table.

With a heavy sigh, he picked up his glass and crossed the room, feeling leaden. He was willing to talk, as long as she didn't get all preachy. He sat hard and picked up the cheddar, trying to bite off the plastic wrapping. She took it from him and used a knife to open the packaging.

"Why don't you have a drink with me?" he asked.

Joybird waved him off and sat. She gave him the cheese and folded her hands in front of her like a therapist.

"Please don't," he begged, but Joybird looked so deflated that he softened. "Birdie," he continued, "I know you want to help, but trust me, there's nothing anyone can do. And Gerry Platt was right. My new pilot sucks."

"Do you think it would help if you found Donna DeLuca?" she tried.

His shoulders slumped, and he turned away, taking a gulp of Jack Daniels. He didn't want to cry—not in front of his kid.

"Dad?" she prodded.

"I told you," he said, hoping to end the conversation, "I missed my one shot." He picked up a paring knife and sliced a hunk of the crumbly cheddar. "I'll never get it back."

"But what if you *could* find her?" Joybird prodded. "What if you got another chance?"

"If I got another chance," he said, popping the cheese in his mouth, "I would take it."

Chapter 12

Joybird loved mornings. And on a crisp autumn day like today, she loved waking early enough to see the sun rise resplendently in blurs of gold and pink over the jagged Manhattan skyline. It filled her with hope—this vision of man-made accomplishment set against the wonder of nature. She took a moment to appreciate it from the garbage-strewn parking lot before she got in her car and drove to Noah Pearlman's apartment building.

She arrived in an almost rapturous mood. Everything felt so new and full of possibilities. Her business. The chance at finding Donna for her father. A meaningful connection with Noah. She had even bought a new sweater in ocean blue, which made her eyes particularly vivid. As usual, she'd chosen a size bigger than she needed so it wouldn't be too clingy across her chest, and she thought it suited her. Joybird shook out her hair, which she wore loose around her shoulders today.

Noah came out of his building lugging two large trash bags of materials.

"Pop the trunk," he called as he approached.

Noah Pearlman was long and lean, with curls even thicker than hers and an impossibly opaque black beard. He was wearing a plaid flannel shirt open over a white tee and faded red shorts, despite the cool weather. He threw his bags in her trunk and dropped himself into the front seat.

"Those things are heavy."

"You're welcome," she responded, before realizing he hadn't actually said thank you, but he didn't seem to notice. "Where do you want to stop for breakfast?" she added.

He ran his hand through his lush hair. "I don't think we have time."

Joybird fought back disappointment as she looked out the windshield, watching a stooped old man make his way slowly to a bench. He was carrying a bagged loaf of white bread, and there were pigeons at his feet before he even sat. Noah noticed him, too, and opened his window.

"Hi, Edmund!" he called.

The man glanced up and waved, looking genuinely delighted at being noticed. Joybird's heart ached with tenderness at this exchange.

"You have the goodness of an angel," she blurted as Noah closed his window.

"Yeah?" he said, looking genuinely pleased. "Thanks."

"I'm glad you reached out."

"Me too."

Joybird tried to make eye contact and share a smile, but he was looking out the windshield, his face still dull with sleep. She imagined he had woken up only minutes ago.

"You sure you don't want to get coffee?" she asked.

"We'll grab some of the swill they serve at the community center. And they have decent bagels." He paused and glanced over at her. "Unless you really want to."

It warmed her, this consideration of her feelings, especially since it was obvious he was still waking up.

"No, it's okay," she said. "I just thought it might be nice to take a few minutes to chat. We never really get to spend time together."

"Oh, sorry," he said. "Am I being a jerk?"

"Not at all."

"Hey, want to see something?" he asked, pulling out his phone.

"Always!" she chirped, and he showed her a text message from a drug-addicted guy named Benny who had taken one of Noah's writing sessions and had just checked himself into rehab. He said he'd be forever grateful to Noah for helping him understand what he needed to do to turn his life around.

"This is amazing," she said, and meant it. She stared at his face and felt a thrill in the pit of her belly. He had such a passion for helping people. She wanted to make him understand that she was cut from the very same cloth. And together . . . well, they could do *anything*.

"It's so gratifying," he admitted.

"I know how you feel," Joybird said, and she hoped he might ask her about her life-coaching business. On her way over, she had imagined him dropping into the seat, eager to tell her how impressed he was with her drive and determination to be a life coach. He would apologize for not responding to her email, but would assure her he'd clicked through to her website and loved it.

He slipped his phone back into his pocket. "I guess we'd better get going."

She put the car into gear and checked her side-view mirror. "Did you happen to notice the decal?" she asked, pulling away from the curb.

"Decal?"

"JoyRide," she prompted. "My new business."

"Oh, right. Congrats. How's it been going?"

"Today is my first day!"

"Hey, cool," he said. "I hope this wasn't an imposition."

She shook her head. "I'm happy to have the time with you." Her voice was clear and distinct, overriding any nerves about putting it out there. She added a smile to show the heart behind the statement.

"You're one of the good ones, Joybird," he said, and gave her arm a pat.

It was just the kind of thing she'd hoped he'd say, and it filled her with so much warmth, she felt weightless. Smiling, she gripped the steering wheel to stay grounded, and wished he would touch her again.

"That means a lot to me," she said, working up even more nerve, "coming from you."

"Will you have time to help me set up?" he asked. "Or do you have to pick up a fare?"

"Client," she corrected. "They're clients now. But, yes, I can spare a few minutes to help." Joybird stole a glance at his appealing profile, enjoying the slant of his nose and the short vertical line of his forehead, which ended at his low, bushy hairline. "How's your writing going?"

"I had another poem accepted," he said, hand over his heart in gratitude. "A new lit mag I was dying to get into."

"Congratulations. What's it about?"

"It's about night," he said. "And what it means to be . . . *unhoused.*" He pronounced the word as if he had invented it.

"Oh!" she exclaimed. "I'd love to read that."

He sat up straighter. "Yeah? I'll send you a link."

She chittered her approval and made a right turn, then a left onto the picturesque Joralemon Street, with its painted brick houses. "Did you see my website?" she asked.

"You have a website?"

"There was a link in my email."

He pulled out his phone again and tapped at it for a few minutes. "Look at that," he said, sounding surprised, and turned his phone toward her to show that he had found it. "Nice picture."

"Thanks. My dad doesn't like it."

He stared back at the image. "Why not? You look pretty."

Pretty, she repeated in her head, to make sure she heard right. He thought she was pretty. Joybird focused on her breathing to make sure she was getting enough oxygen.

"He thinks it's too woo-woo or something," she said.

Noah chuckled. "Your dad sounds like a trip," he said, suppressing a yawn.

"Actually, he's depressed. But I'm trying to help him."

Noah nodded and rubbed his eyes as if struggling to stay focused.

Joybird continued because she wanted to talk about it, wanted to walk through her vision of delivering happiness to her father at last. "I learned that he's been carrying a torch for a certain woman since high school. Can you imagine being in love with someone like that your whole life?" She glanced over and thought he looked like his mind was wandering. Perhaps he was working on a poem or thinking about his day. But Joybird went on, hoping to engage him in her worthy quest. "Anyway, I'm on a mission to find her. So now I'm a sleuth *and* a life coach!"

Noah laughed, as if he thought it was a joke. Joybird decided not to be offended. She probably hadn't explained it well.

"You have other volunteers today?" she asked, wondering how she could steer the conversation in a better direction. She needed at least one more opportunity to signal that she was interested in him.

"Tabitha McCabe," he said.

Joybird felt herself sink. Tabitha McCabe was a lithe, delicately boned blonde, with hair so silky and fine her little pink ears slipped through like baby mice. She had a particular kind of Brooklyn paleness that suggested she was never out in the sunlight. It made her seem impossibly fragile, and Joybird thought she'd seen Noah flirting with her at another event.

"She's a sweetheart," Joybird offered, hoping he agreed with this benign, platonic assessment of Tabitha. When he said nothing, she added, "And beautiful."

He gave a soft chuckle. "I think half my students have a crush on Tabitha."

Joybird wondered if he did too. *Probably,* she thought. Why wouldn't he be more attracted to the fragile blonde beauty than an earnest and sturdy brunette? Joybird swallowed hard, trying to convince herself that she and Noah could have a real connection, and that she stood a chance against Tabitha.

They drove the last few blocks in silence, and when they arrived, Tabitha was sitting on the steps in front of the community center, her mantis-like legs bent in front of her, her head down as she stared into her phone. Joybird put her car in park and looked at Noah. She saw him glance at Tabitha, and told herself that if he bolted from the car to greet her, it meant he was interested. But he turned his head to Joybird and smiled.

"How much time do you have?" he asked.

"Ten or fifteen minutes," she said, wondering if he was trying to get rid of her. "I mean, if you want me to come in."

His eyes went wide. "Why wouldn't I?" he blurted.

"I just . . . I don't know." She tried hard not to glance Tabitha's way.

"Joybird," he said, putting a hand on her arm, "you're one of my favorite people."

"I am?"

Playfully, he wrapped a finger around a lock of her hair. "I've been wanting to tell you that for a while."

She looked down, breathing into the moment and taking in the clean soapy smell of his hand before making steady eye contact. This was everything she'd been waiting for. The air felt charged, magical, as an understanding passed between them, and she lost herself in his dark eyes. Then there was a knock on the glass that broke the spell. It was Tabitha, tapping on Noah's window.

"You guys ready to set up?" she asked.

Noah looked back at Joybird and shrugged as if asking for permission.

"I'll pop the trunk," she said.

Chapter 13

Later, as Joybird set up her car for work, she was still reliving that moment alone with Noah, and her scalp tingled in anticipation. Her dream was coming true! She couldn't think of a better way to begin her work as a joy coach—her specialty.

She pulled up in front of her first client's address, just over the Brooklyn-Queens border, in Howard Beach. It was a neat brick house, and her client, Christopher Catalano, was a twenty-two-year-old with a fresh haircut and a face scraped raw by a recent shave. He wore khakis and a navy blazer—appropriate attire for the job interview he had mentioned on his intake form. When he got into the car, she asked him about it, and he explained that he'd graduated from Oneonta in May and had been working in his father's construction company all summer. It was always meant to be a temporary gig, and now he was on his way to interview with a friend of his dad's at an insurance agency. He was thinking of blowing off the interview and sought advice.

Joybird asked him pointed questions, getting him to focus on big goals and what he really wanted. In the end, it came down to two things: a happy work environment, where he liked the people around him, and good money.

Joybird's phone buzzed with an incoming call. She wasn't going to pick it up, but she took a quick glance at the screen to see who it was. Reuben Ross! Joybird shifted in her seat, excited. He wouldn't be calling unless he had found Donna DeLuca's current last name. This day could turn out to be even more momentous than she had hoped. But she wouldn't call him back until she dropped off her last client, because she wanted to be sure she could give him her full attention. Until then, she would just sit tight and think about how happy her father would be at last. She pictured him beaming with delight, throwing his arms around her in gratitude. Goose bumps rose up her arms.

She turned her attention back to Christopher Catalano. "So what do you think?" she asked. "About the interview?"

"It can't hurt, right?" His eyes shone now, her counsel and advice paying off. "I mean, it could be just the thing."

Joybird got out from behind a slow driver, and the road opened up. With no one in front of her, she was able to time the next light, sailing through just as it went from red to green.

"What if I want the job and I don't get it?" Christopher asked.

"Then you'll have gained valuable interview experience and will do better on the next one."

By the time they reached the insurance agency in Middle Village, Christopher Catalano's energy had transformed. He seemed a little nervous, but she thought that was positive. It meant he was eager to make an impression. She wished him good luck and told him to reach out if he ever needed to talk again.

"Have a joyful day!" she called out the window, deciding this would be her signature sign-off.

Her next client brought her back to Brooklyn. It was Althea Harrison, an attractive woman in her fifties. She had a long, slender neck and was carefully made up, with tasteful false eyelashes and plummy lipstick. She needed a ride to "any Western Union office," and wanted to talk to Joybird about her jealous friends. After Joybird tapped into her phone and determined that there were Western Union kiosks in several neighborhood drugstores, they settled on one about twenty minutes away.

"What do you need Western Union for?" Joybird asked.

"I'm wiring some money to my boyfriend, Ismail, overseas."

That sounded like a potential red flag to Joybird, but she thought it was best to back into the topic from the other end.

"You said your friends are jealous of you?" she asked.

"I had weight-loss surgery and lost over two hundred pounds," Althea said. "Some of my friends can't handle the new me."

"I'm sorry to hear that," Joybird said. "Friendships are important, and we all want our friends to be happy for our successes."

"Exactly! And they can't accept that I have a handsome new boyfriend."

"He lives overseas?"

"In London, England," Althea said, "but he's in Nigeria right now on business."

Oh no, Joybird thought, *this has catfish written all over it.* She studied Althea in her rearview mirror. She was an attractive woman, smartly dressed, with a direct demeanor and intelligent eyes. She didn't seem like the kind of person who would fall prey to such an obvious scammer, but egos could be as delicate as marionettes, and these con men knew just which strings to pull.

"Have your friends met him?" she asked.

"*I* haven't even met him," Althea said. "Not yet. We found each other on Facebook. You want to see a picture of him?"

"Sure," Joybird said, and when she stopped at a light, Althea handed over her cell phone. It showed a photograph of a young shirtless man who looked Mediterranean. With massive biceps and rippling abs, he was clearly a bodybuilder, perhaps even a model. She did not believe this was Ismail, and assumed Althea had never thought to do a reverse image search.

"Handsome," she said. "What does he do for a living?"

"He's an exporter . . . of women's dresses. But my friends don't believe me. They think he's scamming me. They just don't believe I could attract such a good-looking gentleman. To them, I'm still fat old Althea."

Joybird nodded, wondering if the weight loss was at the root of Althea's vulnerability. It might have been a very long time since she had felt attractive. And now here was this guy, who seemed to be a gorgeous young man, paying her all sorts of attention. Naturally, she wanted to believe it.

"Maybe they're just worried about you," Joybird offered, as she turned onto Empire Boulevard. "There are a lot of scammers on the internet."

"But I'm not stupid," Althea said.

"Of course not."

"And I'm a New Yorker. I know when someone's scamming me."

"Tell me more about Ismail," Joybird said. "Do you talk on the phone? Video chat?"

"We talk on the phone every day," she said. "We haven't had a video chat yet because his camera is broken. My friend Debra Conley thinks that means he's a scammer, but a scammer doesn't talk on the phone every day and tell you he loves you."

"Too bad about the camera, though," Joybird said. "It would be nice to FaceTime with your boyfriend."

"I offered to buy him a new iPhone, and he said he didn't feel comfortable with it. That's a real gentleman." She folded her arms.

"Your friends don't see it like that?" Her eyes trained on the road, Joybird saw a parked car jut quickly from the curb, and she slowed to avoid it. The car behind her honked.

"They keep saying, 'Althea, don't be so naive.' I am not naive!"

"I'm sure you've checked him out," Joybird said. "Googled his business . . . did a reverse image search on his picture."

"Reverse image search?" Althea asked.

It was exactly what Joybird hoped she'd say. "You don't know what that is?"

"I'm not that techie."

"I'll show you," Joybird said, and steered into a fast-food-restaurant parking lot, pulling into a space. "Can I see that picture again?"

Althea handed her phone to Joybird, and it took her about three seconds to find the original source of the photo. It belonged to Giovanni Ferretti, a bodybuilder from Brindisi, Italy. She handed the phone back to Althea, who stared down at it.

"I don't understand."

"I know that you speak to Ismail all the time," Joybird said gently, "and that you have real feelings for him. But he's using someone else's picture."

"He told me it was him. This has to be a mistake."

"Let me see that again for a second," Joybird said. Althea passed her back the phone, and Joybird opened the gallery page on the bodybuilder's site, where there were dozens of photographs of him. She handed it back.

"This just doesn't make any sense," Althea said, her eyes moistening. "He told me it was him. He *told* me."

"This happens online all the time," Joybird assured her. "People misrepresent themselves. It's not your fault."

"There has to be an explanation," Althea insisted. "This man is using Ismail's pictures. Or maybe Ismail set up this bodybuilder site for some reason."

Joybird felt Althea's pain deep in her own chest. The woman's heart was breaking in real time, and she was trying desperately to save herself by denying what was right in front of her.

"That's unlikely," Joybird said.

"I'm going to text him," Althea told her, and then dictated into her phone. "Hey, baby. You have a minute to talk now?"

A few minutes later, his response came in, and she read it out loud. "I am going into a business meeting now. Did you wire that money, baby?"

Althea blinked, and tears spilled down both cheeks. "He got into a jam in Nigeria," she said to Joybird, "and he needs money because his credit card was stolen. He asked me to wire him seven thousand dollars. He said he'd repay me as soon as he got back to England."

"Do you think that's wise?"

"I don't know. He really needs the money. If I could just talk to him. I'm sure there's an explanation."

Joybird knew that Althea's head and heart were locked in battle. It was excruciating to cause her this much pain, but it would be worse for her to learn the lesson after losing all that cash.

Joybird used her own phone to google Giovanni Ferretti and found a video of him accepting a bodybuilding award. She increased the volume, and he was speaking in Italian. She turned her phone toward Althea. "This is the man in the photos. Does it sound at all like Ismail?"

Althea watched in stunned silence for several minutes as the man continued speaking in rapid, excited Italian. Her tears turned to sobs, and Joybird stopped the video.

"No," Althea choked out. "That's not him. That's not Ismail."

"What do you want to do?" Joybird asked.

"I want to go home."

Joybird drove to the next light and made a U-turn. She gripped the steering wheel as her passenger wept softly. This was not how she had hoped her day would go. She had wanted to bring joy. But it would have been irresponsible to let this woman get taken advantage of.

"This isn't your fault," Joybird said.

"Of course it's my fault."

"No. I want you to feel proud of yourself for having a big, open heart, ready for love. It's not your fault a scammer took advantage of that. Look at all you've done, Althea. You lost two hundred pounds! You're a strong woman!"

Althea blew her nose. "I thought I was."

"You are! And you'll find love, I promise. Real love." She paused. "Just not on Facebook."

"But where am I supposed to meet someone?"

"At work? Church? Lots of places."

"I work at the makeup counter at Bloomingdales. I don't meet any eligible men there. And I haven't been to church in a while."

"Would you like to go back?"

There was a long silence, and Joybird sensed that Althea was remembering how it felt to be in church. "I think I would," she said softly.

"Althea, do you have a friend who can hold your hand through all this?" Joybird felt sure Althea needed someone to spend time with her. Someone who would remove this scammer from her contacts.

"Debra," she whispered.

"Is she strong too?"

"Like a prizefighter. But we're not talking right now."

"You got into an argument?"

"Over Ismail," Althea choked out. "I said some harsh things. Terrible things."

Joybird turned left onto Bedford Avenue. "What do you think would happen if you showed up and apologized?"

"I think she'd wrap her big old arms around me."

Joybird drove in silence for a few minutes, letting Althea sit with her thoughts of a reconciliation with Debra. At last, she asked, "Althea, what would you like to do now?"

Althea pulled a tissue from her purse and wiped her nose. "I'll give you Debra's address."

Chapter 14

After a late lunch, it was time for Joybird to meet her third client of the day, Riley Wilbanks—the girl she assumed was related to the wealthy socialite. According to her intake form, Riley was fifteen years old, a sophomore at the prestigious Berkeley Carroll School in the Park Slope section of Brooklyn. When Joybird pulled up in front of the ornate doorway arch, kids were spilling out onto the street. She kept her eyes peeled for someone who looked like she was expecting a ride.

Finally, a skinny girl with neon-pink hair and an open jacket stopped on the steps and scanned the parked vehicles. The day had turned cloudy, and a chill blew in, fanning out her jacket. She stuck her hands in the pockets to tame it.

When her eyes alit on Joybird's car, she approached and leaned on the windowsill. Joybird noticed that her nails were bitten, and she wore a T-shirt printed with a cartoon drawing of a tied rope and the words "I literally can knot."

"Riley?" Joybird asked.

The girl tucked her fuchsia hair behind her ear. "I guess you're the spell caster who's supposed to transform me?"

Joybird laughed. "I don't know about that," she said, "but I'm here to help."

Riley opened the back door, threw in her overloaded backpack, slid into the seat, and slammed the door. "I don't need fixing," she said.

"I can see that," Joybird acknowledged. She wanted the girl to feel comfortable.

"And I've been seeing a therapist since I was six, so . . ."

"I'm not a therapist," Joybird said.

"What are you then?"

"I'm a life coach. I'm just here to help you figure out what will make you happier." She paused, and when Riley didn't respond, she added, "I know it sounds corny, but I've helped a lot of folks feel better."

"My mother said you changed her life." The girl put a melodramatic hand to her heart and spoke with breathless sarcasm. "She's like a whole new woman now—she's going to paint again . . . thanks to *you*."

Mother? Joybird turned around to stare at her. "Wait a minute," she said. "Corinne is your *mom*?" She had driven the woman around all day, and she never mentioned having a daughter.

"I know, right?" the girl said, as if they had just agreed on how astonishing this fact was.

"I . . . I thought you were her niece or something. I should have—"

"Don't feel bad," Riley said. "Narcissists don't exude anything maternal. They're only interested in talking about themselves."

This precocious kid was as sharp as a No. 2 pencil on the first day of school, and Joybird knew she'd have to bring her A-plus game. She pivoted around to face the windshield, thinking back to her conversation with Corinne. She had said something about an ex-husband in Brooklyn.

"You live with your dad?" she ventured into the rearview mirror as she started the car.

"Yeah. But I see my mom once a week, and she said it would be 'beneficial' to have you as my driver. I guess she thinks you can cure me of my delusions of adequacy."

Joybird watched as Riley buckled her seat belt, then pulled a packet of chips from her backpack. She yanked it open and began pushing them into her mouth.

Joybird put on her signal and angled away from the curb, waiting for an opening in the traffic. "You think she wants you to change?"

"Corinne thinks I should be more like her—you know, materialistic, shallow, and sex-crazed. Or fatally sad that I'm not."

Sex-crazed. Joybird had come to a similar conclusion about Corinne but thought it was close to tragic that her daughter saw it too.

"Sounds like you're okay with who you are," she observed.

"Please," Riley said. "I'm fifteen. I have a big mouth, and I know how to impress grown-ups. Doesn't mean I've got my shit together." She ate in crunch-punctuated silence for a few minutes, then crumpled the empty chips bag and took one of the fresh water bottles Joybird had supplied for riders. She twisted it open and swigged a long gulp.

"Help yourself, by the way," Joybird joked.

She had meant it good-naturedly, but Riley looked momentarily wounded. "Sorry. Was I supposed to ask?"

"No, it's fine," Joybird said. "I was just kidding."

"Oh, hilarious. You're a regular Johnny Carson . . . or whoever you people think is funny."

"Johnny Carson?" Joybird repeated. "How old do you think I *am*?"

"Don't be offended. I suck at guessing ages. Everybody over thirty looks old to me."

"I'm thirty-*one*," Joybird protested.

Riley shrugged. "See?"

Joybird turned right onto Seventh Avenue, heading toward Flatbush. She decided to keep the conversation focused on Riley. "Tell me what keeps you up at night," she said.

"How do you know I don't sleep like I'm dead?"

Joybird considered pointing out the bitten nails but didn't want to make the girl self-conscious. "You just seem like you don't unplug that easily," she said.

Riley nodded. "That's fair."

"So you want to answer the question?"

The teenager gave a heavy sigh. "I don't know. Everything, I guess." She put her hand on the window and looked out, as if she saw something interesting. But Joybird was pretty sure she was getting lost in whatever had troubled her.

"What about last night?" Joybird said. "What did your mind wander to as you tried to sleep?"

"Same thing it always wanders to on Tuesday nights—Wednesday."

Joybird slowed to let an aggressive driver into her lane. "What's bad about Wednesday?"

"It's the day I'm forced to spend time with the deposed Princess of Sutton Place, soon to be the Marquise de Murray Hill."

Now Joybird understood why this time slot had been reserved for every Wednesday over the next three months. "You don't like being with her?"

"You've met my mom," Riley said, implying that the rest was obvious.

Joybird couldn't argue. She might not enjoy hanging out with Corinne either. And she understood what it was like to have a difficult parent who wasn't always pleasant to spend time with. Joybird endured her father's behavior because she understood there was pain behind it, and she loved him unconditionally. Maybe that was where she could help Riley land—a place of love and sympathy.

"What is it like when you go over there?"

"Dwank," the girl said.

Joybird looked at her in the rearview for clarification.

"Sucks," Riley explained. "First, she asks if I want Berta to make me something to eat. I say no. Then she asks if I have homework. I say yes. And she's like, I'll leave you to it, and she goes into her bedroom, locks the door, and has phone sex with some dude. Or maybe FaceTime sex." She gave a shudder. "I don't even want to think about it. Anyway, after that, we go out for dinner, and then she sends me home, unless I want to stay over, which I pretty much never do."

Phone sex. In front of her young daughter. Joybird hoped it wasn't true.

"Is this conjecture, or . . ."

"Her bedroom is right next to the bathroom. Sometimes I hear her. It's so gross."

Joybird held tight to the steering wheel. This was a lot of sexuality for a kid to be dealing with. "I'm sorry you have to endure that. Did you talk to her about it?"

"Once or twice. She thinks she's being a saint for not actually hooking up with these guys while I'm there."

Joybird cringed. This was definitely too much for a fifteen-year-old, especially since she probably had no say in these court-ordered visitations. "Have you spoken to your father about it?" she asked, hoping there was some adult in Riley's life who knew what was going on.

Riley shook her head. "It would only get her in trouble."

It wasn't the answer Joybird expected. She stopped at a light and angled the rearview to study her. Despite everything, the kid loved her mom and wanted to protect her. Of course she did. That's the way it was with kids and parents, no matter how messed-up they were.

"You have a good heart, Riley," she said.

"Me?"

"You don't want to make your mom's life more difficult." Joybird tapped on her phone to see the address she had programmed in for Riley's drop-off. Of course. It was the Sutton Place building. Corinne hadn't moved yet.

Riley shrugged. "She's an asshole, but she's *my* asshole."

"What about your dad?" Joybird asked. "Do you like spending time with him?"

"We only have 'family time' now, which means Dad, his bigmouthed wife, Emily—who doesn't shut up for like three seconds—and their screaming two-year-old."

"Do you like your little brother?"

"Sister," Riley corrected. "She's okay . . . when she's not throwing a fit."

Joybird paused to consider why she had assumed the baby was a boy, and realized she had been projecting. Like Riley, she had gone to live with her father, his second wife, and her half sibling—in her case, a brother. She reminded herself that this was not about her; it was about her client. Riley held up a piece of candy from the pouch Joybird had affixed to the seat back. "Is this caramel?"

"Butterscotch."

Riley popped the candy in her mouth and rolled it around, sucking and clucking. "You married?"

"Single."

"Boyfriend?"

Joybird thought of Noah, but for some reason the scent of Devon's cologne came alive in her sinuses. Was it still in the car, or had she imagined it? She inhaled deeply, searching for more of it, but found none. She looked in the rearview. "No, no boyfriend. You?"

"Unfortunately not," she said with a long, dramatic sigh.

It was such an adolescent reaction for this sophisticated kid that it touched Joybird's heart. She glanced at her again and saw Riley roll her head back and close her eyes. It looked like she was thinking about her crush.

"Tell me about him," Joybird said.

Riley returned from her reverie. "What?"

"The boy you like."

"How do you know it's a boy and not a girl?" Riley challenged.

Joybird smiled. "You're the one that said 'boyfriend.'"

Riley folded her arms.

"*Is* it a girl?" Joybird asked.

Riley looked as if she was bracing herself to argue, but then sighed, releasing it. "His name is Carter, but everybody calls him Truck."

"Truck?"

"He got run over in eighth grade, and some idiot thought it was funny, so it stuck."

"Was he badly hurt?"

"He's got a limp, and I think he was in a coma for a while, but he's probably the smartest kid in the school, so . . . I guess it's not a big deal."

Joybird thought it probably was a big deal, but she let it go. "Tell me more about him."

"He's a senior. A composer. He has a cockatoo named Luigi he's totally obsessed with."

"Are you in any classes together?" Joybird asked as she turned onto Flatbush Avenue. The sky let loose a few drops onto her windshield, and she stared up at the gray clouds to assess the weather. Maybe she'd get lucky and it would blow over.

"He's a senior, and I'm a sophomore, so no."

"Does he know you like him?" The drops came harder, and Joybird resigned herself to the rainstorm, still hopeful it would be brief. She turned on her windshield wipers and headlights.

"Doubt it."

"Can I make a suggestion?"

"Are you going to tell me to ask him out?"

"I was going to suggest you find a common interest. Like join some club he belongs to." She knew it was just the kind of advice grown-ups always gave to kids, and braced herself for an eye roll. But Riley seemed receptive.

"He's editor in chief of the literary magazine."

"Perfect!" Joybird said. The rain intensified as water cascaded down her windshield and obscured her vision. She turned the wipers to the highest speed and assured herself these kind of downpours usually passed quickly.

"But I don't know," Riley said. "They're a pretty tight squad."

"I bet they'd love to have a smart girl like you."

By the time they reached Corinne's address on Sutton Place, the downpour had eased to a beating, steady rain, and Riley seemed to be in a hopeful mood. Joybird guessed she had already decided she would join the school's literary magazine and was imagining her burgeoning friendship with Truck.

"Can I make one more suggestion?" Joybird asked, before Riley exited the car.

"I guess."

"Today, when your mom asks if you have homework, tell her you'd like her to sit with you while you do it."

Riley scrunched her face. "You think she would?"

"I don't know," Joybird said, though she had a good idea that Corinne needed someone to need her. "But it can't hurt to ask, right?"

"Thanks," Riley said. She got out of the car, hitched her backpack onto her shoulder, and pulled up her hood.

Joybird rolled down the window. "One more thing," she said as Riley walked off. The girl turned to her expectantly.

"Call him Carter," Joybird said.

Riley hesitated as she took that in, rain running down her hood. Then she gave a nod and continued toward the building, stopping to jump gleefully into a puddle with both feet.

Joybird rolled up the window, the interior of the car going steamy and silent against the *thunka-thunk* of the windshield wipers. "Have a joyful day," she whispered.

Chapter 15

Joybird got home in an exuberant mood. Her first day as a life coach had been a shining success. Plus, she had shared a poignant moment with Noah. And even though she hadn't been able to reach Reuben Ross yet, she'd left a message and knew he'd call back with good news any minute, bringing her one step closer to finding Donna DeLuca for her father. It was cause for celebration. She shook out her umbrella in the hall and opened the door to her apartment.

"I'm taking you out for dinner tonight, Dad!" she called, as she hung her wet rain jacket on the coatrack.

"I already had pizza twice this week, big shot."

He was in the recliner reading the *New York Times*. Joybird took in the scene—including two empty beer bottles on the table next to him—and knew he'd been unproductive.

"Not a pizza place," she said. "A real restaurant, with tablecloths and wine and great reviews." She was certain it was just the kind of thing that would lift his mood.

"Didn't know you could afford Manhattan prices," he said. "You been holding out on me?"

"Who said anything about Manhattan?"

He put down the newspaper. "You want to go out for a nice dinner in *Brooklyn*?" He pronounced the word like it had dog shit stuck to its shoe.

"We have some of the best restaurants in the world." She crossed to the kitchen sink to wash her hands.

"If you like greasy calamari and cheap Chianti."

Joybird was pretty sure Brooklyn had the best calamari in the country, but she ignored the teasing. "There's a terrific Middle Eastern fusion place right around the corner. I promise it's as good as any place you went in LA on your expense account." She noticed that evidence of her father's lunch was still on the counter, including an open bag of whole wheat bread, which she sealed with a twist tie and put back in the freezer.

"I don't know," he said, sounding tired.

"Why not?" she asked, though she understood he was stuck in the inertia of depression. His eyes looked dull and sleepy—so different from the shining lights she remembered from the years she lived with him in Los Angeles, when his career was sizzling and everyone wanted him. Back then, his gruffness came off as restless energy, and it drew people to him. Joybird wondered what it would take to resurrect that version of him.

"I just got comfortable," he insisted, as if he hadn't been comfortable all day, lounging in his drawstring bottoms and undershirt.

"I'm not asking you to put on a tuxedo, Dad."

"But pants," he said, like it was an unreasonable request.

"Yes," she said patiently as she wiped down the counter. "You would definitely need to wear pants." She wanted him to shave, too, but knew that would be a losing battle.

"New York is so fucking formal," he said. "You forget that when you're in LA."

She considered changing plans, going to a café where he could wear pajama bottoms, but that simply didn't feel celebratory. "Please, Dad. It'll be fun." She closed the open cabinets and rinsed the dishes in the sink.

"Birdie, this is all very sweet, but let's just order in. It's so much easier."

She understood that the idea of going out—or making any kind of effort—felt overwhelming to him. But that was the paradox of depression. The more you fed it, the hungrier it got. Joybird simply had to intervene.

"It's a big day for me, Dad, and I really want to go out."

"Ask Betty, then. Or one of your ironic hipster pals."

"I want to go out with *you*," she insisted.

"Because I'm such a barrel of laughs?"

"You'll like this restaurant. And you'll feel so much better if you just walk out that door."

"I think that was the last line in *Butch Cassidy and the Sundance Kid*." She studied him, confused.

"Doesn't matter," he said. "I'm not going. Sorry, kid."

Joybird looked at him across the butcher-block counter, wondering if this was the right time to tell him what she'd been up to. It was supposed to be a secret until she actually found Donna DeLuca, but maybe this was the opportunity. After all, it was only a matter of time. And she could see that he desperately needed the jolt.

"Dad," she said, her elbows on the counter, "what if I told you I found Donna DeLuca?"

His face whipped toward her. "What?"

"I don't want to get ahead of myself," she said, "but I have a really good lead. And that's all I'm going to say for now."

His posture tightened. "You found Donna?"

"Not yet, but I'm close. And I promise you"—she paused to swallow against a swelling in her throat—"I will not stop until I find her for you." She looked into his face and saw his eyes go damp. Was her father actually crying? Joybird rested more weight on her arms, her knees going wobbly.

"You're serious?" he asked.

After taking a few steadying breaths, Joybird walked toward him. She thought about reaching for his hand but stopped herself, as he wasn't one for physical affection. Instead, she brought her palms together in a solemn vow. "I promise," she said. "But it could take a little while. I just need you to be patient. And don't ask me any more questions about it. When it happens, I want to surprise you."

He stood and did something Joybird never could have anticipated. He hugged her.

Chapter 16

Sid actually looked forward to dinner out with his daughter. As he showered and dressed, he felt uncharacteristically hopeful, but he tried to temper his enthusiasm. After all, there were a million ways this whole thing could go south. Donna could be remarried. Or in a serious relationship. She could be disdainful of his spiraling career trajectory. And then there was the biggest fear of all—that she wouldn't even remember him.

He told himself it wasn't possible. In his heart, they'd been tied together since that day they first kissed. Surely, she felt at least some of that. She had to.

Sid examined his image in the mirror, trying to see himself through Donna's eyes. With overgrown hair, a patchy gray beard, and eyes red from too much drinking and too little sleep, he looked less like a successful comedy writer and more like a guy who carried his life in a shopping cart and slept on a grate. So after just the slightest hesitation, he rinsed off his razor and got rid of the scruffy growth. Then he dressed as he would want Donna to see him—in a crisp shirt and the insanely expensive blue blazer his ex had talked him into buying from a Rodeo Drive boutique. He finished it off with pressed jeans and his favorite Nikes. He could feel Donna's approval, and it gave his wounded old heart a dose of youth.

He held it there as he went back into the living room to wait for Joybird. By the time she emerged, he was back in the easy chair reading the *New York Times*.

"Dad," she said, sounding surprised, "you look . . . great." A smile spread across her smooth face—she was clearly proud of herself for inspiring his transformation.

"You too," he said, and meant it. For once, she was wearing something that wasn't three sizes too big on her—the kind of cute striped sweater her mother would have worn—and the difference was remarkable. She was, he realized, every bit as lovely as Vanessa. "You should dress like that more often."

"You don't like the way I dress?" she asked, sounding wounded.

He sighed. This was the kind of shit that always got him into trouble with women. Why couldn't they take compliments? Why did they always have to back a guy into a corner?

Sid folded his arms. Joybird needed to find her confidence. He wanted her to be a woman with a strong, indomitable ego. "Why should you give a shit what I think?" he said.

Her mouth turned down. "That sounds like a no."

"Jesus Christ, Birdie, stop it. Let's go." He knew he could have been gentler, but he clung to an almost religious belief that it was a bad idea to play into anyone's neediness, as it only made them weaker.

She put on a brave face, and Sid watched as she worked past the hurt and came out the other side. Joybird opened the tiny closet near the door to extract her coat and umbrella.

"It stopped raining," he said, pointing out the window.

"Did it?" she asked, as if it were something truly miraculous, and just like that, she ricocheted back into ebullience. He'd been right not to coddle her.

They walked out into the brisk October night, where the air was still damp but clean and vaguely electric. It gave Sid a renewed sense of purpose, and suddenly he felt like he just might have the grit to rework that script. If only he tried a little harder, the project could bust down doors and get him back in the writers' room. Donna would be knocked out. And his dear girl would have everything she could dream of.

Feeling like his old self again, Sid started cracking jokes about the Brooklynites they passed—like the hipster who looked like she loomed her own toilet paper, the thug who looked like he would steal it from her, and the enormous woman in an expensive coat who would have been better off spending her money on a treadmill.

Joybird, of course, laughed at none of it. Her impenetrable PC sensibilities were just impossible to crack, but he was keen to keep trying.

"See that guy?" he said, pointing to a drunk leaning against a building. "He's probably some poor schmuck who used to run a corporation until he complimented a chick on her figure."

"Dad, stop," Joybird said. "You're being so unkind."

"They can't even hear me," he insisted.

She tsked, and when they passed two boisterous drag queens sharing a joint, he saw Joybird brace herself for another snide comment. But he simply said, "Wait right here," and approached them.

"You ladies look spectacular," he said.

The redhead gave a twirl to afford him the full view, and Sid gave an appreciative whistle.

"You're cute," she said, mussing his hair.

Sid pointed to the joint. "Looks like you're having a fun night."

"If you're angling for a hit, forget it," she told him. "We just don't know where those lips have been."

"Hey, I wouldn't dream of putting my lips anywhere they don't belong," Sid responded. "I was just wondering if you had one to spare that you could sell me."

The drag queens exchanged a look. "Ten bucks," said the redhead.

As they managed the transaction covertly, the redhead nodded toward Joybird. "That your girlfriend?"

"Nah, she's too old for me," he said. "That's my daughter."

They laughed at his joke, and he said goodbye, walking back to Joybird.

"What was that about?" she asked.

"They sold me a joint."

Joybird was incredulous. "You approached them to buy weed?"

"I smelled pot as we were passing, so I figured it might be a good opportunity."

"I think it's still illegal to buy it on the street," she said, her brow tense as she looked around.

He laughed. "Relax, Birdie. The NYPD has better things to worry about than an old white dude buying a joint from a couple of freaks."

"You can't call them freaks!" Joybird said, looking horrified. "That's so—"

"Calm down. They don't give a shit. They liked me."

"And you made a joke at my expense?" she asked.

"Don't worry about it."

She sighed, releasing her anxiety. "I'm glad you didn't say anything insulting to them."

"Come on, I like drag queens. You can tell them they have nice tits and they take it as a compliment."

Still no laugh. In fact, Joybird barely acknowledged the comment, and they continued on to the dark and cozy restaurant, where the hostess told them there would be a forty-minute wait for a table.

"You okay with that?" Joybird asked him.

"Not really," he muttered, then addressed the hostess about the tall, gray-haired man he had noticed in the corner.

"Is he the owner?"

The hostess nodded. "That's Mr. Ayoub."

In LA, Sid had learned pretty quickly how starry eyed the general public could be about Hollywood . . . and how easy it was to come off as Somebody Important. So he sauntered over and complimented Mr. Ayoub on the restaurant's decor.

"I bet you get a lot of location scouts asking to rent the place out," he said.

"Location scouts?" the man repeated in his soft accent.

"From film studios," Sid explained. "You haven't been hounded?"

"We've only been open a year," he said, clearly intrigued.

"I see."

"Are you in film, Mr. . . ."

"Marcus," Sid offered, shaking his hand, "Sid Marcus. Not exactly."

Mr. Ayoub looked just a little uncomfortable, as if he was trying to decide if it was polite to probe. Sid gave him an open grin.

"Do you mind if I ask?" the restaurateur said.

"I'm a producer," Sid told him, "but on the TV side." It wasn't a lie, but most people didn't understand that it was pretty common for writers to get producer credit. It had nothing to do with development and dealmaking, which was what executive producers did.

"Can I give you my card," Mr. Ayoub said, "in case you hear of anything?"

And that was all it took. Ten minutes later, they had a table.

"That was pretty neat, Dad."

He waved it away. "Almost too fucking easy."

Chapter 17

As Joybird glanced down at her phone, waiting nervously for Reuben Ross's call, her father signaled for the waitress and ordered a bottle of wine.

"I'll pay you back for all of this," he promised her. "With interest."

He looked more relaxed and happy than she had seen him in years, so Joybird simply gave him a grateful smile. Inside, though, a ripple of worry snaked its way through her system. Had it been a mistake to tell her father she was close to tracking down his lost love? What if she'd been wrong and Mr. Ross hadn't found Donna DeLuca's married name? The disappointment might be too much for her father to bear.

They were almost finished with their dinner when the callback finally came. She excused herself to take it outside, just in case. By that point, her father was on his second bottle of wine and discharged her with a grand gesture of noblesse oblige.

"Mr. Ross," Joybird said breathlessly into her phone. "Thank you for calling me back."

"I have some news," he said.

"You found that list with Donna DeLuca's married name?"

"I'm afraid I didn't."

Regret shot through her, and despite the chill, Joybird went clammy. Why, she wondered, had she told her father she had all but found this woman? *Why?* Her mouth went dry at the thought of her failure, and she had to focus on her breathing to keep from drifting away.

"Oh?" was all she could manage to say.

"But I got in touch with this other guy, Frank Strauss—an attorney in Greenwich. You know him?"

"Frank Strauss?"

"Litigator. Hell of a guy. Thought maybe your dad had mentioned—"

"I don't think so."

"Never mind. He remembered Donna and said she married a guy named Ackerman, and now she's divorced and lives in Darien."

"Darien?" she said stupidly, still trying to catch up with the conversation. Joybird's brain had melted down and needed a minute to recover.

"Darien, Connecticut," he said. "Are you okay?"

"Yes," she said, finally understanding what was happening. It was exactly what she had hoped for. He'd gotten her a name and a location. Donna DeLuca was within her reach. "Thank you! Thank you so much. This is . . . I can't even tell you how much I appreciate this."

"Don't worry about it, sweetheart."

Joybird was so choked with emotion that it took her a moment to settle herself before going back to the table and facing her dad. She didn't want to tip her hand yet—there were still too many things that could go wrong—so she needed to play it cool.

If anything showed on her face, Sid was too drunk to notice. After dinner, they emerged into the brisk night, and Joybird welcomed the invigorating wind. But when it started to drizzle, she picked up her pace and hurried her father along. They made it inside just before the skies opened to a spectacular downpour. Drunk and sated, Sid headed right to bed.

Joybird went into her room and opened her laptop to try to find Donna Ackerman on a people-search app. Armed with the right city and state, it was easy. And there she was, with a 203 area code. Joybird filled with skittish excitement. But was it wise to simply make a call? What would she say? And what if the woman wasn't receptive?

Maybe it would be better to see if she could find her on Facebook first and reach out that way. Joybird didn't want to scare her off and was worried about being too aggressive.

She wanted to talk it through with someone and thought of calling Betty, but decided she owed Devon Cato a shout-out first. She had been trying not to feel guilty about blowing him off, but a rumbling of remorse wouldn't leave her alone, no matter how hard she tried to shake it. And she understood why—despite their differences, he had been so kind to her. She sent him a text.

Reuben called with Donna DeLuca's name! Thought you'd want to know

Before waiting to hear back, she opened Facebook. Again, it was a popular name, but this time she had a strategy. First, she found Reuben Ross's page, which was easier now that she knew the spelling of his name and what he looked like. She searched his friends list for Frank Strauss, with a plan to see if Donna Ackerman was among his contacts. But before she could click through, her phone pinged. It was Devon.

Congrats! What's the plan?

She texted back:

Still figuring it out

Joybird clicked on Frank Strauss's Facebook page. As she navigated to his friends list, her phone rang.

"Thought you might want to strategize," Devon said.

Joybird pushed her pillow against the headboard and leaned back. "I'm so relieved this worked out—I kind of jumped the gun and told my father I was closing in on finding her, and I had a moment of panic. I just . . . I didn't want to . . ." She paused, struggling to describe her feelings.

"To disappoint him?" Devon offered.

"Yes," she said, grateful he had found the right word. To Joybird, the idea of disappointing her father was painful to even contemplate.

"We can't let that happen," he said. "So what now?"

"I was thinking of sending her a Facebook message. Something friendly and not overly aggressive."

"Okay, but you'll need a plan B in case she doesn't respond."

Joybird fluffed her pillow, getting more comfortable as she listened to the rain hitting the window in a relentless beat that seemed to beg for a tune to go with it.

"I'll need to think about that," she said.

"You want to meet for a drink?" he asked. "We can knock it around."

She did, but . . . again, the idea of encouraging anything romantic still seemed like a mistake, especially after the recent development with Noah. Besides, with the weather assailing the streets, she felt so cozy and protected in her room.

"It's so awful outside," she said. "And I just got in."

"Breakfast tomorrow?" he asked.

"Don't you have work?"

"Before work," he said. "We can meet someplace near you in Brooklyn Heights—it's on my way."

"Um," Joybird said, stalling as she considered it. She thought about the regret that had been simmering inside her—stubborn and brackish—and realized that there would be nothing wrong with a genial breakfast. "Actually, yes. That would be great."

"What's a convenient place near you?" he asked.

"Starbucks on Montague Street?" she offered, and almost immediately regretted it, as that was where Noah Pearlman worked as a barista.

"Perfect," Devon said before she could take it back. "I'll be there at seven thirty."

Chapter 18

The next morning, Joybird arrived at her local Starbucks to find that Devon had already snagged one of the little round tables directly across from the counter, where Noah was busy serving a line of customers. She caught his eye and gave a small wave, then pulled out the seat across from Devon. As she hung her jacket over the back of the chair, Joybird took a surreptitious glance back at Noah, only to discover he was staring at her. She didn't believe in playing the jealousy game—and would certainly never counsel anyone to do it—but couldn't help feeling this might push him to ask her out.

She turned her attention to Devon and got the impression he had clocked the subtle exchange but chose to ignore it.

"I ordered you a cappuccino," he said, pushing a sleeved paper cup toward her. "I hope that's okay."

He gave a small smile, his eyes fixed on her. Joybird sat and glanced away, self-conscious. "Thank you," she said quickly. "I really appreciate all of this."

"You got me hooked into this mystery," Devon said. "I have to see it through to the end."

Joybird pulled her laptop from her bag and carefully positioned it on the small table. She opened it, accessed Wi-Fi, then navigated to Donna Ackerman's Facebook page and turned it toward Devon.

"So this is the woman who stole your father's heart all those years ago," he said, studying the profile picture.

Joybird wondered if he was as surprised by the photo as she was. Not that Donna Ackerman wasn't attractive, but she looked more like a passably pretty Darien divorcée than some goddess. Still, she had good cheekbones, and Joybird could imagine she had been quite lovely as a young woman. Her father, she assumed, still saw that girl when he looked at this woman's face.

"Did you send her a friend request?" Devon asked.

"You think I should? I was afraid it would seem weird."

He nodded. "The only problem is that if you're not connected, your note won't go to her regular inbox. Good chance she won't even see it."

Joybird agreed, as she had already considered that, and took a first sip of her coffee. She didn't usually order cappuccino, so it was unexpectedly delicious. The cinnamon tasted like a gift, earthy and rich. She savored another sip and caught Devon watching her, clearly amused that she was enjoying it so much.

"Cinnamon," she explained.

He nodded, hand to heart as if she didn't need to say another word, and turned his attention back to Donna, asking Joybird if she'd been able to get a phone number.

"That part was easy. I mean, I don't know if I should assume it's current, but my plan is to give her a few days to respond on Facebook. If I don't hear from her, I'll call."

"Give her a week," Devon said, his hand wrapped around his cup as he watched her drink. "You're really enjoying that."

She shrugged. "I usually get the Americano. This is so . . . indulgent."

He smiled. "If you behave yourself, I'll get you the caramel macchiato next time."

"You think I can handle it?"

"Baby steps," he said.

They talked about her message to Donna DeLuca, and Joybird turned the computer back to herself and read out loud the draft she had started.

"Dear Donna. My dad, John Martin, was a classmate of yours at Paxton, and he remembers you fondly. He had a long, successful career as a TV writer under the name Sid Marcus, but is struggling now and dealing with depression. He saw you recently in Manhattan and regrets not approaching you. At your convenience, could you please call me so we can discuss the possibility of a meeting? I know it would mean a lot to him."

She paused, and Devon's brow tightened in concentration.

"It's terrible, right?" she asked.

"I think you need to be a little more vague, and definitely don't mention seeing her in Manhattan. That could seem stalkerish. Just concentrate on getting her to call you, or at least message back. The trick is to engage her."

He was right, of course, so she deleted most of what she'd written and started another version. As she typed, Devon reached across the table and brushed a lock of hair from her eyes. She ignored the tingle of intimacy and kept typing. Before she was finished, Joybird sensed a presence standing over her and looked up to see Noah Pearlman.

"Hi!" she said, startled.

"Am I interrupting something?"

"It's okay," she said, and introduced the two men.

"Nice to meet you," Devon muttered, his arms folded across his chest.

"Yeah, you too," Noah said, and then addressed Joybird. "I thought you were having a business meeting or something."

He was nosing around for details, and she couldn't imagine any reason for it besides jealousy. Now that she was face to face with the reality of it, Joybird was flustered and embarrassed. She felt like she was back in high school after she'd found out that the two boys she'd been sitting between in trigonometry both liked her. Once she knew the truth, she started sitting in a different seat—right up front near the teacher—so she wouldn't have to deal with the discomfort of their rivalry.

"Um . . . ," she began, not sure what to say.

"It's not business," Devon cut in. "It's personal. Did you need something?" He rested his chin on his hand as if he were completely relaxed. But she could feel his leg jiggling beneath the table.

Noah addressed Joybird. "I don't know if you got the email blast, but we're running another program at the community center this afternoon."

"Oh, sorry," she said, her hand to her throat. "I'm working today. When's the next weekend event?"

"I'll text you," he said.

She smiled. "Thank you! I'll keep an eye out for it."

"Nice to meet you, Kevin," he said, and turned to walk away.

"It's *Devon*," Joybird corrected.

Devon waved it off. "This is Starbucks," he said. "They're trained to get names wrong." He turned his cup toward her to show that it said *Evian* in black marker.

She gave a small laugh. "That can be your watery alter ego."

"Right," he said, considering it. "The diluted version of me—the guy who doesn't get pissed off when a creepy barista approaches to flirt with his date."

Date? Joybird felt her face burn hot. She thought he understood this wasn't anything close to a date.

"Relax," Devon said, when he saw her expression. "I was just kidding. Except for the bit about the creepy barista."

Joybird exhaled, relieved. "He's really a good guy," she explained. "Runs a local volunteer group that helps people use creative writing to feel less marginalized."

"Well, Mr. Good Guy has the hots for you, Joybird . . . in case you hadn't noticed."

"Oh, I don't think so," she said, feeling herself flush. "We're just friends."

"Be careful," he said. "I don't trust him."

Joybird touched her neck, understanding that if Devon saw it, too, it wasn't her imagination. That moment in the car had meant something—Noah Pearlman was attracted to her. She looked up to see Devon staring at her.

"Oh shit," he said, leaning forward for a closer look at her face. "You like him. You like that dude."

"I . . ."

"Oh, fuck me," he said. "Is that why you suggested this place? You wanted to make him jealous?" The change in his expression alarmed her—a mixture of anger and hurt, right on the surface.

"No!" she insisted. "I didn't. You said breakfast, and I . . . it popped into my head. I don't believe in any of that . . . in making someone jealous."

"Maybe not consciously."

"You're not mad, are you?"

He straightened in his chair, agitated. "What do you think this is about?" he said, gesturing between the two of them. "Do you really not get it?"

Joybird felt dizzy with confusion. Hadn't he just acknowledged it wasn't a date? She grabbed the table with both hands to keep herself anchored. Her breath got impossibly shallow, and she tried to slow it down. "I thought it was about finding Donna DeLuca," she whispered.

"No, you didn't. You know I like you." He paused, peering at her until she glanced back up at his eyes, which looked injured. "I think about you so much," he said softly.

She wanted to ask why but worried it would sound like she was fishing for a compliment, so she took another sip of her coffee to buy time. As she considered it, Joybird realized how ironic his attraction was. He liked her because she was so different from the other girls he dated—women who were into designer shoes and expensive purses and other symbols of money and status. He was drawn to her ethos. But that was the very reason she couldn't envision them together. They were so far apart on what they valued.

"I'm just always so happy when I'm around you," he said. "And I think you feel the same way about me."

Joybird wanted to protest, but she couldn't. There was more than chemistry between them. She *liked* him. But they were so incompatible that it made no sense. For either of them.

"We're so different," she said.

"And?"

"And . . . I don't understand why you'd want to go out with me. You're so"—she gestured to indicate the entirety of him—"fancy." She cringed at the word but couldn't think of anything better. *Slick* came to mind, but it felt too insulting. She continued. "And I'm . . . idealistic." Joybird blushed at her own explanation. She hadn't meant to make herself sound superior, but she was too stressed to make it any clearer.

"I get it," he said, his voice even. "You think I should go after someone more like me—superficial and materialistic."

"I didn't say that."

He sighed, releasing tension. "No, it's a fair point," he said. "And the truth is, I've been down that road. A lot. And more than once, I had my heart trampled like roadkill. After the last time, I swore I was done. I thought every woman was just another person to break my heart." Devon looked away for a long beat as if gathering his thoughts, then stared into her face. "But when I wound up in your Uber, I was like . . ." He closed his eyes as though he were revisiting that moment. "Like . . . shit, this girl is different."

He opened his eyes and looked at her. They were silent for a long time as Joybird took it in. His attraction excited and rattled her.

"I don't know what to say to that," she finally whispered.

He shook his head and sighed. "Just ignore it."

"How can I do that?"

He glanced away as if searching for something. When he looked back at her, his expression was resolute. "On second thought, don't ignore it. Keep it simmering on the back burner where you can see it. Because I'm not going to ask you out again—I don't need the rejection—but if you change your mind . . ." He opened his arms to indicate that he would be available to her.

Joybird nodded as she considered his words, wondering what would happen if that simmering pot boiled over.

"Can I ask you something?" she said.

He leaned back in his chair, looking relieved he had said what he needed to. "Always."

Joybird sipped her coffee and put it down gently. "What was her name?"

He blinked, surprised. "Her name?"

"The woman who hurt you so much."

"Ah," he said. "That would be Leona."

"Were you together a long time?"

"Three years. A month after we got engaged, I found out she'd been sleeping with her boss. Didn't even think it was a big deal."

"I'm sorry," Joybird said.

He closed his eyes as if the pain was just too much to bear. "I thought we were . . . everything to each other. I don't know how you come back from that."

His heartache was hard to witness, and her eyes watered in sympathy. It took her a moment to find her voice. "It takes time," she finally said.

"That's what people say, but . . . it feels like permanent damage."

Now it made sense. He liked her *because* they were opposites, not in spite of it. She was more a symbol than a real object of desire—proof that there might be an antidote to what ailed him. She made a private vow. She wouldn't be flattered by his attention, or swayed by her own pulsing desire.

"I'm sorry you're in so much pain," she said.

"Me too." He picked up his coffee and took a long, restorative sip. "So let's get back to your dad's love life."

And they did, putting the finishing touches on Joybird's message to Donna Ackerman.

"You'll let me know if you hear anything," he said, intoning it like a statement, not a question.

"Of course."

"Meanwhile, I'm going to do some reconnaissance. There's an older guy in my office who's lived in Darien forever. I'll see if he knows anything about her."

On their way out the door, Joybird gave Noah a breezy goodbye.

Devon put a proprietary hand on her back and leaned in to whisper, "Be careful with that dude, Joybird. Trust me on this."

Chapter 19

The next morning, Joybird awoke to a curious clucking emanating from the living room. Thick with sleep, it took her a minute to identify it.

Laughter.

She got out of bed and went to see what was going on. There was her father, tapping away at his keyboard, laughing out loud. The night before, he had told her he had a new idea for a comedy and was going to start working on another pilot, from scratch. She didn't know if he would really follow through, so she was thrilled to see him at it. Joybird smiled. She couldn't imagine what the script was really about—all he had said was that it was *Breaking Bad* meets *Seinfeld*, which didn't tell her much. But she had confidence that he knew how to write a funny script. Maybe he'd even go all the way with this one and it would wind up on network television, or HBO. Perhaps it would land at a streaming service. In any case, he would be back in the game. She beamed with pride. She had done this. She had saved her father.

Joybird imagined the show being a hit and getting an Emmy nomination. It was easy to picture her father in a tuxedo, welcomed back into the Hollywood fold at the award ceremony. She knew exactly how much that would mean to him.

Joybird switched the POV of this fantasy, imagining herself watching it from the audience instead of a TV screen. She would be sitting next to him, holding his hand at that tense moment when they opened the envelope. "And the Emmy goes to . . ." Then, when his name was called, she would be the one he hugged. And maybe he would even thank her in his speech. The thought made her gasp out loud.

Her father stopped typing. "Can't you see I'm working?" he barked.

Joybird slipped back to her room to get ready for her third day as a joy coach, feeling like there was nothing she couldn't do.

When she passed back through the living room, his laptop was closed, and he was puttering around in the kitchen, setting things on the counter with more force than necessary.

"Everything okay?" she asked.

"You broke my concentration," he grumbled.

"I'm leaving now," she said. "You'll have a long day to yourself to get lots done."

He released his anger with a sigh. "When I'm in the zone, I can be kind of a dick. Please don't take it personally."

"Don't be silly," she said, hoping to make him laugh. "You're almost always kind of a dick."

He folded his arms and assessed her, looking impressed. "Not bad, baby girl."

Joybird beamed. She so rarely got that kind of appreciation from her father. She tucked the feeling close to her heart, gave him a kiss on the cheek, and left for work.

Her first client of the day was an older woman named Sheila who wanted advice on buying a dress for her niece's wedding. She had taken dressing room photographs of herself in four different gowns, and asked Joybird to look at the pictures and tell her which one to buy. Joybird thought the tiered navy blue dress was the most flattering, but she knew better than to make the decision for her. Instead, she asked Sheila how she felt in each one, trying to buoy her confidence in her own judgment.

"You know," Joybird said, "there's no wrong choice. Pick the dress that makes you feel best."

"The animal print!" Sheila said, bringing her hands together in a clap. "I love it so much."

It was a bold choice, but Joybird understood that if Sheila felt that good in it, she would dazzle. "You're going to have a great time at the wedding," she said.

After that, Joybird had two clients in a row who wanted career advice. Then she picked up Garret Muller, a thirty-four-year-old man who looked like he hadn't washed his stringy hair in a week. On his intake form, he had simply said he wanted advice on his social life. But when he got in her car, he told her he needed to know how to go about finding "a clean prostitute," as his mother had died a few months ago, and now that he had the house to himself, he was ready to have sex. Determined not to judge, Joybird engaged him in conversation about his daily life and got him to admit he was lonely. So she helped him brainstorm on ways he could meet people, and how he might start taking better care of himself to make a good impression. She knew that sometimes the most obvious things were hard to see—like how much easier it would be to get a date if you wore clean clothes and washed your hair.

By the end of the day, Joybird still hadn't heard back from Donna Ackerman, but as she walked home from the outdoor parking lot, she felt the buzz of a text and looked down at her phone. It was from Noah, and she felt a rush of excitement, even though it was only a message about the details on the next weekend event for his organization. She typed out a quick response:

Thanks for the info—I'll be there!

Before hitting send, she scrolled through the emojis, looking for something appropriate to add. It needed to suggest flirtiness, but not too much. She wasn't going to blow him a kiss or send him a face with hearts over the eyes, though those depicted her feelings well enough. A thumbs-up seemed too banal. She settled on a smiling sun—just enough to let him know she'd put some thought into the text. She hoped it conveyed that she was making an effort for him.

Immediately, she saw the gray dots to indicate he was typing a reply. It took several minutes, which she thought was significant. He was putting effort into his message too. When it finally came through, she had to cover her mouth to keep from yelping.

Busy tonight? Want to come by for a drink around 10?

It was followed by a martini glass and the open-smile happy face.

Joybird held the phone to her heart. It had finally happened. Noah Pearlman had asked her out. And yes, she understood that ten p.m. drinks at his place was a booty call, but she also knew he wasn't the type of guy who slept around. If he wanted her in his bed, he wanted her in his life.

Still, she wondered if it was wise to go running over there. Would she look needy and desperate? Maybe it was better to tell him she was tired after a long day of work—because she was—and ask for a rain check. Maybe then he'd propose a more conventional date. On the other hand, she didn't want him to think she was blowing him off. He might get the wrong impression that she was dating Devon.

Joybird fished out her key and let herself into her building. She needed a little time to think about this, maybe go upstairs to Betty for advice.

When she reached her apartment, Joybird saw two pizza boxes on her little kitchen table. Her father was in the living room recliner, and a plate with one slice was balanced on his chest as he sipped from a beer bottle.

She greeted him and hung up her jacket. "You ordered two whole pizzas?" she asked, aware that he always put it on her account.

"Couldn't decide if I wanted plain or pepperoni."

"But that's sixteen slices . . . for two people. And I'm still on a tight budget."

"I can do the math," he said. "Relax. I'll pay you back every penny. That's a promise."

"Dad—" she began, gearing up for one of her gentle life lessons, aware that she needed to tread lightly.

"Besides, they won't deliver a single pizza, so what choice did I have?"

Joybird rubbed her forehead. "What I usually do is run out and pick it up. It's only a couple of blocks away. And it's good exercise."

He took a big bite of his pizza. "You want me to write this pilot or not?" he said, his mouth full.

Joybird couldn't argue with his creative process, so she simply took one of the boxes of pizza and went upstairs to see her wise and wonderful neighbor.

Betty, wearing a black tank top that revealed her soft upper arms, greeted Joybird with delighted surprise and invited her in. It was a cluttered apartment that smelled vaguely of incense. The walls—painted an aggressive yellow—were adorned with an eclectic array of antiwar and pro-environment posters, with a few art prints thrown in. They sat amid an assortment of colorful throw pillows on the living room couch, the pizza box and a bottle of wine on the heavily stained coffee table in front of them, not a coaster in sight. Betty poured them each a glass.

"You look especially happy," Betty said. "I take it all is well with the coaching business?"

"Not just that," Joybird said, grinning.

Betty studied her. "Noah?" she asked. Joybird had been telling her about him for months, so she knew just how much he occupied her thoughts.

Joybird took out her phone and opened the text message. "Look what I got from him."

"Goodness," the older woman said, taking the phone and holding it far from her face so she could focus, "somebody's horny." She handed it back.

"It's more than a booty call," Joybird protested. "He's not like that."

Betty took a slice from the box, put it on a plate, and handed it to Joybird.

"There's nothing wrong with wanting to get laid," she said, taking a slice for herself.

"I know. It's just that I think this is more than that, I really do."

Betty took a bite, then sipped her wine. "Kiddo, if he wanted to pursue a relationship, he'd take you out."

"He knew I was busy today. Yesterday he asked me to volunteer at one of his events, and I told him I couldn't make it. I think I've been on his mind."

"All of a sudden?" Betty asked.

"The other day he told me I was one of his favorite people."

"Uh-huh," Betty said, not sounding particularly impressed.

"And I ran into him yesterday when I was with someone else. I think it made him take me more seriously."

Betty's eyes went melodramatically wide. "Who were you with?"

Joybird looked away. "Devon, the Wall Street guy," she said, hoping Betty wouldn't press her too much on the relationship. She didn't have the energy to go into it. "He's helping me find Donna DeLuca."

"This is the Wall Street guy you turned down for a date?"

"We're friends now . . . sort of."

Betty squinted at her. "But he still has the hots for you."

Joybird took a bite of her pizza, chewed, and swallowed. "We worked all that out."

"Just to be clear, Noah sees you with a flashy, successful guy who wants to get in your pants, and suddenly he notices that you're attractive?"

"That's not a bad thing, is it? I mean, he already said he liked me. I just . . . I'm not good at flirting, so he never looked at me like that. Then when he saw me with another guy . . ." She shrugged.

"You want my advice?" Betty said.

"That's why I'm here."

"You need to ask yourself if you really like this Noah guy or if you just want to get it on with him. Because if you just want to fuck him, then go for it. But if you want something more, don't go running into his bed tonight. Because he'll drop you."

"He's not like that, though. He has a good heart. I've seen it."

"Okay, then. What do you think will happen if you tell him you're too tired to come over tonight?"

"I'm afraid I'll miss my chance with him."

"There you go," Betty said quickly.

"You don't understand. If I turn him down, he'll probably think I'm involved with Devon."

Betty put on her reading glasses and held out her hand. "Let me see your phone for a second."

Joybird handed it to her and watched as the former journalist carefully tapped something into it with a curled index finger. Joybird tried to be patient, but her friend typed so slowly it was excruciating. When she finally handed the phone back, Joybird saw that she had drafted a response to Noah: Would love to see you but I'm exhausted from work. Rain check?

It was exactly what Joybird had considered when she first saw his message. Still, she read it back to herself three times. It was probably the smart thing to do, but she was worried she would blow her one chance with this guy. Maybe a flirty emoji would clarify. But after scrolling through the selections and rejecting every option, she decided to add a line of text instead.

Maybe this weekend?

She read the whole thing back to herself, decided it was perfect, and hit send. It was a test, of course. If he made definitive plans with her, it would mean he was serious about pursuing something. If not, then Betty was right, and the booty call was just about sex.

She left her phone face up on the coffee table as they went back to enjoying their meal. Several minutes later, he responded:

Weekend kind of jammed—will let you know

Chapter 20

The disappointment was physical. Joybird felt it like a plummeting in her gut. But she took a few cleansing breaths and caught herself, deciding there was no reason not to believe him. After all, it was Friday night, and it made perfect sense that his weekend was already booked. She was busy too. On Saturday morning, she had two clients, and on Saturday afternoons, she usually met with a group of life coaches to share ideas. She even had tentative plans for Saturday night: helping an old coworker set up for a political fundraiser, and going out for drinks afterward. On Sunday, she thought she might take her dad for a ride up the Taconic to do some leaf-peeping. He had been in Los Angeles a long time and probably missed the fall foliage.

When she got back from Betty's apartment, she sent a quick text to Devon, telling him she hadn't yet heard back from Donna.

He responded: Can I call in an hour? Got some good intel

Joybird remembered that Devon said he had a coworker who lived in Darien and might know Donna, so she was eager to hear what he had to say. She looked at the clock—it was ten p.m., and she was tired. Devon, she imagined, was out with friends. Or maybe a date. A soft tendril of jealousy wriggled through her, but Joybird reminded herself that he wasn't there for her own ego, waiting in the wings in case she ever changed her mind. If he was on a date, it was a good thing. It would let them move on as friends. And maybe he was taking a positive step in mending his broken heart.

When her phone rang after eleven, Joybird had just dozed off. But she answered and tried to sound awake.

"Shit, I woke you," Devon said. "I'm sorry."

She clamped her jaw against a yawn, impressed that he was perceptive enough to know she'd been faking her liveliness. "It's okay."

"You want to talk tomorrow?" he asked.

She sat up so her voice would sound stronger, propping pillows behind her back. "I'm dying to hear what you found out."

"Good, because I'm dying to tell you—I talked to the older guy in my department who lives in Darien, and he didn't know her, but he put me in touch with a woman in purchasing who also lives there. She's in her early thirties, and I figured there was no chance she'd know Donna. Turns out she's friendly with one of her kids."

Now Joybird was fully alert. This lead could be her break. "Devon, this is—"

"I know! And she's totally down with the whole thing. She thinks it's hilarious that Donna Ackerman is someone's long-lost love, and promised to keep the whole thing on the q.t. So here's the dope. Donna's definitely divorced and single. In terms of hobbies, she's a big tennis player, belongs to a local country club. That won't help us, but this will: she volunteers at a local arts center."

"An arts center?"

"It's open to the public. So I figured if we pop in while she's working there, you can strike up a conversation with her and make your case in person. I think that would be much more effective than trying to do it over the phone. You have such an earnest face, she won't be able to resist."

Now Joybird was more than awake, she was pumped, excited by the possibility, and flattered he thought she was irresistible to the world at large. She was even glad he said "we," because it was comforting to have a partner in this quest, even if she had no intention of dragging him up to Connecticut.

"I wonder if they're open on Sunday," she said. "I was planning to take my dad on a ride upstate to see the foliage."

"A meet-cute!" Devon said. "I hadn't even thought of that."

"What's the place called?" she asked, opening her laptop.

He said it was the Sweet Barn Arts Center, which she quickly navigated to online. The front page of the website gave her exactly what she'd hoped to find.

"There's a show going on right now," she said. "And Sunday is the final day. All I need is a tank of gas and a way to convince my father to get in the car."

"What will you tell him?" he said quickly, his excitement matching hers.

"I'll have to be a little cagey. I don't want to reveal the truth, because there's always a chance she won't be there, and he doesn't handle disappointment well. Plus, I think it would be better for him to be surprised. He was so down on himself for not having the courage to speak to her when he saw her in New York. This would give him the chance for a redo. It's just what he needs."

"I'd like to come," Devon said.

Joybird felt a catch of excitement in her chest, but caught herself. She shouldn't be this eager to spend time with him. "You would?" she said.

"Please. I'm so deep into this caper I have to see it play out."

She wanted to say yes, but then she pictured Devon and her father in the same car, and it made her edgy. What if Sid decided to be irreverent and insulting? Worse, what if he made a game of embarrassing the hell out of her? Teasing was his favorite sport.

"I don't know," she said. "My dad—"

"You think I can't handle your dad?"

"He can be pretty offensive."

"I've been offended before," Devon said. "I survived."

She went quiet, considering how to explain it.

"What?" he pressed. "What are you not telling me?"

"He'll try to embarrass me. And he's really good at it."

Devon laughed. "What is he going to do—show me your naked baby pictures?"

"If only," Joybird said, pushing at her cuticles. What could she say without revealing that she had already talked to her father about him? It was all too humiliating.

"Just let me know what time to pick you up," he said.

"Excuse me?" she asked, confused.

"No reason to take the joymobile when I have a perfectly comfortable Range Rover I hardly ever get to drive."

"I didn't even know you had a car," she said.

"It's mostly for weekends."

More wasted money, she thought—an expensive SUV sitting in a parking space that probably cost him hundreds of dollars a month. Part of her wanted to accept his offer, just to give him a chance to get the car out on the road. But she shook her head, reminding herself that she bore no responsibility for the health of Devon's pricey vehicle.

"It's an imposition," she insisted. "Thank you, but I can't."

"You can," he said. "And I wouldn't have offered if I didn't want to do it. How's eleven a.m.?"

Joybird let out a long breath. She knew she might enjoy being the passenger for once, getting to savor the scenery. That is, if her father could manage to behave himself. And it seemed to mean a lot to Devon.

"Are you sure?" she asked, giving him a way out in case he was just being polite. "You probably have so much to do on the weekends, and friends who want to—"

"Joybird," he interrupted, "go back to sleep. I'll see you Sunday."

Chapter 21

By Sunday morning, there was still no text from Noah, so Joybird assumed his weekend really was as jammed as he had said. She made coffee and waited for her father to wake up.

"Beautiful day for a drive," she said when he padded out of the bedroom in his Dolce & Gabbana robe. The night before, she had mentioned that she'd arranged for them to take a leaf-peeping ride, but all she got was a grunt.

"Have fun," he said, taking the cup she offered.

"We're going together," she insisted. "With my friend Devon."

"My script isn't going to write itself."

"Can't you take a day off?" she asked. "And when was the last time you saw the Northeast foliage?" Her mother, she remembered, had loved the splendor of fall, and Joybird hoped she could tap into some of that nostalgia.

He walked over to the window. "Look, a tree. I'm transformed."

"Come on, Dad. You lived in LA for so long. You must miss seeing the autumn colors."

"You know why New Yorkers are so smug about their damned foliage? Because the weather sucks, and they're trying to convince themselves there's a reason to live in this damp, dank climate besides the pizza." He came back to the table and sat.

Joybird sipped her coffee and studied him. "Is the writing going okay? You seem like you're back in a bad mood."

He rubbed his forehead. "I was moving too fast and wrote myself into a corner. That's what happens when I let myself get too enthusiastic. Now I just . . . I can't nail the beats. I used to be able to pull myself out of this, but . . ." His hand went to his mouth. "I think I've lost it."

Joybird saw his eyes turn sad as he filled with all the losses he'd suffered. She couldn't let him go there. "Maybe you need a break," she said. "Get out of this apartment. I think it'll do you some good."

He seemed to consider it as he sipped his coffee. "That's what my therapist used to say."

"Is that a yes?"

"My therapist was an idiot."

"I don't think you really believe that," Joybird said, noting that his voice had lost its edge. She wondered if he was softening, willing to be convinced. "Please, Dad," she added. "I really want to spend the day with you. And I think you'll like my friend."

"Who is this guy, anyway? Someone you're screwing?"

Joybird kept her face even—she didn't like to give any oxygen to her father's crudeness. Besides, she understood it was a cover for his melancholy.

"He's just a friend," she said. "He's very smart."

"Spare me," he said with a bitter laugh. "The last thing I want to do is spend time cooped up with one of your pungent, boring-as-shit, looms-his-own-caftans, deodorant-rejecting Brooklyn hipsters."

"He's not at all like that. He lives in a condo and works in finance. And he smells wonderful."

"I've met your friends, Birdie. I've never seen anyone like—" He stopped himself and stared hard at her face. "Wait a second. Is this that Wall Street guy? The fat dude?"

"His name is Devon. And he's not fat."

"I thought you didn't want to go out with him."

She clucked. "I told you. We're just friends. There's this art gallery he wanted to pop into up in Darien, and he offered to drive, so . . ."

He laughed again, this time amused. "Okay, okay," he snorted. "Don't say another word."

"You'll come?"

"I've got to meet this guy and see what this whole thing between the two of you is all about." He rose and headed toward his bedroom.

Joybird looked down and let out a long breath, trying not to stress about his apparent plan to make her uncomfortable. After all, this was progress—he was moving out of his despair. And if all went well, he'd soon be face to face with Donna.

"You might want to shave," she called, imagining his long-lost love setting eyes on him for the first time in almost fifty years.

He turned to look at her. "You must really have the hots for this guy."

"It's not that, I . . ."

"Relax," he said. "I won't embarrass you. I'll even change my underwear."

"You mean that?"

He knitted his brow. "I know I'm a slob, but I do change my boxers."

"I meant about not embarrassing me," she said. "I don't know if I can handle it."

"Don't worry about it, Birdie," he said.

Joybird nodded, but before she could even utter a sigh of relief, he added, "You're tougher than you think."

Chapter 22

"If you want me to drive so you two kids can sit back here and make out, just let me know," Sid said as he leaned toward the front seat, where Joybird and Devon were buckling themselves in.

"I don't hate that idea," Devon said.

Sid clapped him on the shoulder. "I like this guy already."

Joybird exhaled, preparing for a long ride. "I knew you would," she said. "He's a good man."

"And not fat," Sid added.

"What?" Devon asked, confused.

Joybird put a hand over her eyes. "Don't pay any attention to him," she said. "Please."

Sid leaned forward. "When she told me she wouldn't go out with you, I assumed you were either stupid, ugly, or fat."

"My father is dying to think I'm a hypocrite," Joybird clarified.

Sid shrugged. "Turns out she's just a commie."

"Are you?" Devon asked.

"No!" she protested.

Devon started the engine with the push of a button. "But maybe commie adjacent?" he asked. He put on his turn signal and pulled away from the curb.

"Oh, god," Joybird said. "Are we there yet?" She hoped her little quip would get a laugh from her father so they could move on.

It did, and Joybird felt herself relax.

"So what's your deal?" Sid said to Devon. "How did you become a capitalist-pig stockbroker?"

"Dad!" Joybird scolded.

"It's okay," Devon said to her. He glanced in his rearview at Sid. "I'm actually a capitalist-pig equity analyst."

"Sounds fancy."

"It's just the nerdy end of the investment spectrum. I research companies and make investment recommendations."

"I bet there's an interesting story to this career choice," Sid observed.

"There's a *story*," Devon said, pointedly leaving out the adjective.

"Your folks, right? They pushed you into business school?"

"That was my choice. Fordham. Though I really didn't know what I wanted to do. I just . . . I wanted to be successful. I had a cousin who worked at Goldman Sachs, and that's where he went to school, so I figured, why not."

Joybird hadn't known any of this and felt a twinge of guilt that she'd never asked him about his background. "What do your parents do?" she said.

"Oh, come on," Sid interrupted. "Don't bullshit a bullshitter. It wasn't your decision."

Devon shrugged as if convincing him was immaterial. "They were pretty chill about my decision. If anything, they wanted me to be a teacher like my mom."

"I don't buy it."

Devon glanced at Joybird. "Why doesn't he believe me?"

"He just doesn't like to admit when he's wrong."

"Not true," Sid protested.

"When have you ever admitted to it?" Joybird asked.

"When have I ever been wrong?"

Joybird knew she could cite a dozen examples without even straining her memory. Just that morning, he'd insisted that the milk he'd left out on the counter hadn't spoiled. And yesterday he had blustered about how stupid it was to charge your cell phone before the battery was completely drained. Even when she showed him an article refuting his point, he wouldn't concede. If she went back further, she could bring up examples from her childhood—like the time he and her mother got into a massive fight when he insisted seat belts in the back of the car made kids *less* safe. But Joybird didn't want to get into an argument with him, so she ignored his comment and addressed Devon.

"Are both your parents teachers?" she asked.

"My dad is a graphic designer who got laid off constantly, through no fault of his own. Growing up, I just knew I wanted something more stable and stupidly thought finance would be easy money."

Joybird took in that explanation and examined it. Of course, it made sense that his career path was more about stability than greed. Maybe she really had been a little judgmental.

"Why an analyst and not a stockbroker?" she asked.

"I tried that route," he said. "Wasn't for me—selling and flattering all the time." He shuddered. "Felt like I was in a straitjacket. So I went to my cousin and asked what I should do. He said, 'Dev, you like being the answer man, so be the answer man. Go into research. Be the brother who knows shit.' And so I did. The end." He glanced toward the back seat via the rearview mirror. "Hey, Sid, you taking notes for a Netflix series?"

Sid pretended to be sleeping. "I'm sorry, what? Were you talking?"

To Joybird, the information was anything but boring, especially since it shined a light on why Devon was so interested in helping her find Donna DeLuca. He liked knowing things and enjoyed chasing down the details.

"I should have understood that about you," she said. "That you really like having answers."

"My cousin says I'm an information junkie," he explained, and they exchanged a look that said they would need to be cryptic in front of her father so he wouldn't suspect the day's true mission. Devon changed the subject, asking her about the coaching business.

"I heard it was your bright idea," Sid interrupted, oozing sarcasm.

"It was a *great* idea, Dad," Joybird insisted.

"Yeah? How much repeat business you got?"

"Too early to tell, but I do have one client who already booked three months' worth of sessions."

Sid laughed. "That must be one fucked-up broad."

"It's a girl, actually," Joybird said. "A teenager. I helped her mother, so . . ."

"A teenager. Jesus. That's going to be a nightmare."

"No, she's a good kid. I think I helped her already."

"Your daughter is excellent at what she does," Devon said over his shoulder. "I got into her Uber in the shittiest mood and *wham*—she lifted me right out of it."

"Well, I live with her every day and look at me. Still a miserable old fuck."

"I'm working on it, Dad," she said.

Traffic was stop and go until they got out of the city. Once they crossed the Throgs Neck Bridge and passed into more open terrain, Joybird began pointing out the foliage—a tapestry of bright golds and flaming oranges, threaded with deep reds—undulating in the breeze. When Sid grudgingly admitted it wasn't terrible, Joybird said she remembered how much her mother had enjoyed the splendor of autumn.

"Well, she was an artist," he said dismissively.

"So are you," Devon said to him.

"Me? I write for TV. What the fuck would I know about art?"

"I bet you know what you like," Devon said.

"Like most barbarians, I have strong opinions."

"Perfect," Devon said, and shot Joybird a subtle look. She understood what he was doing—laying the groundwork for getting her father out of the car and into the gallery. "I was just hoping to get your thoughts on a painting I might buy. I want a gut reaction from someone who doesn't consider himself a connoisseur."

"You struck gold then," Sid muttered.

Joybird studied Devon's face and could tell he was pleased with himself. He must have sensed she was looking at him, because he glanced over and gave her a smile so warm it made her flush. She went back to admiring the scenery.

"How did your parents meet?" Joybird asked Devon, curious to know more about him.

"At a school dance. They both tell the story like it was love at first sight. The earth moved and all that."

"You don't believe them?" she asked.

He rocked his head, considering it. "I think the story got romanticized over the years."

"He probably just grabbed her ass," Sid offered from the back seat. "And the rest is history."

"Ignore him," Joybird said.

"Don't be so prissy," Sid told her. "Back then, there was nothing wrong with grabbing someone's ass. Now you have to ask: 'Miss, may I please place my hand on your posterior?'"

"I don't think that would get you very far," Devon said.

"If you can't grab and you can't ask, I don't know how anybody winds up getting laid."

"You can ask," Devon said, "just be cool about it."

"You say that like it's easy," Sid grumbled.

Devon laughed. "It's definitely not easy, man."

When they arrived at their destination, Devon parked his SUV in one of the last available spots, and the three of them walked through the double doors of the arts center into the crowded studio space. It was a converted post-and-beam barn, with a vaulted timberwork ceiling so high it reminded Joybird of a cathedral. The center of the room was thick with bodies and dimly lit, while the white-painted walls—where the artwork hung—were flooded with high-intensity lighting. Joybird took a quick scan, trying to spot someone who looked like the Facebook profile photo she had seen, but most of the faces were too shadowed for a good look.

Sid folded his arms as he, too, surveyed the crowd, which looked more country club than bohemian, and was decidedly white.

"Almost makes me want to change my name back to John Martin so they'll let me in," he said. Then he looked Devon up and down and laughed. "But have fun. I'm sure they'll make you feel welcome. Maybe Bitsy and Conrad will invite you to join their yacht club."

"I can handle it," Devon said. "But since you're so at home, why don't you take a look around? I'll go see if I can find out about that painting."

Devon and Joybird set off, barging through the middle of the crowd as their heads swiveled from side to side. At last, Joybird saw a woman in a crisp white blouse and a popped collar in the corner of the room, holding a clipboard. She felt her pulse quicken. "I think that's her," she whispered, and considered how she might get Donna into her father's sight line. Joybird decided she would say that they were interested in one of the paintings and had some questions. Then they could lead her in that direction, and before they reached the artwork, Sid would look up and spot her. There would be a hushed moment of recognition—the kind of scene in a movie where the rest of the world fades out and the music swells—and then . . . then he would finally get to approach his long-lost love. Joybird breathed into the ripple of chills that raised goose bumps on her arms.

She and Devon pushed their way through the chattering cluster toward Donna DeLuca Ackerman. But when they got close, they saw that the woman was in her midforties, with a square jaw, and looked nothing like the woman in the photo. Her name badge said "Rachel B."

"Can I help you?" she asked them.

Joybird felt her spirit sink. "Uh, no. Sorry," she said. "I thought you were someone else." For a second, she considered asking Rachel B. if she knew where Donna Ackerman was, but she dismissed it because she didn't want Donna alerted that someone was looking for her. It would be best if the meeting with her father looked accidental.

She turned back to Devon and whispered, "What now?"

They decided they would split up and circle the periphery. Joybird went off to the left, studying the people studying the paintings, which were an eclectic array from local artists, encompassing everything from competent but uninspired landscapes to striking modern art in slashes of color. She discovered two smaller galleries off the main room and even checked out the ladies' room. No Donna.

She was on her way back to her father when Devon stopped her. "You find her?" he asked.

She shook her head and understood he hadn't either.

"And now we have another problem," Devon said, pointing.

She followed the line of his finger, and her eye landed on an oversize canvas depicting two nude women whose breasts were the central focus of the painting. One was a young girl with pert nipples pointing toward the moon, while the other was an old woman with pendulous breasts and pale saucer-size areolas. The artist, she assumed, was trying to make some kind of point, but it eluded Joybird.

Then she realized that Devon wasn't pointing at the painting, but at her father, standing in front of it in close conversation with a wiry woman in a short-sleeved polo shirt. She wore her pale-blonde hair in a blunt bob, and had the tanned, muscular look of a serious golfer, or maybe a tennis player.

"What's going on?" Joybird asked.

"She recognized him—came right up and said she was a big fan of *Down Here*. He's flirting his head off. Now I'm afraid that even if we find Donna and get her within a foot of him, he won't look up."

She watched as her father made the woman laugh. When she touched his arm, he moved in closer. Joybird thought about his three wives, all of whom had dark hair and olive complexions.

"She's really not his type."

"Like that matters," Devon said.

"Doesn't it?"

"She's flirting with him. That makes her his type."

Joybird recalled what her father had said about availability as a motivating factor. Actually, he had said something about getting into the pants of ugly chicks, but the point was that attraction wasn't always the point.

"Should we break it up?" she asked.

"Let's leave it alone for now. We need to ask the staff if Donna's even here."

"I was hoping it wouldn't come down to that. If she gets tipped off someone is looking for her, it defeats the whole idea of an accidental meeting."

"We're running out of options," Devon said.

She knew he was right, so they set off again in search of the woman with the clipboard. On the way, Joybird continued to scan the faces.

When they found Rachel B., Joybird said, "I'm sorry to bother you, but I was wondering if you knew where I could find Donna Ackerman."

"You know, I haven't seen Donna today. Let me find out."

At that, she disappeared into a back room, and Joybird felt deflated. Now, Donna would be alerted that people were looking for her, and she would have to give some kind of explanation.

As they waited, Joybird and Devon continued to scan the crowd. After several minutes, a noise rang out—a loud smack that reverberated through the cavernous space. A hush fell over the room as all faces turned toward the source of the sound. The crowd moved away, creating a path through the center of the hall, so that Joybird could get a clear view of what everyone was staring at. There, beneath the bright light that illuminated the garish nudes, was the sinewy woman in the polo shirt, her hand still in midair. Standing before her, with a red hand-shaped mark on his cheek, was her father.

Joybird heard frantic whispers around her.

Did she slap him?

What did he do?

In this day and age!

"Oh, shit," Devon said. "We'd better get him out of here."

Just then, Rachel B. appeared between them. "Well!" she said cheerfully. "Now I know why I didn't see Donna. She's on vacation."

"Okay, thanks," Joybird said as she raced off.

"But she'll be back next week for the handmade-jewelry exhibit!" Rachel called.

Joybird and Devon dashed over and rushed Sid out the door without saying a word. When they were in the parking lot, she said, "For god's sake, Dad, what did you do to that woman?"

"She was flirting like hell, but as soon as I made a move . . . Jesus fucking Christ." He rubbed the red spot on his cheek.

"Oh, god," Joybird muttered.

"So easy to forget how hung up these WASPs are," he said.

"Did you touch her?" Joybird asked. She didn't want to hear the answer but knew she would need to face the truth in order to work her life-coaching magic.

"Please tell me you didn't grab her ass," Devon said.

"I didn't!" Sid protested. "I swear! She was all over me—stroking my arm, licking her lips. She gave me every damned signal except grinding her hips into me. So I took your advice and used my words."

"Saying what, exactly?" Devon pressed.

"I said, 'By any chance, would you like to fuck an Emmy-winning TV writer?'"

Devon covered his face. "Jesus, Sid."

"I thought it was a good line."

"No, dude. It wasn't."

They got into his car and slammed the doors. Before he started the engine, Devon turned toward the back seat. "You have to read the situation. Be a little more subtle."

"Who makes these fucking rules?"

"Not guys like you." He turned back toward the windshield and started the car.

"'Subtle,'" Sid muttered. "Doesn't sound sexy to me."

Joybird groaned. She was starting to get a clearer picture of why her father had been booted out of Hollywood. It occurred to her that it might be a good thing they hadn't yet found Donna DeLuca, as he needed some lessons on civility first.

"Dad," she implored, "nowadays, if you want to impress a woman, you have to treat her with respect. Honor her space. You understand?"

"I'm not an idiot."

"I just want you to remember it. I know you were an important man for years and years, and things used to be . . . different."

He was silent for a long time, and Joybird could tell he was lost in thought—perhaps remembering his younger days.

"Dad?" she prodded. "You understand?"

"Of course."

"Promise me you'll never do anything like that again."

"I don't need to promise you anything," he said bitterly, and Joybird could feel in her bones that he was disappointed in himself and needed a gentle nudge toward the light.

"Please, Dad. I need to hear you say it."

He folded his arms. "Why?"

Joybird and Devon exchanged a look.

"Just do it, Sid," he said. "It'll mean a lot to her."

"Why does everything have to be so fucking PC?"

"Because we're learning to respect one another," Joybird told him. Sid snorted.

"Come on, man," Devon said. "You can do it."

Sid went quiet again.

"Please, Dad," Joybird begged.

At last, he exhaled. "Okay, okay," he said. "I promise."

At that, Joybird felt the familiar tingle of purpose—the reason she had become a joy coach. She had made a positive difference in someone's life. Of course, she understood that change could be a gradual process, but she also understood that the act of making the promise was significant. It meant he would at least think about his actions the next time he had such an impulse.

She smiled, and Devon glanced at her, giving a surreptitious thumbs-up, and she felt the added satisfaction of successful teamwork.

"Hey, what about that painting?" Sid asked.

"The painting," Devon said, clearly remembering his earlier lie, and stalling as he concocted a way to cover his tracks. "It, uh . . . wasn't there. Someone bought it."

"Too bad. Maybe you should have made an offer on another one."

"There wasn't anything else that caught my interest."

"Oh yeah?" Sid said. "I guess you didn't see the one with the tits."

At first, Sid seemed proud of the joke, but then it landed with a thud, and he folded his arms. Joybird glanced at him in the rearview mirror and saw a mixture of consternation and disappointment, but also something else. A moment later, she understood. He was rewriting it.

Chapter 23

Joybird went up to visit Betty so she could recount the events of the day, hoping her friend might be amenable to doing some life coaching of her own, with a specific target in mind: Sid Marcus. Joybird knew that rehabilitating her incorrigible father would take more than the earnest advice of a well-meaning daughter, and Betty seemed to have a knack for getting him to listen.

"Openhanded?" Betty asked, after Joybird explained about the slap. "He still has a mark."

Betty tsked as she yanked the cork from a bottle of Shiraz. "Don't take this the wrong way," she said, carefully pouring the wine, "because I like your father, but he's a pig." She put down the bottle and folded her arms, studying the glasses as if she could witness the wine breathing.

"He's learning, though," Joybird said.

Betty turned to her and cocked an eyebrow. "Old dog, new tricks?"

Joybird nodded because she knew, given the opportunity, people could always grow and change. "He just needs some guidance."

Betty handed Joybird her wine and sat next to her on the couch. Her perfume, as usual, was an old-fashioned scent that made Joybird think of movies from the 1970s and big hoop earrings.

"I love your spirit," Betty said.

"You know, you're one of the few people who like him."

"He amuses me," she admitted. "But even when he's being a dick, it's clear it comes from a place of pain and that he truly wants to be a better father. Besides, I know how to handle him. You have to call him out on his shit. He actually takes it pretty well."

"From you."

Betty sipped her wine as she took that in. "Fair point. He seems to have a grudging respect for me. But only because I'm not his daughter . . . and not someone he wants to bang."

Joybird nodded. "He listens to you."

"Sometimes."

"Do you think you can help? Because I really want to drive home the lesson about treating women with respect. If he hears it from you . . ."

"Kiddo, it's not going to make a difference."

It hurt Joybird to think Betty really believed that. "It will," she insisted. "I know it. And don't you think he deserves the opportunity to become a better person?"

"Deserves?" Betty asked, her voice thick with skepticism.

Joybird put her hand to her heart. "We all deserve a chance to become our best selves."

Betty gave a gentle laugh. "You would have made a great flower child." She held up the two fingers of a peace symbol.

"Will you do it?" Joybird pleaded.

"For you? Of course," Betty said. "But forgive me if I remain unconvinced that it will do any good."

Her cynicism did nothing to temper Joybird's enthusiasm. In fact, before Betty had even finished her sentence, Joybird was envisioning her father's happy ending.

The next morning, Joybird awoke excited about her week. She had new clients scheduled every day, and so far, two repeats on the calendar— Althea, who had been the victim of a catfish, and Riley, her teenage client. It was almost enough to keep her mind off her plan to drive back up to Connecticut to have a private and frank conversation with Donna Ackerman—her next step in making her father's dreams come true.

In the meantime, she was waiting to hear from Noah, eager to see him at the next Mightier than the Sword event and continue what they'd started.

Althea was standing in front of her building when Joybird pulled up. She was smartly dressed in a belted red jacket, and Joybird studied her body language as she approached the car. There was a different energy to her. Not better or worse, just altered.

"I love that color on you!" Joybird said as Althea got into the back seat. "How have you been doing?"

"It's been an adjustment, but I'm okay."

Althea had indicated that she usually went by subway to her job at Bloomingdales in Manhattan, but she would take a ride today to have another life-coaching session, as the first one had been so helpful. Heart full from the unexpected validation, Joybird put the car in gear.

"Did you work things out with your friend?"

"Oh yes, Debra was very forgiving. I even went to church with her yesterday."

Joybird put on her signal and pulled away from the curb. "And how did that feel?" she asked.

"Healing. I forgave Ismail, prayed for him."

That was a good step, but Joybird understood that he was probably on her mind all the time. "And did you delete him from your social media accounts?"

Althea was quiet except for the whisper of a small sigh. When Joybird stopped at a light, she glanced at her client in the rearview mirror and saw her rummaging through her purse.

"Not right away," she confessed, pulling out a tissue.

Joybird fought the disappointment tugging at her. "Why not?" she asked, keeping her voice light.

"I wanted to give him a chance to explain himself. We were very close. It wasn't like I could just . . . ignore him."

Sure you could have, Joybird thought as the light turned green. "So you've been in touch?"

"He was upset about the money. He said he was in terrible trouble and he'd been counting on me. I asked him about the fake profile pictures, though, and he got mean—said I was a shallow b-i-t-c-h if all I cared about was his looks. I said, 'But you deceived me.' Then he said . . ." She paused to tap at her phone. "I'll read it to you. He said, 'Don't forget I have pictures of you. I don't want to post them online, but if you don't send me the money, what choice do I have?'"

Joybird's knuckles went white as she gripped the steering wheel. Clearly, Althea had sent this horrible man naked pictures. It was a worst-case scenario. She looked again in the rearview and saw tears streaming down Althea's face, ruining her perfect makeup. She dabbed at her cheeks and under her eyes.

"You sent him pictures?" Joybird asked, for confirmation.

Althea nodded. "I trusted him. I thought we were in love."

"You know, he's probably just trying to scare you. I'm sure he doesn't want the kind of legal trouble he could get into."

"Debra's husband, William, is NYPD. He told me he'd take care of it. He said I shouldn't worry."

"Well, thank god," Joybird said, relieved. She didn't know what kind of power a New York City police officer had over a criminal operating out of Nigeria, but she assumed these guys had ways of issuing convincing threats when they needed to.

"He said I had to delete him from my contacts."

Wise advice, Joybird thought. "And did you?"

"I even blocked his phone number. He can't text me anymore."

"I'm really proud of you," Joybird said. "I know this has been hard."

They went on to discuss healthy ways of dealing with loneliness. Joybird wanted Althea to feel comfortable being alone so she wouldn't rush into another bad situation. Althea agreed with everything she said and seemed to be on the right track. It was gratifying.

"And you should probably be careful about men who approach you on Facebook," Joybird said, as she pulled over on Sixtieth Street, near Lexington Avenue, around the corner from the main entrance to Bloomingdales.

"Oh, absolutely," Althea said. "I've been messaging with a very lovely gentleman named Neil, but I'm taking it slow."

Joybird's heart sank, and it took her a moment to find something to say. "Maybe you should concentrate on meeting someone local, someone your friends know."

"It's hard at my age."

"I understand, but you're a bright, attractive woman and—"

"And Neil says age is just a number."

Joybird put the car in park and turned to face Althea. She had fixed her makeup and wore the same beatific smile she'd had when she first talked about Ismail.

"What does Debra have to say about all this?"

"Oh, I haven't told her about Neil yet. It's all very new. But I knew you would understand. You want to see his picture?"

Chapter 24

On Wednesday, as Joybird waited in front of the Berkeley Carroll School for Riley Wilbanks, she felt the buzz of an incoming text and looked down to discover it was from Noah. A trill of excitement charged through her before she discovered it wasn't a personal message but a group text inviting his friends to hear him read at a poetry event the following night in Prospect Heights. Still, she was happy because it meant she would get to spend time with him in a social setting. Joybird sent a private message to her old roommate, Zabeen, who lived in that neighborhood, and they arranged to meet up at the venue. Maybe Betty would want to come, too, as it would be an opportunity for her to meet Noah and see him in his element.

Joybird was so involved in texting Noah to say that yes, she'd be happy to come and was looking forward to it, that she didn't see Riley approaching. All at once, the rear door swung open and a cool October breeze blew in along with the girl's youthful energy.

"I'm happy to see you!" Joybird gushed, setting her phone aside. It was, she knew, important for this girl to feel appreciated.

Riley's expression turned dubious. "Why?"

Joybird smiled, ignoring the knee-jerk cynicism, and gave the girl a moment to settle in. "Tell me what's new and exciting in your life," she said.

"*My* life?"

"You seemed like you were in a good mood."

"I was. But now I'm going to see Corinne, and I'm not looking forward to the shit show." She opened her backpack and started rummaging through it.

"Things didn't go well last week?" Joybird asked. She started the engine and put on her turn signal. "Did you tell her you'd like her to help you with your homework?"

"It's not that," Riley said as she pulled out a bag of chips and yanked it open.

"What, then?"

The girl sighed and ate two chips before responding. "She's getting ready to move, and I'm supposed to pack up my room and throw away *at least* half of my stuff. It's not fair."

Joybird knew that children of divorce who got shuttled from house to house could get overly attached to their possessions, which became their port in a storm. She pulled away from the curb and merged into traffic.

"Will your new room be a lot smaller?"

"I think it's *bigger*. She's just going all Marie Kondo or some shit. I don't get why that should be *my* problem."

"But you'll get to take your favorite things, so that's positive."

Riley grunted, as if she didn't want to hear anything that might pull her from her funk.

"No offense," she said, "but you're like one of those everything-is-rainbows-and-unicorns people. It's annoying AF."

It wasn't too far from the truth, but Joybird had decided a long time ago not to apologize for her outlook on life.

"Are you having trouble figuring out what to bring and what to discard?" she asked.

"I don't want to 'discard' anything. It's my stuff. If I didn't want it, I wouldn't have it in the first place."

"What are some of the things you're worried about losing?"

Riley stopped talking as she continued eating her chips, and Joybird waited. Finally, the girl mumbled, "I don't want to talk about this."

Joybird stopped at a red light and glanced at her in the rearview mirror. "What *do* you want to talk about?"

Riley poured the last crumbs from the packet into her mouth and then crumpled it. She licked her fingers. "I joined the literary mag club."

"Great! How's it going?"

Riley's face lit up and she let out a joyous gasp, as if a jolt of electricity had just surged through her. "I can't even."

Joybird smiled and glanced back, amused that this articulate kid had suddenly lost her ability to express herself. The pivot in her mood seemed to fill the car with oxygen.

"Can I have this?" Riley asked, holding up a bottle of water.

"Of course," Joybird said, and waited for her to say more about the literary magazine.

Riley wiped her mouth with the back of her hand. "Okay, so like, the first day, Carter gave me this story to proofread. He didn't ask me to edit it or anything, but I fixed two really whack sentences and showed him a paragraph I thought should just be deleted. I mean, I thought it was really obvious, because it had nothing to do with the rest of the story, which was about two sisters, but then there was this bit about a shiny teapot, and it was a sort of show-offy, look-how-great-I-can-write tangent. But Carter was like, 'Wow, you're a great editor, Riley.' And then the next day, he sat right next to me at lunch, and I was just dying."

"How wonderful!" Joybird said, delighted to hear this precocious, sophisticated kid descend into normal teenage rapture.

"And my friend Kat said, 'He's totally into you,' and I was like, 'I don't know,' and she said, 'Dude, he *likes* you.' So . . . whatever. I'm just really . . . ugh. He's got so much rizz."

The last part was uttered with such desperate, melodramatic, adolescent lovesickness that it filled Joybird with nostalgia as she remembered her own teenage years. They went on to talk about boyfriends, and Riley admitted she'd never had a real one, unless you counted Javier, who she went out with in seventh grade, which she *totally didn't*.

"Do you think Carter will ask me out?" she said.

"That's a tough call from my end. What do you think?"

"Kat says he almost definitely will."

"If he does," Joybird said, "what will you—"

Riley's phone rang. "Shit," she said. "I forgot to text Corinne that I'm on my way." She answered it. "Hey, Mom . . . Yeah, I'm in the car . . . I don't know. Soon, I guess . . . No, I don't. It's *my stuff* . . . Really? . . . *Really?* Yeah, that would be cool . . . I don't know, let me put you on speaker." She paused, and held the phone toward the front seat. "My mom wants to talk to you," she said to Joybird.

"Hey, Corinne," Joybird said over her shoulder.

"Since I'm moving to that Murray Hill apartment next week," Corinne said, without preamble or greeting, "I took your advice, and I'm making a clean start, getting rid of everything that weighed me down."

Joybird frowned. She hadn't said anything like that. Corinne was throwing her under the bus, making it her fault Riley had to discard her prized possessions. She didn't want to call her on it and have a confrontation, but she also didn't want to let it go.

"You know," she said, "I don't think it's necessary to—"

"But I got an idea," Corinne interrupted. "Since you live in Brooklyn and her dad lives in Brooklyn, you could bring some of her stuff there. I'll pay you, of course. A win-win, right?"

Joybird rubbed her forehead. Corinne was so assertive that she made it hard to turn down her proposal, but Joybird needed a moment to think about it.

"Does her father know about this?"

"Of course! I called, and he said it was fine."

Joybird thought about it as she considered her schedule. "Is the stuff ready to load? Because I have another client, and I don't have much time."

"I'll get the porter to bring up a handcart," Corinne said. "It'll be fast."

"Okay, just . . . I can't make the drop-off for a couple of hours. Is that all right?"

They finished making the arrangements, and by the time Joybird arrived at the Sutton Place address, there was a uniformed man with a handcart standing near the entrance. Joybird strained to see how much stuff there was, and she could make out four cartons. It was a lot, but she understood how important it was to Riley.

When she pulled over and popped the trunk, the man heaved two large black trash bags from behind him.

"Am I taking all of that?" she asked, wondering if it would fit in her trunk.

"Yes, ma'am," he said. "And Miss Corinne asked if you could wait just a few minutes. Jacques is coming down with the rest."

"The rest?"

Riley opened the back door and got out. "Thanks, dude!" she called as she dashed into the building.

Joybird felt stuck—manipulated by Corinne into an untenable position. She turned to the man stuffing the bags into her car. "I can only take what will fit in my trunk."

"We'll do our best," he said, then went to get the handcart with the boxes. When he finished loading everything into her car, they were still waiting for Jacques to come down with the rest.

Joybird took the opportunity to finish her text to Noah, then checked the time. She had another client in Brooklyn to get back to, and if she hit traffic, she would be late. She considered just taking off, but worried how it would affect Riley. She texted to Corinne that the car was fully loaded, and she had to leave.

Corinne texted back: We just have a few more things. Coming right down. Don't leave.

Joybird bit her lip, considering how to reply. Finally, she typed: I can only wait two more minutes. So sorry

There was no response. After three minutes, she texted again.

Have to leave now. Maybe you can bring the rest to Murray Hill and I can take it next time

The response was quick.

He is getting on the elevator now!

Joybird sighed and watched the minutes tick by on her phone. It had to be the world's slowest elevator. At last, Jacques emerged from the building carrying two shopping bags and a carton. The men were able to fit one of the bags into the trunk, but the rest had to go on the front seat next to Joybird so the back seat would stay open for her next client.

Later that day, when she reached Barry Wilbanks's impressive house in the Bay Ridge section of Brooklyn, Joybird pulled the car up to align the trunk with the neat brick path that went straight from the steps to the front door. She got out, carrying the items from the front seat, and trudged up the stairs. Carefully balancing the box, she rang the bell.

After a minute, an attractive woman opened the door. She was in her midthirties and had a round face with narrow blue eyes. Her dirty-blonde hair was pulled back in a ponytail, and there was a toddler balanced on her hip. Joybird assumed this was Riley's stepmom, Emily, and her half sister.

"Can I help you?" the woman asked.

"I'm Joybird. I'm here with Riley's stuff?"

The woman looked confused. "I'm sorry?"

"Weren't you told I was coming?"

She looked past Joybird at the car, and the baby girl balled her fist around the V-neck of her shirt. "No. What's going on?"

Joybird told the woman she was a life coach, then recounted her conversation with Corinne and explained that she had Riley's things in her car.

"Oh, god," Emily said, frowning. "How much stuff is there?"

"Quite a bit."

"Of course," she muttered under her breath, then said to Joybird, "Look, this doesn't make any sense. I spoke to Barry an hour ago, and he didn't say anything about it."

"Can you call him?" Joybird asked, certain Corinne had told the truth about clearing this with Riley's father.

"He's in surgery now," Emily said.

"Oh," Joybird said, surprised by the woman's calm. "I'm sorry. I hope he's okay."

Emily looked confused by the response and then collected herself. "No, no. He's not *having* surgery. He's *performing* it. He's an orthopedist."

"I see," Joybird said, and hesitated. "I'm sure Corinne cleared it with him. She promised me she did."

The woman gave a small laugh, as if she didn't quite believe it. "You may as well come in," she said, seeing Joybird struggle with the boxes in her arms. "I'm Emily," she continued as she led Joybird into an immaculate designer living room in shades of white and beige, "and this is Isabella."

"She's precious," Joybird said as she put down the heavy items and took in the pristine room. "Wow, this is like something from a magazine. How do you keep it so perfect?"

"Don't be fooled," Emily said. "This is just for show. The playroom is a mess."

They continued on to a family room with a television and bins of toys. Emily put the baby down on a colorful mat and handed her a plastic Mickey Mouse puzzle.

Emily turned her attention back to Joybird. "I want you to do me a favor, as Riley's life coach. Go up those stairs," she said, pointing, "and open the closed door that's just past the bathroom. Take a look and then come down and tell me what you would do if you were me."

Joybird hesitated, confused. What could be up there that the woman wanted her to see? "I don't, uh . . ."

"Please. You'll see what I mean."

Joybird did as she was asked, trying to prepare herself for what could be behind the door. She imagined it was Riley's bedroom and that either it was too tiny to accommodate all the items in her car or was simply already packed with possessions.

In fact, the sight of the room made Joybird gasp. It looked . . . ransacked. But also, filled way beyond capacity. There was a four-poster bed in the middle, and on its south end was a lopsided mound of clothes, including patterned pajamas, a pink bra, dark-colored jeans, numerous T-shirts, a pair of purple shorts, a striped dress, teal panties, a tie-dyed sweatshirt, and more. The pile also contained a bright-green wig, two spiral notebooks, a collection of partially shredded lined papers, a desiccated ballet slipper, the power cord to a laptop computer, and several glossy textbooks. The scene was repeated on the floor, which also held dirty socks and food-encrusted plates and cups, as well as two opened boxes of Always sanitary pads, one crumpled dollar bill, a soccer ball, and a ukulele. There was no clear space to walk from the door to the bed. Against the left wall was a cubby-type shelving unit, with most of the boxes half-pulled out and overflowing with clothes. There was another shelf messily stacked with books and knickknacks, and a dresser that held a pile of haphazardly stacked stuffed animals reaching almost to the ceiling. On one wall was a flat-screen TV connected to a partially buried gaming console. A basket of clean, folded laundry stood valiantly near the door, next to an empty trash can lined with a plastic bag. The distinct scent of Febreze permeated the space.

Joybird closed the door and went downstairs. Emily was sitting cross-legged on the floor facing Isabella.

"I understand why you wanted me to see that," Joybird announced, still confused about why Barry Wilbanks would have agreed to let her bring over even more things.

Emily stood and dusted her hands.

"Shocking, right?"

"How did it get that bad?"

"Her father refuses to hold her accountable, and there's only so much I can do without being the wicked stepmother. So nothing ever gets better—only worse."

"Why do you think he agreed to let me bring over another carload of junk?"

"Please," Emily said, "there is no way he agreed to it."

Joybird tucked her hair behind her ear, wondering where the breakdown in communication had occurred. Corinne had seemed so certain that Barry Wilbanks had given her the green light.

"I never could have imagined it would be that bad," Joybird said to Emily.

"Did you notice the only clean thing in the room is the trash can? She never throws anything away."

Joybird shook her head. She didn't quite understand the psychology of hoarding. It was commonly associated with obsessive-compulsive disorder, but she believed it was something more pernicious, tied to abandonment issues.

"She needs help," Joybird said.

"Tell me about it."

Thinking about all the stuff in her car, Joybird understood why Corinne insisted on getting rid of it. Still, she never should have agreed to take it.

"What do you want me to do with my car full of her things?"

Emily shrugged. "Take it to a dump?"

"I can't!" she cried, hoping the woman would soften. "That would do real psychological damage. She would feel so betrayed." The thought of causing Riley so much pain made her eyes water.

Emily exhaled. "Of course, I know. I'm sorry. I just . . . what would you do if you were me?"

"Talk to the psychologist at her school? Get the names of some good doctors?"

"We're on that," Emily said. "She already sees someone. I meant, with the stuff in the car."

Joybird thought for a minute. "Is there room in the garage?"

A few minutes later, as she made trips between the garage and her car, unloading her trunk, Joybird understood the nature of the compromise—it was entirely likely Barry Wilbanks would throw away Riley's things the first chance he got. She hoped he would be gentle about it, but knew there wasn't anything she could do to affect him. It was out of her hands.

Meanwhile, she couldn't understand why Corinne had seemed so sure she had Barry's permission to bring over all that stuff. It just seemed so unlikely he would agree to it. In her mind, Joybird replayed her short conversation with Corinne, wondering if it was possible she might have misinterpreted what the woman had said about getting her ex's permission. But there was no way. It wasn't until later, when she was recounting the whole incident to Betty and heard the words coming out of her own mouth, that Joybird finally understood Corinne had flat-out lied. It couldn't have been more obvious.

Joybird knew exactly why she hadn't seen it—her sunny faith in people sometimes blinded her to bad behavior. But she shrugged it off as a small price to pay for the privilege of living her life in the bright, white light of optimism.

Chapter 25

The next night, Joybird got ready for Noah's poetry reading, excited that her neighbor Betty had agreed to come along. She put on a black-and-gold-trimmed sweater she had bought online not realizing how formfitting it would be. Still, it was flattering, and she paired it with dark skinny jeans and boots. The effect bordered on seductive, and Joybird felt a ripple of nerves as she studied herself in the mirror. It was too much, wasn't it? People would cluck and whisper. *She thinks she's all that.* Joybird considered what else was in her closet, but when she heard voices in the living room, she knew Betty had arrived, and went out to get her opinion.

"Damn, kiddo," said Betty, who was wearing a black leather jacket, black concert shirt, and bright-red jeans. With her white hair, the effect was dramatic—the world's coolest moto-grandma.

"It's not too much?"

"No such thing."

"You look great too," Joybird said.

"Never mind me," Betty said. "I'm just trying to stay a little bit relevant. But you. You are rocking those boots."

Sid interrupted with a theatrical cough-cough to remind them of his presence.

"What's the matter?" Betty asked. "Don't you like Joybird's outfit?"

"No, it's fine," he said. "I just didn't know people went to poetry readings to get action. Maybe I should tag along."

Betty gave his shoulder a backhanded swipe. "Say something nice to your daughter, Sid."

"I thought I just did."

She folded her arms expectantly, like a teacher waiting for a student to behave. Her cloud of white hair had the effect of defiant cotton candy.

"Okay, okay," he said, and turned to Joybird. "This getup is definitely going to get you noticed."

Joybird looked nervously at Betty. "Should I change?"

"Oh, hell no. You look gorgeous. And, kiddo, you're allowed to be sexy. It's not against the law."

"But will people think—"

"Fuck 'em," Betty said. "Fuck what people think. Put it out there. You deserve to be your beautiful, smoking-hot self."

Joybird stood, frozen, trying to make a decision. On the one hand, she definitely wanted Noah to notice her. On the other, standing out made her feel jittery and self-conscious. If she weren't so curvy, the outfit would be fine, but she was no Tabitha McCabe, who wore her clothes like a hanger. "Maybe I'll keep my jacket on," she said, reaching for it.

"You keep your jacket on, and I'll break both your hands," Betty said, then turned to Sid. "You coming?"

He shook his head. "Why would I do that?"

"You said—"

"I was *kidding*. Jesus."

"What are you going to do—sit here by yourself in the dark and get drunk?"

"Don't be ridiculous," he said. "I'll keep a light on."

"It's fine," Joybird assured Betty.

She said it so quickly that Sid looked at her suspiciously. "You don't want me to come?"

"It's just not your kind of thing, Dad—Brooklynites reading poetry."

"When you say it like that, it sounds kind of hilarious."

"So grab your jacket," Betty said. "It'll do you good to get out of the apartment."

Joybird exhaled, trying to calm her skittering nerves. She really was worried her father would misbehave, but managed to convince herself all would be well. After all, Betty would be there to keep him in line, maybe even find a teachable moment to help him learn to be a better human being. Plus, it would be a great chance to spend time together doing something social.

Still, when Sid replied, "Why the hell not?" her stomach tightened into an obstinate fist.

Joybird forced a smile, and he laughed at her obvious discomfort. "Think of all the inspiration I'll get for my pilot," he said.

"You're going to put my friends into your sitcom?"

"Don't think of it as a sitcom. Think of it as *Portlandia* meets *Schitt's Creek* meets self-important-hipster Brooklyn poets."

Betty snorted at his attempt to reduce Joybird's friends to a ridiculous trope. "That stinks like horseshit," she challenged.

"Yes," he said. "But studio executives love the smell of horseshit in a script. It smells like . . . ratings."

Chapter 26

The reading was in a dank, low-ceilinged room down a steep flight of steps under a pub. When they arrived, Joybird's friend Zabeen was already there with her significant other, Shawna. They had snagged a table at the front of the room and saved seats, so Joybird led Betty and her father around the clots of chitchatters to their table and made the introductions. When she pulled out a chair to sit, Betty caught her arm.

"Jacket off," she commanded, close to Joybird's ear.

"I don't know, Betty."

"What is it the kids say? YOLO? C'mon, be a brave girl."

Joybird nodded, because she understood she was being timid, fearing the judgment of others. And that was no way to live. She pulled off her jacket and bent to hang it over the back of her chair. When she straightened, she noticed Noah coming through the doorway and clocked his reaction as he saw her, his eyes moving from her face to her chest, down to her thighs and boots, then back up again. She gave a wave, and he approached.

"I'm so glad you came," he said, then leaned in. "You look beautiful."

His warm breath sent a shiver down her neck, and she knew Betty had been right. Hiding her body had made no sense.

"Thank you," she said, glad the room was too dimly lit for him to see her blushing. Then she introduced him to everyone at the table.

"Are you one of the 'poets'?" Sid asked him, putting air quotes around the word.

"I am," Noah said proudly, oblivious to the jibe.

"So what do you write about—being woke to racism, being woke to sexism, being woke to—"

"The poem I'm reading tonight is about the despair of being unhoused."

"Perfect!" Sid said, as if he expected unintended hilarity.

Nervous, Joybird glanced at Noah's face, but she could see that he was deaf to her father's sarcasm. Relieved, she invited him to sit with them.

"What do you do, Noah?" Sid asked as the younger man took the empty seat next to Joybird. "Because apparently, my daughter doesn't go for men who make a living."

"He works as a barista," Joybird said, hoping to cut off the conversation.

"To support myself," Noah added. "But I'm really a writer."

Sid tutted. "My condolences."

"Thanks," Noah said with a laugh. "I guess."

"You know what Dorothy Parker said about that?" Sid asked him.

The poet shrugged but looked interested.

Sid leaned in. "She said, 'If you have any young friends who aspire to become writers, shoot them now, while they're happy.'"

Betty gave him a disapproving look. "That's not the whole quote, Sid."

"I got the gist," he insisted.

Joybird wondered what she could say to change the subject and take Noah out of the hot seat, but before she could manage it, he responded to her father.

"Point taken," he said. "But I wouldn't be a writer if it wasn't a compulsion."

"God help you, then," Sid told him.

Joybird glanced at Noah's face, worried, but he seemed at ease. "My dad is a writer too," she explained.

"Oh?" Noah said, his face lighting up. "What do you write?"

"Nothing you'd like, I promise."

"Are you a novelist?" Noah asked.

"If only."

"He's a TV-comedy writer," Joybird explained, careful to use present tense.

"And isn't he just hilarious?" Betty asked.

Zabeen turned to Sid. "Didn't you write *Down Here*?"

He snapped his fingers at a passing waitress. "What does a guy have to do to get a drink in this joint?"

Joybird knew he was doing schtick, pretending he didn't want to talk about his accomplishments to call more attention to them. It worked, of course, and Noah's hand flew to his chest.

"I loved *Down Here*!" he gushed. "I used to watch it as a kid. Did you really write that?"

"I admit to nothing until I've had at least two glasses of scotch."

Noah turned to Joybird. "You didn't tell me your father was a famous writer."

"She's not exactly proud of her old man," he interjected.

"Of course I'm proud of you," Joybird insisted; then said to Noah, "We never got around to talking about our families."

"We'll have to fix that," he said, leaning close, and Joybird flushed with delight.

Sid snorted. "Get a room, you two."

That was the moment Noah reached under the table for Joybird's hand. She reacted with a gentle squeeze, and a drama was set in motion. He got a better grip on her hand and held fast, not releasing her until a waitress came to take the drinks order. By then, Joybird was nearly numb with happiness.

A few minutes later, the host took the stage to welcome the crowd and introduce the first poet.

It was a young woman whose poem was about following a snail to the ocean. Joybird listened intently, nodding, even though the metaphor was nonsensical. The whole crowd seemed to be playing along, pretending she was saying something deep. When the host came back on stage to introduce another poet, Sid muttered, "What's next? *Myrtle the Turtle*?"

But it wasn't. The next poet was a woman who had been sexually abused as a child and then assaulted as an adult. Joybird glanced at her father to gauge his reaction and could see that his jaw was set tight, as if he were ready to be outraged at the lies and manipulation. When it quickly became apparent that this writer had welled her own pain, his expression changed, becoming concerned and then stricken. It was no wonder. The poem was raw and emotional, taking the listener on a journey as the woman found her voice and began recovering her own body.

When she got to the part where she demanded—*demanded*—the right to be who she was and dress how she wanted, Joybird sat up a little straighter. And when she got to the part where she demanded—*demanded*—her right to be safe in this world, a hush fell over the room, and every woman was transfixed. Tears spilled down Joybird's cheeks. Her friends Zabeen and Shawna were also crying. Betty grabbed a cocktail napkin to wipe her face.

Joybird turned to look at her father and saw that his eyes were wet, as well. This touched her, but when he realized he was being watched, his demeanor changed as he tried to look uninterested.

Joybird understood that he'd been embarrassed by his own emotions. After a moment, though, he generously reached out to give her hand a pat. It struck Joybird as his way of admitting he'd been affected, and she interpreted that as an important breakthrough.

By the time it was Noah's turn to read, the audience was emotional and primed, and his personal story of homelessness and addiction and recovery seemed to touch everyone in the room. Joybird glanced at her father to see if his cynicism about Noah had abated. He caught her eye and gave a small shrug as if to say *Maybe, just this once, I was wrong.*

Chapter 27

The next day, Joybird felt like Riley—giddy and excited, pressing Betty for insights on Noah's level of interest in her.

"He definitely has the hots for you, kiddo," she observed.

"Is that all you saw?" Joybird asked, disappointed. "Physical attraction?"

"What did you expect me to see?"

Now Joybird felt silly. She had assumed the chemistry between them—an alchemy of desire and deep, personal connection—was strong enough to be sensed from one corner of the room to the other. But examining it in daylight, she realized it was ridiculous to presume it was obvious to anyone but her and Noah.

She sighed. "I don't know."

"Look, I can't possibly make a judgment about his feelings for you. But if you got a strong vibe, trust your gut."

Joybird nodded. She needed to talk about this—to say it out loud. "Something special passed between us, Betty. I'm sure of it. The night felt . . . magical."

Her friend smiled gently. "I'm happy for you. Just try not to let it cloud your judgment."

"You mean I shouldn't rush into his bed," Joybird clarified, remembering their conversation about booty calls.

"Not if your tender heart's on the line."

Joybird nodded and promised she would hold out for a real date, no matter what. And why shouldn't she? Her dream was to be Noah's girlfriend, not merely his lover.

For the rest of the day, Joybird was acutely aware of her phone's silence. So when it buzzed the next morning, she felt a jolt of excitement. But it wasn't Noah; it was Devon. Her disappointment quickly gave way to curiosity about why he was reaching out, but also gratitude; he was becoming a trusted friend.

Still, she was puzzled by his question about what time they were leaving for Connecticut, as they hadn't made plans to go together. In fact, she had made up her mind that she couldn't possibly impose on him again. Her plan was to drive alone to finally connect with Donna DeLuca Ackerman and open up about her father's feelings for her.

She texted back: I can't put you out like that! I'm sure you have better things to do with your Saturday

His response was quick: I set the day aside. Totally want to see that jewelry exhibit—Mom's birthday is next week

Joybird couldn't argue with that. Plus, she was grateful for the company, as it would get her out of her own head and keep her from perseverating on Noah. When Devon once again insisted on driving, she didn't put up a fight, agreeing that she needed a break from the steering wheel.

An hour later, he texted to say he was waiting outside, so she slipped a denim jacket over her cinnamon-print Old Navy dress, grabbed her purse, and edged toward the door.

"Bye!" she chirped. "Going out for a bit."

Her father seemed to notice she was trying to slip out quickly. "Where are *you* heading?" he asked.

"I, uh . . . I'm going shopping with Devon." Joybird hated the tangled web of lying and feared he might say he wanted to come along. But Sid just squinted at her, dubious, as if he knew something was up.

"What's that look on your face?" he pressed.

"Nothing. I'm just . . . you know. I got to go."

"You dating two dudes at once?"

She closed her eyes, summoning patience. "Dad," she chided.

"Take it from someone who's been on the receiving end of that bullshit. It's nothing but trouble."

"I told you—Devon and I are just friends."

"Sooner or later, you're going to have to decide between these guys," he said. "I vote for Wall Street."

"See you later, Dad."

Outside, the brisk wind took her by surprise, chilling her bare legs, and Joybird wondered if she should go back for her long jacket. But she didn't want to have another conversation with her father, and Devon was already waiting for her. So she opened the door and got in, bracing for the feel of the cold leather against her thighs. But the upholstery felt buttery and warm, enveloping her in comfort.

"You turned on the seat warmer," she said.

Devon shrugged. "It's chilly."

"And what's that smell?" she asked, realizing something other than his cologne had wafted toward her.

He reached into the back seat and grabbed a white paper bag. "Coffee," he said, handing it to her. "And muffins."

She opened the bag and inhaled the scent of blueberries and spiced apples. "That's so thoughtful."

He shrugged. "I stopped into that Starbucks."

"Which Starbucks?" she asked, her heart skittering, as she knew Noah had the Saturday-morning shift. In fact, she had been thinking about popping in herself, but worried how contrived it would look, since he hadn't yet reached out to her.

"*Your* Starbucks. Where that dude works."

"Oh?" she asked, wondering if Noah had recognized him as the man she'd been sitting with.

"Guy's a trip. Told me to give you a message, since we're spending the day together."

Joybird shifted uncomfortably, wondering how the conversation had gone from buying coffee to telling Noah they were spending the day together. She hoped Devon hadn't left him with the impression they were dating.

"What was the message?" she asked.

He studied her, and she could tell he was less than pleased. "You really think I'm going to be his messenger boy? Fuck that guy."

This was more animosity than Joybird had expected. "I'm sure he didn't mean anything by it."

"I'm sure he *did*. He was marking his territory."

Despite herself, this news gave Joybird a giddy jolt. Noah hadn't called her, but he was thinking about her.

"You don't have to look so happy about it," Devon added, putting his car into gear.

"Are you mad?"

"Yeah," he admitted. "I don't like that guy, and it pisses me off that you think he's hot shit."

Joybird considered telling him about the poetry reading, explaining that Noah was someone who had truly suffered and was now giving back. But she just said, "You know, he runs a local literary program for underprivileged people."

"I guess he's a saint, then."

His jaw was so tense it made her squirm. There was nothing to do but change the subject and try to cheer him up. "I don't want to talk about him," she said. "And I'm sure you don't, either."

"You got *that* right."

"Tell me about your mom. Her birthday is coming up?"

He nodded. "After everything she went through, I want to give her something a little different. Something unique, like her. I thought handmade jewelry would be just right."

"She's okay now?" Joybird asked, remembering what Devon had said about his mother's chemotherapy.

"She's great. It was just a long road back. Harder than either she or Dad expected." There was a catch in his voice, and she intuited that there was a time he was worried she might not make it.

"I'm glad she came through it. And it's so sweet you want to give her something special." This man really had a good heart. He was compassionate, considerate, generous. And given his heartbreak over his last relationship, she could understand why Noah had fired up so much anger in him. There were still a lot of raw emotions he hadn't worked through.

"I was hoping you could help me pick something out," he said.

"Of course!"

"Also, how do you feel about stopping at a farm stand on the way back? I wanted to get some apples and bake her a pie."

"You know how to make apple pie?" Joybird asked. Devon was full of surprises.

He laughed. "You sound so shocked."

"I am!"

"I don't really know how to cook," he said. "But I know how to bake pie. My grandma taught me. What about you?"

"I know how to cook," she countered. "But I don't know how to bake pie."

He gave an easy laugh. "Want to learn?"

"Love to," she said, and meant it. It always seemed like such a homey skill.

For the rest of the ride, they discussed how she would approach Donna Ackerman and what she would say. By the time they arrived, Joybird felt ready.

Inside the arts center, individual displays were set up in an artistic, upscale version of a flea market. The artists themselves were standing beside their pieces, answering questions and making sales.

This time, it didn't take long for Joybird to spot the woman whose profile she had studied on Facebook. It was Donna Ackerman in the flesh, having an animated discussion with one of the artists and a few patrons. Joybird and Devon decided to give her time to finish her conversation while they shopped for something suitable for his mother.

They went from display to display—there was so much to admire. When Joybird stopped to pick up the price tag on a triple-strand necklace of turquoise and hammered silver, Devon stopped her.

"No looking at prices," he said.

"Seriously?" she asked. Joybird didn't know how to shop without considering cost.

"Let me worry about that," he said. "I just want your gut reactions."

And so she let her eye wander from one piece to the next and found herself enjoying the fantasy of shopping purely on aesthetics. A gold necklace caught her eye, as the chain held a butterfly pendant—delicate but striking—accented with tiny diamonds and colorful gemstones. It was one of the prettiest pieces of jewelry she'd ever seen, and Joybird tried to imagine owning something so exquisite.

"You like that?" he asked as she fingered the necklace, watching the gems catch the light.

"It's beautiful," she said. "But is this your mother's taste?" Joybird had noticed Devon stopping at pieces that had a more handmade, folk art look.

"Maybe not," he said. "But it's very pretty."

"Stick with something you can really see her wearing," Joybird said, as she reluctantly released the delicate necklace and moved on.

After several minutes, she saw Donna Ackerman extricate herself from her conversation, and gracefully cross the floor to the other end of the gallery. She wore a royal blue cotton blouse, crisply pressed and turned up at the sleeves to reveal a plaid cuff. There was a dignity to her bearing, and Joybird could understand why her father was drawn to this woman.

Devon clocked Joybird's sight line. "Now's your chance," he said, and gave her arm a supportive squeeze.

She nodded and set off, catching up with Donna as she was inspecting a display of handmade clutch purses decorated with colored glass.

"Excuse me," Joybird said. "Are you Donna?" She knew the answer, but she and Devon had decided it would be best to look unsure, to mitigate any possible stalker vibe.

"Yes, can I help you?"

Her voice was deep and strong, making it immediately clear this woman was not easily intimidated. Joybird realized her concern about frightening Donna with an ambush had been unjustified.

"My name is Joybird Martin," she said. "And my father grew up here in Connecticut. I think he knew you in high school."

"Oh?" Donna said. "Where did he go to school?"

"Paxton Academy. Graduated in '72."

"Then I would certainly know him. What's his name?"

"Back then, he was John Martin."

Donna looked off in the distance as if searching her memory. "Sure, I remember John. No, Johnny. We called him Johnny. Nice-looking boy."

Joybird couldn't help smiling. This was the best possible response. "He thought you were cute too."

Donna cocked her head, amused. "Now how would you know that?"

"Well"—Joybird paused for a breath—"he talked about you."

"He did?"

This was the delicate part that could come off as creepy. But there was nothing to do but go for it. "He never told you, but he had a terrible crush on you."

Her eyes went wide. "I had no idea."

"He always regretted not asking you out."

"And he told you this?" She seemed truly confounded by this information.

"We were having a talk about long-lost loves," Joybird said, not wanting to tell the woman her father had seen her at a restaurant in Manhattan, as she and Devon had decided it might sound menacing.

"I'm flattered," Donna said. "This is all news to me. Also, my god, it's so long ago."

"Right," Joybird said, assuming the woman did not remember the single kiss all those years past. It had meant so much to her father, but Donna might have forgotten it by the very next day.

"So how is he?" she asked.

"At the moment, not great. He had a pretty brilliant career as a TV writer, under the name Sid Marcus. That's what he goes by now."

Donna looked thoughtful. "I think I heard that one of our classmates was in Hollywood and doing quite well."

"Unfortunately, it all kind of tanked after his divorce." Joybird was careful with language here. She could have said, *after his last divorce,* but thought it wise to hold back on revealing his sordid marital history.

"I'm sorry to hear that," Donna said, playing with one of her rings, and Joybird detected a change in tone. Clearly, the word *divorce* had piqued her interest. She fingered the pink-quartz strand around her neck. "Is he still in LA?"

Joybird didn't want to get ahead of herself, but that question—and the body language—seemed pretty pointed. Donna was on the market.

"No," she said. "He came back to New York to . . . heal. He's been staying with me in Brooklyn."

"Did he send you to find me?"

Joybird shook her head. "I'm doing this on my own," she explained. "I'm on a mission to cheer him up, and I thought . . ."

"You thought you'd try to fix us up on a date?" Donna asked.

Joybird responded with a nod and shrug, and Donna gave a small laugh.

"That's very sweet. But there's one problem—and you're probably too young to understand. In his mind, I'm still seventeen. I think it might crush him to discover I'm just as old as he is."

"I don't think so," Joybird said, holding tight to the truth that he did, in fact, know exactly how his beloved Donna DeLuca had aged. "I think he'll still see the girl in you."

"You're darling to think so. How did you find me, anyway?"

"Facebook," Joybird said, leaving out all the legwork it took to find her married name.

"Of course," Donna said. "Nobody's anonymous anymore."

"So what do you think?" Joybird asked. "Would you be willing to meet him for dinner one night? Maybe in Manhattan? Or he could come to Connecticut?"

"I don't know," Donna said. "It's a little uncomfortable to make plans like this without even speaking to him. I don't know what he's like. I barely even remember him from high school."

"Want to see a picture?" Joybird said quickly, as she could sense cold feet overtaking Donna's initial interest.

"Why not?"

Joybird opened a photo on her phone. It was a professional headshot of her father from a conference he spoke at ten years ago. Joybird understood that he looked a bit older now, but thought if he shaved and combed his hair, the picture would still be a good likeness. Importantly, he was in a suit and tie, looking respectable. She handed it to Donna.

The woman studied the image, her brow knitting in thought. "This is John Martin? I don't think I would have recognized him."

Joybird decided she had made the right decision not to tell Donna he had recognized her. It would have revealed too much about his obsession.

"He's got a really sharp sense of humor," Joybird said.

"I can imagine."

"He was the head writer for *Down Here*. Won an Emmy."

Donna's expression opened as her palm flew to her chest. "I had no idea! I used to watch that with my children. That was a terrific show. He's so talented."

"So will you do it?" Joybird asked. "Will you meet him?"

Donna handed the phone back. "Let me think about it for a few days."

"Of course," Joybird said, disappointed. "But I really—"

"In fact, I have to be in the city next week. So if I decide to do this, maybe that would be a good time."

To Joybird, that sounded like a win. She seized the opportunity to exchange contact info with Donna, who promised she would be in touch either way.

"Well?" Devon said when she returned. "How did it go?"

"I don't want to get my hopes up, but . . ." She held up crossed fingers to illustrate her hopefulness.

"I knew you could do it!" he said, and wrapped her in a hug that felt even better than the buttery warmth of heated seats, and there was that alluring scent again. Only, this close, it made her heart race.

Chapter 28

Joybird was in Devon's gleaming kitchen when her cell phone buzzed. She couldn't make a dash for it since she was standing next to him while they both pressed dough into pie tins, her fingertips deep in the fleshy softness as she tried to make an identical twin to his near-perfect creation. Besides, Devon would suspect it was only because she assumed it was Noah, and he wouldn't be wrong. She continued working her fingers into the dough.

"You're dying to get that, aren't you?" he asked, glancing at her face.

She blushed at being read so easily. "Not really," she lied, hoping he wouldn't press it.

"Good." He wiped his hands on a dish towel. "Let's slice those apples."

Afterward, while the pies were baking, he poured them each a glass of crisp Chandon Blanc de Pinot Noir, which he insisted was not champagne, and they toasted to Donna DeLuca. As she sipped the bubbly white wine, Joybird relayed her conversation with the Connecticut divorcée nearly word for word, and Devon agreed there was a very good chance the woman would be willing to meet with Sid, a.k.a. John Martin. The oven timer buzzed, and Devon put on mitts to slide out the pies as they continued talking. The conversation itself—as well as the steamy sweet aroma of the cooked apples—engaged Joybird enough to take Noah off her mind for several long minutes. But as soon as Devon excused himself to the bathroom, she waited for the sound of the door shutting and reached for her phone.

She had been right—the text was from Noah. She quieted her nerves and read it.

Did you get my msg about coming by 2nite? Maybe 10? Would love to see you 💜

The heart emoji almost did her in. He was putting himself out there, and it meant everything. On the other hand, she knew Betty had been right—it was important to hold out for an actual date. Surely, he would understand. Joybird exhaled to steady herself. There was little time to think . . . or let her courage fizzle. She typed: Would love to see you too, but have my heart set on a real date. More meaningful! LMK when you have time 💜

Damn, it was bold. She took a sip of wine to fortify herself, pausing to enjoy the dance of sparkle on her tongue, and hit send. Devon reemerged just as she dropped her phone back in her bag, and seemed distracted by the sweetness filling the air.

"Mm," he said. "Smells good in here."

She turned to face him. "Thank you for teaching me how to bake an apple pie. It might become my new hobby." It had been Devon's idea to bake two of them, so they could eat one today and he could bring the other to his mom tomorrow. It also gave her the chance to learn by doing.

He picked up his wineglass. "I'll drink to that," he said.

Again, she tipped her drink toward his, and they both sipped. When she looked into his eyes, they were focused on her lips, and she felt his desire shoot through her, landing with a gentle but insistent push. Their eyes locked, and she expected him to look away, self-conscious. But he seemed delighted she had caught him. Maybe even amused.

"What do you think?" he asked, nodding toward the glass.

She turned her attention back to the drink. "It tastes like . . . a celebration. I don't understand why people spend hundreds of dollars on champagne when they can have this."

He gave a small laugh. "Most girls would be impressed if I brought out a bottle of Dom Perignon. But you're genuinely happier to indulge in the value wine."

"I am!" she said, smiling. "The expensive stuff would have made me cranky."

"Okay, then I hope you won't be too upset with me when I give you this." He reached behind himself, then produced a small black rectangle tied with a red ribbon.

"What is this?" she asked, looking down at the box he had placed in her hand.

"Open it."

Joybird hesitated. Why was he giving her a gift? She hoped it was nothing indulgent, but at the same time felt the giddy excitement of her childhood. All those emotions came rushing back to her. She remembered the sweetest moments, right before she opened a gift, when the package in her hands held nothing but promise—the chance for a love-starved child to feel treasured and wanted. When her mother was alive, birthdays and Christmases were simply the fulfillment of dreams. The doll she had coveted. The toys advertised on her favorite TV shows. The game that seemed impossibly fun. Wishes granted.

That changed when she lived with her grandparents and gifts became practical—winter coats and backpacks and pencil cases. She learned to choke back disappointment and act delighted. When presents from her father arrived, it was more difficult. They were rare enough to make her gasp with excitement. But inside, there would be something just babyish enough to be vaguely insulting. She later put the pieces together and understood he hadn't even picked them out himself. That was why they were so sporadic—she got presents from her father only when he was involved with a woman tender enough to think of his poor little girl back east.

Joybird looked down at the glossy black box from Devon, carefully tied with a shiny bow. She savored the moment, not even daring to guess what was inside. Then, at last, she pulled at the ribbon and opened it.

It took a second for her to realize what she was looking at, and then Joybird's hand flew to her mouth. It was the gold butterfly necklace she had admired in the arts center—the one with the glistening stones, which looked even more brilliant here in Devon's kitchen, catching the overhead lights and reflecting them back like sparklers. Her voice caught in her throat as she gasped.

She looked up into Devon's face. He wore the tiniest, most joyful smile, and his dark eyes were filled with expectant hope. He was waiting for her to say something.

"Devon," she began. "Devon . . ." The words just wouldn't come.

"Can I put it on you?" he asked.

She realized, then, that she was crying, because no one had ever done anything this kind for her. Part of her wanted to say *No, it's too much—I can't.* But that hungry inner child coveted everything about this precious gift. So she took a jagged breath and nodded.

Devon carefully pulled the delicate strand from the box and went behind her to clasp it at the back of her neck. His warm fingertips sent a shiver down her body.

There was no mirror in the room, so she could only imagine how it looked on her. Joybird touched the piece on her throat, trying to visualize it. Devon stepped around to face her. He held her shoulders and stared at the necklace, then at her eyes. Finally, his gaze settled back on her mouth as if that was where it was meant to be all along. His hands seem to grow warmer.

As he continued staring, she knew what he wanted—to kiss her. He was waiting for a signal that it was okay.

Her yes came in the form of a subtle tilt back of her head as she moved her face closer to his. He lowered his head toward hers, and— after a momentary pause that was just long enough for her body to respond with urgent heat—their lips connected as his strong arms pulled her in.

This kiss, this kiss, she thought. At once, she realized she'd been expecting it, hoping for it, wanting it. But she never could have imagined it would feel this tender, this wonderful, this inevitable.

He pulled away and smiled, then simply said one word.

"Pie?"

And that was it. There was no more kissing, no overtures, no invitation to the bedroom. But at that moment, something shifted between them. Something significant. It was as if they had made a pact—a mutual agreement. It wasn't until later—after they had eaten a light bite, then way too much pie, and he had driven her home, and they arranged to see each other next weekend, and there was another kiss as sublime as the first one—that she realized what it was. They were in a relationship.

Chapter 29

Walking up the stairs to her apartment, Joybird's legs got heavier with each step as a feeling of regret began to weigh on her. How had this happened? She hadn't meant to become Devon's girlfriend. One minute they were baking pies, and the next it was as if they'd materialized on the other side of the Rubicon.

Joybird tried to shake off the thought. Maybe she was reading too much into it.

But no. The evening had ended with the agreement to see each other again next weekend and the assumption that they were officially part of each other's lives. And she had let it happen.

It was the kiss, of course. That changed everything.

How had she succumbed to it so easily, when she had no intention of being romantically involved with him? It made no sense. But then her fingers flew to her throat, and she knew. The necklace. He had bought her an expensive present, and she had fallen for it.

She wanted to think it wasn't the necklace itself, but his thoughtfulness and generosity that had won her over. Yet she had enjoyed being in that expensive apartment, with its modern kitchen and designer furniture. Had she been seduced by the gleam of opulence? Was it really that easy to slide into such shallow waters?

She would need time alone to think about all this—to examine her motivations and understand her feelings. But when Joybird put her key in the lock and pushed open the heavy door to her apartment, there was a Grateful Dead song playing, and the scent of weed wafted toward her. In the living room, her father and Betty sat facing one another, a bong between them on the coffee table. Joybird just wanted to go into her room and shut the door.

"How was your day, kiddo?" Betty asked, her eyes narrow.

"I was just shopping with Devon," Joybird said quickly, hoping Betty wouldn't accidentally blurt out the true purpose of her day trip. "It was fine."

"You've been gone since this morning," her father observed. "Where'd you go shopping—Milan?"

"We picked up some apples and baked pie," Joybird said, holding up the wrapped tin. Devon had insisted she bring the leftovers home.

"You have homemade apple pie in there?" Betty asked, rubbing her hands together.

Joybird put down the pie and hung up her jacket. "I'll cut you guys a couple of slices," she said.

"Just give us the whole thing and a couple of forks," her father said, clearly consumed with a severe case of the munchies.

"You sure?" Joybird asked.

"Would you prefer we used our hands?"

Joybird sighed, in no mood to argue. She retrieved forks from the kitchen and did as he asked, but when she bent to put the leftover pie on the coffee table, the necklace hung down from her throat, the butterfly sparkling with vanity as it hovered over the surface.

"What is that?" her father asked.

Betty leaned forward for a closer look at the brilliant stones. "Ooh, pretty. Are those rubies?"

"It's nothing," Joybird said, straightening. "Just a new necklace."

"Did Wall Street buy you that?" her father pressed. "He must really have the hots for you."

"Goddamn it, Dad! Have you learned nothing?" Joybird snapped.

He drew back, unaccustomed to being challenged by her. "What did I say?" he asked defensively, looking to Betty for help.

"I don't want to hear any more talk of my love life from you. Not one more word! It's none of your damned business."

With that, Joybird stormed off to her room and shut the door.

Breathless, she leaned against the wall to calm herself down. Joybird had never yelled at her father before. In the heat of the moment, it had been exhilarating. But now she wondered how much damage she had done to his already-broken ego.

It'll be okay, she told herself. *He's stoned. And besides, you're going to deliver Donna to him, and everything will be wonderful.*

She sat on the edge of her bed and became aware of the scent of cooked apples as well as Devon's earthy cologne clinging to the fabric of her dress. She pulled it off and threw it into the laundry basket in the corner. Wearing only her bra and panties, Joybird approached the mirror to study the effect of the necklace on her bare skin. It was striking, even sensual, against the smooth flesh of her throat. She felt ashamed of how much she loved it.

Joybird heard her cell phone buzz and pulled it from her purse. It was a text from Noah, reacting to her last message.

Wow. Never expected that from you.

She read it over and over, trying to decipher exactly what he meant. If there had been any friendly emojis, she could interpret the "Wow" to mean he was impressed. But this seemed like a rebuke. Hoping she was wrong, Joybird typed back: ??

After several minutes, she got her answer.

You seem like such a cool girl. Didn't expect you to be into the whole patriarchal transactional dating scene

It was a gut punch, and Joybird hung her head. He was right. She had become exactly the person she never wanted to be. *But no,* she told herself. She *hadn't* changed. Because despite her momentary lapse in judgment,

Noah was the one she wanted. Not Devon. Noah, the poet, the activist, the sensitive mentor to the needy and broken. Noah, who would be able to see and appreciate the good in her. Fingering the necklace, Joybird took a few deep breaths and typed out her response.

> It's just that I really like you and want us to have something special

Joybird could barely breathe as she waited for his reply. Would he reject her? Tell her to get lost? By the time it came through, she was lightheaded and dizzy.

> I want that too

A tear escaped down her cheek. She started to type out a long response, but backspaced over it. Ultimately, she sent the simplest message she could: ❤

He wrote back: I really want to hold you now

A warmth radiated through her. It was the best thing he could have said. She responded: Me too

His response appeared in seconds: So come over

Her fingers hovered over her phone as she let the joy of this moment wash over her, and then she typed: OK

Chapter 30

Joybird arrived at Noah's apartment in her ocean-blue sweater and denim jacket, paired with the skinny jeans and boots she knew he liked. The butterfly necklace was in her room, pooled into her jewelry box.

She pushed the buzzer, and the door opened quickly. Noah was in a Feel the Bern T-shirt from 2016, with basketball shorts and bare feet. He hugged her, and she felt enveloped in warmth and gratitude.

"I'm so glad you're here," he said.

"Me too."

The apartment had a college-student vibe—dirty and disorganized, with threadbare furniture. Joybird wasn't about to judge Noah for this. He'd had a rough time in his teens and twenties, and started fresh only a few years ago. So of course his development was a little arrested. He was still catching up.

A guy in his twenties—clean-shaven but with long hair—sat on a futon in the living room, playing a videogame.

"That's my roommate, Ratner. Ratner, this is Joybird."

"Hey," he replied, barely looking up. Thighs splayed open, he leaned toward the screen as if his body could affect the action of the game.

"You want something to drink?" Noah asked her. "White wine?"

"That would be great," she said.

"Wait right here."

As he disappeared into the kitchen, she took off her jacket and draped it over her arm. Then she simply stood there, watching Ratner play *Warzone* until Noah came back and handed her a refrigerator-cold glass of white wine. His own drink seemed to be club soda or seltzer, and she assumed he was a teetotaler due to his history with addiction. She was grateful he didn't seem to mind that she needed the wine.

"Let me show you my room," he said, taking her by the hand and leading her there.

She was glad to see it was considerably cleaner than the rest of the apartment, with a queen-size bed covered in a blue-plaid comforter, and neat sand-colored furniture, including a small desk with a tall stack of notebooks, and a crammed but organized bookshelf. His bed abutted a wall that was painted a rich matte brown, contrasting with the soft white of the other walls. He shut the door and took a long sip of his drink. She laid her jacket on the chair.

"My oasis," he said. "What do you think?"

"I like it," she told him, deciding it was more her style than Devon's sleek decorator apartment with its designer furniture.

He put his glass down on a piece of cardboard that seemed to serve as his dresser's coaster. She did the same. The idea, she knew, was for them to have their hands free.

He opened his arms, and she moved in for his embrace, resting her head on his chest. She didn't mean to compare him to Devon, but since she had been in his arms only hours earlier, it was impossible not to. Noah was taller and leaner. She didn't detect any cologne, but he smelled like lemons and fresh laundry, and that was lovely. He bent his head over hers, and she could feel his beard on her face.

"I've wanted this for a long time," she admitted, holding him tight.

"Really?" he backed away to look at her face, and his expression was so delighted, it made her smile.

He kissed her then, eager and hungry, his tongue frantic. She could feel his erection pressing against her, and though she willed him to slow down, her body was ready and responsive, shivering at the force of his desire. Noah's hand went to her breast, and they continued kissing, their breath getting quicker as Joybird grew warmer. He pulled away.

"It might not surprise you to know I'd love to see you naked," he said, his eyes on her breasts.

"Oh," she said, flustered. "That's . . . a little fast for me."

He drew back, pulling his lips tight. "I'm sorry!" he said. "I can be clumsy about all this." He looked deeply into her eyes as if searching her face for help.

"It's okay," she said. "Really."

He sat on the bed. "Should we just talk for a bit?" he asked, patting the spot next to him.

"Why don't you read me one of your poems?" she suggested.

His eyes brightened. "Really?"

"I'd love it."

"You're an amazing girl, Joybird," he said, and sweet pleasure spread through her like warm tea and honey.

Noah went to his desk and scanned his notebooks until he found the one he was after. He pulled it out and flipped the pages. "Found it," he said, smiling. "Are you ready?"

She nodded, and he leaned against his desk and read aloud. The poem was called "When I Am a Man," and it detailed all the ways he would change when he was not so awed in the face of beauty, made clumsy by his desire. As the poem went on, it got more specific, describing a white neck, lovely and frail, a cheek like cool, pale stone, and hair like summer rays spun into silk. Joybird tensed. The poem, it seemed to her, was about a lanky blonde. Joybird was glad Noah hadn't shown any interest in Tabitha that day at the community center. Still, she couldn't help feeling a pang of jealousy that he was attracted to someone so different from her.

"Well?" he said, closing the book.

"I love it," she choked out. "Is it . . . about someone in particular?"

"Oh!" he said, nearly gasping. "No, it isn't. I mean, it is. But she's someone I knew a long time ago." He stopped and shook his head. "And here I go again, clumsy as fuck. You see what I mean?"

He gave a small self-deprecating laugh, and Joybird released her worry. It was silly to be jealous. He was here with her in his bedroom, trying so endearingly to seduce her.

"It's a wonderful poem, Noah," she said. "You're so talented."

He put the book down and approached her on the bed. "I'm crazy about you, Joybird. I've been thinking about you so much."

She absorbed the words, playing them over and over as she flushed with excitement. "I've been thinking about you, too."

"Is it okay if I kiss you again?" he asked.

"Of course!"

He sat next to her and leaned in, placing his lips gently on hers. Within seconds, his tongue was in motion, and his hands were all over her. He was exactly as awkward as he had written about, but she forgave him. His passion was so earnest and uncontrolled. The next time, she knew, they would be able to take it more slowly and gently.

She gave in to her desire, returning his ardor, and just like that, he was on top of her, burying his face in her neck. They kissed and kissed, fully dressed, until the fever was too much to bear, and articles of clothing were yanked and pulled and thrown to the floor. A condom appeared from nowhere, and he quickly glided it on.

Before doing anything else, he made eye contact. "Okay?" he asked.

"Yes!" she breathed.

At that, he stopped holding back, and it was everything she had wanted. Joybird could feel him falling for her. The thought brought her to the very brink.

"Joybird," he said, "your breasts are amazing. They're an entire poem."

And then, despite herself, the scent of Devon came from nowhere, and it was like a wave she couldn't stop.

When it finally receded like a muscled undertow, Joybird told herself that that wisp of Devon meant nothing. This was where she belonged—in Noah's bed, in Noah's life, a new relationship blossoming. It was beautiful.

He ran his smooth hand over her breast. "An entire poem," he said again, and fell asleep.

Chapter 31

The next morning, Joybird tiptoed quietly into the apartment so her father wouldn't know she had stayed out overnight. She understood he probably wouldn't care—not really—but he'd relish teasing her about it, especially since she'd been prickly with him the night before. As crusty as he was, he expected nothing but kindness and respect from his daughter. And in truth, she felt like she owed it to him. After all, he'd lost just about everything. She was the last refuge in the storm of his life.

Joybird could hear the soft snores coming from his bedroom and knew he was in a dead sleep. It was no wonder. From the mess in the apartment, it was clear he'd been up late partying with Betty.

She took a luxurious hot shower and was straightening up when she heard her phone buzzing by her bedside. She made a dash for it, expecting an affectionate text from Noah, but it was Devon.

What did Sid think of the pie?

Joybird hesitated before responding, wondering what she was going to do about him. She'd need to tell him something, but what? That she wasn't his girlfriend? It seemed absurd, because of course she wasn't. And she couldn't very well tell him she'd slept with Noah last night. It would stir all the hurt from his past.

So she simply went into the living room, took a picture of the empty pie tin with two forks resting in it, and sent it with the caption: What pie?

He wrote back: Ha! Hope my mom feels the same

This, she decided, was exactly how she would deal with Devon. She would go on being friendly with him, but if he tried to kiss her again—or made any kind of move—she would say she wanted to keep their relationship in the friend zone. It was such a simple solution that she wondered why it had seemed so fraught. She plugged her phone back in and resumed her work straightening the apartment.

By the time her father ambled into the kitchen, eyes bloodshot and hair pointing madly in every direction, the place was back in order, a fresh pot of coffee ready.

"What time did *you* get in?" he said, scratching his stomach through his robe.

"You want some coffee?" she asked.

Sounding hungover, he grunted assent and sat at the table. She put a steaming mug in front of him and turned back to the sink to finish washing the dishes.

"So which one was it?" he asked.

"Excuse me?"

"Which dude—Wall Street or poet?"

She kept her back to him and continued scrubbing. "Can we please not talk about my love life?"

"If you're going to be seeing a new guy, I think I should know. Unless it was a one-night stand. Is that what it was? Because if you just needed to get laid, I understand."

She whirled around. "No, Dad. It wasn't a one-night stand. I was with Noah, okay? And he really means a lot to me. So please, don't get ugly about this."

He held up his hands in surrender. "Who's getting ugly? I'm all for it. May you two be very happy together and raise a brood of artisanal Brooklyn kids with names like Basket and Weave."

She sighed and went back to the dishes.

"I only hope he feels the same way about you," he muttered, just loud enough for her to hear over the running water.

"Of course he does," she said, working at the remnants of a grilled cheese sandwich encrusted on her favorite frying pan, which seemed scratched and ruined.

"Because that Wall Street guy is really putting in an effort."

She took three deep breaths and held up the frying pan. In her most controlled voice, she said, "You don't use a metal fork on a nonstick pan."

"Well . . . someone's being a little snot," he said, clearly still simmering over her attitude the night before. He folded his arms in righteous indignation.

"I just want a tiny bit of consideration, Dad. That's all."

"Oh yeah?" he said. "Like you had consideration for me last night?" He glared at her, trying to look mad, and she understood. He was wounded. Her father wasn't used to being challenged by her, and felt like he'd been disrespected. His pain rattled her nerves, and she looked away, blaming herself. Joybird tried to steady her breathing, coaching herself to stay grounded so she wouldn't float from her body.

She turned her back to him and opened the faucet to full force, attempting to drown out whatever he might say next as she resumed the futile effort of trying to salvage the frying pan.

"Birdie," he called over the rushing water, but she ignored him, squirting a line of blue dish soap into the pan.

"Hey!" he called, louder.

"I'd rather not talk right now," she said as gently as she could.

"Your phone is ringing."

"What?" she shut off the water and heard it, coming from her bedroom. She pulled off the rubber gloves and ran into her room to answer it.

"Hello?" she said breathlessly, expecting to hear Noah's voice. She'd been so excited she hadn't even registered the name on the caller ID.

"Joybird?" said a woman's voice. "It's Donna Ackerman."

"Donna," Joybird sputtered quietly, readjusting her expectations. She shut her door, sat on the edge of her bed, and collected herself. The timing was perfect, as she had just abraded her father's raw wounds. Now, she might have the salve to cure him. "I'm happy to hear from you."

"I thought about what you said and kicked it around with a friend and decided that yes, I'll do it. I'll meet with your father."

Joybird gasped, and tears spilled down her cheeks. She had done it! "You will?" she said, just to make sure she heard it right.

"I have tickets to a matinee on Wednesday, and I figured as long as I'm in the city, it wouldn't hurt to take a trip out to Brooklyn."

It took Joybird a moment to absorb the information, but once she did, they discussed the details and decided that since Joybird would be in Manhattan that afternoon dropping off her regular client, she would swing by to pick up Donna and take her back to Brooklyn.

The plans firm, she went back to the kitchen and faced her father. It was a big moment, and she was searching for just the right words.

"Well," he said, before she could speak. "You look better. Let me guess. You and the poet are going to start a rooftop honeybee farm and open Brooklyn's first organic, fair-trade mead distillery."

Joybird shook her head and smiled. "I found her," she said.

He cocked his head. "Huh?"

Joybird crouched down and grabbed his hands. She looked straight into his eyes, her face wet with tears. "I did it, Dad. I found her for you. I found Donna DeLuca."

Chapter 32

The Donna news was so exciting that it very nearly overshadowed Joybird's anxiety about not hearing from Noah. As Sunday rolled into Monday, she wondered if maybe it was some kind of a test. Or not really a test, but Noah's conscious rejection of the traditional patriarchal dating norms. Perhaps he was eagerly waiting to hear from *her*.

Yes, she decided. That was almost definitely it. And so, before she headed out to see her first client of the day, she typed out a text, backspaced over it, typed out another, backspaced over that, and finally settled on a simple and honest message:

Thinking about you ❤

There. It had the perfect tone, and she knew he would reply quickly. She didn't need to worry. She pressed her phone into the holder on her dashboard and started her workday.

By the time she dropped off her last client and returned home, there was still no response from Noah. Devon, on the other hand, had messaged her several times about the Donna DeLuca news. He was eager to help, and even offered to come to the apartment on Wednesday and make sure her father was sober and ready for Donna when she arrived.

After stalling and stalling, Joybird finally accepted his offer via text message because she couldn't think of any way to turn him down without some kind of explanation. And there was nothing she could possibly say that wouldn't devastate him. The only thing to do was go on being his friend, while making it perfectly clear there could be nothing more between them.

By Tuesday, there was still no word from Noah, and it was getting more difficult to believe the night had meant as much to him as it had to her. But no, she told herself. It couldn't possibly have been her imagination. He was crazy about her—he had said so himself. And the lovemaking had been so special! She could feel how much it meant to him. There had to be some simple explanation. Maybe he was busy at work and thought he'd responded. That had once happened to her when her friend Hannah had reached out to make plans, and until Hannah sent a second text, Joybird was absolutely certain she had responded. So she decided to try again and be more direct. She sent him a message that he couldn't ignore.

Can't wait to see you again. This weekend maybe?

By that night, Joybird was in Betty's cluttered apartment holding back tears as her friend poured her a tall glass of wine.

"What should I do?" Joybird pleaded. "Should I just call him? Stop by Starbucks when he's working?"

"Oh, kiddo," Betty said, handing Joybird her glass. "He knows you're waiting to hear from him. If he wants to pursue this, he will."

"But when? I mean, how much time do I give him?"

"I used to have a Wednesday rule," Betty said, sitting beside Joybird on the couch. "If I went out with a guy Saturday night and I didn't hear from him by Wednesday, it meant he wasn't interested or wasn't worth my time."

"But that's tomorrow," Joybird said, feeling like it was much, much too soon to give up on Noah.

"The good news," Betty said, "is that you'll be too distracted by bringing Sid and Donna together to give it much thought."

"Right," Joybird said, though she knew that even when she wasn't consciously thinking about Noah, he was right there, simmering beneath the surface.

Her cell phone buzzed, and she avoided Betty's gaze as she made a desperate grab for it. But it was a text from Devon. And at the sight of his name, the lingering scent of him materialized in her sinuses again. She tried to push it away, but the feeling of that kiss came back in a warm rush, from the moment their lips touched to the moment he pulled away and looked at her. *Saw* her.

"Noah?" Betty asked.

Joybird shook her head. "Devon."

"You're blushing."

She realized, then, that she had just spent nearly two whole seconds not thinking about Noah, and a troubling thought began to snake its way inside. Had she made a terrible mistake?

Joybird reached for the wine, poured herself another glass, and shook it off.

"Let's talk about Donna and Dad," she said, and smiled, willing her heart to follow along. Everything was going to be wonderful.

Chapter 33

Normally, Joybird loved the sound of wind whooshing and howling outside her window. It reminded her that she was, in fact, safe, sheltered, and protected. But today, as fierce gusts shook leaves from Brooklyn's steadfast trees, she had a worrying thought. What if a storm blew in and Donna canceled her plans for the day? *But no,* she told herself, *that's not going to happen.* Even wealthy Connecticut suburbanites didn't blow off expensive tickets to a Broadway musical. Donna had probably ordered them months ago. A little storm wouldn't keep her at home. It was all going to work out.

The wind blew in something else, as well—a shift in Joybird's perception. It suddenly seemed so clear. Noah was not going to call. Not after ignoring two texts from her. Yet his message was now obvious. The night in which she had invested so much of herself was nothing to him. Just sex. Once again, Joybird had been blinded by her sunny faith in people.

But it was worse than that. Noah's rejection opened a chronic wound, reminding Joybird there was something about her that was inherently unlovable.

Her phone began to sing its morning alarm, prodding her to get out of bed and start her day. There were clients waiting, responsibilities to meet. She hit snooze three times before finally dragging herself into the shower. She hated feeling this way.

The rushing water helped, cleansing her of negativity. *Be positive,* she told herself. *That's who you are. A person who rejects feelings of sorrow, regret, and hurt. A person who focuses on possibilities, on the full bounty of life.* She envisioned the sadness pouring down the drain and washing away, leaving her scrubbed, fresh, and new. She was not going to wallow in pain. Especially not today, of all days. She was going to deliver Donna DeLuca to her father! It would be a beautiful moment. A crowning achievement in her life. By the time Joybird picked up her first client of the day, she was renewed. Even the rain felt promising, like it would bring good luck.

Just to be sure, she texted Donna to confirm the time and place of their rendezvous and got an immediate response. They were all set.

See? Joybird told herself, as if she were speaking to a client. *It's all good.*

Later, as she waited in front of the Berkeley Carroll School for Riley Wilbanks, Devon texted again to confirm their plans. He had promised to go to her apartment to help her father get ready. Ostensibly, his job was stylist—helping to choose the right slacks and shoes. In reality, Joybird was grateful he'd be there to make sure her dad didn't get stoned or drunk before Donna showed up. She sent back a cheerful thumbs-up along with the message, Thanks again! He responded with a heart emoji, and her gut churned with guilt. She supposed they'd need to have a frank talk eventually, but she didn't want to think about that now.

Joybird glanced at the school's doorway, watching the kids spill out. It had just stopped raining, and the afternoon light was crisp and shimmering, as if the sun were proud of burning off the clouds. Her eyes landed on two kids leaning against a railing, their arms around one another. The girl was Riley—her neon-pink hair particularly vivid in the slanted light—and the boy, she presumed, was Carter. He was tall and narrow, with limbs he hadn't yet grown into, and he struck her as the preppie version of a teen heartthrob, with a sharp jaw and shiny brown hair falling across his forehead. He wore jeans and a wine red hoodie.

Riley looked up and saw Joybird's car. She said something to the boy, and they kissed on the lips, their bodies pressed together. When they came apart, they looked at each other for a few seconds, smiling, before Riley bounced away toward the car.

Only a week ago, Joybird realized, Riley had been pining for him, desperately searching for signs he liked her. And now, it seemed, they were an item. If Joybird hadn't gotten a glimpse into Riley's neuroses, she would have been happy for her. But this, she knew, could be trouble. If the girl clung to this boy the way she clung to her possessions, it might end badly.

But maybe not. Maybe this was a chance for Riley to feel loved, wanted, and secure. Maybe it was just the thing to help her grow. In any case, Joybird would try to guide her to take it slowly.

"Oh my god," Riley said when she got into the car. "Did you see?"

"I did."

"That's Carter."

"I kind of figured." She twisted around to face the back seat and saw what looked like a hickey on Riley's neck. "I guess you have a boyfriend now."

"I do. I have a boyfriend." A laugh of joy escaped from her.

"That must have happened fast."

"I guess. I mean, he asked me out on Friday, and on Saturday we went to the park and walked around all day, talking. And then we went for pizza, and on Sunday we talked on the phone for like three hours. Yesterday he gave me this." She held out her wrist to show Joybird a narrow silver bracelet that had the word "one" engraved into it.

"One?" Joybird asked.

"We're so alike, we kept saying, 'We're like one person.' I couldn't believe he found this." She took back her wrist and studied it. "It's like a dream," she whispered.

Joybird understood, then, that it was probably too late to caution the girl to slow down. It would simply sound like the kind of thing grown-ups always said, because they Just Didn't Get It. Still, she had a queasy feeling in her stomach about the relationship. But perhaps that was projection. *Carter isn't Noah,* she told herself. After all, the boy was clearly enamored. So she let it go and spent the rest of the ride indulging Riley as she prattled on about her new boyfriend.

Later, after Joybird had dropped the happy rider off at her mother's new apartment building—a modern high-rise in the Murray Hill neighborhood—she headed across town and up to Broadway, where she was meeting Donna outside the Marquis Theatre.

She thought she had arrived early enough to find a place to pull over in front of the theater, but after circling the block twice, she finally pulled over a full city block east of the address and texted Donna to let her know where to find her. She wasn't worried when she didn't hear back right away. The show was probably still in progress, and Donna, like all good audience members, had dutifully turned off her cell phone. She would see the message after the show let out and she powered it up again.

It had been a long time since Joybird opened her Duolingo app to continue her efforts to learn Spanish, but today seemed like the right time to get back to it. She went over the last few lessons she had already completed, just to refresh her memory, and then moved on to a new section.

By the time she was done, Joybird realized she had been waiting half an hour, and there was still no text from Donna. She decided to call one last time, but it went to voicemail.

Joybird tried to ignore the gnawing fear that something had happened to change Donna's mind. She had to find out.

After turning on her hazard lights, Joybird abandoned her car and dashed down the block toward the theater, hoping she could make it there and back before her car got towed.

By the time she reached the theater, sweating and out of breath, she saw stragglers standing around beneath the awning. The show had already let out, and Donna was not in sight.

Joybird was about to rush back to her car when she saw a group of women huddled at the stage door, getting their Playbills autographed. And there she was, in a beautiful cream-colored cashmere coat, smiling broadly as the star handed back her program.

"Donna!" Joybird called. "Donna!"

The woman turned around. "Oh, hello," she said casually.

"I've been calling and texting."

Her expression fell. "I'm so sorry!" she said. "I forgot to turn my phone back on. I got so caught up, and I love getting autographs. I collect them."

"It's okay," Joybird said. "It's just that I'm illegally parked and . . ."

Donna bit her lip and apologized again, then said goodbye to her two friends and set off with Joybird.

Donna, in expensive high-heeled boots, was not the type of woman to be rushed, so they ambled to the illegally parked car at an excruciatingly slow pace. And when Joybird saw it, comfortably nestled right where she'd left it, with no NYPD cruiser in sight, she sighed, relieved, and filled with ebullient joy. This wonderful thing was about to happen.

Chapter 34

Sid rose when he heard them coming up the stairs. This was it—Joybird was about to deliver Donna DeLuca at last—and his heart thudded.

"Ready?" Devon asked as he straightened Sid's tie.

"I think so."

Betty handed him the bouquet of flowers she had bought and squared his shoulders toward the door before stepping behind him, next to Devon.

He heard his daughter's key in the lock, and then the door opened.

"Dad," Joybird said, and he stepped forward, waiting for her to move aside so he and Donna could lock eyes. He imagined a self-conscious smile, an unsure hug, and then, later, laughing about how awkward it had all been.

After all these years, he finally figured out that their one kiss hadn't been as significant for her as it had for him, but he prayed she at least remembered it. At Paxton, she'd been famous for having a genius-level memory, so there was hope.

It had happened at a classmate's party. Santana was playing on the stereo, and Sid—who was Johnny then—had gone into the kitchen looking for something to drink. A girl handed him a rum and Coke, which everyone was drinking that year. Just then, Donna walked into the room, and all heads turned. She wore a sunny-yellow turtleneck sweater tucked into hip huggers, her dark hair spilling like liquid satin around her shoulders. She ignored everyone else, marching right toward

Johnny, who had stopped breathing by that point, certain his heart would shatter like a dry ice experiment. Until that moment, they'd never even said hello, though they were in the same chemistry class.

Donna grabbed the drink from his hand and took a sip before shoving it back at him.

"Putrid," she pronounced.

"Like gym socks," he agreed, which was the cleverest rejoinder he could think of at the moment, as teenage hormones were zinging through his system like they were eager to escape. For a young man trying to look cool, it was a tough inner storm to weather. He felt as if his whole life had just been suctioned into a vortex. This girl. This goddess. There was nothing else.

Some guy behind them guffawed in agreement about the drink. "It sucks 'cause the Coke's flatter than Stephanie Valentine's chest," he joked, referring to a lithe and pretty girl the jocks loved to tease because they all liked her.

When Johnny saw Donna roll her eyes at the comment, he knew it was his chance. "Doesn't suck as much as your mother," he said to the guy. It wasn't his best line, but he turned back to Donna to see if it had made an impression on her.

"You know," she said to the guy, her eyes lit with dark mischief, "when I told your mother drinks were on the house, she got out a ladder."

It took the boy a minute to get the joke, but then he whined, "Hey," sounding wounded, which struck Donna and young Johnny as the funniest thing ever. He motioned for her to follow him as he crossed the room toward the refrigerator.

"There's a rumor going around that you got a ninety-eight on the chem midterm," she said, changing the subject.

He turned to her, surprised she even knew they were in the same class. "Where'd you hear that?"

"You learn a lot if you pay attention."

"Is that why you came to talk to me—because I'm good at science?"

She shrugged. "I don't like idiots."

He scoffed. "You might be at the wrong party."

Donna flipped her hair and looked around. "I'm only here because of Michael Wilde, but I saw him talking to Vicky Imperioli."

Johnny opened the refrigerator and, as expected, found a secret stash of Budweiser. He took two and handed one to her. "Want to make him jealous?" he asked, not sure if she was serious about Michael Wilde.

"Why not?"

They grabbed their jackets, then slipped out the back door and sat on a cold concrete step, sipping their beers.

"Why are *you* here?" she asked him.

"I *like* idiots," he said.

"Because they make you feel smarter?"

"Yeah."

Donna took a swig of her beer. "That's bullshit," she said matter-of-factly.

"How do you know?" he asked.

"'Cause you like *me*, and I got a hundred on the chem test."

He believed it. The girl was brilliant. Also, she was right—even then, he had exactly zero tolerance for idiots, and smart girls set his blood on fire.

"Maybe I like you because you're beautiful," he said. "You ever think of that?"

She squinted at him. "I think it doesn't hurt. But looks only go so far with you."

"You think I'm deep?" he asked, congratulating himself. This was going better than he had hoped. Girls loved guys who were deep. It was practically all they talked about.

But Donna shook her head. "Nope."

He looked at her, wondering if she was teasing him. "No?"

"I think it's your insecure ego. You walk around like you think you're hot shit, but deep inside, you're worried you're not. So you go after smart girls because if they think you're hot shit, then you really must be."

Johnny gasped. Literally. This was 1971—years before the explosion of self-help books changed the way people spoke about human behavior—and he'd never heard anything like it. Forget pop psychology. Donna DeLuca was peering right into his soul, offering the most astute observation he'd ever heard, and it blew his mind.

"You want to get high?" he asked, pulling a joint from his jacket.

She did. And as they passed the joint back and forth, they had a conversation that ricocheted from one topic to another—music, movies, families—and they were in such perfect sync it felt like magic. And then, when Johnny leaned in for a kiss, he knew—with more true confidence than he'd ever felt—that he'd been born for that very moment. They both had. Donna went liquid in his arms, like she was pouring into him.

And sure, they were pretty high at that point, but when they came up for air and looked at each other, they were stunned. It was as if they'd both been infinitesimally small until that moment—minute concentrations of heat and matter—when the collision created an entire universe.

"What was that?" she asked, breathless.

"The big bang, I think."

Donna gazed into the night sky. "And now there are stars."

Looking back, it was hard for Sid to understand why that had been the end of it. He didn't call her the next day or the day after that. He didn't approach her in the hallway or talk to her after chem. Maybe he was afraid of ruining that perfect moment, or of discovering it wasn't what he thought it was. Maybe he believed he didn't deserve that kind of happiness.

Sid sighed, certain they still hadn't written the self-help book on his miserable psychology. But now, he had the chance to fix all of it.

He looked over at Joybird, who milked the moment, studying him. She glanced around, and Sid could tell she was surprised to see the apartment looking so fresh and tidy. Indeed, the three of them—Betty, Devon, and Sid—had been hard at work getting everything just so. Devon had run out for fresh daisies, which now sat in two white vases on the counter between the living room and the kitchen, creating the effect of separating the two spaces. Sid ran his hand through his recently cut hair, and hoped the clothes Devon had selected for him—smooth khakis and a pale-blue sweater—made the right impression. James Taylor's "Fire and Rain" played softly in the background. Sid had wanted to put on Santana, but Betty talked him out of it—said it had the wrong vibe.

Joybird smiled at her father, and they shared a moment as he filled his chest with air. Then, at last, she stepped aside, revealing the woman of the hour.

"Dad . . . say hello to Donna."

Chapter 35

Joybird looked back at her father's face expectantly, trying to imagine how he felt. But the smile melted, replaced by a look of utter confusion. He blinked in what seemed like a blitzkrieg of bewilderment.

"Who is *that*?" he yelped, his face crumpling.

"It's Donna," Joybird said. "Donna DeLuca."

Sid shook his head, color draining from his visage. "Like . . . hell . . . it is," he said through labored breaths.

Joybird watched as he bent at the waist trying to fill his lungs. She wanted to say something—anything—but couldn't speak.

Sid looked up and addressed Donna. "Miss, I'm very sorry. I don't mean to offend you, but I don't know what's going on here."

Joybird was just as confused. She looked from Sid to the Connecticut divorcée she had just presented.

"You thought I was Donna DeLuca?" the woman asked.

Joybird's armpits went damp. How had this all gone so wrong? "You're not?"

"My maiden name is Brown."

"Brown?"

"Donna DeLuca was a *terror*. They called her Mean Donna." The woman looked lost in a memory. "I was Nice Donna."

"I don't understand," Joybird said.

"Donna DeLuca married some guy named Sabato or Sabatini. Something like that. A famous oboist."

"An oboist?" Joybird asked, trying to catch up.

Donna looked at Sid. "Johnny," she said, her face pained, "I mean, Sid . . . this is so . . . I don't know what to say. I hope you're not too disappointed."

Joybird looked in her father's wrecked eyes and could tell that *disappointed* didn't come within a thousand miles of describing how he felt. In fact, she'd never seen a more profoundly wounded expression on anyone in her life.

Sid dropped the flowers on the floor, then pushed past them and out the door.

As Donna backed away, Joybird stood in the middle of the room, staring at the door, trying to make sense of it all. She almost felt like she was in some twisted nightmare, about to wake up and make her father reappear to change what had just happened.

She heard a sniffling behind her and turned to see Donna Ackerman née Brown dabbing her nose with a tissue.

"This is so humiliating," Donna said.

"No!" cried Joybird. "It's all my fault. I'm so sorry."

"It's no one's fault," Betty reassured her. "Just a misunderstanding."

"She's right," Devon said.

Donna shook her head. "I should have known," she muttered. "Donna DeLuca looked like a movie star. I wasn't in her league. I was just—"

"You're a beautiful woman!" Joybird insisted. "That's why I thought you were . . ." She trailed off, sensing the compliment was hitting an impenetrable barrier. Donna was far too distraught.

"I have to go," she choked out, turning away from them.

Joybird tried to think of something to say to make her feel better, but nothing came. She looked at Devon, who shrugged sympathetically.

"I'll drive you home," Joybird finally said. "It's the least I can do."

"No, dear. I can't. I need to . . . I'll take the train. I'll be fine."

Joybird offered about ten more awkward apologies, but it was clear Donna just wanted to escape the scene as quickly as possible. She wouldn't even accept Joybird's offer to drive her to Grand Central Station, wouldn't let Devon or Betty walk her out.

And just like that, Nice Donna was gone.

Chapter 36

"What have I done?" Joybird muttered, sinking into the easy chair. Betty had left, and she was alone with Devon. "That poor woman."

"She'll be fine," Devon assured her. "I bet she'll laugh about this later."

Joybird tried to let that thought lift her, but it was impossible. "And my father?"

"He'll get over it too."

She shook her head. "I don't know. He has nothing now. Less than nothing, because he let himself have hope and now that's gone. I'm not sure he can recover from this." Even in his absence, she could feel the sadness—a choking dust hovering in the ether.

"You can't blame yourself."

"Who else is to blame?" Tears spilled down her cheeks. Devon grabbed a paper napkin from the kitchen counter and handed it to her.

"Me?" he offered. "Reuben Ross?"

Joybird blotted her face. "I should have confirmed her identity. It would have been so easy. It just never occurred to me there were two Donnas in his—"

"Stop it," he said. "You can't beat yourself up."

Joybird inhaled, trying to collect herself. She reached for her phone and called her father's number, but heard it ringing from his bedroom. Despondent, she hung up. "Where do you think he is now?"

"Getting drunk, probably."

"Should I go look for him?"

He sat on the arm of the chair. "There are probably a thousand bars in Brooklyn."

"I could start at O'Keefe's and work my way out." She peered at him with desperate eyes, as if he might agree that exhausting herself on a ridiculous quest could solve something.

"Don't you think that'll be a waste of time?" he said gently.

She let out a sigh. "What else can I do?"

"Stay right here and have dinner with me while we wait," he said, and took out his phone. "Mexican okay?"

Joybird hesitated. This was all so benign, so harmless. Yet it couldn't have been more complicated. She had slept with Noah, which she now realized was a terrible mistake. But she couldn't simply move forward with Devon as if it had never happened . . . or could she?

Joybird decided there was simply too much on her plate right now to think about it, so she shrugged her assent. "Shrimp tacos sound about right," she said.

Over dinner, Devon tried to lighten the mood by asking if she, too, had ever harbored a secret crush like the one her father had on Donna DeLuca. Joybird admitted obsessing over Skip Lipman in fifth grade. She watched carefully to see if any unreasonable jealousy registered on his face, as she knew that people with betrayal issues could be a little irrational. But Devon seemed to take it in good humor, so she relaxed, explaining that Skip's actual name was Joshua, but that she and her best friend Amanda had made up substitute first names for their crushes so they could talk about them in public.

Devon told her his first crush was Fernanda Morales. But she was in eighth grade, and he was in seventh, so they were like star-crossed lovers, despite how much time he spent in her house playing *Super Mario World* with her younger brother, Miguel.

Joybird asked about his family, and Devon added to what he had already told her about his parents. He also talked about his younger brother, Cal, who was a head taller than him and lived in Silicon Valley, making crazy money as a programmer.

Devon mentioned Joybird's mother, which few people did, so she was happy to open up. One of her only vivid memories was making art projects together at the kitchen table. Once, her mom made an elephant out of nothing but glitter and glue, and Joybird had thought it was the most beautiful thing she'd ever seen.

"I wish I still had it," she whispered.

It was close to midnight when Joybird realized it was time to let Devon off the hook. She really didn't want him to leave, because she knew she could get a terrible call any minute. The police? A hospital? The thought of dealing with it alone was overwhelming. Still, she'd imposed on him long enough. So Joybird announced that she was tired and added, "I'm sure he'll walk in the door any minute. You don't have to stick around."

"I'll sleep on the couch," he said, his eyes tender with concern, "so you don't have to be alone."

Yes, she thought. *Please.* But Joybird shook her head. "I can't ask you to do that," she said.

He gave a small laugh. "You don't have to ask. I'm doing it."

"But you have work tomorrow."

"Don't worry about it."

Joybird was so choked with gratitude she couldn't speak, so she simply fetched some clean bed linens and a spare pillow, and got him set up on the couch. As she settled into her own cool mattress, trying to get comfortable under the soft sheets, she envisioned him walking into her room and slipping in beside her. She imagined him surrounding her with his warm arms, his gentle heat, and that intoxicating cologne. And though she conjured the imagery to help combat her anxiety, she soon found herself stirring with desire. She kicked at the sheets, rejecting her feelings. *This isn't about you,* she told herself. *It's about your father.*

Less than an hour later, as she still yanked at the covers trying to sleep, her cell phone rang. She grabbed it in a panic, noting an unfamiliar number on the caller ID.

"Joybird?" said a woman's voice. "This is Carol Ross."

Carol Ross? It took Joybird a moment to process the information. This was Reuben Ross's wife, whom she had visited in Queens.

"Is . . . is everything okay?" Joybird sputtered.

"Your father showed up at my doorstep, drunk as a skunk." She was speaking quietly, yet her voice was laced with indignity.

"He's there now?"

"He sitting in my kitchen with a cup of coffee. But frankly, I don't want him here. Reuben's away on business, and this is not acceptable."

"I'm so sorry," Joybird said. "Is he all right?"

"No, he's *sloshed*. Showed up babbling incoherently. I told him he had to leave, but then he started crying that his life was over and said he had nowhere to go, so . . ." She paused to let out a breath. "I can put him in a cab, or you can come get him. You tell me."

Joybird looked up and saw Devon standing sleepily in the doorway to her bedroom—no shirt, no shoes, no eyeglasses. She put her hand over the phone and whispered, "My father's at the Rosses' house in Forest Hills."

Devon rubbed his eyes and peered into her room, as if he was trying to make out her form in the darkness. Joybird, backlit from the glow coming in through the window, felt like her sight line gave her an unfair advantage, and she tried not to notice how effortlessly sexy he looked—strong and vulnerable at the same time.

"What should I do?" she asked.

He yawned and cleared the sleep from his throat, then cocked his head toward the front door with a shrug. "Let's go get him."

Chapter 37

Later, Sid wouldn't be able to recall how he'd made it to the Rosses' house in such a drunken stupor, as the journey was just a series of vague images. He knew he'd been on a subway at some point, falling from one side to the other, and then in a taxi. He couldn't remember talking to the driver, but knew he must have given him the Rosses' address, which was embedded deep in his hippocampus, as they'd lived there for over thirty years. He supposed he'd paid for the ride, as he recalled cursing at a credit card that refused to come out of his wallet.

"Oh, for god's sake," Carol had said at the sight of him, and he'd started to weep in self-loathing. Somehow, he remembered something from a lifetime ago—a drunken pass he'd made at Carol during a party. Afterward, he hadn't remembered much about it and tried to pretend it never happened. That was the part that angered her most. *Don't flatter yourself,* he had said, instead of apologizing.

Now, all he could do was apologize. "I'm so sorry, Carol. I'm such an asshole. I'm so sorry. So fucking sorry."

She tsked and let him in, and next thing he knew, he'd fallen asleep, his head plastered to the kitchen table. Sometime later, a rude hand shook at his shoulder.

"Dad!" Joybird said, trying to rouse him. "Wake up, Dad."

"Come on, Sid," Devon said. "We're taking you home."

Then his hands were under Sid's armpits, hoisting him to his feet.

After that, Sid was in the back seat of Joybird's car, though all he could recall about the ride was that they wouldn't agree to drop him at a bar.

When the car finally came to a stop, he awoke with a snort. "Where's Reuben?" he barked, remembering his earlier fury.

"We're home, Dad."

"I want to kill that bastard," he said, without much conviction.

"You're not killing anyone. You're going to sleep."

Right, he thought. *Time to sleep.* And at that, Sid decided he didn't want to kill Reuben Ross anymore. Not really. After all, the guy had tried to help, connecting with another classmate who claimed to remember Donna. But when Sid was wallowing in his victimhood, he needed somewhere to direct his rage, and imagined his fist connecting with the guy's jaw. His favorite part of the fantasy was when Reuben hit him back with a quick punch square in the nose. He saw himself collapsed and bloodied, and it was just what he wanted—to feel some physical pain that might overpower the emotional agony pulling him under.

"I'm putting a trash can next to your bed," Joybird explained, pulling off his shoes, "in case you need to vomit."

"I never even touched her," Sid mumbled.

"What?" Joybird asked.

"Carol Ross. I swear, I never laid a hand on her."

"Good night, Dad," his daughter said, and shut the door.

Chapter 38

"I got my first tattoo!" Riley sang as she threw her backpack into the car.

It was a week after the Donna Ackerman fiasco, and the days had felt like sludge as Joybird pushed her way through them, telling herself it would get better. But her father was stuck in a dark place, refusing to talk and barely coming out of his room. The more Joybird tried to cheer him up, the angrier he got. So she decided to give him space as she waited for her last shot at finding Donna DeLuca—the Paxton yearbook she had ordered. She called the school to get an idea of when she might expect it, and they said it had been shipped out two days ago.

But right now she had to focus on the fragile teenager in her car.

"A tattoo?" she repeated, sounding more shocked than she had intended, and she immediately regretted it. Showing disapproval was not an appropriate response. But she was jittery from worry and lack of sleep, and couldn't quite control her reaction. This kid was way too young for a tattoo.

Fortunately, Riley didn't even notice. She slid into the car and held out her forearm. "I did it for Carter. Look!"

Joybird peered down expecting something romantic, like a heart, but saw a carefully rendered purple-and-gold baseball cap with the word *ONE* on the front. Beneath it were tiny marks she could barely make out, but discerned that they were the teenagers' first initials, *R & C*. The skin around the artwork was still red and raw.

"He got the same one," Riley explained. "We designed it together. Carter thought it would prove our love. Now no one can question it."

Why, Joybird wondered, did they have to prove their love? She imagined the boy talking Riley into this, insisting it was them against the world. The whole thing felt . . . unhealthy.

"And the hat?" she asked.

"There's this great song about a magic purple hat, and we thought it would be cool. It's from this obscure indie band Carter's really into."

Joybird tried to keep her expression even but could see that Riley had been completely consumed by this relationship. Of course, that wasn't unusual for teenagers—they could be so intense—but this felt different. A possessive guy and a fragile girl with attachment issues.

"Did your parents give permission?" she asked.

"Are you kidding? My father would kill me for even asking. But Carter knew a guy who would do it anyway."

"So your father still doesn't know?"

Riley sat back. "Mom does."

"You showed it to her?"

"Not on purpose. We were at my grandparents' place, and she saw it when I pushed up my sleeves to wash my hands."

Joybird pictured the scenario and thought there was a pretty good chance the kid had wanted to get caught. She waited until Riley buckled in and then pulled the car away from the curb.

"What did she say?"

"She thought it was cute. Romantic. But made me promise not to show Didi and Grandpa because they think tats are 'common,' and they'd blame her."

Joybird fought the urge to roll her eyes. Corinne needed to step up and be the adult. But she just said, "'Common'?"

"It's how they say 'trashy.' To Deidre and Milton, it's the worst possible insult."

Joybird got the picture. These people were New York City's version of royalty—Upper East Siders with generational wealth.

Nearly everything was déclassé to them. No wonder Corinne was such a hot mess.

"When are you going to show your father?" she asked, hoping at least one parent would take responsibility for this troubled kid.

"Maybe never."

"Never's a long time."

"Deep," Riley said. "You should put that on a pillow."

Joybird ignored the dig as Riley rummaged through her backpack and pulled out a bag of chips. Or rather, Pirate's Booty—a change of pace. Joybird wondered if that, too, was Carter's influence.

"I'm glad you showed me," Joybird said, trying to win the girl back. Not that she wanted to be Riley's psychotherapist. Life coaching was one thing—dealing with mental health issues was above her pay grade.

Besides, Joybird was starting to feel pretty shaky about her skills. Not only did she blame herself for sending her father into a self-destructive spiral, but she knew all the sunny talk in her arsenal wouldn't fix it. Unless she was able to find his long-lost love, he might never recover.

The night before, she had confessed as much to Devon, as they had settled into a comfortable friendship and were talking a lot. She still hadn't told him about Noah—only that she wasn't quite ready to take their relationship to the next level, and he seemed okay with that. But her feelings for Devon were growing deeper and deeper, the physical attraction impossible to ignore. Eventually, she would simply have to confess, and wrap it in the kind of apology he could accept. She just had to find the right time.

Meanwhile, she enjoyed his friendship. Devon was compassionate . . . wise . . . insightful. When he had suggested hiring a private investigator to find Donna, she'd given it some good thought.

"Maybe," she'd said, not wanting to admit it would probably be too expensive, because she knew Devon would offer to pay for it and she didn't want to go there.

"You're not giving up, are you?" he'd said.

She'd explained that she had ordered the Paxton yearbook and was expecting it any day. "I think there might be some clues in there," she'd added, "especially since we now know Donna married an oboist."

"Want to see something?" Riley asked, interrupting her thoughts.

When Joybird stopped at a light, the girl leaned forward to show her a picture on her phone. It was her arm and Carter's arm side by side, their matching tattoos aligned.

"You can't even tell whose arm is whose!" Riley gushed.

"Cool," Joybird said, though she didn't think it was cool at all that the girl had fused her identity with her boyfriend's. She thought about all that trash Riley couldn't bear to part with and wondered what would happen when the boyfriend broke up with her, which Joybird assumed was inevitable. She kept two hands on the wheel as she tried to work out how she could intervene to alert the parents to the hazards on the horizon. Maybe she'd stop in when she dropped Riley off and try to get Corinne alone for a few minutes. A face-to-face would be better than a phone call.

For the rest of the ride, Joybird let Riley chatter on about Carter— the music he was into . . . the anime he was into . . . the video games he was into . . . the crazy things his cockatoo Luigi could do . . .

"Hey, you know what?" Joybird said when they arrived at the building's grand entrance. "I'm going to pop up with you and use the bathroom." It was the perfect excuse to come upstairs and talk to Corinne.

She got the doorman's permission to leave the car parked for a few minutes on the brick-paved driveway and followed Riley to the elevator.

When they reached the apartment, Riley put her key in the lock and swung open the door. "I'm home!" she called. "And I brought Suzy Sunshine."

It was, Joybird figured, Corinne's nickname for her.

She followed Riley into the apartment, and the first thing that struck her was the abundance of actual sunshine flooding in through the wall of windows. The second thing she noticed was that there was company. Corinne, dressed in an artist's smock, stood in the middle of the living room in front of an elderly couple seated in blue-velvet chairs. The woman looked like an older version of Corinne—stick thin with a papery complexion and wispy silver hair. The man had broad shoulders and an austere shaved head.

"Oh," Corinne said, surprised. "I didn't know you were coming up."

"Sorry," Joybird said. "I should have texted first."

"She just has to pee," Riley explained.

"Riley," the older woman chided. "Really, now."

"Joybird," Corinne said, "may I introduce my parents, Deidre and Milton Floyd."

The couple said nothing. They just glared at Joybird disapprovingly.

"I . . . I don't mean to intrude," Joybird stammered.

Corinne waved away her concern. "As long as you're here, maybe you can explain to my parents why I need to express myself through art."

"We don't need to involve strangers in family business," said her father.

"But Joybird is the one who suggested I start painting. This whole thing was her idea."

Great, Joybird thought. Corinne was throwing her under another bus—and this one was a private jitney with bespoke first-class seats.

Milton Floyd rose, and Joybird immediately understood why Corinne had such a tumultuous relationship with him. He was about six foot five, with a commanding presence—like a four-star general in a Savile Row suit. He shimmered with privilege and disdain.

"You?" he said to Joybird. "You did this?"

"She's a very creative woman," Joybird stammered. "She needed an outlet to express herself."

"Did you know she paints vaginas?" demanded Deidre Floyd.

"I've moved on from landscapes," Corinne explained. "It feels more . . . authentic." She swept her hand toward the wall, indicating an oversize canvas with slashes of pink and red paint. Though it was highly stylized, there was no mistaking that it was a vagina, especially with the stubs of angry black pubic hair. It was defiantly vulgar, as if Corinne had meant it to be offensive. Still, Joybird was surprised by the artistry. The woman was more talented than she had expected.

They all looked at Joybird, awaiting a comment. She finally said, "It's so . . . vivid. I'm impressed."

"'Impressed'?" repeated Deidre Floyd, her hand to her heart.

Milton Floyd folded his arms and looked at Corinne. "You let this *cabdriver* influence your life?"

"She's an Uber driver, Daddy."

"For god's sake, Corinne."

"I'm . . . I'm a life coach," Joybird cut in.

Milton Floyd looked her up and down, and Joybird suddenly wished she hadn't grabbed a pair of jeans off the floor that morning. But it had been a rough week, and the best she could manage was to don nearly clean clothes and tuck her hair under a hat.

He tutted and turned back to his daughter. "She looks like a vagabond."

"She helped me," Corinne said, "when you threw me out of the apartment. And now she's helping Riley."

"You're letting this Uber driver counsel my granddaughter?"

"I'm a life coach," Joybird repeated.

"Miss," Milton Floyd said, "I don't even know what that means."

"She gives great advice," Riley said. "*Real* advice. Not like my therapist, who just says, 'And how does that make you feel?'"

"What kind of 'great advice'?" he demanded, his brow tightening.

"She helped me get a boyfriend."

Oh no, Joybird thought. *Not this.*

"You have a boyfriend?" said her grandmother.

"I told you, Didi. *Carter.*"

"You're too young for a boyfriend," said the grandfather.

"I am not."

Joybird stood frozen, trying to think of anything she could possibly say to diffuse the escalating argument.

"Don't get excited, Milt," his wife piped in. "I'm sure it's not serious."

"It *is* serious," insisted Riley.

"Look what you've done!" the man bellowed at Joybird.

"Please, Milt," Deidre said. "She doesn't know what serious means. She's just a child."

"They're really cute together," Corinne insisted.

"I'm not a child, and I understand what serious means," Riley said, her voice rising. "You have to accept that—I'm *fifteen years old*, I'm in a serious relationship, and it's the best thing that's ever happened in my entire life." She sounded like she was on the brink of hysteria.

"Dear," her grandmother began, "what looks serious at fifteen—"

"Stop it!" Riley cried, tears flowing. "Just stop condescending to me!"

Milton looked at Joybird. "Is this your idea of helping?"

"Grandpa!" Riley screeched.

"Lower your voice, young lady," he said.

"Grandpa!" she repeated. "I have a serious boyfriend! Stop acting like my feelings don't matter."

"You do not have a serious boyfriend, Riley," he said, as if he could make any statement true by uttering it.

"I do too!"

He clenched his teeth, appalled by the back talk. "No," he simply said, and Riley lost it.

"I do too! I do too! I do too, you old fart! Look!" At that, she pushed up her sleeve and showed her grandparents the tattoo.

It took a moment for the Floyds to realize what they were looking at. And then, it was as if a giant straw had sucked all the oxygen from the room. An eerie quiet descended, like the hush before an explosion.

The gigantic Milton Floyd took a step toward Joybird, and she felt herself floating away. *No,* she thought, trying to catch a deep breath so she wouldn't disassociate. *Not now. Please.* She tried to root herself to the ground, prepared for the fury of his booming outrage. But before he could speak, her fear became an entity. It broke the tether connecting her to Earth, and Joybird left her body, hovering far above the scene like an ethereal drone. She was no longer there, a participant in the conversation, but an essence who could hear the voices floating through space.

When Milton Floyd finally spoke, it was not the booming fury of a powerful judge, but something more frightening—a voice as contained as a trained assassin's.

"Miss," he said, so slowly and carefully it could be neither questioned nor misunderstood, "it's time for you to leave."

Chapter 39

Joybird didn't even remember getting to the elevator and leaving the building. She just knew she found herself in her car, wishing she could go straight home to recover. But she had one more client that day and needed to meet her responsibilities.

She sat for several minutes, trying to find herself. She touched her cheeks, patted her thighs. *Yes,* she thought. *I'm here. I'm in my body. I'm okay.*

She was able to focus enough to remember that her last client for the day was a fifty-eight-year-old divorced bank manager who wanted Joybird to help him get up the nerve to ask out a twenty-three-year-old coworker. But she wasn't quite ready to face him, as her confidence had been slammed to the ground and stomped on.

You're doing your best, she told herself. *So what if those people judge you? You did right by Corinne, and you'll find a way to help Riley too. You'll also do right by your father! In the meantime, keep going, Joybird. You've got this.*

Another deep, cleansing breath, and she nearly eradicated her anxiety. Joybird started the car and set off to pick up her client, Lewis Schmidt. She was focused and ready.

In the beginning of the conversation, Lewis kept turning the talk back to his philosophy that age was just a number, trying to get Joybird to agree with him. She wouldn't, as her goal was to get him to understand it would be inappropriate to pursue someone so young.

"I'm not her boss," he explained, as if that were the only issue.

"Still, it could be uncomfortable for her."

"Do you think she might say yes, though? Maybe Sofia likes older men. And anyway, I'm a pretty young fifty-eight." He ran his hand through his dense salt-and-pepper hair, as if it were proof of his vitality.

"But you're still thirty-five years older than her, Lewis. That's a lot."

"But isn't age just a number?" he repeated, for the fourth or fifth time.

"If you really believed that, you wouldn't keep bringing it up."

"I've totally fallen for this girl," he said, and then corrected himself. "Woman, I mean. I think about her all the time. I know I can make her happy."

Joybird tried to find out if there were any age-appropriate women in his life. When that didn't work, she asked more questions and learned he had two sons in their twenties and a thirty-one-year-old daughter.

"What would you tell your daughter if a sixty-six-year-old man asked her out?"

"This is different."

"How? It's the same age difference."

"I'm so vital, though," he insisted. "Look at me. I could pass for midforties."

Joybird glanced at him in the rearview mirror, noting his puffy eyelids and softening jawline, and didn't think he could pass for midforties, but she kept that to herself. "Well then, picture your daughter when she graduated from college. What would you have said if she came home and announced she was dating a fifty-eight-year-old professor?"

"My daughter," he said to himself, and went quiet for several moments. Joybird could tell he was really thinking about it—picturing his tender girl with someone so much older.

"I don't know," he finally admitted, and again went quiet as the truth sank in. "Honestly, I don't."

"You know," she said gently, "Sofia is someone's daughter too."

Joybird glanced at his face again, and it was as if she could see the delusion of his dream slipping from his eyes. She couldn't help feeling sorry for the guy. He'd been holding so tight to his fantasy and would need time to grieve its loss.

"Twenty-three is very young," he admitted, sounding forlorn.

"You okay?" she asked.

There was a long pause as he struggled to speak. "I'm just a lonely guy," he finally admitted.

"I know. But there are so many age-appropriate women out there—kind and beautiful women—who would love to date a guy like you."

They spent the rest of the ride talking about the different ways he could meet women, and by the time she dropped him off, he seemed encouraged, despite the undercurrent of loss. Still, Joybird knew he might later decide that he and the twenty-three-year-old were meant for one another, but she hoped it was at least a step in the right direction, if not an actual breakthrough.

Joybird drove back home and parked her car in the lot, wondering what she might find when she walked through the door of her apartment. Her father, she assumed, would be in his room, either drunk or stoned . . . or both.

When she got into the building, Joybird went to check her mailbox, hoping the Paxton yearbook had arrived. It would be just the thing to lift her spirits.

Sure enough, it was there, infusing Joybird with a second wind. She held the package to her chest for a moment before tucking it under her arm and bounding upstairs, a tingle of hope lightening her steps.

"I'm home!" she called as she walked into the apartment. She dropped her keys by the door and set down the yearbook, ready to deal with whatever state her father was in. "Dad?"

He wasn't in the living room, so she knocked on the door of his bedroom. When there was no answer, she pushed it open, steadying herself for what she might find. To her surprise, though, the bed was empty. She hoped it was a good sign but feared he was out drinking again. She went back into the living room and texted him.

You okay? Where are you?

While she waited for a reply, Joybird pulled off her hat, shrugged out of her jacket, and tore open the package from Paxton Prep. She stared down at the book's embossed navy blue cover, wondering if the task of combing it for clues would settle her nerves while she waited to hear from her father. Before she could open it, though, she heard the ping of a text message and grabbed her phone. But it wasn't from Sid—it was from Devon.

How was your day? Dad okay?

Fearing it might be another long night, Joybird kicked off her shoes and settled on the couch to reply. And that's when she saw it—a note on the coffee table, written in Betty's distinctive script. Joybird shook her head, wondering what it was with baby boomers and handwritten notes. A text would have taken seconds. She picked it up and read.

> Talked the old boy into going back to the restaurant
> where he saw Donna DeLuca. Long shot, but worth
> a try in case she's a regular there. Either way, it's a
> chance for us to enjoy a nice meal and an evening in
> the city. Now go take some time for yourself, kiddo.
> Love, Betty

Joybird let out a long, cleansing breath. She liked the advice very much. It inspired her to pick up the phone and call Devon, instead of texting. She filled him in on everything, including the arrival of the yearbook.

"Do you want to come over?" she asked. "We can go through it together." Joybird took a fortifying inhale. It was time. She either had to tell Devon about Noah, or stop this train before it picked up more speed. Both options were so uncomfortable they crowded her throat, making it hard to swallow.

"I've got a better idea," he said, and suggested they meet at a tavern on Henry Street for dinner.

"Yes!" she blurted, without hesitation, because now, the pressure was off. Alone in her apartment—the bedroom beckoning—she'd have no choice but to face her dilemma. But in a public place, where her father was the topic of conversation, she could continue to play it by ear. Either it was the right time to come clean . . . or not.

Chapter 40

When Joybird arrived at the restaurant, Devon was waiting at the door. She clocked the look on his face when she came into view, and it wasn't her imagination—he lit up. Joybird's pulse flittered and skipped.

He greeted her with a hug, and she took the opportunity to get a deep whiff of his scent. She couldn't imagine any man smelling better than this.

By necessity, they took the least romantic table in the pub, as it was under a low-hanging chandelier, giving them enough light to study the yearbook. They slid into the booth side by side so they could peruse the pages together, and Devon ordered them a bottle of wine.

"Should we get started?" she asked. Joybird had resisted the urge to get a sneak peek at the contents, as she knew it would be more fun to make discoveries along with Devon.

He gave a nod. "I want to see Sid first."

Joybird opened the book to the middle and found her father's picture.

"There he is," she said, "John Martin."

Joybird put a finger on the black-and-white image of her father, young and handsome, wearing long sideburns and a wide collar under his Paxton blazer. The boy in the picture next to him wore a silly bow tie and an even sillier grin. Devon laughed.

"The seventies. Jesus!" He put his face closer to the page to read the mouse-type blurb under her father's name. "This is interesting . . ."

She squinted to see what he was looking at. It said: *Swim Team; Tennis Club; Year Book Editor. In the fall, John expects to attend Dartmouth College as a journalism major.*

"'Interesting'?" Joybird prodded.

"Most yearbooks don't have information on the students' college plans."

"It's *Paxton*," she said pointedly, as their reputation rested on the placement of their graduates.

Devon rubbed his hands together. "It could open another road leading to Donna DeLuca," he said. "Let's take a look."

They paused to smile at each other, and then Devon began flipping the pages backward as Joybird scanned the faces.

"Stop!" Joybird said. "That's her." She didn't even need to see the name, as the girl's beauty was just as luminous as her father had described. Only he'd insisted she was a cross between Cindy Crawford and Sophia Loren, but Joybird thought she was nearly a dead ringer for Brooke Shields. Then she noticed something else. Donna DeLuca looked like an even prettier version of her pretty mom. Her father, she realized, had spent his whole life searching for a substitute.

"Hello, Donna," Devon said.

"I've never seen a more beautiful girl," Joybird gushed.

Devon smiled, looking her square in the eyes. "I have."

"Oh, stop," she said, blushing. Joybird knew she wasn't nearly as gorgeous as Donna DeLuca, but was grateful Devon thought so. Or even that he was kind enough to pretend he did.

"Here we go," he said, and read aloud. "Drama Club (president); Chess Club; French Club; Synchronized Swimming. In the fall, Donna expects to attend the University of Rochester as a business major."

Joybird nodded. "Okay," she said. "Let's tuck that away and see if we can find that oboist."

"What did the other Donna say his name was?"

"She wasn't sure, but she thought it was something like Sabatini."

Devon flipped to the names starting with *S*, and they looked for any boy with a last name that was even vaguely Italian. The only one they could find was Richard Salerno, but he was pure jock, and there was nothing in his bio about being in the orchestra.

They went back to the beginning of the book and looked through it, page by page, for any information on the orchestra. There was no list of members, but there were three photographs from some concert. One showed a couple of flutists and another, the string section. Joybird brought her face close to the third photo, which had a boy on a viola in the foreground. Behind him, though, she saw what looked like an oboe. She could barely make out the face of the long-haired boy playing it, his slender fingers wrapped around the instrument.

She took out her phone and snapped a picture of the image.

"What are you doing?" Devon asked.

"I'm going to text this to Reuben Ross and see if he recognizes this boy." She sent the image and felt a tingle of satisfaction. "I feel like we're getting close, don't you?"

While waiting to hear back from Reuben, they ordered dinner. Devon shifted to the other side of the table to make it easier to talk. They toasted to finding the right Donna this time and getting Sid his happily ever after.

"I didn't get to thank you for last week," she said.

"You don't have to."

Joybird shook her head. "It's just . . . look, I wanted to tell you . . . I'm sorry I judged you when we first met. It wasn't right."

"No, it was pretty fair," he said. "There are a lot of assholes on Wall Street. In fact, you'd probably hate most of the guys I work with."

She shuddered, picturing a room full of men like Milton Floyd, Riley's grandfather. "Probably."

"Still, I wanted to ask if you would consider coming with me to a work thing."

"A work thing?"

"My boss's wife is throwing him a surprise fiftieth birthday party at a rooftop bar in Manhattan, and she invited the whole department."

Joybird felt an immediate chill, as the anxiety of the scene in Corinne's apartment came flooding back. She imagined Devon's boss and his wife as perfect doppelgängers for the Floyds. Tense, she looked away. Joybird wanted to do this favor for him, but it felt like a blueprint for a panic attack.

"What's the matter?" he asked, clearly sensing her distress.

"I . . . I don't know if I'm really comfortable with that," she stammered.

"Too fast?" he asked, assuming he was pushing too hard on this new relationship. His expression bordered on dejection.

"It's not you," she assured him. "I'm just not comfortable with people like that. Do you mind very much if I don't go?"

"I don't want to pressure you," he said, "but you shouldn't feel uncomfortable. These people are not better than you."

She nodded, trying to let it sink in.

"I mean it, Joybird," he said, taking her hand. "No one is better than you."

She wanted to find comfort in that, but she could still feel Milton Floyd's disdain, still track her own trajectory toward disassociating. It was too much, especially on top of her conflict about this relationship.

"It's just . . . I can't." She felt her eyes water, and he squeezed her hand.

"It's okay," he said. "But let me know if you change your mind."

She nodded and took a sip of her wine. Just then, her cell phone rang. She picked it up and looked at the caller ID. It was Reuben Ross. She put it on speaker.

"I just got that picture you sent," he said.

"And?" she asked. "Can you identify the kid playing the oboe?"

"I can," he said.

"Great!" Joybird said, excited. "What's his name?"

Reuben cleared his throat. "Cindy Rosenberg."

◆ ◆ ◆

Later, as Devon walked Joybird back to her apartment, he told her he hoped she wasn't too upset about not finding the oboist. "It was always a long shot that he was someone from high school," he added.

Joybird nodded, suppressing a yawn. She was exhausted. "I was just hoping we would get lucky."

"But maybe we can use the book to track down other friends. Or we can contact the University of Rochester alumni association."

"Wait a minute," Joybird said, as a thought took hold. "Rochester. That's where the Eastman School of Music is."

Devon squinted in concentration. "Eastman?"

Joybird shook off the sleepiness with a wave of excitement. "It's a prestigious conservatory," she explained, "like Julliard. But it's part of the University of Rochester. Isn't there a good chance she met him there?"

"I suppose."

"Maybe tomorrow we can figure out how to track down any oboists who graduated from Eastman around the same time as Donna."

"Hang on a second," Devon said, pulling out his cell phone. They stopped under an awning as he tapped into the Google search bar. "Shit. There are a lot of orchestras in New York," he said. "And we don't even know if he lives here."

"Try the Eastman Wiki page," she said. "Maybe they list notable alumni."

Sure enough, at the bottom of the page there was a long list of names, and as they scrolled down, they struck gold: *Vincent Sebastiani, oboist.*

Devon clicked through and saw that he played for the New York Philharmonic.

"This has to be the guy, right?" he said.

Joybird pulled out her own phone and googled "Donna Sebastiani." She switched to the images tab and almost yelped in triumph, because there she was—Donna DeLuca—all grown up in a crisp, professional headshot. She looked mature, confident, complicated, and maybe even more beautiful than the girl in the yearbook. The photo linked to the board of directors page for a big company called International Creative Associates.

Joybird turned her phone toward Devon, who read Donna's title out loud: "Executive Vice President of Publishing and Media Rights." He let out a long whistle. "I guess Donna DeLuca is more than a pretty face."

Chapter 41

After studying the musician's bio and determining Vincent and Donna had been divorced for years, they walked back to Joybird's apartment, discussing what to do next. They agreed it would be best to keep their discovery from Sid for now, as another disappointment might push him right over the edge. First, they would make contact with Donna and be sure she was willing to meet with him.

When they reached Joybird's building, she hesitated, wondering if she should invite Devon inside. She wanted to, but she was nervous. It didn't feel like the right time to tell him about Noah, and she wasn't sure it would be fair to take him into her bed without owning up. Of course, it was possible he'd never find out. Likely, even. In that case, wasn't it better not to tell him? Joybird paused to consider that. In reality, what good could come of telling him? Wasn't it more about unloading her guilt than protecting his heart? She needed more time to think about this.

But then, Devon leaned in for a kiss, and suddenly, her hormones were in control. She pressed herself into him, and he brought her even closer as the heat radiated in unstoppable waves. The closeness was too much, but not enough. Not nearly enough.

"Devon," she said, breathless, her skin alert as his lips found her neck. "I have to—"

He lingered in that spot for a moment and then pulled away, staring deep into her eyes. "I'll call you tomorrow."

"Really? I . . ."

"We're both tired," he said.

He was right, of course. She was exhausted, ready to collapse. It was the wrong time to make this decision.

He put a thumb under her chin and gave her another kiss—this one more chaste. And then he was gone.

Chapter 42

Sid sat next to Betty at his daughter's small kitchen table. They were so focused on his laptop screen they barely noticed that the container of ice cream between them had started to melt. Sid absently stuck a spoon in as he watched Betty put her fingers on the keyboard and type in a better search phrase. He had to concede that the former journalist was a better researcher than he was. Also, a lot smarter and feistier than he had expected. And her taste in music wasn't half-bad.

Their task was interrupted by the sound of Joybird's key in the door. Betty looked up.

"Hey, kiddo," she said cheerfully when Joybird entered. "Fun night out?"

"Fun?" Joybird repeated, as if the question had taken her by surprise.

Sid looked at her. "It's not against the law," he said.

"No, of course not."

Sid studied her face. It was clear she didn't want to talk about it, so of course, he pressed. Besides, if he put her in the hot seat, it would throw her off the scent of what had just happened between him and Betty. They had considered it a one-off—like the scratching of an itch—the kind of thing that would never happen again. And anyway, he certainly didn't want to involve Joybird.

"Were you with Wall Street?" he asked, intuiting the truth. Because why else would she look uncomfortable and embarrassed? He wished she would get over this notion that having money made someone unsuitable for her.

"His name is Devon."

"I hope he took you someplace expensive."

Joybird gave a restrained sigh, as if she didn't want to let on that she found the line of questioning invasive. "We had a very nice dinner. Everything all right here?" She turned her back and carefully tucked something into the hall closet.

"Why didn't you invite him up and throw us out?" Sid asked, changing the subject.

"Dad, please," Joybird said.

Betty jumped in before he could continue his needling. "I had this idea about hiring a private detective to find Donna DeLuca," she explained, pointing at the computer screen.

"Really?" Joybird said, looking distressed by this news.

"What's the matter?" Betty asked.

"Nothing. It just . . . sounds expensive."

"That's why we're bargain hunting."

"We're looking for someone like my last ex-wife—" Sid added, "Cheap and dirty."

Betty laughed, but Joybird stayed serious.

"Relax," Sid told her. "You won't be out a dime. Betty is lending me the money."

"I insisted," Betty said.

Joybird continued to look troubled, as if she was still uncomfortable with their mission. But at last she shrugged it off, told them she was tired, and went to bed.

Chapter 43

Joybird hadn't wanted to let on that she'd already tracked down Donna, as she knew her father wouldn't be able to handle another disappointment if it didn't work out. Still, it seemed wrong to let him go through the trouble and expense of hiring someone when she'd already done the sleuthing. For now, though, there was nothing to do but let him spin his wheels. Tomorrow, she would tell Betty and enlist her help in hitting the brakes.

Joybird climbed into bed, intent on envisioning a happy ending for her father and Donna DeLuca. But no matter how hard she tried to focus, she kept drifting back to that kiss from Devon. That thrilling and beautiful kiss. It filled her with lightness, carrying Joybird on a warm and welcoming current into the sleepy kingdom of her night.

The next morning, Joybird waited until she was in her car before tapping in the number for the New York offices of International Creative Associates. When she finally got through to an actual person, she asked for Donna Sebastiani and was connected with an assistant.

"She's in a meeting," the woman said after Joybird introduced herself. "May I ask what this is in reference to?"

Joybird took a steadying breath. She had assumed it wouldn't be easy to get through to such a high-level executive, so she gave her planned response. "I'm calling on behalf of an old friend of hers from Paxton Prep."

"Paxton Prep?" said the assistant.

"Paxton Academy," Joybird clarified. "Where she attended high school. There's an old friend of hers who's kind of . . . sick." This, she decided, wasn't really a lie, as her father's bouts with depression qualified as a mental illness. "And . . . well, I really need to speak with her. It's important."

Joybird held her breath as the assistant paused. In that tiny space of time, she imagined Donna getting on the phone and gasping at the mention of "John Martin," maybe even getting choked up. *I'd always wondered what happened to Johnny,* she might say. Or *I've been following his career from the very beginning.*

"Why don't you give me your number," the assistant said, "and I'll have her get back to you."

It was disappointing but, of course, not unexpected. Joybird gave the woman her number and decided there was a fifty-fifty chance Donna would actually call back. And if she didn't, well, Joybird would just keep trying.

As she was reviewing her schedule for the day, her phone buzzed with a text. It was Noah—after all this time. Joybird steadied herself. No matter how sincerely he apologized, she was not going to let him off the hook for ghosting her after they slept together.

She opened the message and was so taken aback it took her a moment to realize what she was looking at. Noah had not sent her a personal note, but had included her in a group text to all the volunteers who helped out with his literacy organization, asking if anyone was free to work.

What the hell?

Joybird didn't like to harbor anger or resentment, but *come on.* He had to know she'd been waiting to hear from him. She gritted her teeth and considered ignoring the message. It was probably the smart thing to do. But no, not this time. Joybird decided she needed to assert herself in some small way. So she typed the coldest reply she could muster: Sorry, busy. It was as close as she could get to *fuck off.*

Normally, she would have had second thoughts about being so curt, but this time, she knew she wasn't overreacting. Noah's behavior was inexcusable.

She started her car and was about to pull out of the lot when another text came in from him. This one was private. It said simply: I miss you

For a moment—just one quick, terrible moment—her heart seized at the words. But almost immediately, she recognized it as emotional muscle memory and grunted in disgust. First at herself, and then, more vehemently, at Noah.

"You've got to be kidding me," she said out loud. Joybird shook her head, feeling justified in her righteous anger. She was done with him.

She put her phone into the holder on her dashboard and tapped on the map, which she'd programmed for her first client of the day. It was Althea Harrison, the woman who'd been catfished by a guy overseas and then gotten herself into another suspicious situation. Joybird hoped she'd moved on, and that she'd found love closer to home.

As she pulled out of the lot, her cell phone buzzed with a call. It was Noah. She hit ignore. He called again. She put the phone on *do not disturb.*

Althea was outside waiting for her, looking as put together as always. She wore a belted camel coat, and her hair was swept to the side in a new style. Her makeup, as usual, was on point—just as you'd expect from a lady who works the cosmetics counter at Bloomingdales. But today, according to her intake form, she was having lunch with a gentleman she'd recently met.

"His name is Theodore," she explained, after she'd settled into the back seat. "He's a friend of my cousin Ruby's. I met him at her birthday party."

Joybird was delighted Althea seemed to be done meeting men on Facebook.

"The last time we spoke," she said, "you were seeing someone named Neil."

"Oh, Neil," Althea said with a dismissive wave. "Let me tell you how that went down. After I was done with Ismail, I couldn't get him out of my head. All those lies! And what if he was doing to other women what he did to me? So I unblocked him on Facebook just to see who he was talking to."

Oh, no, Joybird thought. This man with his fake pictures and his blackmail was a terrible obsession. But she let Althea go on.

"I found this lady named Jasmine who was leaving messages on his page. So I reached out to tell her what happened. I even showed her that site you found—with that Italian bodybuilder whose pictures Ismail used. Turns out, this lady, Jasmine, had already sent him money—twenty-two thousand dollars! Can you imagine? That poor thing. She was wrecked, Joybird. I felt terrible, but I knew I did the right thing."

"You did," Joybird assured her. "I just hope you blocked him again after that, so you can move on."

"Oh, I moved on, all right. I mean, I didn't block him—I'm keeping tabs on that monster. But let me tell you, I made up my mind then and there I would never get involved with another man who asked for money."

"Wise move."

"So that's when I broke up with Neil."

Right, Joybird thought. Another catfish, just as she had suspected. She was sorry Althea had to keep learning the hard way, but glad she was coming around. The next step would be to find someone who fulfilled her enough to extinguish her obsession with Ismail once and for all.

"So no more Facebook connections after Neil?" Joybird asked.

"Only one—but it was someone I knew. An old boyfriend, Gordon, who recently got divorced. We started chatting on Facebook and got along like old times. When he suggested we meet for coffee, I was so happy. I dated him back when I was fat, and was so proud to show up at the coffee shop looking slim. I thought we had a lovely time, catching up, laughing. But you wouldn't believe what he said to me at the end of the date."

"What?" Joybird asked.

"He said he liked me better big. Can you imagine? So anyway, that was that."

Joybird glanced back at Althea. She really admired this woman, who was determined to find love. She weathered disappointment after disappointment and just kept going.

The rest of the session was uneventful, and Joybird realized Althea really didn't want advice at this point. She just wanted to share her excitement over Theodore, and Joybird was happy to comply.

When they reached the restaurant, Joybird wished her luck and watched as Althea was greeted by a man holding flowers. He was on the short side, with a kind, round face, and Joybird thought he looked smitten. She hoped this was Althea's happily ever after.

Before driving off, Joybird checked her phone and discovered that Noah had called three more times. This was getting ridiculous. But at least he was sampling a taste of his own medicine. As she continued on to her next client, she thought about those awful men who had tried to take advantage of Althea. Noah, she decided, was in that category. He hadn't asked for money, but he had used her for sex, pretending there was something more between them. It was despicable.

A few minutes later, he called again. This time, she picked up, ready to tell him to leave her alone. She hit speaker.

"What do you want, Noah?"

"I know you're mad at me," he said. "And I don't blame you."

It didn't sound like an apology. "Okay."

"I meant to call you. I really did, but . . . something happened."

Like what? she thought. *Did you break both your hands and lose your voice? Were you kidnapped and tied up in a warehouse someplace?* She let out a breath. "I'm listening."

"I was contacted by an old friend who was in trouble. She'd been on the wagon for two years but was using again."

"An old girlfriend?"

There was a pause, as if he hadn't expected her to connect the dots so easily. "Well . . . yeah," he said. "But she really needed me. I had to help her, Joybird. She was such a mess. I got her back into rehab."

Joybird imagined the scenario. Surely he could have found a minute to shoot her a text. That is, unless he was caught up in the heart-pounding drama of reconnecting with someone he loved. "I understand you were busy," she said, "but you *ghosted* me."

"I shouldn't have done that. I'm so, so sorry. I guess . . . it was a confusing time for me."

"Because you still have feelings for her?"

He went quiet, and Joybird knew she was right. "Well?" she pressed.

Noah cleared his throat. "You can't just turn that kind of thing off, you know? But I'm not seeing her, I swear. That's been over a long time. And I miss you so much."

Joybird was unmoved. "I'm not a consolation prize."

"Of course not," he said. "I respect and value you. And I've been thinking about you so much. Can I see you? I think I can explain this all better in person."

She believed his excuse about the old girlfriend showing up, strung out and needing help. But she knew there was more to it, knew that he'd reduced her to zero once this woman was back in his life. Joybird closed her eyes against childhood memories of abandonment. *Never again,* she thought. Not if she could help it.

"Please, Joybird," he added. "Our night together meant everything to me. I even wrote a poem about it."

She looked inward, trying to find any part of her that was eager to leave Devon for Noah, and came up empty. It warmed her, this certainty. Even after all those months of obsessing over this guy, she had no desire to reconnect with him.

"I'm sorry, but no. I won't see you, Noah. Thank you for calling. Good luck."

"Wait a second," he said. "I'm just asking for a few minutes. I'll come over and—"

"No," she said definitively. "Do not come over."

"No?" he repeated, and she could tell he was surprised by the force of her response. "Are you seeing someone?"

She debated whether she should tell the truth. After all, it really wasn't any of his business. And besides, she needed him to know it was his behavior and not her circumstances that made her turn him down.

"It doesn't matter," she said.

"Is it that Devon guy?"

"I have to get back to work," she told him.

"Please," he begged, "let me call you later. We have so much unfinished business."

"Goodbye, Noah," she said, and hung up.

Chapter 44

Later, she texted Devon to tell him she had put in a call to Donna, adding, So now we wait.

He texted back, suggesting that a dinner together at his place would help fill the time, and Joybird tingled. She was ready for this. So very ready.

It was hard to get through the rest of the day, even harder to play it cool when she got home and found her father in front of his computer, back at work on that pilot, which he had decided to make into an intergenerational comedy. He said he'd heard it was the hot thing, and he was living it, so why not?

"I'm going out tonight," she said.

"Getting busy with Wall Street?" he asked.

She ignored the question. "What about you? Is Betty stopping by?"

"I don't need a babysitter," he said. "Besides, I'm working on this script. I'm just going to order a pizza and see how far I can get."

Joybird thought that was good news. Clearly, his focus on hiring a private investigator to find Donna had brightened his outlook. Now, Joybird had to be certain she could get the big-wheel executive to agree to see him.

Meanwhile, she needed to tell Betty the latest, so she went upstairs to visit her friend, who opened the door wearing a Ramones concert T-shirt, a dish towel in her hands. Joybird smelled something delicious.

"Am I interrupting you?"

"Not at all. Just trying a new mushroom-risotto recipe. Come in."

Joybird followed her into the cluttered kitchen, which didn't have more than one square foot of counter space on which to work. The rest was taken up with canisters, spice bottles, small appliances, cute salt and pepper shakers, two utensil cups, a ceramic cookie jar shaped like a teapot, a knife block, and a white bowl filled with red apples. There was a tiny bottle of truffle oil and a container of grated parmesan cheese next to the stove. Marvin Gaye's "I Heard It Through the Grapevine" played quietly from an iPhone speaker.

While Betty stood over the pot, stirring the risotto, Joybird explained how she and Devon had tracked down Donna DeLuca.

"I don't want to tell my father yet, in case I can't get her to agree to see him. I just don't think he can handle another disappointment."

"Wise move," Betty said. "That woman's got his whole heart."

"I know he's imagining a happily ever after with her."

"If he gets it," Betty said, "it'll restore his faith in the world." She ladled some broth into the risotto, watching intently as she stirred. The scene felt homey and familiar to Joybird, who closed her eyes, trying to conjure an image of her mother in a similar setting.

"You okay, kiddo?"

Joybird snapped back from her reverie. "I was just wondering if you could stall Dad on hiring a private investigator," Joybird said. "I don't want him borrowing money for such an unnecessary expense."

"Consider it done. I'll tell him I have an old friend who's a private detective who will do it for free. It's not even a total lie, because I really do know a retired investigative journalist who does that kind of work."

Betty continued stirring as she asked Joybird what else was going on in her life. "Are you still hung up on that Noah guy, or . . ."

"That's definitely over," Joybird said, and explained the day's drama. Then she told Betty about her plans to see Devon that very night.

"You chose the right one," Betty said. She pulled out a spoonful of risotto and held it toward Joybird, who tasted it.

"Oh my god, that's heaven."

Betty tasted it, too, then added a rounded spoonful of parmesan cheese to the pot. "You two going to get it on tonight?"

Joybird took a deep, long breath, trying to oxygenate every cell. "I hope so," she said, still feeling his warm lips on her neck.

"I'll invite your dad up here so you can have the apartment to yourselves."

"Don't bother," Joybird told her. "I'm going to his place. Besides, Dad is working on his script tonight. I think he's hunkering down."

◆　◆　◆

As his daughter was getting dressed to go out, Sid stared at his computer, thinking about slaughtering a darling he'd been trying to write around for the past hour. When his cell phone rang, he lunged for it.

"Whatever it is," he said, instead of hello, "the answer is yes."

"Good," Betty said, "because I made the best risotto you'll ever taste."

"I'll bring a shovel," he said, and hung up.

Joybird came in just as he was closing his laptop. "Going somewhere?" she asked.

"To Betty's. She made risotto."

"I thought you were working tonight."

"I'm not allowed to take a break for dinner?"

"I didn't say that. I just thought you were in the zone."

He shook his head. "Trust me, I need the distraction."

Joybird smiled. "I'm glad, Dad. I think this friendship is good for both of you."

Sid held back a chuckle, because he knew Joybird was thinking Betty might be the first platonic woman friend he'd ever had, and that it was the perfect way for him to learn respect and boundaries. What she didn't realize was that with Betty, boundaries could be a blurry thing. He headed for the door.

"Have a good time," Joybird said.

"Pretty sure I will."

Chapter 45

"Duck a l'orange?" Joybird repeated.

"Don't you like duck?" Devon asked. The table was set for two, a pair of tall candles in the center. Tea lights were lit all along the gleaming kitchen counter.

"I'm just . . . surprised. You said you didn't really cook."

He laughed. "Don't be impressed. I have a chef friend who made it and got everything set up for me. For *us*. But I made the salad." He patted his chest at the last part, puffed with pride, and Joybird smiled.

She took a moment to appreciate all he had done for her, and compared it to her one night with Noah, in which he barely remembered to ask if she wanted a drink while she stood watching his roommate play video games. If she had any lingering reservations about not disclosing her one-night stand with Noah to Devon, this clinched it. Noah was nothing to her. A nonentity. What happened between them was like an insignificant crack in the sidewalk. All she had to do was step over it.

"It's beautiful," Joybird said to Devon, her eyes going damp. She took a deep breath and let herself enjoy it.

Over dinner, they talked about what they might do if Donna Sebastiani didn't return Joybird's call.

"I could just show up at her office building, but I don't think that would go over well."

"Maybe Reuben could call her."

Joybird thought that was a great idea and stored it away. Meanwhile, she asked Devon about his day, his family, and how his mother was doing. He asked about her life-coaching business and said he was impressed with how quickly she had made it all work. He also asked if she'd given any more thought to accompanying him to his boss's birthday party.

"I don't . . . I don't know," she said, still far too traumatized by her experience with Riley's terrible grandparents to feel comfortable.

"It's okay," he said. "I just want you to know the invitation stands. You can change your mind anytime."

Later, it was Joybird who suggested they move to the bedroom. They'd been sitting on the sofa in front of the electric fireplace, which she learned he could turn on and off with a switch. But it didn't take long for her to lose her fascination with his command of modern appliances and become more interested in his other talents. One kiss had led to another, and then another. His desire fed hers until they were both panting in such fevered frenzy that nothing in the world felt as important as connecting, flesh to heated flesh.

He wanted her. She wanted him.

To Joybird, it felt like so much more than sex. His touch was sparked; his fingertips seemed to contain everything she ever wished a man would say to her. Joybird had never felt so beautiful, so sexy, so loved. They came together, and he was so patient that she was nearly embarrassed.

"It's okay," she said as he held back. "This is . . . wonderful. It's all wonderful. You can—"

"Nope," he said. "Not yet." He put his face into her neck, found the spot that made her shiver, then ran his hand down her belly into her wetness. That touch again. And again and again. She gasped and bucked and cried out, sure it had never been this good.

Afterward, as Joybird lay in his arms, relaxed and blissful, he asked if she was hungry.

She shook her head. "Are you?"

"I can wait," he said, pulling her close. "I don't really want to move."

They stayed like that until her cell phone rang. She wanted to ignore it, but worried it could be her father calling with some kind of emergency. So she picked it up to glance at the screen and saw that it was Noah. She grunted and rejected the call.

"Who was that?" Devon asked.

"Don't worry about it," she said.

"That's not an answer."

She sighed and realized that withholding the truth gave it more weight. "It was Noah."

"The coffee shop dude? Why is he calling you?"

"Just . . . he's running one of those literacy events this weekend. He's probably calling to see if I'll help out." It was only a partial lie, Joybird decided. After all, he *had* contacted her about an upcoming event.

Devon squinted at her. "You don't have something going on with this guy, do you?"

"No," she said, which was true. It just wasn't the entire truth. "Of course not."

"But you would tell me if you did?"

She paused to swallow against a knot in her throat. "Devon, I'm not seeing Noah. I promise."

It was evasive, but now that she and Devon had slept together, she couldn't possibly tell him about her stupid mistake. He'd be devastated. Joybird's heart raced. Should she have told him when she had the chance?

He brought her in his arms, kissed her head, and held on for dear life. "Joybird . . . ," he muttered, his voice cracking with emotion. He couldn't seem to find any way to finish the thought, so she just said, "Me too."

Chapter 46

By the next afternoon, Donna Sebastiani still hadn't called back, so Joybird phoned again, left another message, and went to pick up her next client—a fragile twenty-something mother who had just received a cancer diagnosis. Though her prognosis was good, she needed to talk through her fears, her anxieties, her plans.

When Joybird's phone buzzed during the session, she was certain it was Donna, but she didn't want to risk glancing at the screen while her client was talking. Then she heard the ping of a voicemail and ignored that too.

She managed to keep her mind on her job and helped the young mother work through balancing her family's expectations with what she really wanted. She dropped the woman at her destination, hoping she'd been able to help.

After taking a moment to center herself, Joybird picked up her phone, concerned about missing her chance to connect with Donna. But the call had been from Corinne Wilbanks, who left a breathless voicemail saying she was in the middle of a crisis and that Joybird had to call her back immediately. Her voice sounded shaky, and Joybird wondered what might constitute an emergency for the self-centered Corinne. Then another message from her came in. This one was a text: 911

Joybird hoped it was a matter of Corinne being overly dramatic, but she called back as fast as she could.

"Where are you?" Corinne barked.

"What do you mean, where am I?"

"I'm in Brooklyn," Corinne said, "at my ex's. Are you close by? Something's wrong with Riley."

"Slow down," Joybird said. "Tell me what's going on."

"Some high drama at school. I think some girl told Carter that Riley was messing around with this boy from her AP English class—which she insists she wasn't—and it seems like he believed this girl and broke up with her, and I don't know what the hell is going on. She locked herself in her room and won't talk to Barry or Emily, so they called me, and she won't talk to me either. Can you come over?"

Joybird went tense in concern, as she hoped Riley wasn't thinking about hurting herself. The girl was so tightly wound.

She wanted to help, of course, but her schedule was jammed. And unlike most life coaches, she couldn't call clients at the last minute to reschedule, because they relied on her for a ride.

"Give me a second," Joybird said, examining her calendar. She was in midtown, and her next client was in Prospect Heights, which wasn't all that far from the Wilbankses' house. If she left right now, hit no traffic, and didn't spend more than fifteen minutes with Riley, she might actually make it in time.

"Please!" Corinne said. "It's an emergency."

"Okay, okay," Joybird said. "I'll be there as fast as I can."

As she drove—trying her best to weave around the traffic—Joybird decided that this might be the best thing that could have happened, because now Riley's parents would understand how precarious their daughter's situation was. Maybe they would even involve her psychotherapist, who would be more equipped than Joybird to navigate these difficult issues. In the meantime, though, the challenge would be getting Riley to agree to talk to her.

She found a parking spot just up the block from the familiar brick house and did her best run-walk to the door. To her surprise, it was Riley who opened it. She wore an oversize white sweatshirt—presumably

Carter's—with the sleeves pulled down over her hands. Though her eyes were puffy from crying, she didn't look sad.

"I'm okay," Riley said. "I don't know why the idiots thought they needed to call you."

"What's going on?"

Joybird heard a male voice call from behind her. "Tell her to come in!"

"Join the party," Riley said, and led Joybird into the pristine living room, where Riley's divorced parents and her stepmom were all seated. The toddler girl, Joybird assumed, was napping.

Barry stood, shook Joybird's hand, and introduced himself.

"I'm sorry we got you out here," he said. "Apparently, everything is okay now. Riley just got off the phone with Carter."

"He said he was sorry he didn't believe me. He knew I would never cheat on him," Riley explained, and managed a smile.

"Can I get you something to drink?" Emily offered.

"I'm fine," Joybird said. "I can't stay long." She turned to Riley. "Do you want to talk about what happened?"

"It was this toxic bitch Lily, who's always up in everyone's business."

"Carter's ex," Corinne explained.

Joybird turned to Riley for clarification. "Lily is Carter's ex-girlfriend?"

"He hates her."

"But he believed her when she lied about you and some other boy?"

"She's very manipulative," Riley said. "That girl loves to fuck with people. And she's got an IQ of like a million, so she's extremely good at it. Classic psychopath."

And yet, Joybird thought, Carter had dated her. She was starting to get a picture of him as someone who was drawn to smart, damaged girls.

"But you worked it out with him just now?"

Riley nodded. "He called to apologize. Once he had time to clear his head, he realized Lily had manipulated him." She looked around the room. "Is anyone else in the mood for mac and cheese?"

"Just a minute," Joybird said. "I want to address how you cut yourself off from everyone when you were upset."

Riley rolled her eyes. "I just needed space."

"You should have told us that," her father said.

"You wouldn't even talk," Corinne added. "It was creepy."

"Concerning," Barry clarified.

Riley snorted at their worry. "You guys don't understand how annoying you can be."

Her stepmother said, "We care about you, Riley."

Corinne shot her daggers, as if she had no right to speak in this conversation. It kept the atmosphere charged with tension.

"I was upset, okay?" Riley said, pacing and gesticulating. "I'm allowed to be upset. My boyfriend thought I was cheating on him. And he broke up with me! It was just . . . ugh. You guys don't understand."

"I do understand," Corinne said. "Love is hard. Love is heartbreaking."

Joybird caught Barry and Emily exchanging a look. She could only imagine the conversations these two had about Corinne when she wasn't in the room.

"Listen," Joybird said to Riley, "I know it can feel like the adults are ganging up on you. But when you're feeling that terrible, it's not the time to cut yourself off. That's when you need people the most."

"The next time—" her father began.

"There's not going to be a next time," Riley said. "He's never going to doubt me again."

"I mean the next time you're upset about something."

"Fine," Riley said. "I promise I won't be such a dick next time. Now can we have some mac and cheese?"

At that, Joybird excused herself, explaining she was running late for her next client. She told Riley she would see her the following week and dashed out the door.

Chapter 47

When Joybird dropped off her last client of the day at a Midtown Manhattan address, she realized she wasn't far from the offices of International Creative Associates and wondered if she should do a drive-by on the off chance she might catch a glimpse of the elusive Donna Sebastiani. She didn't know what she hoped to glean from a quick look, but it felt almost irresistible . . . if maybe just a tiny bit stalkerish. She put her car in gear and set off.

Coming to a stop at a traffic light, Joybird had a clear view of the building's double brass doors, set back from the road. It was rush hour, and people were pouring from the building, but it didn't take long for her to spot a tall woman in a buttery-brown coat with a single black button at the neck. The wind blew her lush dark hair from her face, and there was no question that this was Donna. She was stunning, regal, and carried herself with the ease and confidence of a woman who never stopped to worry what anyone thought of her.

Though she looked just like her photograph, there was an element that felt surprising—maybe even disappointing—and Joybird realized what it was. Donna had the visage of someone who was locked down, not prone to kindness. Joybird assumed there had to be an inner layer of tenderness, but the exterior hardness was disconcerting. She tried to picture what had happened when the assistant said someone named Joybird Martin had called about an old friend from Paxton. It was impossible to imagine this jagged rock formation softening at the news, curious to return the call. Now, there was no question Joybird would have to involve Reuben Ross in the negotiation to put Donna and her father in the same room.

When she got home, Joybird was surprised to find her father in the easy chair, thumbing through the Paxton yearbook. She froze, realizing she had forgotten to pull it from the hall closet and hide it in a better spot. She hadn't wanted him to find it and track down Donna before she got a chance to intercede and make sure the woman was willing to see him. She was now less confident than ever that this might happen.

Then Joybird noticed a bottle of Jack Daniels on the table next to him—never a good sign. He was unshaven, unshowered, and unashamed.

"Everything okay?" she asked.

"Why were you hiding this from me?" he demanded, holding up the yearbook. Clearly, he'd been waiting for her to walk through the door so he could make this self-righteous accusation.

"Uh . . . I . . . I wasn't hiding it."

"The hell you weren't!"

"Take it easy," she said, aware that the alcohol fueled his bad temper.

"I thought you *wanted* me to find Donna."

"I do!" she protested. "Of course I do."

"Are you going to pretend this wound up in the back of the closet by accident?"

Joybird hesitated, wondering if she should tell him the truth—that she had already tracked down Donna, but thought it best to protect him from the information until she was absolutely sure the aloof executive would agree to see him.

"I . . . um . . ." She paused, searching for a partial truth that might calm him. "I ordered it to help me find Donna, but it had no clues, so . . . I just put it away."

He took a swig of his Jack Daniels, right from the bottle, then roughly opened the book to the page with Donna's picture. "Look at her," he muttered, wiping his eyes, which were wet with tears.

His pain was palpable. Joybird sat in the chair next to him and took his hand. "Dad, I swear I am doing everything possible to find Donna."

He put a gentle finger on the face in the yearbook. "Did you ever see a girl like this?"

"She's beautiful."

"Also smart and funny. No, not funny—clever, which is a thousand times better. And insightful, determined." He paused to take another pull from the bottle, then looked back down at the image. "Did I tell you I kissed her once? At a party."

"You did."

He rubbed his forehead as if trying to conjure the past. "Why didn't I ever ask her out after that?" he said, like he was questioning his younger self.

"I don't know, Dad."

"It's like . . . like I was this close to my dream and I just . . . let it go. Who *does* that?"

"Lots of people."

"They do?" he asked, genuinely surprised. "Why?"

The question was so earnest that Joybird's own eyes went damp. She'd never seen her father this vulnerable.

"Fear of rejection?" she offered, understanding that Donna had probably always been an intimidating and formidable presence.

He closed his eyes, disappearing into the past. "That would have killed me." He hiccuped against a sob, and Joybird handed him a tissue.

"I know," she said softly.

"What a wimp," he muttered, shaking his head. "I should have done it. Back in high school, I mean. I should have taken that fucking risk. Isn't that exactly what kids are supposed to do?"

"It was a learning experience," she said. "I'm sure it helped you later on."

He looked at Joybird as if he was really seeing her, appreciating her, before peering back down at Donna's picture.

"Maybe we should put this away," Joybird said gently, trying to pry the book from his hands.

"Are you crazy?" he demanded. "This is my key to finding her."

"I combed over every page," she insisted, worried he might indeed find some clue that would lead him straight to Donna. She could imagine the whole thing playing out in disastrous slow motion as he flew into a manic rage, culminating in a bender that landed him in jail or the hospital.

"But *I'm* the one who can find the clues," he insisted. "That's why you should have shown it to me. None of this has any meaning to you."

"Did you . . . find something?" she asked.

"I remembered two girls she was friends with," he said, tapping at the book. "I bet at least one of them knows how to track down Donna. Maybe you can help me find them on Facebook or Instacart."

"*-gram*," she corrected.

"What?"

"Insta*gram*. You wouldn't be able to find them on Instacart unless they were delivering groceries."

"If they can deliver Donna, that's all that matters."

Joybird offered a gentle laugh and tried to get him to give up the book. "Seriously," she said, "let's put this away. We can give the information to the private investigator."

"Why shouldn't I contact them myself?" he asked.

"Because you want to surprise Donna, don't you? If she gets word you're nosing around, it might scare her off."

He put his hand on his chest as if protecting his heart. "That would be calamitous."

"Right," Joybird said, "we have to approach this carefully."

He held tight to the book. "I'll give this to Betty so she can pass it to the private investigator."

"You want me to bring it upstairs?"

"Tell her to come down."

Joybird hesitated, but he was dug in, so she relented and reached out to her neighbor. When Betty arrived, Sid filled her in, then handed over the yearbook, along with a note he had scribbled with the names of the girls he had remembered. "I think I should talk to him," Sid said.

"Talk to who?" Betty asked.

"Are you stoned?" he said. "Your friend. The private eye."

Joybird worried that their subterfuge about the investigator had been blown, but Betty collected herself quickly. "Oh, right," she said. "My friend."

"Can you get him on the phone?" Sid asked.

"Now?"

"Why not? I have valuable data to share." He tapped his head to show just where it was stored. Betty glanced at Joybird, who shrugged.

"Good idea," Betty finally said. "I'll text him and see if he's available." She took out her phone and started beating at it with her fingers, clucking with frustration.

"Let Joybird do it," Sid said. "Our generation could thumb its way across country but not, apparently, across a cell phone."

Betty handed her phone to Joybird, who pretended to send a text to the private investigator. Of course, her father was completely unaware he was being handled. As he settled in to spend the evening with Betty, waiting for a call that would never come, Joybird wafted out the door like a scent, floating toward another date with Devon.

Chapter 48

On Sunday morning, Joybird and Devon went to a local diner for breakfast. They had spent the whole night together for the first time and were both giddy with the newness of discovering one another. He seemed charmed by every little thing about her—how kind she was to the waitress, the way she ordered her eggs (one over easy, one sunny-side up), her intuitiveness about his feelings. And she was floored by his compassion, generosity, and intelligence. She was even starting to appreciate his ambition—that drive to succeed and prove his worth. When he talked about his job, she understood his frustrations, as his boss was like a tyrannical father, dispensing approval in tiny, miserly doses.

"Do you think about changing jobs?" she asked.

"Not yet," he said. "I'm on track for a promotion, so as long as I keep impressing Bryant and he doesn't decide to be a dick, I'll be in good shape."

"And then you'll leave?"

"Maybe."

That surprised her. "Wouldn't you want to get away from that guy the first chance you got?"

"You're assuming other bosses aren't as bad. That's not really the way it works. The trick is to become a department head. That's my goal."

She could see it playing out and understood exactly how proud he'd feel, and how seriously he'd take his responsibilities. "You'll be so good at it," she said.

A warm smile bloomed across his face as he reached over to touch her cheek. There was so much love in the gesture, her heart was filled with gratitude, nearly ready to burst. She hoped the feeling would last and last and last.

It was only November, but a light snow had begun to fall. They turned toward the window simultaneously to admire it and then back at each other, grinning. The temperature was climbing, and soon it would turn to rain. But for this one romantic moment, it felt like the snow was falling just for them.

They were halfway through their meal when Joybird's phone buzzed.

"It's Reuben," she said, looking down at the screen. A couple of days earlier, she had asked him if he would intervene with Donna, and he had placed a call to her office, explaining that he was an old classmate. Devon looked as excited as she felt. Joybird set the phone between them, putting it on speaker.

"She just called me back," Reuben said, excited. "On a Sunday! I didn't expect—"

"How did she sound?" Devon asked.

"Like she was busy and didn't want to spend too much time on the phone. It was all very rushed, but she said she remembered Johnny Martin really well."

Devon reached across the table and gave Joybird's arm a squeeze. She shifted in her seat, almost too excited to contain herself. This was really happening!

"Does she know he changed his name to Sid Marcus?" she asked.

"Said she's followed his career all this time."

Joybird felt herself overflowing with relief. This was exactly what she had hoped for. "And?" she pressed.

"I asked if we could set up a meeting, and she said, 'Let me talk to the daughter first.'"

Joybird furrowed her brow. "I don't understand."

"I couldn't really get much out of her," Reuben said. "I told her your father had been depressed, so maybe she wants to get a read on how fragile he is before they meet."

"I guess that makes sense."

"She said she has time in her schedule tomorrow at one fifty-five p.m. She wants you to come to her office."

Joybird almost snorted. She'd heard of people scheduling meetings at odd times to ensure attendees wouldn't be late, but this seemed especially anal. "One fifty-five?" she repeated, just to be sure she'd gotten it right.

"She was very clear that you have to be on time because she's got another meeting."

Joybird tapped the calendar app on her phone and saw that her afternoon was free. "Okay," she said, "I can do that. But what about Dad? I mean, can I bring him?"

"She didn't say, but it can't hurt. Let him wait outside while you talk to her. I'll bet if he's there, she'll agree to see him."

Joybird thought it was odd that Donna wanted to talk to her first, but told herself to be happy about this. It was all going to work out. She'd go in to see Donna, who would probably want assurances that her father was stable and not some kind of creepy crackpot.

She got the details from Reuben and thanked him profusely.

"You did it!" Devon said, when she got off the phone.

"You think so?"

"You found Donna DeLuca. You got an appointment to see her. The rest will be up to her and Sid."

"I'm a little intimidated by that woman," she admitted.

"Because of the scheduling weirdness?"

Joybird had been too embarrassed to tell Devon about driving by Donna's office. But now she realized he wouldn't judge her for it. She took a sip of coffee and wiped her mouth. "I have a confession," she said, biting her lip. "I kind of stalked her."

Devon raised a curious eyebrow, amused.

"I was in midtown at rush hour," Joybird went on, "so I drove by her office, and I actually got to see her in the flesh. She's . . . got a vibe."

"What kind of vibe?"

Joybird thought about that for a moment, trying to find the right word. "Imperious," she finally said.

Devon looked delighted at this.

"Why are you smiling?" Joybird asked.

"Anyone else would have described her as a bitch," he said.

Joybird felt a warm glow, seeing herself through this man's eyes. She was so enchanted that she almost didn't notice a group entering the restaurant, led by the lanky blonde Tabitha McCabe, a fellow volunteer for Noah's organization. Then she realized there were several familiar faces in the assemblage, and Joybird remembered that this was the morning of Noah's event. They had probably just wrapped up and were going out for brunch together.

Tabitha shook the snow from her coat and waved from across the restaurant. Joybird waved back.

"Who's that?" Devon asked, and Joybird wondered if this was just his natural nosiness—his need to be The Answer Man—or a kind of possessiveness, more related to his fear of betrayal. Maybe, she thought, once he got comfortable enough to understand she wasn't like his past girlfriends, he'd relax and not feel the need to know every small detail of her life.

"Tabitha McCabe," she said. "Friend of Noah's."

"Noah?" Devon repeated, his expression turning dark, and she knew she'd been right not to tell him what had happened. He wouldn't have been able to handle it.

"Can't we just forget about him?" she asked.

"I don't think so," Devon said. "Look."

He nodded toward the door, and Joybird turned. There was Noah, surrounded by an entourage. She tried to pivot away before he caught her looking, but it was too late.

Please don't come over, she thought, her back to him. *Please.* But then there he was, looming over their table, his thick black beard flecked with snow.

"Hey," he said. "I've been trying to reach you."

Joybird tensed. "You remember Devon," she said, ignoring his statement and trying to sound casual.

"I knew it," Noah seethed. "I knew you were seeing this dude. It's why you didn't want to talk to me."

"If she doesn't want to talk to you," Devon said, "then what are you doing here?"

"Joybird," Noah begged, "please. I know I was kind of a dick, but if you knew how sorry I was."

"I don't want to have this conversation," she said to him, aware that the more he talked, the more questions Devon would ask.

"I'm only working until five tomorrow," Noah said. "Maybe afterwards we can meet for—"

Devon stood. "She made herself very clear. She doesn't want to talk to you. Now leave us the hell alone, or things are going to get very serious between you and me. Understand?"

Noah put his hands up. "I don't want to fight with you, bro. That's not my jam."

Devon remained standing, giving Noah the death glare until he backed away.

Joybird put her head in her hands. "I'm so sorry," she whispered.

"Guy can't take no for an answer."

"It's okay," she said, reaching for his hand. "I'm not taking his calls, and I'm definitely not meeting up with him."

"If he bothers you . . ."

"He's harmless, I swear." She glanced back at the table of Noah's entourage, which seemed to have turned into an impromptu poetry reading, as one of the girls had stood up and was reciting a depressing verse about a dead cat. When she finished, there was a smattering of applause from her group, and then Noah stood.

"I have one," he said, his voice booming across the restaurant. Joybird got the impression he wanted her to hear, and she went on alert, recalling that he'd said he'd written a poem about her. "It's new— inspired by a very special lady in my life."

At that, he made pointed eye contact with Joybird and her palms went sweaty. *Oh, no,* she thought. *No, no, no!* She looked at Devon's face, which was laser focused on Noah.

"Let's go," she said, her heart hammering. "I don't want to hear this."

"What's going on?" he pressed. "Did he write a love poem for you or something?"

"Please," she begged, "let's get out of here. I'll explain everything outside."

His face was stony, but she stood and put on her coat. "Come on." She picked up the check from the table, but Devon snatched it from her hand, threw down some cash, and followed her outside.

The snow had turned to a slushy mix, wetting her hair. Joybird pushed it out of her face, then grabbed Devon's arm and led him to a nearby awning. A hard rock formed in her throat, but there was only one thing to do. She had to tell him about Noah.

"You have something to say?" he asked her.

"Give me a minute," Joybird pleaded, trying to find the right words. She knew it would bring up the trauma of past betrayals. But maybe if she softened it with a heartfelt explanation, it wouldn't be so bad. After all, Devon was the one she had chosen, the one who meant everything to her. If she could get that across, he'd forgive her.

"There's something I didn't tell you about Noah," she began. "Before you and I were together—"

"Fuck me. You slept with him?" He looked incredulous, as if he couldn't believe what he was hearing.

"It was before—"

"You lied to me," he said, his eyes dark with anger.

"No! Not really. I mean, it was in the past, so—"

"How far in the past?" His voice was hard and bitter.

She searched his face for softness, for any signs he might forgive her, and found none. Joybird inhaled against a staccato breath. *Don't cry,* she told herself, but a single sob escaped. Before she could collapse into a puddle, she turned from him and filled her lungs one, two, three times.

When at last she made eye contact, wiping her damp face, he seemed to have disappeared inside his own pain. Joybird's throat went even tighter. She thought she'd understood how damaged he'd been by infidelity, but looking at his face now, she could see it went even deeper than she imagined.

"How far in the past?" he repeated.

"Don't ask me that."

"Goddamn it, Joybird." He looked so hurt it broke her in half. She had done this.

"It was just one time. And it's irrelevant. He means nothing to me."

"It's not . . . irrelevant . . . to me," he said slowly, his teeth clenched.

"But it should be," she pleaded. "You're the one I . . . I have feelings for." She'd wanted to say *love,* because it was what she truly felt, but knew this wasn't the right time to make that proclamation.

"Such strong feelings that you lied to me?"

"Yes!" she cried. "Because I didn't want to upset you."

Devon hung his head, and when he brought it back up, she saw a tear behind his glasses. As it ran down his face, he wiped his nose with the back of his hand—a gesture wholly unlike him. Then he stood taller, as if trying to regain his composure, and Joybird waited for him to say something.

Then, finally, he did.

"You don't always get what you want." Devon waited a single beat, unable to look at her, then turned and walked away.

"Devon!" she said, but he ignored her. "I'm sorry!" she called. "I'm so, so sorry."

Chapter 49

"I called Devon three times and left messages," Joybird told Betty. It was a few hours later, and they were in the aging hippie's cluttered living room, surrounded by the detritus of her decades as a reporter and journalism professor. "I sent five texts. What can I do?"

Betty pulled off the bandanna she'd been wearing as a headband and released her soft white hair, which fell just short of her shoulders. "He might need a little space, kiddo."

Joybird had been over it in her mind again and again. But no matter how many ways she imagined it, she couldn't picture a scenario in which she told Devon the truth about Noah and he accepted it with magnanimity.

"What would you have done?" Joybird asked. "Would you have told him when it first came up?"

Betty shrugged. "I'm a let-the-chips-fall-where-they-may kind of gal." She poured a glass of wine and handed it to Joybird, who couldn't ever remember feeling so tortured. Devon was in misery, and it was her fault.

"But he's so *hurt*," she insisted, putting the wineglass down on the table.

"Sometimes we have to hurt people," Betty explained, and Joybird stared. It was one of the most incomprehensible statements she'd ever heard.

"Do you really believe that?"

"C'mon," Betty said, "you can't *always* make people happy."

"Why not?"

"That's a burden no one should have to carry."

Joybird closed her eyes and rubbed her forehead, remembering what it felt like to be in Devon's arms, how happy they'd been just a few hours ago. She could still smell his fragrance buried deep in her sinuses.

"We're so good together," she said, as if it might help explain something.

"I know."

"What should I do? Should I call him again? Should I go to his apartment?"

Betty sat next to her on the couch. "Do you want to smoke a joint?"

"What good would that do?" Joybird asked.

"I think you just need to chill out for a while—let him sleep on it," Betty said. "He might feel differently tomorrow."

That meant they'd both be tortured all night. Surely, there had to be *something* she could do now.

Joybird's phone rang, and her heart lurched. She closed her eyes in silent prayer. *Devon. Please, let it be Devon saying all he'd needed was a little time.* His voice would be soothing and strong. He'd say he forgave her and that he was sorry, too, and surely, they could work all this out.

She opened her eyes and dashed for the phone, but when she looked at the screen, hope spilled from her grasp like dry sand. It wasn't Devon. It was Corinne Wilbanks again.

Joybird wanted to let it go to voicemail, as she was just too bereft to deal with the woman's drama. But no, there might be a problem with Riley, and she couldn't live with herself if she ignored that.

"Not Devon?" Betty asked.

Joybird shook her head. "Riley's mom," she said, her voice flat. It rang again.

"You going to answer?"

Joybird sighed and tapped the green button.

"I need you to get Riley tomorrow," Corinne said without preamble.

"What?" Joybird asked. The woman had a way of barking orders without bothering to explain. "Can you back up a little? Is everything okay?"

"Of course everything's okay. You know Riley. She bounces back like nothing ever happened."

Joybird sighed. This woman didn't understand her daughter one bit.

"But something came up for Wednesday," Corinne continued. "Something important. I wanted to switch to Thursday, but Barry said it would be *inconvenient*. He's such a pill."

Right, Joybird thought. *Barry is the pill, not you.* "So you need me to pick up Riley from school tomorrow afternoon?" she asked.

"If you can't do it, I'll have to hire an Uber, but we both know she'd be better off in your car, in case she decides to go off the rails again."

Joybird understood she was being manipulated with guilt, and it didn't escape her notice that Corinne hadn't mentioned what was so pressing that she had to cancel her regularly scheduled night with her daughter. If it was anyone else, Joybird might have assumed it was some kind of emergency, like a doctor's appointment. But knowing Corinne, it was probably a hot date she didn't want to miss.

She thought about her scheduled appointment with Donna Sebastiani and knew she could use it as an excuse to blow Corinne off. But in truth, the meeting would probably last less than ten minutes, leaving her plenty of time to pick up Riley. Besides, Joybird knew the girl was in a fragile state, and she feared turning down this request could be risky.

"Well?" Corinne asked, her voice impatient. "Can you do it or not?"

"Fine," Joybird said. "I'll be there."

When she got off the phone, Betty smiled and patted her hand. "One day, you'll tell that woman to go jump in a lake."

Joybird held back a laugh. It was such an old-fashioned expression. She'd only ever heard one other person say it—her dad.

"I know," Joybird said. "But the girl. And it's not really that inconvenient for me."

Betty opened a small hinged box on the coffee table and pulled out a joint. She lit it and took a drag. "That kid is lucky to have you," she frogged out, the smoke still in her lungs. "We all are." She held out the joint to Joybird, who shook her off.

As Betty finally exhaled, Joybird thanked her and wondered if her father felt the same way. Soon enough, she'd find out.

Chapter 50

Joybird left her car in a lot three blocks from Donna's office—the cheapest parking she could find in that part of midtown. She checked the time and trotted to the address, hoping she'd find her father waiting there, as they had arranged to meet up in front of the building so they could go in together. Joybird figured it was the only chance he had at getting past security, since she was the one with the appointment.

Unfortunately, he wasn't there yet. She stood on the pavement in front of the courtyard, looking left and right to catch any sight of him. A brisk breeze blew across the expanse, and Joybird turned up the collar of her coat, then dug her hands deep into her pockets. After several minutes, she pulled out her phone and sent him a text: Are you close?

He responded: ish

Joybird checked the time again, fearing Donna wouldn't agree to see her if she was even a minute late. She stalled a few more minutes, then sent another text: I don't think I should wait any longer

Sid texted that he was still at the florist two blocks away, adding: Go on up without me.

She responded: How will you get upstairs?

He told her not to worry, insisting he was confident he could finagle his way past security.

Joybird was less convinced. Everything was riding on this meeting, and if her father wasn't right there in the waiting room after her brief chat with Donna, he might miss his chance. Still, she had no choice but to go in alone. She took a deep breath to settle her nerves and entered the building. After showing the security guard her ID, she was given an adhesive badge along with instructions to take the south elevator to the eleventh floor, which she did.

When the doors dinged open, a slender young woman was waiting for her. "Ms. Martin?" she asked.

Joybird noted that everything this woman was wearing—from the pristine knit dress to the stylish designer shoes—looked brand new. It left her feeling shabby in the gray blazer she had bought for herself several years ago, when the state senator she worked for promoted her to office manager. But this staffer seemed friendlier than the woman who had answered the phone at Donna's office, and Joybird tried to use that to relax a little. This whole thing was so nerve racking.

"I'm Keiko," said the young woman, and she led Joybird down a long hallway and around several corners. Joybird focused on the route, memorizing it so she could text her father instructions for finding the office. Finally, they reached a set of wide glass doors leading to an empty waiting room decorated in warm autumn colors, and Keiko swiped her key card to unlock the door, then held it open for Joybird.

"Can I get you something to drink?"

"I'm fine," Joybird said, though she was parched from nerves. She had no concrete reason to think Donna DeLuca Sebastiani would be unkind to her, yet her body was on high alert, ready for an attack. She tried to tell herself she was being ridiculous. Donna had already said she remembered Johnny Martin, hadn't she? That stiff demeanor Joybird had witnessed could be meaningless. Maybe she'd just been having a bad day.

Please, Joybird thought, *let Donna be kind and warm. Let her be eager to meet with her long-lost friend.*

"Have a seat," Keiko said. "Fiona will come out to get you." Then she disappeared behind a pale wood door.

Joybird lowered herself onto the spongy couch and texted her father the coordinates while nervously jiggling her foot.

Sid arrived at the building several minutes later with a solid plan for getting past security. He knew that ICA represented some of the biggest names in television, so he decided he would simply wait at the front of the building until he recognized someone he knew—or had at least crossed paths with at some point—and follow them past security. He thought it helped that he was holding a massive bouquet. Who could be suspicious of a man with flowers? He made a mental note that it might make a good gimmick if he ever needed to slip a con man into a script. He'd give him an extravagant spray of colorful blooms. Maybe a large cake box.

Sid thought he recognized Aaron Bell, a prickly yet well-connected writer he had worked with in the nineties. But since they hadn't parted on the best of terms—and Aaron almost certainly wasn't important enough to be able to sail past security—Sid laid low. He needed someone recognizable.

In the waiting room, Joybird attempted to calm herself with square breathing techniques. She rose from the couch and tried to peer down the hallway and see if her father was coming, but it was quiet. She texted him again, and he wrote back: Relax, I'll be up in a few.

Just then, the wood door opened and another woman appeared. This one was a little older and certainly more weary, her eyes ringed in dark circles. Joybird wondered just how challenging it would be to work for someone like Donna Sebastiani.

"Joybird Martin?" she said, in a voice Joybird recognized. It was the woman she had spoken with on the phone. "Donna will see you now."

Sid was starting to get pretty jittery himself, but then he saw his opportunity. It was Danny Strauss, an actor who'd played a kid on a sitcom Sid had worked on nearly twenty years ago. Of course, he was all grown up now—a funny-looking boy who'd bloomed into a funny-looking character actor, famous enough to turn heads.

"Danny!" he called, his voice assertive and delighted. The actor turned to look at him, confused.

"Sid Marcus," he boomed. "I wrote all your favorite episodes of *Judge Linda.*"

Danny laughed appreciatively, pretending he remembered him. "Good to see you, Sid."

"Can't believe I'm running into you," Sid told him. "I was just talking about you to Halsey."

"Oh?" Danny said, clearly intrigued. Halsey Aikens was one of the biggest agents in the business. She had never represented Sid, but he kept that to himself.

"Her birthday's today," he said, holding up the bouquet, and saw a twinge of concern cross Danny's face, as if he were wondering if he was supposed to remember his agent's birthday with flowers.

Sid continued talking—dropping names and mentioning studios like he had the biggest deal in the world cooking—as he followed Danny Strauss to the security desk. The actor signed in, and they strolled together to the south elevators like two guys who owned the world. Sid was ad-libbing, bouncing from one incoherent anecdote to the next, as the poor guy tried to follow his train of thought, certain the final point would be about some lead role Danny was perfect for. As a writer whose job it was to invent storylines, lying came as easily to Sid as sidling up to a bar and opening his mouth.

He got into the elevator with Danny, continuing his line of bullshit. When the doors opened on the eleventh floor, he shook the actor's hand and said goodbye, leaving him standing there in utter bewilderment.

Sid felt bad for the poor guy, but he needed to focus. He took a deep breath, trying to settle himself, and wished he had stopped for a belt of scotch. *Too late now,* he thought, and followed Joybird's instructions until he got to the glass doors she had described. They were, of course, locked. He peered into the waiting room, and Joybird was gone—already facing Donna to answer whatever questions she had.

He stood there in the empty hallway, waiting for someone he could con into opening the door. It seemed that Donna was a pretty big deal, so he figured if he told someone the flowers were for her birthday, they'd let him in for fear of getting into trouble. Problem was, the hallway was so deserted, he half expected to see tumbleweeds blow by.

Donna Sebastiani sat before a window, backlit, ignoring Joybird and Fiona as they entered. She was wearing a wireless earpiece and seemed to be listening to someone.

"I don't think so," she said curtly to the person on the other end of the phone, and motioned for Joybird to approach. Fiona slipped silently out the door and shut it behind her.

Joybird lowered herself into a black microfiber chair while taking in the stark decor of the office. Donna sat behind a gleaming white desk in front of bright white walls, which were adorned with massive photos of famous faces, artistically captured in black and white. The left side of the room had a wall-to-wall bookcase, the spines conspicuously vibrant in the monochromatic room. Donna wore a dandelion-colored blazer with military-style epaulets, and Joybird wondered if she was consciously trying to project the image of a couture army general. Behind her, the skyline of Manhattan stood at attention.

"No, Nick," Donna said to her caller. "We're not at that stage yet . . . Yes . . . Okay, I have an appointment. Email me." She tapped at her earpiece to end the call and turned her attention to Joybird.

"So," she said, "you're Johnny Martin's daughter."

◆ ◆ ◆

Sid was growing impatient. Where the hell were all the workers—chained to their desks? At last, he saw a young woman slip out a door and into the bathroom across the hall. He tried to strategize what he might do when she came out. Would it spook her if he called out?

Then a young man pushing a mail cart rounded the corner, and Sid sighed, relieved.

"Excuse me," he said to the kid. "Can you help me? I left the waiting room to find a bathroom, and now I'm locked out."

"What?" the young man said, trying to catch up.

"Donna Sebastiani," Sid explained, holding up the flowers. "Do you mind?"

At the mention of Donna's name, the kid's face went cold in fear, and he ran to unlock the door faster than a man dodging a bullet.

◆ ◆ ◆

"What a vivid color," Joybird chirped, pointing to Donna's yellow-orange blazer. "You're like the sun itself!" Donna's expression stayed hard, and Joybird continued, already flustered. "Thank you so much for seeing me. I know you're busy, but it's going to mean so much to my father."

Donna folded her hands and sat back. Up close, her beauty seemed chiseled, unreal. Only the small lines forming around her eyes and lips added humanity. "Is that so?" she said.

It sounded like a challenge—as if the woman didn't believe her—and Joybird felt her pulse quicken. "You know, he's had a crush on you for all these years."

Donna laughed. "Johnny Martin? Cocky Johnny Martin had a crush on me?"

"I don't know if he ever stopped thinking about you."

"Oh, please," Donna said. "That's a whole lot of crap."

This was worse than Joybird had expected. "No!" she insisted. "It isn't. Trust me on this. Dad's carried a torch for you his whole life."

"Listen, I don't know what kind of game you two are playing, but I promise there's nothing I can or would do for his career."

Joybird tried to take a deep breath, but her lungs were unyielding. This woman had made up her mind that this whole thing was an opportunistic setup. "This isn't about his career. I swear!"

"You think I don't know what happened to Sid Marcus? Trust me, I hear everything. The only reason I agreed to see you was to let you pass this little tidbit on to him: *His career is over.*"

"This has nothing to do with his career," Joybird said. "Honestly. He was telling me about this party at high school. He said he kissed you and never had the courage to ask you out. He's regretted it ever since."

"You think I'm an idiot?"

"Of course not!"

"Listen to me—I've got hyperthymesia. You know what that is?"

"I . . . I don't."

"It means I can remember practically every damned thing that ever happened to me, and I recall that party with perfect clarity."

"So you remember the kiss?"

"Oh, I remember the kiss, all right. I also remember telling Johnny I had a crush on Michael Wilde—a bass player who was at the party. You know what he said?"

Joybird shrugged.

"He said, 'Let's make him jealous.' Then we went outside, sat on the stoop, and smoked a joint. And that's when your father pounced."

"What . . . what do you mean 'pounced'?" Joybird asked, getting panicky. She thought about men like Brett Kavanaugh. About her father's problem with boundaries. If this was one of those stories, she didn't think she'd be able to handle it.

"I mean he kissed me!"

Joybird paused, trying to understand. "Is that all?"

Donna's nostrils flared. "I was *high*. And he knew I had a crush on another boy."

"Maybe he thought he was winning you over."

"Maybe he thought he could get a girl stoned and take advantage."

"But if all he did was kiss you," Joybird protested, certain the woman's outrage was completely unreasonable. She could imagine two teenage kids sitting together and sharing a joint, getting along. At some point, the smitten boy leans in for a kiss. It all sounded so wholesome—like a Norman Rockwell painting, but with weed.

"There was more," Donna said.

Joybird's palms went damp. "More?"

"After that, we went inside and sat on the sofa, and that son of a bitch put his arm around me in front of God and everyone."

This was getting weirder by the second, and Joybird blinked, trying to make sense of it. What could be more innocent than a besotted boy putting his arm around a girl?

"Is that what you're mad about?" she asked, not sure she understood why the woman was outraged at something so benign.

"Everyone thought we were together! It ruined my chances with Michael Wilde. My whole life could have been different! Do you know he won a Grammy?"

It seemed like a joke. But no, the woman actually believed what she was saying—the rage and paranoia were palpable. Now Joybird understood what was going on. Donna Sebastiani had a thing for musicians. Also, she was batshit crazy. The trait her father had interpreted as strength had morphed into . . . what? Narcissism? Psychosis?

"This all happened decades ago," Joybird said.

"So?"

"So it's a long time to hold a grudge, don't you think?"

Donna stood. "This meeting is over."

"Wait!" Joybird said, not ready to give up. She had made a promise to her father and needed to see this through, mental illness or not. "You don't understand. He's in love with you. He spent his whole life regretting that he didn't ask you out after that party. He's been married three times, trying to find another Donna DeLuca. This has nothing to do with his career. You have to believe me. He's been thinking about you for more than forty years. Will you at least meet with him? Please?"

"I wouldn't meet with that bastard if he was Brad fucking Pitt."

Joybird heard a sound behind her and turned to see the door burst open. There—holding a bouquet the size of a large toddler—was her heartsick old man.

"Who the hell are you?" Donna asked.

It was happening. He was face to face with her, breathing the same air. Sid smiled, ecstatic.

"It's me, Donna. It's Johnny!"

He studied her face—her perfect, beautiful face—waiting for recognition, followed by a delighted laugh. But she just said, "Get out of here before I call security."

"Donna, please," he begged. "Don't you remember me?"

"That's the problem," she said. "I do."

"I don't understand," he said, trying to get his bearings. She seemed so angry. So very, very angry.

"You ruined my life, you son of a bitch."

"How . . . how did I ruin your life?" he stammered.

"Michael Wilde," she spat.

Confused, he glanced over at Joybird, who shrugged. "Michael Wilde?" he said to Donna.

"Don't pretend you don't remember."

Joybird laid a hand on his arm. "I think we should go, Dad," she said.

"Can't we just talk?" he asked Donna.

"Get out," she seethed.

"I brought you flowers," he told her.

"You really have some goddamned nerve," she said. "I'm not falling for any of this. Take that ridiculous bouquet and get the hell out of my office, you pathetic, talentless hack."

Sid stood frozen in place, trying to understand what was going on. "Donna," he pleaded.

Her jaw went as hard as ice. "Leave," she said through her teeth, and at last, he did.

Chapter 51

Joybird lingered behind in Donna's office, compelled to stand up for her father. The formidable woman came out from behind her desk and took a step toward Joybird, who balled her fists to keep herself from disassociating.

"You know," she said to Donna, "for all these years, my father's been kicking himself for being too scared to ask you on a date. But now, I don't think it was fear at all. I think it was self-preservation."

Donna folded her arms. "What is that supposed to mean?"

"It means you're cruel." It was one of the boldest things Joybird had ever said to another person. She held her breath, waiting for the world to come crashing down around her. But the only thing that happened was a subtle shift in the craziness behind Donna's eyes. And just like that, her aura of invincibility slipped away, and Joybird could see that she was just a bitter, old narcissist, terrified of having her self-image challenged.

"I may be a bitch," Donna said, looking Joybird up and down, "but you dress like shit."

Joybird shook her head. The woman wasn't just mean—she was hopeless and petty.

So that was the end of it. Joybird knew she had a tendency to see silver linings that looked dull gray to other people, but at this moment, she felt very grateful her father had spent a lifetime avoiding this woman.

As Joybird left Donna's office and dashed into the waiting room, she tried to figure out how to convince her father that he had dodged a particularly explosive bullet, but he wasn't there. She ran out the glass doors, down the corridor, and all the way to the elevator. He was gone.

She tried to tell herself he'd be standing outside on the pavement waiting for her, but she knew it was unlikely. She pictured him heading to the nearest bar and getting so drunk her worst nightmares would come true.

When she got outside the building, she saw something that made her heart sink. The huge wrapped bouquet was lying in the middle of the sidewalk. Joybird approached and stared at it, then peered up and down the block.

A man unloading cartons from a truck clocked her concern and called out to her, "You looking for the old guy who dropped those?"

"I am!" she cried.

He pointed up the street. "I think he got on the subway."

The subway. Joybird was bereft. She didn't know where he was headed, but she understood he was ready to derail.

Chapter 52

Joybird sat on a bench in the courtyard in front of Donna's office building and sent her father a text, which he didn't answer. Then she called Betty and explained the whole scene in Donna DeLuca's office, up to the point where her father walked out and disappeared. Betty promised she would try to reach him.

"But what should I do in the meantime?" Joybird pleaded.

"There's nothing you *can* do, kiddo."

She got off the phone and sat for several more minutes on the hard bench, her butt getting colder and colder until she had no choice but to get up and trudge to the parking lot. As she walked, Joybird realized it was probably a good thing she had agreed to a session with Riley that afternoon. It would distract her from worrying about her father.

Once she got in the car and started heading downtown toward the Brooklyn Bridge, Joybird found herself navigating toward the Merrill Lynch building, where Devon worked. And then there she was, idling in her little blue Honda again amid all those gleaming black SUVs—just like the first time they met.

She took out her phone and composed a text: Met with Donna. It didn't go well. Thought you'd want to know

Instead of hitting send, she stared down at it, wondering how terrible she would feel if he didn't respond. At last, she decided it was worth the risk, and tapped the button.

Almost immediately, she saw the dots indicating he was composing a reply. And then there it was: You ok?

She clasped the phone to her chest. He still cared. She looked down at the message and typed her response: No. Then she thought for a moment and added: I'm parked in front of your building

She hit send and waited. Then waited some more. Joybird saw no indication he was typing a reply. Maybe he was coming downstairs? She shut off her engine and stared at the glass doors to the building. After several more minutes, she asked herself how long it could take to ride the elevator down from his office. At last, she had to face the truth. He was ignoring her. Joybird reached into the back of the car, where she kept her tissues, and blew her nose. It was all too much. She needed to get out of there.

Unfortunately, she'd been boxed in by a Land Rover. She gave a polite honk, then a less polite one, and was about to tap her horn for a third time when she saw the door of the building open. And there he was—coatless despite the cold weather—in his perfect suit with his perfect posture and his ridiculous glasses.

Joybird grabbed another tissue and tried to tidy her face before he approached. Then the passenger door opened, and he slid inside, a whoosh of cold air following him.

"I didn't think you were coming," she said.

Devon slammed the door closed, his body rigid with tension. "I was in the middle of something with Bryant," he said. "I got out as fast as I could."

"Are *you* okay?" she asked.

"Not even a little."

She studied his face and saw about ten miles of pain in his eyes. "Is it work . . . or me?"

"Both."

"Devon, I'm so sorry. I never wanted to hurt you."

He stared out the window, unable to look her in the eye. "I know."

"Do you think you can forgive me?" she asked.

"I'm trying," he said, and that was all it took. After one sputtering inhale, she broke. Everything she'd been holding back burst forth, and she bent at the waist, heaving great sobs.

Devon gently rubbed her back. "Babe," he said, and it was so tender it made her cry even harder.

"Do you want to tell me what happened with your father?"

She did. She wanted to tell him everything. But it took several more minutes for her to quiet her sobbing before she could get it out. Then she told him the whole story, mindful of the ticking clock, because he had to get back to work and she had only a few minutes before she'd need to head across the bridge for Riley.

He clucked sympathetically as she filled in nearly every detail, including her inability to find her father.

"I know you're worried about him," Devon said.

"There's nothing I can do."

"There isn't," he agreed.

Joybird was emotionally exhausted from the subject of her father and Donna. "Tell me about you," she said. "It sounds like you're having a bad day at work."

"Bryant is being even more of a dick than usual. I can't do anything right. He always makes me feel like I'm one step away from losing that promotion, and maybe even my job."

"I don't like that guy," she muttered, feeling protective.

"Me neither," he said. "But I'm hoping this surprise party will turn his mood around."

"That's tonight?" she recalled.

"Five thirty sharp," he said. "His wife took the whole penthouse at the Davida Hotel for happy hour and gave us very specific instructions."

Joybird felt a heaviness in her chest as she looked down, pushing at her cuticles, waiting for what might come next.

"I really want you to be there," he said.

"You do?" She closed her eyes as she absorbed this revelation. Devon was still in this with her, and that meant everything. The problem was, she'd need to get past her anxiety about facing a room full of Milton Floyds. It was a dangerous hill to climb, especially when she was still reeling from the trauma of her meeting with Donna Sebastiani, and worried her father might be drunk and suicidal.

Her phone pinged to remind her about Riley's appointment.

"Can I count on you?" he said. "I'm under so much pressure from Bryant, and I think if I show up with you, it'll make a statement, you know? Please, Joybird. I need you."

"I understand," she said, feeling his pain in every cell. "But can I just think about it for a little while?"

"What is there to think about? I'm asking you to do this one thing for me."

"Please," she said, "I've got to get Riley now. I'll call you afterward."

He said nothing for a long minute as they sat side by side, an eddy of pain swirling around them. Joybird's appointment reminder pinged again, and Devon sighed, expelling so much dismay the car filled with the weight of despair. Then he opened the door and left.

Joybird didn't want to move. She let her head roll back as she gripped the steering wheel, her eyes closed. How had she made such a terrible mess of things?

The car behind her honked, jolting Joybird from her reverie. She looked at the clock, and realized there wasn't another minute to waste. Riley would be waiting for her. Joybird started the car, but before she pulled out, she rolled down her window and looked back at Devon walking toward the building, his posture so defeated it fractured her heart. And just like that, she knew she couldn't do this to him.

"Devon!" she called.

He stopped and turned toward her.

Joybird took a sharp inhale, the cold air a shock to her lungs. "I'll do it," she said. "I'll be there."

He stood straighter, a smile blooming across his face. "You will?" he asked, sounding like he couldn't believe his good fortune, and Joybird knew she'd made the right decision.

"Five thirty sharp?" she confirmed.

"You can't be late," he said.

She understood. If she wrecked the surprise, it would ruin the party . . . and maybe even his career.

"I promise," she said.

◆ ◆ ◆

The traffic on the Brooklyn Bridge was maddening. When it came to a dead stop, she took the opportunity to dictate a text to Riley.

Running a few minutes late

There was no response, and Joybird figured the girl was just too busy making out with Carter to bother replying. But when she pulled up in front of the school, there was no sign of her. She sent another text.

I'm here

Still nothing. Joybird scanned the kids milling around the entrance, until she saw a familiar figure way off in the distance. It looked like Carter, though she couldn't be sure. He was having an intimate conversation with a petite, dark-haired girl. She pulled on his jacket flirtatiously, and when he stepped forward, Joybird detected a limp. It had to be him.

"Carter!" Joybird called out the window, but he didn't hear. She tried again, using his nickname. "Truck!"

At that, he looked up and said something to the girl before stepping forward.

"Where's Riley?" Joybird called.

He shrugged. "I heard she left early."

Left early? Joybird scanned her messages to make sure she hadn't missed anything. She texted Corinne.

I'm at Riley's school but she's not here

Seconds later, Corinne responded: We just got to the hospital

Joybird typed back several question marks as her imagination ran away with her. Why would Corinne be at the hospital? Was Riley okay? *Chill,* she coached herself. It could be nothing. But a wave of nausea hit, and in the five minutes it took for Corinne to respond, Joybird's heart beat several thousand times. At last, a text came through.

Riley took pills. We're at Lenox Hill.

Pills? Joybird fought a wave of fevered fear as her scalp prickled in alarm. But she couldn't waste any time indulging her anxiety. She screeched out of the spot and headed back to the bridge in the direction of the hospital, praying the girl could be saved.

Chapter 53

The traffic going back into Manhattan was almost as slow as it had been in the other direction. Joybird put her phone on speaker and called Betty to tell her what was going on, but it went to voicemail.

"Riley's at Lenox Hill," she said through tears. "She tried to . . . she tried to kill herself." She paused, feeling like she was drowning, because the next part was so hard to say it threatened to pull her under. "It's my fault, Betty. I'm the one who coached her to flirt with that boy and . . . oh, god. I'm on my way there now. But what if . . ."

Joybird couldn't even finish the sentence, and by the time she reached the hospital, it felt like a lifetime had gone by. She parked illegally and ran into the emergency entrance, jockeying through the crowd to reach the reception desk.

"I'm looking for Riley Wilbanks," she said breathlessly.

"Are you a family member?" the woman asked.

"No, but . . . I just spoke to her mother and . . . I . . . never mind." Joybird moved aside to lean against the wall and text Corinne.

I'm in the ER waiting room. How is she?

Joybird stared down at her phone, her hands shaking as she waited for a response. At last, a message came through: Don't know yet.

What happened? Joybird wrote.

Corinne responded: Carter broke up with her so she took a cab to my apartment. When I came home, I found her on the bathroom floor.

Joybird pictured the scene—Riley raiding Corinne's medicine cabinet, which probably had enough controlled substances to kill half of Manhattan. She imagined the girl with a water bottle, throwing pills down her throat until she got so sleepy that she sank to the cold, hard floor.

Joybird began to pace wildly. *Please,* she thought. *Please. Let them save her.*

Lowering herself into one of the hard plastic chairs, Joybird played out what might happen next. Riley awaking with her mother, father, and stepmother at her bedside. Or a doctor waylaying the stricken parents in the hallway to say *We did everything we could.*

Joybird stayed glued to the chair, losing track of time. That is, until an aristocratic couple pushed their way into the chaos of the ER waiting room and stopped, as if expecting a maître d' to lead them to a table. It was Deidre and Milton Floyd. The wife tightened the belt of her Burberry coat. The husband locked eyes with Joybird. He whispered something to his wife, and beckoned Joybird over. She took a deep breath and approached.

"What's going on?" Milton demanded.

"I don't know. They won't let me in."

"This is your fault," Deidre muttered, dabbing her nose with a tissue.

Joybird blinked. "Excuse me?"

"You heard me," the woman said, glaring at her with so much animus it made Joybird tremble. "It's your fault—this whole mess."

Joybird nodded, her gut clenching. "I know," she choked out. "But . . . I think we all share some responsibility, don't you?"

"How dare you!" Milton Floyd said, wagging a finger in her face. "That girl is my granddaughter."

Joybird heard someone call her name, and looked up to see Betty enter the room. Only she wasn't alone.

"Dad?" Joybird cried. "Oh my god, Dad!" She ran and fell into his arms. "You're safe."

◆ ◆ ◆

Sid held the back of his daughter's head as she sobbed. "Shh, Birdie," he said. "It's okay. I'm all right."

"How's the kid?" Betty asked.

"I don't know yet," Joybird said. "We're waiting for news." She introduced them to the Floyds, who fell into practiced gentility before heading off to see if they could get an update. Joybird ushered her father and Betty to some empty seats, then filled them in on what little she knew.

"She's young," Betty said. "Kids are resilient." She shrugged, as if apologizing for offering such a banal sentiment.

Sid, of course, wasn't having it. "Please," he said, because he didn't think unrealistic optimism would help his daughter get through this mess.

Betty glared a warning. "Not now," she said through her teeth.

"I'm just saying that sometimes people die and it's no one's fault."

Joybird's face crumpled. "Michael Jackson," she whispered, her voice quavering.

Sid leaned in. "What did you say, Birdie?"

She was so overwhelmed, it took her a moment to respond. "I just mean . . . sometimes it *is* someone's fault."

"Stop it now," her father said to her. "You're not God."

"Neither was that doctor who shot Michael Jackson full of propofol."

He stood, getting angry, and walked in a quick circle, as if trying to figure out how to protect his daughter from herself. "You didn't shoot the kid full of propofol!" he insisted.

"Daddy, please," she said, clearly upset that he was getting so agitated. "Sit."

But he couldn't sit. He was too wound up, too defensive on her behalf. Joybird would never hurt anyone. Never! She was the most gentle, compassionate, tenderhearted person he'd ever known, and she didn't need to blame herself for this. "Nothing about this is your fault, you hear me? Nothing!"

Before Joybird could respond, the Floyds approached and Milton said, "They want us to wait out here."

"It's touch and go," Deidre squeaked out. She looked so diminished that Sid felt a deep pang of sympathy. He could imagine he'd feel the exact same way if anything ever happened to Joybird. He scraped over two chairs and invited the couple to sit with them.

The man thanked him, so Sid leaned in, assuming they would have some kind of father-to-father connection. "Would you please tell my daughter this is not her fault, " he said.

The man bristled. "I'll do no such thing."

Surprised, Sid sat up straighter. "You can't seriously blame Joybird for this," he said, getting angry.

"Everything was fine until my daughter mistook this . . . this *driver* for a therapist."

Furious, Sid was ready to leap from his chair. "You want a daughter to blame?" he said. "Look a little closer to home."

The indignant patriarch stood. The pugnacious TV writer stood. They stared each other down. And though Milton Floyd towered over him, Sid wanted the son of a bitch to take a swing so he'd have an excuse to break his nose.

Before that could happen, Joybird jumped up and inserted herself between the two furious men. "Sit down, you two. For god's sake!"

The men were caught off guard, and both took a step back. Just then, Joybird pivoted toward the swinging door and called out, "Corinne!"

They all turned to look as the trembling woman entered the waiting room.

"Darling," said Deidre, "how is she? How is Riley?"

"She's awake," Corinne said, her expression stoic, though her eyes were rimmed in red. "They said she's going to be okay."

Her parents gave her something that resembled an embrace. Joybird fell into Betty's arms, and then into her father's. He held tight as he felt the muscles of her back relax in relief. His sweet girl.

"Can we see her?" Deidre asked.

"Not yet," Corinne said, and turned to Joybird. "She's asking for you."

Milton Floyd's face turned so red Sid thought he might drop dead of a stroke right there. "What!" he demanded.

"I'm sorry, Daddy," Corinne said. "She needs Joybird."

Joybird dragged a chair to the bedside, while Riley's parents and stepmom waited outside the room. The girl was wan, her lips pale and chapped.

"How do you feel?" Joybird asked.

"Like shit."

Riley looked so small and young in the hospital bed, an IV line threaded into her thin white arm. Joybird patted her hand. "They said you're going to be okay."

Riley shook her head. "Carter broke up with me."

"I know."

She sniffled. "Can I have a tissue?"

Joybird reached for the box and handed it to her. Riley put it on her lap, wiped her nose, then pushed the button to raise the back of the bed. "I don't know how I go on without him."

"Heartbreak sucks," Joybird said. "But it gets easier, I promise."

"I wanted to die . . . but I also didn't," Riley admitted.

"I understand."

"Mostly," Riley continued, "I wanted to hurt Carter. He went back with Lily. Can you believe it?"

She could. She'd seen them together. "That must be painful."

"I wanted him to feel so bad. I wanted them all to feel bad."

"Your friends?" Joybird pressed.

"And Mom. Dad. Emily. Milton and Deidre."

"Isabella?" Joybird asked, remembering the name of Riley's baby sister.

"Not Isabella. I guess it would have sucked for her if I died."

It would have sucked for everyone, Joybird thought, but knew the girl would have a hard time believing it. So she just said, "They all love you."

"They're really fucked up."

"I know."

"I got dealt a pretty crappy hand," Riley said. "I mean, for a privileged white kid."

Joybird couldn't argue. "I'm sorry about that," she said, understanding how alone the kid felt in her misery. "But you know, lots of people get dealt crappy hands."

"You?" Riley asked.

Joybird shrugged. The girl knew absolutely nothing about her. "My dad left when I was six—then two years later, my mom died, so . . ."

Riley sat up straighter. "You shitting me? I thought you grew up on a unicorn farm or something."

Joybird laughed. "I've needed to create my own unicorn farm."

"Where nobody can hurt you?"

"I still get hurt, Riley," she said.

They sat quietly for several minutes, listening to the bustle outside the room. There was an announcement calling a doctor to the trauma bay.

"What's going to happen to me?" Riley asked.

"You'll probably see a bunch of doctors and get all pissed off and think nothing is helping. But every day you'll feel just a tiny bit better." She hoped she was right. It would, she knew, be a long haul for this kid.

"I'm tired."

"Okay," Joybird said. She patted Riley's pink hair. "I'll see you soon."

She left and joined up with Corinne, who walked her back out to the waiting room, where the Floyds avoided eye contact. They simply clocked her presence, then followed Corinne back to Riley's bedside.

"How did she seem?" Betty asked when the three of them were alone.

"About how I expected."

"You think she'll be okay?" her father asked.

"I don't know. Maybe. It's not going to be easy for her."

Sid looked at his daughter, his eyes soft with sympathy. "You can't blame yourself, Birdie. I mean it."

"Of course I can."

Sid studied her long and hard as if trying to figure something out. "Did I do this to you?" he finally said.

"That's immaterial," Betty piped in, and they both looked at her. She addressed Joybird. "The problem is, you think you have no value if you're not fixing people. But you do, kiddo."

"This broad knows what she's talking about," Sid added.

Joybird nodded, taking it in, realizing they were right. She'd spent her whole life trying to make people happy, and there was a certain desperation to it. It was something she needed to work on.

"Thank you," she said. "It's just hard not to worry about people."

"You're allowed to worry," her father said. "Just don't take it on as your personal responsibility."

"But the whole thing with Donna . . ."

"Not your fault," he said quickly. "She's a crazyass bitch."

"When you left, I thought you'd go straight to a bar, and . . . I don't know."

He nodded. "Betty talked me down. She met me at that bar in Grand Central. I was about to get on a train to Connecticut."

"What for?" Joybird asked.

"I'm not even sure," he said. "My head was spinning. I thought if I took a trip to Paxton and walked around, I'd be able to figure it all out.

Then Betty showed up. I guess I wanted her to talk me out of boarding the train, and she did. We both decided I'd already wasted too many years of my life obsessing about that psycho."

"So it's over?" Joybird asked.

Sid and Betty looked at each other, and Joybird caught something pass between them. "What's going on?" she asked.

"We need to tell her," Betty said to Sid, and he nodded.

"Joybird," he began, leaning in, "Betty and I think you need to get on with your life, without your old man underfoot."

"What do you mean?"

"I'm moving in with her, Birdie."

Joybird could barely process what she was hearing. She looked from her father to Betty, who took his hand.

"We've been getting it on for a little while now," Betty told her.

"Hooking up?" she asked, for clarification.

"At first, we were just fucking, but . . ." Sid shrugged. "She's all right. She's grown on me."

"He's a total pain in the ass," Betty said, "but he amuses me."

"And we get each other," Sid added.

Betty nodded. "And the sex is—"

"Stop!" Joybird said, covering her ears. "I don't want to hear this."

"I know I wasn't exactly the best roommate," her father said, as if she'd be glad to be rid of him.

In truth, she'd loved having him there and had fretted about losing him again. But she never could have foreseen he'd be right upstairs. It felt like the fulfillment of a wish she hadn't even known she'd had.

"Plus," her father said, "now you and Wall Street can make all the noise you want."

Joybird swallowed hard. "I think I messed that up," she muttered, realizing Devon had no idea what was going on. She had never even called, and he was probably at the party right now, thinking she didn't give a damn about him.

"I'm sure you can still fix it," Betty said.

"He wanted me to go with him to a surprise party for his boss tonight."

"So?" her father said. "What's keeping you?"

"Everyone has to be there by five thirty, or they'll ruin the surprise."

"It's only ten after five," Betty said. "I think you can make it."

Joybird thought about the location of the party, twenty-five blocks away. If there was no traffic, it wouldn't be a problem. But it was rush hour.

"I don't know," Joybird said, even as she realized it was worth a shot. Because if she showed up before Rick Bryant arrived, Devon would pull her into his arms, elated she'd kept her promise. It might not completely make up for her mistake with Noah, but it would go a long way. She took a deep breath, visualizing her happy ending.

Without even thinking about it, Sid reached out and tied the scarf that was draped around her neck—a gesture of fatherly affection that seemed to surprise even him.

"Go," he said to her, and she did.

Chapter 54

Joybird bolted out of the hospital toward her car, certain she'd have a ticket for parking illegally. But it didn't matter. Riley was alive. Her father had made a happy landing, despite Donna DeLuca. And Devon was about to learn he could count on her.

There was only one problem. Her car wasn't there. That's when Joybird realized she had parked in a tow-away zone. She looked up the street, and could have sworn she saw the backside of her sky-blue Honda being pulled away.

Now what could she do? Joybird pictured getting into a yellow taxi, barking out the address and yelling, "Step on it," like they did in old-timey movies. But the driver would only inch out into the creeping traffic, with no motivation to weave and honk and bully his way through the mean streets of the Upper East Side.

But of course, there was a better choice: the subway. Joybird could hop on a number six train and reach the Davida Hotel in minutes. In fact, it was a much faster option than driving. She almost wanted to thank the Department of Transportation for towing her car, because now she had an actual shot at arriving on time.

She ran all the way to the subway entrance and dashed down the stairs, panting. Joybird had the subway app open on her phone before she even reached the turnstile, where a clot of people stood trying to get through.

"What's going on?" Joybird asked.

"The OMNY readers are down," someone called. "You need a MetroCard."

A MetroCard? Joybird hadn't used one in so long. She glanced over her shoulder at the kiosks where they were sold, and a long line had formed. Panicked, she pulled out her wallet, hoping she still had one in her purse. And there it was, like a golden ticket.

The turnstile line moved slowly, but at last it was her turn to swipe her card. She ran it through, and the display prompted her to **PLEASE SWIPE AGAIN**. She did so, then got an unwelcome message: **INSUFFICIENT FUNDS**.

Crazed with frustration, she got in line at the kiosk and finally made her way to the subway platform just as a train pulled out. *Damn.* There would be another one in just a few minutes, but the clock was ticking.

As she waited, Joybird refused to check the time. What good would it do? At this point, it would take a miracle for her to reach the party before Bryant arrived. And what then? She supposed she could arrive late and miss the surprise. But by that point, Devon would have fallen into despair, and she'd be right back where she started from. She considered trying to text him, but decided that telling him she'd be late would make him even more anxious, not to mention utterly disappointed in her. Eventually, she hoped, she'd be able to explain herself. But there was no way to cover it all in a text.

Hurry, Joybird thought, staring down the tunnel. *Hurry!*

At last, the train pulled into the station, and Joybird elbowed her way on, sweating and desperate. When she reached the Fifty-First Street Station, she exited the subway car and hurried up the stairs heading out to the street. The sky was darkening now, and she glanced around to get her bearings. She ran the two blocks to the hotel, pushed her way inside, and found the elevator leading to the penthouse. Just before the doors pinged closed, an elegant-looking couple entered. He was on the short side, with a big head and slicked hair. The woman—an attractive redhead—held on to his arm. Could this be Devon's boss, Rick Bryant, and his wife? And was Joybird in danger of ruining the surprise? That would be catastrophic. Her jaw tensed as a hard knot formed in her throat.

Joybird told herself the odds were against it. But when she looked at the time—five forty-five—she realized the odds were, in fact, a disturbingly safe bet.

She backed into the corner of the elevator, trying to make herself as invisible as a random stranger who just happened to be headed to the same place. The woman glanced over her shoulder with a tight smile that seemed to say *I don't know who you are, but when I said 5:30 sharp, I meant it. Now keep your damned mouth shut.*

Joybird gave her a nod, and felt a pulse throbbing in her neck. She took a quiet breath, trying to calm herself.

"I don't know why we couldn't just go to Alberto's," the man complained to the woman. He sounded bitter, querulous. Every bit as bad-tempered as Devon had said.

"It's a big birthday," his wife told him. "I wanted to do something special."

He grunted. "Do you know how much pressure I'm under—with Cliff, with the department? Not sure I can even stomach what they charge for a bottle of wine here."

"It'll be good to relax," she said.

"You really expect me to relax?"

"Rick," she pleaded.

"No," he said. "I mean it. I can't. Let's just go."

"Honey—"

"We're leaving," he said irritably, and reached for the elevator's lobby button. "I'm not in the mood."

The woman looked panicked and desperate as she tried to grab his hand.

"Moods change," said Joybird loudly, and the couple whirled around to look at her.

"Excuse me?" The man sounded affronted.

Joybird knew that inserting herself in their business was a risk. After all, the wife had already shot her a dirty look. But at this point, there didn't seem to be anything to lose, because if the man refused to change his mind about leaving, his wife would need to spoil the surprise in order to get him to the party.

"I'm just saying, this woman clearly loves you and wants to do something special for you to show it."

"I don't see how it's any of your business."

"It's not, but—"

"No offense, lady, but maybe you should shut up."

Joybird wanted to laugh at his attempt to intimidate her with his bluster. Not that it wouldn't have worked with her on nearly any other day of her life. In fact, on any other day of her life, Joybird might have started disassociating about now. But she had just stood up to Milton Floyd. Hell, she had stood up to Donna DeLuca! She was not about to back down from this important confrontation.

"And maybe you should let her in," she said.

He snorted. "What are you—an expert on my marriage?"

"It's just that you seem stressed," Joybird said.

At that, the man appeared to deflate, looking overwhelmed. "An understatement," he admitted.

"And you think leaving will make you feel better?"

He glanced at his wife, who shrugged. "She has a point," the woman said.

Rick Bryant seemed to soften. "I just don't see how an overpriced dinner is going to make me feel better."

"Let's give it a shot," his wife said, and at that, the doors opened to the penthouse—a chic, atmospherically lit space crowded with well-dressed bodies.

"Surprise!" they shouted in unison, and Devon's boss grabbed his large head in shock as he stepped into the room. For a moment, he seemed frozen, but then he bent over, laughing. When he finally stood, he looked into his wife's pretty face.

"I'm such a shit," he told her. "I don't know how you put up with me."

"Me neither," she said, grinning.

Amid the laughter and cheers, Joybird remained in the elevator, trying to see past the couple into the crowd. The doors dinged and began to close, but she blocked them with her hand as she scanned the assemblage of men and women raising champagne flutes. Where was Devon? It was hard to make out the faces, but then she saw a glint of light reflect off the glasses of someone pushing his way through the mass.

She moved to the threshold, using her body to keep the elevator doors open as she waited for him to see her. When their eyes met, she held her breath. Was he angry that she'd arrived late? Furious that she hadn't called? Discouraged and disappointed?

He looked confused at first. Then ten different expressions crossed his face before settling on the one Joybird had hoped to see. He smiled. But it wasn't just any smile. It was the one he'd worn in bed, after they'd made love and he rested the tip of his finger in the center of the butterfly hanging down from her neck.

At the time, she'd thought no one had ever given her a more beautiful gift. But now, as she stepped forward and pulled off her scarf—aware that the tiny jewels caught the light and splintered it in every direction—she knew he'd given her something far more precious.

"You're here," he said, taking her in his arms.

"Sorry I'm late," Joybird said. "When I went to—"

"Don't," he said gently. "Not now. Let me get you a glass of champagne."

She knew he was right. There would be plenty of time to talk about what had happened with Riley, with her father and Betty, and most importantly, between the two of them. For now, there was celebrating to do.

Later, when the party was breaking up—the crowd thinning as relaxed and sated revelers grabbed purses and coats and headed for the door—Devon and Joybird were still on the dance floor, holding tight.

The DJ had been playing one slow song after another, and the night felt magical. Joybird melted into him and wished the feeling could go on forever.

"I guess we should leave," she said into Devon's shoulder.

He kissed the top of her head and pulled her in tighter. "I need another minute."

She understood that he felt the same way she did, savoring this bubble of time, floating blissfully between their past and their future, where they'd need to find their way to a place of unfettered trust and forgiveness.

When the music began to fade, with Louis Armstrong softly finishing his reverie about this wonderful world, they pulled apart at last.

Devon took her hand, and they walked toward Rick Bryant and his wife, Hope, who were saying goodbye to the guests as they left. Since the couple had been densely surrounded for the entire party, it was the first chance Devon got to introduce them to Joybird.

"What a lovely name," Hope said, warmly shaking Joybird's hand. "It suits you."

"Yours too!" Joybird gushed, delighted by the compliment.

"I guess I should thank you for what you said in the elevator," Rick told her.

His wife nodded. "We both should."

"I was happy to help," Joybird said.

Devon gave her hand an affectionate squeeze. "What happened in the elevator?" he asked the three of them.

Rick laughed. "I guess you two have a lot to talk about."

Devon put his arm around Joybird and brought her closer. "Always," he said.

They left the party then, and walked out into the cool enchantment of a Manhattan night, excitement whooshing through the streets like it was in a hurry to meet the next day. But Joybird was happy to amble slowly and gratefully. She hooked her arm through Devon's and leaned into him.

"Where's your car?" he asked, looking around.

It occurred to Joybird she had no idea. Tomorrow, she'd need to go online and figure out where it had been towed. For now, they needed another way forward. So she led Devon toward the subway to catch a train that would rumble and lurch through the darkness, carrying them into the light of their destination.

And as they traveled—the future as inevitable as the sun rising resplendently over a seedy New York City impound lot—she told him everything that had happened in the few hours since they'd talked in her car, starting with Riley and ending with her attempts to reach the party by five thirty.

"I'm sorry," she said, as they sat side by side in the subway car. "I didn't want to disappoint you again."

"I know."

"You must have given up on me."

Devon looked away. "For a hot minute there, I thought I might," he said, and she understood they weren't talking about the party anymore.

"But somehow," he continued, "I just knew everything would work out."

The subway screeched to a stop, and they exited. As the couple ascended the stairs toward the fresh night, Devon stopped to inhale, as if enjoying the scent of the wind. Joybird breathed it in, too, eager to share the experience, and she understood why it pleased him. The air smelled as clean and familiar as optimism.

Epilogue

When the call came in, Betty was out—teaching a journalism class at the New School in downtown Manhattan. She'd finagled a part-time position for Sid, too, and so far he didn't hate it. There were even one or two kids in his TV-writing class with a pinch of promise. The money, of course, was shit, which was why this call was so important. He just needed one last break so he could leave his sweet girl a nest egg. It wouldn't make up for all the years he'd been a miserable father, but it was something.

"We love the concept, Sid," said Joel Wallace, the new comedy development guy at Sony TV. "Really, so fresh. Just what we're looking for. What do you say we schedule a Zoom meeting about the next step?"

"Why not!" Sid answered, a little too buoyantly, and hoped it sounded more enthusiastic than desperate. He took a quiet breath. *Do not blow this,* he told himself.

"I just have a few notes, if you don't mind."

Notes. At this stage, it wasn't a good sign. It meant the sale was contingent on jumping through hoops and barking on command. But Sid had run this obstacle course before and could be as obedient as a border collie.

"I'm all ears," he said, and listened carefully as the pseudocreative executive proceeded to fleece his painstakingly constructed pilot script.

He'd written a modern intergenerational comedy featuring a father and daughter with such opposite personalities it became a sort of updated iteration of *The Odd Couple*. It was, of course, inspired by the past year of his life, only instead of a washed-up comedy writer, the father who landed on his daughter's Brooklyn Heights doorstep was a conservative congressman who'd been caught with his hand in the cookie jar and lost everything. And instead of a life coach, the daughter was a Reiki healer who worked out of her apartment, allowing a comedy-rich stream of kooky guest characters to weave in and out of the story.

Joel Wallace thought the cynical congressman wouldn't be relatable enough, and told Sid it would be better to make him a truck driver who was losing his eyesight and forced to retire.

"A blind truck driver?" Sid asked, wondering how the hell he was supposed to make that funny.

"Disabilities are very on trend right now," Joel explained. "And if we can find the right visually impaired actor, the audience will love it."

"Okay," Sid muttered slowly as he rubbed his forehead, trying to imagine anyone laughing at this scenario.

"And could you make the daughter an English lit professor?"

"English lit?"

"Or philosophy. Something like that—you're the writer. Point is, we're thinking about an updated *Frasier* kind of dynamic, where the father is working class and the daughter is sort of overeducated."

They already fucking made Frasier, Sid thought, but he said, "I'll work on it."

"And we're not sure about Brooklyn. Maybe Buffalo? Or even Pittsburgh?"

"I really like Brooklyn for this project," Sid countered, feeling like a little pushback was in order.

"Um . . . okay, sure. Let's leave it Brooklyn for now. We can always change that when we bring in a showrunner."

Bring in a showrunner? It meant they weren't even considering Sid for the position. The room grew warm, and he pulled at his shirt, wishing he still had an agent. He was going to have to make some calls.

When he got off the phone, Sid opened the cupboard where he kept a bottle of Jack and grabbed it by the neck. He stared at it, anticipating the warm and welcome burn down his throat. *But no,* he thought. He was going to have to do this thing—this godawful thing—absolutely sober. Even if it killed him.

"Why?" Betty asked when she got home a few hours later. "Why do you have to do it?" She shrugged out of her denim jacket and slung it over the back of a chair.

"It's my one shot," he explained. "Everyone else turned it down."

"Do you even want to write a derivative *Frasier* reboot?"

"Fuck no."

"So don't."

"But Joybird—"

"Joybird is fine," Betty interrupted. "She's got a thriving business. She's happy. She's in love. She doesn't need your money."

"She *thinks* she doesn't need it."

Betty sat next to him on the soft sofa and took both his hands. "Trust me, she wants *you,* not your cash."

Sid stared at her, listening hard and trying to take it all the way in, because he felt like she was telling him more than she was saying. "I don't get it," he said, even as he sensed fissures forming in his mental roadblock.

"I think you do."

"You're saying I should give up my dreams?"

"*This* dream, Sid. This TV-comedy-writer dream."

He looked out the window, where a streetlight pulsated as if begging for someone to give it a tap and set it right.

"And do what?" he asked.

Betty cocked her head, waiting for him to see a different kind of light. He concentrated, but could only vaguely sense it shimmering in the distance.

"Help me," he begged.

"*Rocky Hill,*" she said, "your novel."

And then there it was—the blazing, brilliant, white-hot sun. He couldn't face it head on—not yet—but he'd been talking about this book for years and had even explained the premise to Betty more than once. But it always felt like something for later—something he needed to put off until he'd crossed one hurdle, and then the next, and the one after that. Now, he wondered if Betty was right and he could just give it all up and pursue this dream.

"What if it's not any good?" he asked, voicing his greatest fear.

She shrugged. "You'll rewrite it."

"You know, the chances of it being a success—"

"Who cares? Just write the damned thing."

Just write the damned thing. It echoed in his head while he played it out, and suddenly Sid felt like he'd smoked a whole joint, his muscles going loose and easy as his Hollywood ambitions turned to vapor. He leaned back, wondering if this feeling was real, if he'd be able to hold on to it after this heady conversation became a memory.

"Besides," Betty added, "won't it feel good to tell the guy at Sony to go fuck himself?"

The doorbell buzzed, and Betty nodded toward it. "That'll be Joybird. I ran into her in the lobby, and she said she wanted to come up and ask us something."

Sid stood and opened the door for his daughter, who wore a shimmery green sweater that actually fit, as well as a bright smile. Her happiness these days was genuine, not the forced cheer she'd worn for so long to drive her heart forward. Sid considered how far she'd come in the past year. Her business had grown too large to contain in her Honda, so now, in addition to the JoyRide services, she offered life coaching from her apartment via Zoom. Meanwhile, her relationship with Devon continued to blossom.

After they'd greeted each other with hugs, Betty poured three glasses of wine, and they took seats in the cluttered living room.

"What did you want to talk about?" Betty asked.

"Christmas."

Sid looked out the window as if to confirm there hadn't been a glitch in the space-time continuum. "It's only September."

"I know, but Devon's family plans ahead, especially since his brother has to fly in from California. Anyway, they want you to come."

"Both of us?" Betty said.

Joybird nodded. "I hope you'll say yes. I know you usually go to your sister's in Vermont."

"I'd love an excuse not to." She glanced at Sid. "What do you think?"

He looked at his daughter. "You sure they want us?"

"Of course! It was his mom's idea. She's dying to meet you both."

Sid shrugged. "All right, then. Why not?"

Joybird couldn't contain her happiness, and her eyes went moist with emotion, as if her greatest dream had just come true. Betty gave Sid a look that said, *See? I told you so.* Then she turned to Joybird.

"Your father has some news."

"Good news?" Joybird asked.

"Well, good news and bad news," he said. "I've decided to finally write my novel." He paused for effect. "But I won't be selling any more scripts to Hollywood."

Joybird studied him. "And what's the bad news?"

For a second, he thought she was making a joke. But when he looked into his daughter's earnest blue eyes, he understood she was serious, and the last of his trepidations began to disintegrate.

"Never mind," he said, after a beat.

"So there is no bad news?" she asked.

Sid nearly choked on emotion. "No bad news," he confirmed, and Joybird smiled. He realized, then, how grateful he was. Not just for his daughter's untethered optimism, but for Betty's well-grounded grace. It made him think about the health scare he'd had before he left Los Angeles, when he had a stent procedure to fix his damaged heart. But of course, it was just the first step. And now, as he looked from Betty to Joybird, Sid Marcus could finally feel his heart beating in perfect sync with his life. At last, he was home.

Acknowledgments

Some books just seem to write themselves. This was not one of them.

The idea for *Joyride* started nearly a decade ago as a flash of inspiration that bears little resemblance to this story. At that point, it was an embryonic concept that couldn't quite make the leap from a flutter in my chest to a full-blown book. It felt more like a scene from a stage play or a multicamera sitcom than a novel.

Still, I was determined. So I pushed and pulled and tugged, making piles of notes. When I finally figured out how to turn that flash into a book, I went to feverish work, cranking out the first two hundred sweaty pages in a matter of months. Then I put it aside to write two more books—*Take My Husband* and *Divorce Towers*—both of which demanded to be written as novels from the very first spark.

When I went back to *Joyride*, it was a struggle to regain my stride, but I worked doggedly until I finally had a finished draft and was madly in love. Unfortunately, my beta readers didn't feel the same. They all agreed there was something there—perhaps even something wonderful—but insisted the book was too flawed to go out into the world.

I listened and revised and showed it to more beta readers, keeping at it until, at last, I knew *Joyride* had arrived.

All this is to say that I could not have done it without my very smart, insightful, honest, talented, and gracious beta readers. These include Susan Henderson, Saralee Rosenberg, Jordan Rosenfeld, Robin

Slick, David Henry Sterry, and Max Weiss. I thank them from the depths of my heart.

I also owe a massive debt of gratitude to Tommie Hannigan, who patiently answered my many questions about the Uber-driving business. Additional megathanks to Corie Skolnick and, of course, Pete Harris.

Joyride is my tenth published book, but it marks an exciting rebirth for my career, as it connected me with Ann Leslie Tuttle, my fabulous new literary agent. Her enthusiasm for this novel buoyed me more than I can possibly express. And lord, is she a smarty!

Huge thanks to all the hardworking, dedicated, and professional folks at Montlake for getting behind this book and giving it the best home in the world. And most especially to executive editor Maria Gomez for her savvy insights, heartwarming positivity, and limitless vision. I couldn't ask for a better champion. And how lucky I was to get the talented Keyren Gerlach Burgess as my developmental editor!

Finally, a grateful shout-out to the additional friends and family who cheered me on, including Ron Block, Jane Brody, Myfanwy Collins, Deb Conley, Susan DiPlacido, Wendy DeAngelis, Arielle Eckstut, Amy Ferris, Myka Hanson, Bev Jackson, Cookie Kanterman, Caroline Leavitt, Andrea Meister, Jeannie Moon, Lauren Rico, Linda Schreyer, and my three wonderkids, Max, Ethan, and Rook. As always, the biggest thanks of all to my husband, Mike, for bringing the joy to this ride.

About the Author

Ellen Meister is a novelist, book coach, screenwriter, and creative writing instructor who started her career writing advertising copy. Her novels include *Divorce Towers, Take My Husband, The Rooftop Party, Love Sold Separately, Dorothy Parker Drank Here,* and *Farewell, Dorothy Parker,* among others. Meister's essays have been published by the *New York Times, Newsday,* the *Wall Street Journal* blog, the Huffington Post (now HuffPost), the Daily Beast, *Long Island Woman, Writer's Digest,* and *Publishers Weekly.* Career highlights include interviews on NPR, being selected for the prestigious Indie Next List by the American Booksellers Association, having her work translated into foreign languages, and receiving a TV series option from HBO.

Meister lives in New York and publicly speaks about her books, fiction writing, and America's most celebrated literary wit, Dorothy Parker. For more information, visit her website at https://ellenmeister.com.